JOHNNY TREMAIN

YEARLING BOOKS are designed especially to entertain and enlighten young people. Patricia Reilly Giff, consultant to this series, received her bachelor's degree from Marymount College and a master's degree in history from St. John's University. She holds a Professional Diploma in Reading and a Doctorate of Humane Letters from Hofstra University. She was a teacher and reading consultant for many years, and is the author of numerous books for young readers.

For a complete listing of all Yearling titles, write to
Dell Readers Service,
P.O. Box 1045,
South Holland, IL 60473.

JOHNNY TREMAIN

awarded

the JOHN NEWBERY MEDAL

as

*'The most distinguished contribution
to American literature for children'*

in the year of its publication

JOHNNY TREMAIN
A NOVEL FOR
OLD & YOUNG

written by ESTHER FORBES

ILLUSTRATIONS BY LYND WARD

A YEARLING BOOK

Published by
Bantam Doubleday Dell Books for Young Readers
a division of
Bantam Doubleday Dell Publishing Group, Inc.
1540 Broadway
New York, New York 10036

The late Esther Forbes bequeathed the royalties from the sale of her works to the American Antiquarian Society, Worcester, Massachusetts, where she had done most of her historical research.

The trademark Yearling® is registered in the U.S. Patent and Trademark Office.

The trademark Dell® is registered in the U.S. Patent and Trademark Office.

Reprinted by arrangement with Houghton Mifflin Company

ISBN: 0-440-22024-6

Printed in the United States of America

Previous Yearling Edition and Laurel-Leaf Edition

June 1996

10 9 8 7 6 5 4 3 2 1

OPM

To Pamela, Emily, John
and Molly Taylor

Contents

I. Up and About

ON ROCKY ISLANDS gulls woke. Time to be about their business. Silently they floated in on the town, but when their icy eyes sighted the first dead fish, first bits of garbage about the ships and wharves, they began to scream and quarrel.

The cocks in Boston back yards had long before cried the coming of day. Now the hens were also awake, scratching, clucking, laying eggs.

Cats in malt houses, granaries, ship holds, mansions and hovels caught a last mouse, settled down to wash their fur and sleep. Cats did not work by day.

In stables horses shook their halters and whinnied.

In barns cows lowed to be milked.

Boston slowly opened its eyes, stretched, and woke. The sun struck in horizontally from the east, flashing upon weathervanes — brass cocks and arrows, here a glass-eyed Indian, there a copper grasshopper — and the bells in the steeples cling-clanged, telling the people it was time to be up and about.

In hundreds of houses sleepy women woke sleepier children. Get up and to work. Ephraim, get to the pump, fetch Mother water. Ann, get to the barn, milk the cow and drive her to the Common. Start the fire, Silas. Put on a clean shirt, James. Dolly, if you aren't up before I count ten . . .

And so, in a crooked little house at the head of Hancock's Wharf on crowded Fish Street, Mrs. Lapham stood at the foot of a ladder leading to the attic where her father-in-law's apprentices slept. These boys were luckier than most apprentices. Their master was too feeble to climb ladders; the middle-aged mistress too stout. It was only her bellows that could penetrate to their quarters — not her heavy hands.

'Boys?'

No answer.

'Dove?'

'Coming, ma'am.' Dove turned over for one more snooze.

Frustrated, she shook the ladder she was too heavy to climb. She wished she could shake 'them limbs of Satan.'

'Dusty Miller — let me hear your voice.'

'Here it is,' piped Dusty pertly.

Her voice changed to pleading.

'Johnny — you get them two lazy lug-a-beds up. Get them down here. You pull that worthless Dove right out'er bed. You give Dusty a kick for me. I'm waiting for him to fetch fresh water so's I can get on with breakfast.'

Johnny Tremain was on his feet. He did not bother to answer his mistress. He turned to the fat, pale, almost white-haired boy still wallowing in bed.

'Hear that, Dove?'

'Oh — you ... leave me lay, can't you?' Grumbling, he swung his legs out of the bed the three boys shared.

Johnny was already in his leather breeches, pulling on his coarse shirt, tucking in the tails. He was a rather skinny boy, neither large nor small for fourteen. He had a thin, sleep-flushed face, light eyes, a wry mouth, and fair, lank hair. Although two years younger than the swinish Dove, inches shorter, pounds lighter, he knew, and old Mr. Lapham knew, busy Mrs. Lapham and her four daughters and Dove and Dusty also knew, that Johnny Tremain was boss of the attic, and almost of the house.

Dusty Miller was eleven. It was easy for Johnny to say, 'Look sharp, Dusty,' and little Dusty looked sharp. But Dove (his first name had long ago been forgotten) hated the way the younger apprentice lorded it over him, telling him when to go to bed, when to get up, criticizing his work in the silversmith's shop as though he were already a master smith. Hadn't he been working four years for Mr. Lapham and Johnny only two? Why did the boy have to be so infernally smart with his hands — and his tongue?

'Look here, Johnny, I'm not getting up 'cause you tell me to. I'm getting up 'cause Mrs. Lapham tells me to.'

'All right,' said Johnny blandly, 'just so you're up.'

There was only one window in the attic. Johnny always stood before it as he dressed. He liked this view down the length of Hancock's Wharf. Counting houses, shops, stores, sail lofts, and one great ship after another, home again after their voyaging, content as cows waiting to be milked. He watched the gulls, so fierce and beautiful, fighting and screaming among the ships. Beyond the wharf was the sea and the rocky islands where gulls nested.

He knew to the fraction of a moment how long it would take the two other boys to get into their clothes. Swinging about, he leaped for the head of the ladder, hardly looking where he went. One of Dove's big feet got there first. Johnny stumbled, caught himself, and swung silently about at Dove.

'Gosh, Johnny. I'm sorry,' snickered Dove.

'Sorry, eh? . . . you're going to be a lot sorrier . . .'

'I just didn't notice . . .'

'You do that again and I'll beat you up again. You overgrown pig-of-a-louse. You . . .' He went on from there. Mr. Lapham was strict about his boys swearing, but Johnny could get along very well without. Whatever a 'pig-of-a-louse' was, it did describe the whitish, flaccid, parasitic Dove.

Little Dusty froze as the older boys quarreled. He knew Johnny could beat up Dove any time he chose. He worshiped Johnny and did not like Dove, but he and Dove were bound together by their common servitude to Johnny's autocratic rule. Half of Dusty sympathized with one boy, half of him with the other, in this quarrel. It seemed to him that everybody liked Johnny. Old Mr. Lapham because he was so clever at his work.

Mrs. Lapham because he was reliable. The four Lapham girls because he sassed them so — and then grinned. Most of the boys in the other shops around Hancock's Wharf liked Johnny, although some of them fought him on sight. Only Dove hated him. Sometimes he would get Dusty in a corner, tell him in a hoarse whisper how he was going to get a pair of scissors and cut out Johnny Tremain's heart. But he never dared do more than trip him — and then whine out of it.

'Someday,' said Johnny, his good nature restored, 'I'll kill you, Dove. In the meantime, you have your uses. You get out the buckets and run to North Square and fetch back drinking water.'

The Laphams were on the edge of the sea. Their well was brackish.

'Look here — Mrs. Lapham said Dusty was to go and . . .'

'Get along with you. Don't you go arguing with me.'

Fetching water, sweeping, helping in the kitchen, tending the annealing furnace in the shop were the unskilled work the boys did. Already Johnny was so useful at his bench he could never be spared for such labor. It was over a year since he had carried charcoal or a bucket of water, touched a broom or helped Mrs. Lapham brew ale. His ability made him semi-sacred. He knew his power and reveled in it. He could have easily made friends with stupid Dove, for Dove was lonely and admired Johnny as well as envied him. Johnny preferred to bully him.

Johnny, followed by his subdued slaves, slipped down the ladder with an easy flop. To his left was Mr. Lapham's bedroom. The door was closed. Old master did not go to work these days until after breakfast. Starting the boys off, getting things going, he left to his bustling daughter-in-law. Johnny knew the old man (whom he liked) was already up and dressed. He took this time every day to read the Bible.

To his right, the only other bedroom was open. It was here Mrs. Lapham slept with her four 'poor fatherless girls,' as she called them. The two biggest and most capable were already in the kitchen helping their mother.

Cilla was sitting on the edge of one of the unmade beds, brushing Isannah's hair. It was wonderful hair, seemingly spun out of gold. It was the most wonderful thing in the whole house. Gently Cilla brushed and brushed, her little oddly shaped face turned away, pretending she did not know that Johnny was there. He knew neither Cilla nor Isannah would politely wish him the conventional 'good morning.' He was lingering for his morning insult.

Cilla never lifted her eyes as she put down her brush and very deliberately picked up a hair ribbon (the Laphams couldn't afford such luxuries, but somehow Cilla always managed to keep her little sister in hair ribbons). Very carefully she began to tie the child's halo of pale curls. She spoke to Isannah in so low a voice it was almost a whisper.

'There goes that *wonderful* Johnny Tremain.'

Isannah took her cue, already so excited she was jumping up and down.

'Johnny worth-his-weight-in-gold Tremain.'

'If you don't think he is wonderful — ask him, Isannah.'

'Oh, just how *wonderful* are you, Johnny?'

Johnny said nothing, stood there and grinned.

The two youngest Laphams were always insulting him, not only about how smart he was, but how smart he thought he was. He didn't care. Every now and then they would say something that irritated him and then together they would shout, 'Johnny's mad.'

As an apprentice he was little more than a slave until he had served his master seven years. He had no wages. The very clothes upon his back belonged to his master, but he did not, as he himself said, 'take much.'

There were only four real rooms in the Lapham house, the two bedrooms on the second floor, the kitchen and the workshop on the first. Johnny paused in the lower entry. In the kitchen he could see his formidable mistress bent double over the hearth. Madge, in time, would look like her mother, but at eighteen she was handsome in a coarse-grained, red-faced, thick-waisted way.

Dorcas was sixteen, built like Madge, but not so loud-voiced, nor as roughly good-natured. Poor Dorcas thirsted for elegance. She would rub flour on her face, trying to look pale, like the fashionable ladies she saw on the street. She wore her clothes so tight (hoping to look ethereal), she looked apoplectic. How they all had laughed when her stays burst in the middle of meeting with a loud pop! She did not call her mother 'Ma,' but 'Mother,' or 'Respected Mother'; and in her efforts to avoid the rough, easy speech of her associates on Hancock's Wharf she talked (when she remembered it) in a painfully prissy, proper way.

Johnny thought Madge pretty bad, and Dorcas even worse. But he was philosophical about them. He wouldn't mind having them for sisters. They certainly were good hard workers — except when Dorcas tried too hard to be elegant.

It had already been decided that when he grew up to be a really great silversmith (as Mr. Lapham said he would), he was to marry Cilla and together they would inherit Grandpa's silver business. Cilla was just his age. This idea seemed only mildly offensive to both of them. Johnny had no particular objections. Smart apprentices were always getting ahead by marrying into their masters' families. He had been flattered when Mrs. Lapham had told him that he might marry any one of her girls. Of course, Madge and Dorcas (they were fine, big buxom girls) would make better wives. But didn't he think they were a little old for him? True, Cilla was just a mite spindly — but she was coming along fine. Isannah was so weakly it didn't seem worth making any plans for her maturity. So it was to be Cilla.

Johnny had often heard Mrs. Lapham say that Isannah was hardly worth the bother she was to raise. The little girl, her beautiful brown eyes wide with interest, never seemed to mind these remarks of her mother, but they made Cilla cry. Cilla loved Isannah. She was proud when people stopped her on the street and said, 'Is that little angel your sister?' She did not mind that there were so many things Isannah could not 'keep down' — like pork gravy, mince pies, new beer. If Isannah got wet, she had a cold — if a cold, a fever.

First Johnny, with a customary 'Look sharp,' got the sulky Dove and his buckets headed for North Square. Then he took the key to the shop out of his pocket as though he owned it. Dusty, good and quiet as a mouse, followed him.

'Look sharp, Dusty,' Johnny said. 'Get the annealing furnace going. Get to the coal house. Fetch in charcoal. You'll have to do it by yourself. I want to get this buckle mended before breakfast.'

Already the day's bustle had begun up and down the wharf: A man was crying fish. Sailors were heave-hoing at their ropes. A woman was yelling that her son had fallen into the water. A parrot said distinctly, 'King Hancock.'

Johnny could smell hemp and spices, tar and salt water, the sun drying fish. He liked his wharf. He sat at his own bench, before him the innumerable tools of his trade. The tools fitted into his strong, thin hands: his hands fitted the tools. Mr. Lapham was always telling him to give God thanks who had seen fit to make him so good an artisan — not to take it out in lording it over the other boys. That was one of the things Johnny 'did not let bother him much.'

Dove came back, his thick lower lip thrust out. The water had slopped over his breeches, down his legs.

'Mrs. Lapham does not want you in the kitchen?' — Johnny did not even look up from his buckle.

'Naw.'

'Well, then, this spoon you finished yesterday afternoon has to be melted down — made over. You beat it to the wrong gauge.'

'Did Mr. Lapham say 'twas wrong?'

'No, but it is. It is supposed to match this spoon. Look at it.' Dove looked. There was no argument.

'So get out a crucible. 'Soon as Dusty's got the furnace going, you melt it down and try again.'

I'd like to get *you* in a crucible, thought Dove, and melt you down. I'd beat you to the proper gauge... Two years younger than me and look at him!

It was Isannah who ran in to tell them that Grandpa was in his chair and breakfast was on the table. The soft brown eyes combined oddly with the flying fair hair. She *did* look rather like a little angel, Johnny thought — just as people were always telling Cilla on the street — and so graceful. She seemed to float about rather than run.

No one, to see her, would ever guess the number of things she couldn't keep down.

- 2 -

Mr. Lapham, as befitted his venerable years and his dignity as master of the house, sat in an armchair at the head of the table. He was a peaceful, kind, remote old man. Although his daughter-in-law was always nagging him to collect bills, finish work when promised, and discipline his apprentices, nothing she said seemed to touch him. He did not even bother to listen.

His dull, groping eyes lingered kindly over his boys as they trooped in for breakfast.

'Good morning, Dove, Dusty. Good morning, Johnny.'

'Good morning, sir.'

He took his time blessing the meal. He was a deacon at the Cockerel Church and very pious.

Breakfast was good, although no more than a poor artisan could afford — milk and ale, gruel, sausages, and corn bread. Everything was plentiful and well cooked. The kitchen was as clean or cleaner than many of those in the great houses. Every member of the household had a clean shirt or petticoat. Mrs. Lapham was a great manager, but she cared nothing for genteel manners and was the first to laugh at Dorcas's 'If it please you, Mother — just a touch more maple syrup for me.' 'Gimme that there syrup pitcher' was good enough for her.

When the meal was over, Mr. Lapham told Madge to hand him the family Bible.

'Johnny, I'm going to ask you to read to us today.'

Of the three boys, only Johnny read easily and well. His mother had lived long enough to see to that. Dove stumbled shamefully. Dusty usually had the first chapter of Genesis, so that by reading the same thing over and over he might eventually learn.

Madge and Dorcas never cared even to try to read. Mrs. Lapham could not so much as write her name. 'Book larning,' she declared, 'scalded no pigs.' Cilla was so anxious to learn (and teach Isannah) that whenever Johnny read she leaned over the book and shaped the words to herself as he said them. They sat beside each other at table. To help her Johnny always kept a finger on the lines as he read.

Johnny now opened the book, keeping it between himself and Cilla.

'Where, sir, shall I read?'

Mr. Lapham's selections for his boys were sometimes designed to point out some fault in a member of his household, especially in the reader. Dove was always being asked to read about sluggards and going to ants.

Johnny was told where to begin in Leviticus.

'*Ye shall make you no idols nor graven image, neither rear you up a standing image...*' (What was old master driving at? Couldn't a silversmith put a dragon's snout on a chocolate pot?)

Soon the surging roll of the words, the pleasure of the sound of his voice coming so clearly out of his mouth, made him stop looking for possible object lessons in the text. Cilla was leaning over him, breathing hard in her efforts to keep up. Mrs. Lapham sat agape. Soon she'd be saying it was just like having a preacher live with them to hear Johnny Tremain read Holy Writ.

'Finish with the nineteenth verse.'

'*... And I will break the pride of your power; and I will make your heaven as iron, and your earth as brass.*'

'Turn to Proverbs eleven, second verse.'

'*When pride cometh, then cometh shame: but with the lowly is wisdom.*'

'Proverbs sixteen, eighteenth.'

'*Pride goeth before destruction, and an haughty spirit before a fall.*'

'Now close the book. Stand up and expound to us all the meaning of God's Word.'

Johnny stood up. His skin was thin and he could feel himself flush. So the old gentleman was after him for his pride again, was he?

'It is all another way of saying — God's way of saying — that pride goeth before a fall.'

'Yes, and why?'

'Because God doesn't like pride.' Johnny sounded sulky.

'Do you think God would like you?'

'Not especially.'

Dusty was the first to snicker.

'What does God like?'

'Humble people,' said Johnny wrathfully. 'He sends punishments to people who are too proud.'

'Now, Johnny, I want you to raise your right hand and repeat after me, "I, Johnny Tremain..."'

'I, Johnny Tremain...'

'Swear from this day onward...'

'Swear from this day onward...'

'To walk more humbly and modestly before God and man.'

'To walk more humbly and modestly before God and man.'

'Just because some folks are not so smart' (the old master gave Dove and Dusty a pitying glance), 'it's no reason why other folks should go around rubbing their noses in their own stupidities.'

Either Dove or Dusty kicked Johnny under the table. Madge and Dorcas were giggling. Mrs. Lapham was already scraping the trenchers clean, getting on with her work. She did not hold much by Grandpa's soul-searchings.

The master, followed by Dove and Dusty, left for the shop.

Johnny heard Cilla give an exaggeratedly pious sigh. He stopped.

'When the meek inherit the earth,' she said, 'I doubt Johnny gets as much as one divot of sod.'

This was too much for Johnny. He turned on the little girls.

'*When* they do!' he stormed. 'Cill, you can just about keep your mouth shut until then.'

'You know you did look pretty funny standing up there, and saying all those humble things Grandpa told you to.'

Isannah was almost jumping out of her pinafore in glee.

'Johnny's mad,' she chanted. 'Johnny's mad.'

'Yes,' murmured Cilla, looking at him critically, 'you're right, baby dear. His ears are red. That always means he's mad.'

'Johnny's ears are red,' squealed Isannah.

Johnny stalked out of the kitchen as stiff-legged as a fighting tom-cat. His ears were scarlet.

- 3 -

He decided to do nothing that would lay him open to such criticism for at least a morning, but he couldn't help it. First, if he had not jumped on Dusty, the furnace would have gone out. Then he had to explain to his master how badly Dove had done the spoon. Although he tried to sound humble, he was soon behaving perfectly naturally, standing over Mr. Lapham with his notebook in his hand, reading off exactly how those spoons had been ordered.

Mr. Lapham was a fine craftsman. His weakness was that he never wrote down what was ordered or even listened very carefully. If a patron ordered a sauceboat, he would get a fine one — perhaps a month after it had been promised. Sometimes it weighed a little more, sometimes a little less, than it was supposed to. Sometimes it had splayed feet when a gadroon edge had been asked for. Mrs. Lapham herself had told Johnny he must always be on hand and write down exactly what the order was. This was necessary, but it did seem cheeky to see the fourteen-year-old boy standing there, telling his master what he was supposed to do.

Johnny, having started everybody off on his work (even Mr.

Lapham), decided to go to the coal house and see if he should order more charcoal. It was such things Mr. Lapham never thought about until too late.

There were two basketfuls of charcoal and at least half another scattered over the floor. That was the other boys' fault. Johnny himself was too valuable to carry charcoal. He started to yell for Dusty, thought better of it, and went to work arranging the dirty stuff himself.

When *he* was a master craftsman, he wasn't going to buy charcoal by the basket. He was going to own his own willows — say, out in Milton. That would save — say, twopence a basket. In a year — he began to figure. And he wouldn't take just any boy whose father or mother wanted him to be a silversmith. He'd pick and choose. He saw himself sitting at his bench, his shop crowded with boys with mothers, boys with fathers, all begging to be allowed to work for him. He'd not talk to the parents — only to the boys. What church did they go to? King's Chapel? All right. Describe to me at least one piece of silver you see used every Lord's Supper. If they could not answer that, he'd know they hadn't got silver in their blood. But how could he find which boys had nice hands . . .?

'Johnny!' It was Madge's voice that pulled him out of his reverie.

He wiped his black hands on his leather breeches and stepped out into the sunlight of the tiny back yard.

'What is it, my girl?' He often thus arrogantly addressed his master's granddaughters — really his own mistresses.

'Ma sent me. Johnny, it's Mr. Hancock himself. He's in the shop ordering something. Stand by and listen or Grandpa will get it wrong.'

Dorcas next flung herself upon him, too excited to be elegant.

'Johnny, hurry, hurry! It's Mr. Hancock. He's ordering a sugar basin. Can't you go faster? Shake a leg.'

Isannah was jumping about him like a wild thing.

'Help, help!' she shrieked.

But it was Cilla who thought to offer him her clean apron for a towel as he washed off the charcoal at the yard pump.

Oh, but he must hurry! And there was Mrs. Lapham tapping at him from the kitchen window. Slowly he approached the house, the girls chattering about him.

Close to the shop door was a tiny African holding a slender gray horse by the bridle. Johnny noted the Hancock arms on the door of the gig. He felt so good he could not help saying to the black child, 'Mind that horse doesn't trample our flowers.'

There were no flowers in the Laphams' yard.

'Oh, no, sir,' said little Jehu, rolling his eyes. He thought, from the attention this boy was receiving from his escorting ladies, he must be a boy of consequence.

Johnny slipped into the shop so quietly that Mr. Hancock did not even look up. It was he who owned this great wharf, the warehouses, many of the fine ships tied up along it. He owned sail lofts and shops, and also dwelling houses standing at the head of the wharf. He owned the Lapham house. He was the richest man in New England. Such a wealthy patron might lift the Laphams from poverty to affluence.

Mr. Hancock was comfortably seated in the one armchair which was kept in the shop for patrons. (When I'm master, thought Johnny, there are going to be two armchairs — and I'll sit in one.)

Unobtrusively Johnny got his notebook and pencil. Dove and Dusty were paralyzed into complete inaction. 'Do something,' Johnny muttered to them, determined his master's shop should look busy. Dusty could not take his eyes off the green velvet coat, sprigged white waistcoat, silver buttons and buckles on the great man, but he picked up a soldering iron and nervously dropped it.

' . . . and to be done next Monday — a week from today,' Mr. Hancock was saying. 'I want it as a birthday present to my venerable Aunt Lydia Hancock. This is the creamer of the set. Only this morning a clumsy maid melted the sugar basin. I want you to make me a new one. I want it about so high . . . so broad . . .' Johnny glanced at the delicate, lace-ruffled, gesturing hands, guessed the inches, and wrote it down.

Mr. Lapham was looking down at his own gnarled fingers. He nodded and said nothing. He did not even glance at the cream pitcher as Mr. Hancock set it down on a workbench. Johnny's hard, delicate hands, so curiously strong and mature for his age, reached quickly to touch the beautiful thing. It was almost as much by touch as by sight he judged fine silver. It was indeed old-fashioned, more elaborate than the present mode. The garlands on it were rounded out in repoussé work. Mr. Lapham would have to do the repousséing. Johnny hadn't been taught that. He looked at the handle. A sugar basin would have to have two such handles and they would be larger than the one on the creamer. He'd shape it in wax, make a mold. He had cast hundreds of small things since he had gone to work for Mr. Lapham, but nothing so intricate and beautiful as the woman with folded wings whose body formed the handle. He thought he had never seen anything quite so enchanting as this pitcher. It must have been the work of one of the great smiths of forty or fifty years ago. Although he had not intended to address Mr. Hancock, he had said, before he thought, 'John Coney, sir?'

Mr. Hancock turned to him. He had a handsome face, a little worn, as though either his health was bad or he did not sleep well.

'Look at the mark, boy.'

Johnny turned it over, expecting to see the familiar rabbit of the great Mr. Coney. Instead, there was a pellet, and 'L,' and a pellet.

'Your master made that creamer — forty years ago. He made the entire set.'

'*You* made it!' He had never guessed there had been a time when Mr. Lapham could do such beautiful work.

At last Mr. Lapham raised his protuberant eyes. 'I remember when your uncle, Mr. Thomas Hancock, sir, ordered that set. "Make it big, and make it handsome," he said, "bigger and handsomer than anything in Boston. As big and handsome as my lady is. Make it as rich as I am."'

John Hancock laughed. 'That is just the way my uncle used to talk.' He was so sure of his own good breeding, he could laugh affectionately at the rich-quick vulgarities of the uncle who had adopted him and from whom he had inherited his fortune.

He stood up — a tall, slender man, who stooped as he stood and walked. The fine clothes seemed a little pathetic. He had a soft voice, and low.

'But you have not as yet said whether or not you can make my sugar basin for me — and have it done by Monday next? Of course I thought first of you — because you made the original. But there are other silversmiths. Perhaps you would rather not undertake...'

Mr. Lapham was in a study. 'I've got the time, the materials, and the boys to help. I can get right at it. But honestly, sir... I don't know. Perhaps I haven't got the skill any more. I've not done anything so fine for thirty years. I'm not what I used to be, and...'

Although neither of the two men could see the door leading from the hall into the shop, Johnny could. There was Mrs. Lapham in her morning apron, her face purple with excitement, and all four girls crowded about her listening, gesturing at Johnny. 'Say yes,' all five faces (big and little) mouthed at him. 'Yes... yes... yes.'

So they had forgotten morning prayers, had they? Wanted him to take charge.

'We can do it, Mr. Hancock.'

'*Bless me*,' exclaimed the gentleman, not accustomed to apprentices who settled matters while their masters pondered.

'Yes, sir. And you shall have it delivered at your own house a week from today, seven o'clock Monday morning. And it's going to be just exactly right.'

Mr. Lapham looked at Johnny gratefully. 'Certainly, sir. I'm humbly grateful for your august patronage.' He was not a proud man. He was relieved that Johnny had stepped in and settled matters.

Mr. Hancock bowed and turned to go, but none of the boys

thought to run ahead and open the door for him, so Mrs. Lapham, apron and all, barged in, her red arms bare to the elbow, her felt slippers flapping at her bare heels, and did (or overdid) the courtesies for them all.

Hardly was the door closed than there was a rap on it. Little Jehu came mincing in, a glitter of bright colors. He solemnly laid three pieces of silver on the nearest bench and recited his piece.

'My master, Mr. John Hancock, Esquire, bids me leave these coins — one for each of the poor work-boys — hoping they will drink his health and be diligent at their benches.' Then he was gone.

'Hoping they will vote for him — when they are grown up and have enough property.'

'Don't you ever vote for Mr. Hancock, sir?' asked Johnny.

'I never do. I don't hold much with these fellows that are always trying to stir up trouble between us and England. Maybe English rule ain't always perfect, but it's good enough for me. Fellows like Mr. Hancock and Sam Adams, calling themselves patriots and talking too much. Not reading God's Word — like their parents did — which tells us to be humble. But he's my landlord and I don't say much.'

Johnny was not listening. He sat with the pitcher in his hand. To think the poor, humble old fellow *once* had been able to make things like that! Well, he was going to turn the trick again before he died — even if Johnny had to stand over him and make him.

- 4 -

The sun stood directly overhead, pressing its heat down upon the town as though it held an enormous brass basin. There was not wind enough to take a catboat from Hancock's Wharf to Noddle Island.

In the Lapham shop windows and doors were left open to

catch what breeze might come up the wharf, but there wasn't any breeze.

Old Mr. Lapham had worked well in the morning. He said if Johnny could do the handles, he himself could get the basin done in time, but after dinner he had gone down to the old willow behind the coal house, put a basket over his head, and gone to sleep. Dove and Dusty had, therefore, left to go swimming. Johnny was making out of wax an exact replica of the pitcher handle, only enlarging it. He tried again and again, never quite satisfied with his work, but confident that he could do it.

It was long past dinner hour when he crossed the entry into the kitchen. The fire was out. The table cleared except for his place. Cilla had evidently been left to wait on him whenever he felt like eating. The success of Mr. Hancock's order was so dependent upon him, no one would scold him today because he chose to be an hour late. Johnny took his seat and Cilla put down the slate she had been drawing on. She gave him a piece of cold meat pie, a flat loaf of rye bread, dried apples, and ran down cellar to fetch him a flagon of cold ale. He drank the ale, and then more leisurely began on the pie.

With hardly a word Cilla went back to the settle where Isannah was sprawled and picked up her slate. She drew very well. It would be just about nothing, Johnny thought, to teach that girl to write.

'She's doing it for you, Johnny,' Isannah said at last.

'What are you doing for me, Cil?'

'She's designing you a beautiful mark so when you are man-grown and master smith you can stamp your silver with it.'

'I've five more years to go. No matter how good my work may be, I have to mark it with your grandpa's old pellets and "L's."'

'Johnny's forgotten morning prayers and all those wonderful humble people,' said Cilla. 'Look, I've got your "J" and "T" sort of entwined.'

'Too hard to read. Then, too' (he could not imagine why he came out with this secret), 'when I'm master smith I'm going to use all three of my initials.'

'All *three?*'

'J. L. T.'

Neither of the girls had ever heard of a poor working boy with three names. 'You're not making up?' Cilla asked, almost respectfully. 'I've heard tell of folk with three names, but I never saw one before.'

'Look at me, my girl.' He got up to go back to the shop.

'Wait, Johnny. What is that middle name? It begins with "L."'

'As far as you are concerned, it ends with "L" too.'

'I'll bet it's something so awful you are ashamed of it, like "Ladybug" or "Leapfrog." I'll bet it's "Lamentable."'

Johnny grinned, untempted by her insults.

In the shop it was so hot he could not handle the wax. The solitude in which he worked depressed him a little. For the first time he was afraid he could not get the handles right. All the shops had stopped work because of the heat. He could hear the other boys running and splashing, diving off the wharf into the cold water. He locked the shop. Now even Mr. Lapham would have to ask him if he wanted to get in, and he ran off to swim. Later, after sunset, he could get on with the model, even if he had to work by lamplight.

- 5 -

When at last he blew out his lamp, Johnny had made an exact replica of the winged woman, only larger. He looked at it and knew that it was not, for some reason, quite right. Instead of going up to the attic to sleep, he crossed into the kitchen and got an old mattress. The clock struck midnight and he was asleep.

He woke and it was still dark night. Someone was in the room with him and he thought of thieves.

'Who's there!' he yelled roughly.

'It's me. Johnny, I wasn't going to wake you up, if you were already asleep, but . . .'

'What's wrong, Cilla?'

'Johnny . . . it's Isannah. She's sick again.'

'What does her mother say?'

Cilla began to cry. 'I don't want to tell her. She'd just say p-p-p-oor Ba-a-Baby wasn't worth raising.'

Johnny was tired. At the moment he had a sneaking sympathy with Mrs. Lapham's point of view.

'What seems to be wrong?'

'She's so hot. She says if she can't get a breath of air, she'll throw up.' This was a very old, but dire threat.

'There might be a little down at the end of the wharf. Fetch her down.'

Seemed it was always like this. Whenever things went wrong and he was tired, Cilla was after him to help her nurse Isannah. Nevertheless he carried her in his thin, strong arms. She was a tiny child for eight. The whity-gold hair that he secretly admired so much got into his mouth and he wished she was bald. Isannah giggled. On one side of the deserted wharf were warehouses, on the other were ships. Not a person was abroad except themselves. The child grew heavier and heavier.

'Want to walk now, Isannah? You'd be cooler walking.'

'I like to ride.'

'Well — just so *you* are satisfied.'

'Johnny,' said Cilla crossly, 'are you being sarcastic to baby?'

'Yes.'

'How do you feel, dear?'

'I feel like I'm going to throw up.'

'Oh, you get down, then,' said Johnny. 'That settles it.' But he carried her to the very end of the wharf.

Suddenly he felt cool fingers of air lifting the wet, fair hair on his forehead. The perspiration under his arms, dripping down his chest, evaporated and the prickly sensation was delightful.

Isannah cried, 'The wind, the wind! Blow, wind, blow!'

It did not blow, but flowed over them and cooled them. The three sat in a row, their feet dangling over the water below. They

sat well apart at first, with arms outstretched, soaking themselves in the freshness of the sea air.

For a long time they sat and said nothing, then Isannah put
her head in Cilla's lap. Cilla leaned against Johnny. The two
girls were almost asleep. Johnny was wide awake.

'Johnny,' murmured Isannah, 'tell us a story?'

'I don't know any.'

'Johnny,' said Cilla, 'tell us the story of your middle name?'

'It isn't a story; it's just a fact.'

'What is it?'

Although by daytime and if Cilla had teased him, he never
would have told, the darkness of the night, the remoteness of the
place where they sat, an affection he felt for the girls and they for
him, made everything seem different.

After a long pause he said, 'It is Lyte.'

'So you are really John Lyte Tremain?'

'No. My baptized Bible name is Jonathan. I've always been
called Johnny. That's the way my papers were made out to your
grandpa. I am Jonathan Lyte Tremain.'

'Why, that's just like Merchant Lyte?'

'Just like.'

'You don't suppose you are related?'

'I do suppose. But I don't know. Lyte's not a common name.
And we are both Jonathan. Of course I've thought about it . . .
some —— When I see him rolling around in his coach, strutting
about with his laces and gold-headed canes. But I don't aim
ever to think too much about it.'

Isannah was almost asleep. 'Tell more, Johnny,' she murmured.

'Merchant Lyte is so very rich . . .'

'How rich? Like Mr. Hancock?'

'Not quite. Almost. He's so rich gold and silver are like dust
to him.'

'You mean at Lyte Mansion Mrs. Lyte sweeps up gold and
silver in a dustpan?'

'Mrs. Lyte doesn't sweep, you silly, not with her own fair hands.

For one thing, she's dead, and for another, if she weren't she'd just snap her fingers and maids would come running — in frilly starched caps. They'd curtsy and squeak, "Yes, ma'am," "No, ma'am," and "If it please you, ma'am." Then Mrs. Lyte would say, "You dirty sluts, look at that gold dust under the bed! I could write my name in the silver dust on the mirror over that mantel. Fetch your mops and rags, you bow-legged, cross-eyed, chattering monkeys."'

'Diamonds, too?'

'To clean up diamonds they need brooms.'

'Oh, Johnny! Tell more.'

'Once the rubies spilled and the cook (a monstrous fine woman — I've seen her) thought they were currants. She put them in a fruit cake, and Merchant Lyte broke a front tooth on one.'

'A fact, Johnny?'

'Well, it's a fact that Merchant Lyte's got a broken front tooth. I saw it as I stood watching him.'

Cilla said, 'You watch him much?'

He answered, a little miserably, 'It's just like I can't help it. I don't mean ever to think of him.'

Isannah murmured, 'What do they do with their pearls?'

'They drink their pearls.'

'What?'

'Like a queen of Egypt my mother told me of — before she died. She drank her pearls in vinegar — just to show off. That Lavinia Lyte is always showing off too.'

Isannah was asleep.

'You never speak of your mother, Johnny. She hadn't been dead more'n a few weeks when you first came here. You never talked about her at all. Was that because you liked her so much — or not at all.'

There was a long pause. 'Liked her so much,' he said at last. 'We had been living at Townsend, Maine. She got a living for us both by sewing. But when she knew she had to die (she had death inside of her and she knew it), she wanted me taught skilled work, and all I wanted was to be a silversmith. That's why we came to Boston, so's to get me a proper master. She could still sew, but she coughed all the time. Even when she was so weak she could hardly hold a needle, she kept on and on, teaching me reading and writing and all that. She was determined I shouldn't grow up untaught — like Dove and Dusty. She wanted me to be something.'

'That's why you work so hard?'

'That's why. Mrs. Lapham promised your grandpa would take me on just as soon as she was buried. She died — and he did. That's all.'

'What was her name? And how come she — a poor sewing woman — was so well learned?'

"Roundabout here she called herself just Mrs. Tremain, but she was born Lavinia Lyte. She came of gentlefolk.'

'Just like Mr. Lyte's daughter?'

'Yes. She told me once that for over a hundred years Lytes have favored Jonathan and Lavinia as names.'

'Johnny, didn't she ever go to those rich relatives and say, "Here I am"?'

'No. And she told me not to — ever. Unless... only, if I'd got to the end of everything. She'd say, "Johnny, if there is not one thing left for you and you have no trade and no health, and God Himself has turned away His face from you, then go to Merchant Lyte and show him your cup and tell him your mother told you before she died that you are kin to him. He will know the kinship, she said, and in pity he may help you." '

'Your cup?'

'She said I wasn't to sell it — ever. I was to go hungry and cold first.'

'Where is your cup?'

'In my sea chest in the attic. That's why I keep it locked.'

'Will you show me your cup?'

'If you swear by your hope of Heaven and your fear of Hell never, never to mention any of this to anyone. Never tell my true name, nor that I have a cup.'

'But Isannah?'

'If she's heard anything, she'll think it was a story I made up —
like those rubies in the fruit cake.'

Now it was close to morning. Far off a cock crew. Near-by
another answered. The dawn breeze came up from off the sea
and the black night turned gray. Cilla was shivering and stood
up. Johnny shouldered Isannah.

- 6 -

He kept his word to Cilla, and, as he was putting the little girl
back to bed, he slipped to the attic, unlocked his chest, and
brought down the cup in the flannel bag his mother had made.
He opened the door from the shop to the wharf. Although still
dark inside the house, outside it was growing lighter and
lighter.

Gulls flew in from the islands looking for food.

Cilla joined him and he motioned her to follow him out into
the twilight of the new day. He drew his cup from its bag.

As a small child he had thought it was the most beautiful thing
in the world. It was the reason why he had begged his mother to
apprentice him to a silversmith (and there were none in Townsend, Maine). Now he was more critical of the cup. He thought
it too chunky. On one side was engraved the crest of the Lytes.
This was an eye rising up from the sea. From it rays of light (or
lashes) streamed out, half-covering the surface of the cup. It
was this emblem Merchant Lyte had on everything he owned —
carved above his counting house on Long Wharf, engraved on all
his silver — even on dog collars and harnesses. Miss Lavinia had
it stamped on her Spanish-leather gloves. Johnny knew it was
cut on the slate gravestones of the Lyte family on Copp's Hill.

'The same as his,' said Cilla in wonder.

'And the same motto. Look!'

She read the words in her halting manner: 'Let there be
Lyte.'

And miraculously, as she stumbled over these words, there was light, for the sun came up out of the sea.

The children stood and looked at each other. The girl's face showed her excitement — and her fatigue. It was a pointed, sweet little face, her eyes a lighter brown than Isannah's and her hair not so strikingly pale.

Johnny whispered, 'Just like the sun coming up yonder out of the sea, pushing rays of light ahead of it.'

Cilla (evidently thinking Johnny was getting beyond himself) said, 'Might it not just as well be a *setting* eye?' It was the first sour remark she had made to him all the night.

'No, no. My mother said it is a rising eye. But I was to keep whist and mum about it — unless even God has turned away His face. And Cilla . . . you promised.'

'By my hope of Heaven and my fear of Hell.'

II. *The Pride of Your Power*

THE WEEK wore on, each day as hot as the one before, for it was July. Every day after dinner Mr. Lapham took a long nap under his basket snoring as gently as he did everything else. Johnny would let him sleep for an hour, then wake him up, scold him, and get him to work. His work was beautiful. The body of the sugar basin was quickly completed and he began repousséing on it the rich garlands of fruit with the same skill he had had forty years before.

Johnny's own work did not satisfy him as well. He had exactly enlarged the handle in his wax model. Mrs. Lapham and the girls, even Mr. Lapham, said it was fine, and he could go ahead and cast it in silver. It was only Johnny himself who was dissatisfied.

Friday evening, when the light was failing and work over, Johnny took the silver pitcher and his own wax model and left the shop. He was in Fish Street, in a minute stopping outside the silver shop of Paul Revere. He didn't dare knock, but he knew that any moment now the silversmith would be closing his shop, leaving for his dwelling in near-by North Square. He was so prosperous a smith that he did not live and work in the same place.

So at last he saw Mr. Revere, a stocky, ruddy man, with fine, dark eyes, shutting his shop, taking out his key preparing to lock up.

'Good evening, Mr. Revere.' The man smiled with a quick flash of white teeth. He had a quick smile and a quick face and body.

'Good evening, Johnny Tremain.' The boy had long admired Mr. Revere as the best craftsman in Boston. He had no idea Mr. Revere knew his name. He did not know all the master silversmiths had an eye on him.

'Mr. Revere, I'd like to talk with you.'

'Man to man,' Mr. Revere agreed, opening his shop door, motioning Johnny to follow him.

Johnny's eyes flew about the shop, taking in the fine anvils, the hood upon the annealing furnace, the neat nests of crucibles. It was just such a shop he would himself have when he was man-grown. Not much like Mr. Lapham's.

Although Paul Revere was as busy a man as there was in all Boston, he took everything so easily in his stride (doing the one thing after another) that he never seemed rushed, so now, because an apprentice stopped him on the street and said he wanted to talk to him, he appeared to have all the time in the world.

'Sir,' said Johnny, 'it's a matter of handles.' He took the silver pitcher out of the cloth he had wrapped it in and his own wax model and explained Mr. Hancock's order.

'So you want to talk to me as a silversmith to silversmith, do you?' He had Johnny's wax model in his hands — delicate hands to go with such heavy wrists. 'What does your master say of your work?'

'Mr. Lapham won't even look at it much. But he says it's good enough and I can go ahead and cast tomorrow. I've *got* to cast tomorrow because it's Saturday and we can't work Sunday, and it must be done Monday at seven. Although my master thinks it's all right, I'm not sure . . .'

'He is wrong and you are right. Look, you've just copied the handle on the pitcher too slavishly — just enlarged it. Don't you see that your winged woman looks coarse in comparison? I'd have the figures the same size on both pieces — fill in with a scroll. Then, too, your curve is wrong. The basin is so much

bigger you cannot use the same curve. Yours looks hunched up
and awkward. It's all a matter of proportion.' He took up a
piece of paper and a pencil and drew off what he meant with
one sure sweep of his hand. 'I'd use a curve more like that —
see? This is what I meant when I said I'd add a scroll or two
below the figure of the winged woman — not just enlarge her
so she looks like a Boston fishwife in comparison to the angel on
the pitcher. See?'

'I see.'

The man looked at him a little curiously.

'There was a time,' he said, 'when your own master could
have shown you that.'

'Mr. Lapham is . . . well . . . he's feeble.'

'Not doing very much work these days?'

'Not what *you'd* call much.' Johnny felt on the defensive.
'Not much fine hollow ware. Plenty of buckles, spoons, and
such.'

'How many boys?'

'Three of us, sir.'

'I'd hardly think he'd need three. Now, if he wants to cut
down, you tell him from me that I'll buy your unexpired time.
I think between us we could make some fine things — you and I.'

The boy flushed. To think the great Paul Revere wanted him!

'Tell your master I'll pay a bit more than is usual for you.
Don't let him shunt one of those other boys off on me.'

He stood up. It was time for Johnny to go.

'I couldn't leave the Laphams, sir,' he said as he thanked Mr.
Revere. 'If it wasn't for me, nothing would ever get done.
They'd just about starve.'

'I see. You're right, of course. But if the old gentleman dies
or you ever want a new master, remember my offer. So . . .' and
he turned to shake hands; 'may we meet again.'

- *2* -

By Saturday noon, Johnny, following Mr. Revere's advice and his curve, had got the model of the handle exactly right. He could tell with his eyes closed. It felt perfect. He rapidly made a duplicate, for when the molten silver was poured in on the wax, it would melt and float away, so he made a model for each handle.

Now, no matter how long it took him (and if all went well it should not be too long), he must get his handles cast, cleaned, and soldered to the basin itself which Mr. Lapham had made. Of course, on Sunday the shop would be locked up all day, the furnace cold. Mr. Lapham would as always escort his household, dressed in Sunday best, to the Cockerel Church and after that back for a cold dinner. Whether they went again or not to afternoon meeting, the master left for each to decide. He himself always went. Madge and Dorcas usually entertained their beaux. Mrs. Lapham slept. Cilla would take Isannah out along the little beach. Johnny, Dove, and Dusty were apt to steal off for a swim, although Mr. Lapham had no idea of it. He thought they sat quietly at home and that Johnny read the Bible out loud to them.

So Sunday was out. But if he got up at three or four Monday morning, he would have time to clean his work before he took it over to Mr. Hancock at seven.

After Saturday dinner, Mr. Lapham as usual prepared for a snooze, stretched out in the one armchair in the shop, with his basket over his head to keep off the flies. Perhaps Johnny's tyranny during the week had irritated the old gentleman — who never believed it made the least difference to anyone when anything was finished.

'Dove, Dusty,' Johnny was yelling, 'build up the furnace, fetch in charcoal. Hi! you lazy, good-for-nothing dish-mops.'

Dove ran out to the coal house. There was a queer, pleased look on his face when he returned.

'Charcoal all gone, Master Johnny.'

'Gone!'

'Yep. I haven't said anything because you always like to take charge of things like that 'round here.'

'Get a basket! Quick! Run to Mr. Hamblin over on Long Wharf. Try Mrs. Hitchbourn down on Hitchbourn's Wharf. You've got to get charcoal. Hurry!'

Dove did not hurry. It was getting on toward sunset when at last he came back, pushing his big basket on a wheelbarrow.

It was the worst-looking charcoal Johnny had ever seen.

'This isn't what we silversmiths use. This is fourth-rate stuff — fit for iron — maybe. You know that, Dove.'

'Naw. Not me. I don't know anything — see? You're always telling me.'

'I want willow charcoal.'

'You never said so.'

'I'll go myself, but this delay means we'll be working in lamp-light and up to midnight. You are the stupidest animal God ever made — if He made you, which I doubt. Why your mother didn't drown you when you were a pup, I can't imagine. Come Lord's day and I have a spare moment, I'm going to give you such a hiding for your infernal low-down skulking tricks, you'll be...'

The basket over Mr. Lapham's head moved. He laid it down.

'Boys,' he said mildly, 'you quarrel all the time.'

Johnny, in angry mouthfuls, told him what he thought about Dove and the charcoal, and threw in a cutting remark about Dusty.

The old master said, 'Dove, I want to speak to Johnny alone.' And then, 'Johnny, I don't want you to be always riding them boys so hard. Dove tries, but he's stupid. Ain't his fault, is it? If God had wanted him bright He would have made him that way. We're all poor worms. You're getting above yourself — like I tried to point out to you. God is going to send you a dire punishment for your pride.'

'Yes, sir.'

'One trouble with you is you haven't been up against any boys

as good as yourself — or better, maybe. Because you're the best
young one in this shop — or on Hancock's Wharf — you think
you're the best one in the world.'

Johnny was so anxious to be on with the work — tediously
delayed by Dove's tricks — he hardly listened.

'And, boy, don't you go get all fretted up over what's after all
nothing but an order for silver. It's sinful to let yourself go so
over mundane things. Now I want you to set quietly and
memorize them verses I had you read about pride. Work's over
for the day.'

'*What?*'

'Yep. It always was the old-fashioned way to start Lord's
Day at sunset on Saturday and I've decided to re-establish the
habit in my house.'

'Mr. Lapham, we've *got* to work this evening. We've promised
Mr. Hancock.'

'I doubt God cares even a little bit whether Mr. Hancock has
any silver. It's better to break faith with him, isn't it, than
with the Lord?'

Johnny was tired. His head was ringing. His hands shook a
little. He walked out of the shop, slamming the door after him,
and stormed into the kitchen. He knew Mrs. Lapham did not
take much stock in her father-in-law's pious ways. She and all
four girls were in the kitchen. Madge was frying corn meal,
Dorcas wringing out a cheesecloth. Cilla was setting the table,
and Isannah playing with the cat.

Mrs. Lapham looked at him. 'Boy, have you seen a ghost?'

Johnny sat and told his story. He was beyond his customary
abusive eloquence.

The girls stared at him with piteous open mouths. Mrs.
Lapham's jaw set grimly.

'Dorcas, *shut that door*. Don't let your grandpa hear. Johnny —
how many more work-hours will you need?'

'Seven — maybe. I can get two Monday morning.'

'You shall have them. Sabbath or no Sabbath, that sugar
basin is going to be done on time. I'm not letting any old-

fashioned, fussy notions upset the best order we've had for ten years. And if Mr. Hancock is pleased, he may come again and again. I can't have my poor, fatherless girls starve just to please Grandpa. Listen now to me.'

Sunday afternoon Mr. Lapham was not only going to the second service, as usual, but there was to be a meeting of the deacons, a cold supper afterward, and a prayer service at the pastor's. 'That's where you get them five hours, Johnny — tomorrow afternoon.'

Johnny knew that working on the Sabbath was against the law as well as against all his religious training. He might very well go to the stocks or to Hell for it, but when Mrs. Lapham said, 'Darest to, Johnny?' he said, 'I darest.'

'Not a word to the old gentleman, mind.'

'Not a word.'

'Girls, if you so much as peep . . .'

'Oh, no, Ma.'

Dove and Dusty were to be bribed into service by the promise of delivering the basin to Mr. Hancock when done. He always gave money to boys who brought things to the house.

Mrs. Lapham was breathing hard, but she had the matter well in hand. It was settled.

'Isannah,' she said quietly, 'you call Grandpa and the boys in to supper. Cilla, run down cellar and fetch cold ale.'

Her mouth and the folds about it, even her nose and eyes, were like iron.

- 3 -

Sunday afternoon and the work went forward with never a hitch. Even Dove and Dusty were good and obedient, although Dove was half-threatening to tell 'old Grandpa' when he got home. Johnny did not care what his master might say — only, please God, the basin were done and Mr. Hancock come again and again with his rich orders. If Mr. Lapham was angry, he could sell Johnny's time to Paul Revere.

The four girls, still dressed in their pretty go-to-meeting frocks, watched him with fascinated, admiring eyes. Their mother sent them out-of-doors. Did the smoke from the furnace show from the wharf? From Fish Street? Did they hear any comments?

Having found for himself the proper willow charcoal, Johnny went quickly ahead with his casting. He set his two wax models in wet sand. The furnace was piping hot. His hands were very sure. He was confident he could do the work, yet inside he was keyed up and jumpy.

Mrs. Lapham fussed about him and he ordered her to do simple things.

'Not the draft yet, Mrs. Lapham . . . now get to work with the bellows.'

Once he even told her to 'look sharp,' and she took it with a humble 'Yes, Johnny.'

'Now fetch me the crucible.'

She turned to Dove. 'Which one does he want, boy?'

'I'll get her down.'

Dove went to the shelves where the crucibles for melting silver were kept. Johnny did not see Dove standing on a stool, reaching far back and carefully taking out a cracked crucible. Dusty saw him and giggled. He knew the crack in it was so small it was hard even to see. It might stand the heat of the furnace, but the chances were that it would not. That was why Mr. Lapham had put it so far back. Both he and Dove thought it would just about serve Johnny Tremain right — after the insufferable way he had been bossing everybody — if the crucible gave way and the hot silver did spill all over the top of the furnace. It would certainly make Johnny look like a fool, after all his fussing.

Johnny took the cracked crucible in his trusting hands, put in it silver ingots, set it on top of the furnace.

Cilla flew in. 'Ma, there's a man looking at our chimney.'

'How's he dressed?'

'Seafaring man.'

'No seafaring man ever objected to a little Sabbath-breaking. But mind if you see any deacons or constables.'

The work went on.

Isannah sat with the cat in her lap. 'Johnny's going to Hell,' she said firmly. Johnny himself thought this was possible.

He called to Mrs. Lapham to 'look sharp' and put the old silver turnip watch where he could see it. The silver must be run at a certain speed and be allowed to cool for just so long.

Mrs. Lapham was so slavishly eager to help him, he almost felt fond of her. He did not notice Dusty and Dove snickering in a corner.

Some of the beeswax he had used for his models had been left too near the furnace. It had melted and run over the floor. Johnny had been taught to clean up as he went along, but today he was in too much of a hurry to bother.

'Johnny,' cried Mrs. Lapham, 'isn't it time to pour? Look, the silver is melted and begun to wink.' It was true.

He moved forward delicately, his right hand outstretched. The crucible began to settle — collapse, the silver was running over the top of the furnace like spilled milk. Johnny jumped toward it, his right hand still outstretched. Something happened, he never knew exactly what. His feet went out from under him. His hand came down on the top of the furnace.

The burn was so terrible he at first felt no pain, but stood stupidly looking at his hand. For one second, before the metal cooled, the inside of his right hand, from wrist to fingertips, was coated with solid silver. He looked at the back of his hand. It was as always. Then he smelled burned flesh. The room blackened and tipped around him. He heard a roaring in his ears.

When he came to, he was stretched out upon the floor. Dorcas was trying to pour brandy down his throat. Mrs. Lapham had plunged the burned hand into a panful of flour and was yelling at Madge to hurry with her bread poultice.

He saw Cilla's face. It was literally green. 'Ma,' she said, licking her white lips, 'shall I run for Doctor Warren?'

'No — no . . . oh, wait, I've got to think. I don't want any of them doctors to know we was breaking Sabbath Day. And we don't need no doctor for just a burn. Cilla, you run down the wharf and you fetch that old midwife, Gran' Hopper. These old women know better than any doctor how to cure things like this. Johnny, how you feel?'

'All right.'

'Hurt yet?'

'Not yet.'

He knew it would later.

-4-

Johnny lay in the 'birth and death room.' This was hardly more than a closet with a tiny window off the kitchen, used for storage except in times of sickness. His hand had been done up in a linseed poultice. The smell of the linseed was stifling, and now, on the second day, the pain had really begun. His arm throbbed to the shoulder. Gran' Hopper was in the kitchen, talking to Mrs. Lapham.

'Mind you keep that poultice wet. Just leave it wrapped up and wet it now and then with lime water. There's more luck than anything else in things like this is. If it don't come along good, I'll make a charm.'

Not many years before, Gran' Hopper would have been hanged for a witch. She had the traditional venerable years, the toothless cackle, the mustache. Nor was she above resorting to charms. But she had had vast experience. No doctor in Boston knew more than she about midwifery and children's diseases. So far she had done as well as any of them, except for one thing. The hand had been allowed to draw together — turn in on itself. It was less painful than if it had been held out flat.

By the fourth day ulceration had set in. This was considered

Nature's way of healing an injury. Gran' Hopper gave him laudanum and more laudanum. There followed drowsy days and nights that ran together, a ceaseless roaring in the ears. There was nothing left of him but the pain and the drug.

The fever abated and with it the doses of the drug. Johnny had not once looked at his hand since he had stood before the furnace and seen it lined with silver. Gran' Hopper said on the next day she would unwrap it and see, as she cheerfully put it, 'what was left.'

Thus far the pain and the drug and the fever had dulled his mind. He had not thought about the future, for of what use to anyone was a cripple-handed silversmith? But that night Gran' Hopper's words haunted him. Next day she would see 'what was left.'

He was utterly unprepared for the sight of his hand when finally it was unwrapped and lay in the midwife's aproned lap. Mrs. Lapham, Madge, Dorcas, all had crowded into the little birth and death room. Cilla and Isannah were in the kitchen, too frightened to go near him.

'My!' said Madge, 'isn't that funny-looking? The top part, Johnny, looks all right, although a little narrow, but, Johnny, your thumb and palm have grown together.'

This was true. He bent and twisted his fingers. He could not get the thumb to meet the forefinger. Such a hand was completely useless. For the first time he faced the fact that his hand was crippled.

'Oh, let me *see!*' Dorcas was leaning over him. She gave her most elegant little screech of horror, just like a great lady who has seen a mouse.

'My!' said Mrs. Lapham, 'that's worse than anything I had imagined. Now isn't that a shame! Bright boy like Johnny just ruined. No more good than a horse with sprung knees.'

Johnny did not stay to hear more. That morning he had dressed (with Mrs. Lapham's competent help) for the first time. He got up, stood facing them stiffly, his bad hand jammed into his breeches pocket.

'I'm going out,' he said thickly.

Cilla and Isannah sat close together in a frightened huddle, staring at him, not daring to speak. He said rudely, 'You should have come in too — and seen the fun.'

Cilla gaped at him, tried to say something, but only swallowed.

'You two — sitting there — looking like a couple of fishes.'

He slammed the front door after him. He had always been bad about slamming doors. In the fresh air he felt better. He pretended not to hear Mrs. Lapham calling him from a window to come right back. All Fish Street could hear when Mrs. Lapham called. He paid no heed.

He walked all over Boston, his hand thrust deep in his breeches pocket. Instinctively he wanted to tire himself out (which was easy in his weakened condition) so he could not think.

When he came back, there was something queer about the silence of the kitchen. No one reproved him because he had disobeyed Mrs. Lapham. He knew they had been talking about him.

Cilla, for one of the first times in her life, tried to be polite to him.

'Oh, Johnny,' she whispered, 'I'm sorrier than I was ever sorry before.'

Isannah said, 'Is it true, like Ma says, you'll be only good for picking rags?'

Cilla turned on Isannah. 'You're crazy! Johnny isn't going to pick rags... But oh, Johnny, it's so awful and I'm so sorry and...'

Johnny's face was crimson. 'Will you stop talking about it!'

Isannah went on — 'Madge says it looks awful...'

'If either of you girls,' he stormed, 'ever mention that I've even got a hand, I'll... I'll... just get on a ship and never come back. I'm not going to have you mucking about with your infernal cry-baby "Oh how dreadfuls." '

So he went to the shop.

He saw with anger that Dove was sitting at his bench, daring to use his tools. He had not been in the shop for a month. Of

course it should be expected that Dove would use his bench —
for a little while — just until he was back at it himself.

Mr. Lapham had looked up from his work, blinked gently,
shook his head and sighed. Dusty was making a terrific din in
one corner.

Johnny stood and watched Dove's clumsy work as long as he
could in silence. At last he burst out.

'Dove, don't hold your crimping iron like that . . .'

Dove leaned back. His fat, white face grinned up at him with
exaggerated innocence.

'Thank you, Master Johnny. I know I'm not as good as you
are. Won't you please to show me just how I should hold my
crimping iron?'

Johnny walked out of the shop by the door leading to the
wharf. He'd never show anybody again how to hold a crimping
iron. If you can't do, you had best shut up. He started to slam
the door, thought better of it. If you can't do, you'd best not
slam doors.

So he strolled the length of the wharf. There was a big ship
in from Jamaica. He idly watched porters rolling barrels of
molasses out of its hold. A sailor was trying to sell an old lady
a parrot. He saw John Hancock standing in a group of men.
The sugar basin had never been delivered. When Mr. Lapham
had discovered the evil that had gone on in his absence and the
terrible punishment God had meted out to Johnny Tremain,
he had ordered the whole thing melted down and he himself had
gone over to Mr. Hancock, returned the cream pitcher, and
merely said he had found it impossible to make a sugar basin.
No explanation.

The boy was accustomed to working from eight to twelve,
sometimes fourteen hours in a day. He had no holidays, no
Saturday afternoons. He had often imagined to himself the
pleasure it would be just to stroll once down Hancock's Wharf,
as he was strolling now. Nothing to do. His hands in his pockets.
Other boys — friends of his — would look up from their work,
envy his idleness. Here and there he did see a familiar face.

He believed every one of them was talking about his burn — pitying him. There was not a boy on the wharf Johnny did not know. He had made friends with some and enemies of others, and had played or fought with all of them. He saw Saul and Dicer packing salt herrings in a tub; Andy, his leather thimble strapped to his palm, sewing a sail; Tom Drinker (the local bully) coopering a barrel. This was Johnny's world, but now he walked through it an alien. They knew what had happened. They did not envy Johnny's idleness. He saw one nudge another. They were whispering about him — daring to pity him. Dicer's master, the herring-pickler, yelled some kind remark to him, but Johnny did not answer. Seemingly in one month he had become a stranger, an outcast on Hancock's Wharf. He was maimed and they were whole.

At the end of the wharf, under the derrick used for unloading the largest ships, he stripped off his clothes and dove into the water. There was not another working boy in Boston who was out swimming in the middle of the afternoon. Only once or twice in a summer — on days of unendurable heat, teachers dismissed school, masters closed shops, and the boys ran down to the wharves to swim. Sometimes, like Mr. Lapham's boys, they swam secretly, silently, on Sunday afternoons, but usually only after dusk had fallen and the day's work was over.

Johnny dove and swam. But it was curious to be alone. He did not like the feeling of being thus cut off from his normal life.

Yet one thing gave him great pleasure. Once in the water, his bad hand was as good as the other. Swimming, he could forget it.

- 5 -

At first Mrs. Lapham tended to humor the 'poor boy.' As he preferred the birth and death room to the attic with Dove and Dusty, she had let him stay on. He had never in all his life slept in a bed alone — much less a whole room. He wanted to be alone.

There was one trouble with his new quarters. When Mrs. Lapham came down to start breakfast, she always began by getting him up.

'Get into your clothes — you lazy boy. Stop by at Deacon Parson's for a quart of milk. Get to the town pump.'

Soon enough she was addressing him as a 'lazy good-for-nothing,' a 'lug-a-bed,' a 'worthless limb of Satan.' Such words poured out of her absent-mindedly, but never in the old days had she called Johnny such names.

The boy least necessary in the shop had always done chores. Now both Dove and Dusty were more valuable than Johnny Tremain. Every morning he put on the heavy wooden yoke, trudged over to North Square for drinking water. Now for the first time he learned to handle a broom properly. He carried in charcoal for the annealing furnace in the shop and wood for the cooking hearth in the kitchen, and as he moved restlessly about doing (and often failing to do) this humble work, Cilla and Isannah watched him and said little. Never a single insult. He had made it clear to them he wanted to be left alone.

Madge and Dorcas found innumerable small tasks for him, now he 'wasn't doing anything.' Once fat Madge made him sit before her, holding a skein of yarn from which she wound a ball. He was miserable with his crippled hand stretched out for all the world to see. When she mentioned it, he threw the yarn at her head and walked off.

One day Mr. Lapham called to him and led him to a bench under the old willow behind the coal house. The old man had never once berated him for Sabbath-breaking, never reminded him how often he had pointed out that pride goeth before a fall.

'My boy,' he said mildly, 'soon it will be September. Summer is over.' Johnny nodded. 'And I feel I must talk with you. When I signed for you, Johnny, there was a mutual contract between your mother and myself. She's dead, so the contract is now between you and me. I promised to feed and clothe you, keep you in good discipline, and as far as your capacity permitted to teach you the silversmith's arts and mysteries.... I ... I never had a boy so quick to teach, but ... And you promised to serve me diligently for seven years, to keep my secrets and my honor. You've done all that, Johnny. But ... but now ... I can't keep my contract with you. I can't teach a cripple-handed boy to be a silversmith.'

Johnny said nothing.

'Mrs. L. is right,' the old man went on.

'You mean she wants you to get rid of me?'

'Not exactly, but she does think it is an extravagance for a poor household to keep a boy just for chores. But I've told her' — there was an unexpected glint of determination in the groping old eyes — 'I've told her as long as you wish you are to stay with us. I won't ever ... turn you out. I mind the time your mother came to my shop with you ... she was a sweet lady ... very genteel. She said your heart was fastened on being a silversmith. She said you was a bright boy — you always was that. Now, Johnny, it's for your own good I'm talking to you. You've got to learn another way of supporting yourself. I want you to go around, look about the shops, and find out a respectable trade where a bad hand won't matter too much. You're a bright boy, Johnny. Maybe a ropemaker or a cooper or a weaver could teach you his craft. That hand of yours will soon be strong enough, but will always be sort of doubled in on itself.'

Johnny started to look at his hand, but quickly thrust it back in his pocket.

'You're right,' he said. 'I've got to go.'

'I don't want you to feel hurried about leaving us, Johnny. You're just about earning your keep by the odd jobs you do, spite of what Mrs. L. says. You look about you quietly and find a trade to your fancy and a master you think you'd like. You can tell him from me I'll give the rest of your time away for nothing.'

It was less than two months ago Mr. Revere was promising something extra for his time.

'Mrs. L. doesn't like it the way you loiter off and go swimming; but you loiter and swim all you have a mind — just so you get the chores done and settle down real hard to finding yourself a new trade. And one more thing I have on my mind.'

'Yes, sir.'

'I want you to forgive Dove like a Christian.'

'Forgive him? Why?'

'Why, that when you asked for a crucible he handed you the old cracked one.'

'You mean . . . he did it on purpose?'

'No, no, Johnny, he only meant to humiliate you. He tells me (Mrs. L. made me question him) that he was that offended by your Sabbath-breaking he thought it fitting that you should learn a lesson. I can't help but admit I'm encouraged with that much piety in *one* of my boys.'

Johnny's voice sounded strangled. 'Mr. Lapham, I'm going to get him for that . . .'

'Hush, hush, boy. I say, and Bible says, forgive. He was real repentant when he told me. Never meant to harm you. He was in tears.'

'He's going to be in a lot more of those tears 'fore I'm done with him. That scabby, white louse, that hypocritical . . .'

'Hold your tongue, boy. I thought misfortune had taught you patience.'

'It has,' said Johnny. 'If I have to, I'll wait ten years to get that Dove.'

But he quieted himself instantly and thanked his master for his kindness. As he walked past the shop, he saw Dove and Dusty hanging idly out of the shop window. They were looking for him.

Dove said: 'Will Mr. Johnny Tremain be so kind as to fetch us drinking water? Mrs. Lapham says *we* are too valuable to leave our benches. She told us we were to send you.'

Without a word he went to the back entry, put on the heavy yoke.

Understandably, the sight of Johnny wielding a broom, carrying charcoal, firewood, water, had not quickly lost its fascination for his erstwhile slaves. They were still hanging out of the window.

'Look sharp, Johnny.'

'Hey, boy, look sharp.'

Giggles. A low whistle.

Johnny said nothing.

III. *An Earth of Brass*

WEEKS wore on. September was ending. A large part of every day Johnny spent doing what he called 'looking for work.' He did not really want to follow any trade but his own. He looked down on soap-boilers, leather-dressers, ropemakers, and such. He did not begin his hunt along Hancock's Wharf and Fish Street, where he and his story were well known and the masters would have been apt to employ him from pity. He went to the far ends of Boston.

Mr. Lapham had told him to stand about and watch the different artisans at their trades until he was sure it was work he could do. Then he was to address the master politely, explain about his bad hand, and ask to be taken on. But Johnny was too impatient, too unthinking and too scornful. He barged into shop after shop along the great wharves and up and down Cornhill and Orange, Ann, and Ship Streets, Dock Square, King and Queen Streets — 'Did the master want another boy?' — keeping his hand hidden in his pocket.

His quickness and address struck everyone favorably, and so an old clockmaker eagerly agreed to take him on — especially when he told him that he had already served Mr. Lapham two years.

'But why, my boy, is Mr. Lapham ready to part with you, now that you must be of value to him?'

'I've a bad hand.'

'Let me see it.'

He did not want to show his hand, but the masters always insisted. He would take it out of the pocket where he always kept it, with a flourish, display it to the sickening curiosity of the master, apprentices, journeymen, lady customers. After such an experience he would sometimes loiter and swim for the rest of the day. Sometimes he would grit his teeth and plunge headlong into the next shop.

He rarely bothered to look at the signs over the door which indicated what work was done inside. A pair of scissors for a tailor, a gold lamb for a wool weaver, a basin for a barber, a painted wooden book for a bookbinder, a large swinging compass for an instrument-maker. Although more and more people were learning how to read, the artisans still had signs above their shops, not wishing to lose a possible patron merely because he happened to be illiterate.

Having been told by one clockmaker he would not suit, Johnny walked in on two more and got the same answer.

A butcher (his sign was a gilded ox skull) would have employed him, but the idea of slaughtering animals sickened him. He was a fine craftsman to the tips of his fingers — even to the tips of his maimed hand.

Now he never came home for the hearty midday dinner. Mrs. Lapham, Madge, and Dorcas were always pointing out how much he ate and how little he did. He knew Mrs. Lapham was looking around for a grown-up silversmith who would come in as a partner for Grandpa, and she had said (looking straight at Johnny) she would not ask him to sleep in the attic with the two boys. He was to have the birth and death room. 'I declare,' she said one day, 'no business can be run with just a feeble old man and three of the most worthless boys in Boston — eating their heads off.'

Seems she was negotiating with a Mr. Tweedie — newly arrived from Baltimore. He had arrived alone, but she must make sure he really was a bachelor or a widower. Obviously, whatever partner she found for her father-in-law must marry one of her 'poor fatherless girls.' The shop must stay in the family.

So Johnny ate as little as he could, and did not come home at noon. But someone would usually slip a piece of hard bread, cheese, jerked beef, or salt fish and johnnycake in the pocket of his jacket as it hung on its hook. He knew it was Cilla, but he never spoke to her about it. His unhappiness was so great he felt himself completely cut off from the rest of the world.

But sometimes, as he lay in the sun on Beacon Hill or Copp's Hill (among the graves), or curled himself upon a coil of rope along a wharf, eating the food she had managed to get for him, he would dream of the great things he would do for her — when he was man-grown. There were three things she longed for — a gold necklace; a gray pony with a basket cart; a little sailboat. He dreamed of himself as successful — rich. Never as the ditch-digger and ragpicker Mrs. Lapham was always suggesting to him.

Some days there was no food in his pocket. Then he went hungry.

On one such day, he was strolling up Salt Lane. Here about him and on Union Street were printing offices. It was noon, and all over Boston work had stopped and everyone, except himself, had either gone home for dinner or to one of the famous taverns. Above one tiny shop he saw a sign that attracted him. It was a little man in bright blue coat and red breeches, solemnly gazing at Salt Lane through a spyglass. So this was where the *Boston Observer* was published. The Laphams took no newspaper, but he had heard Mr. Lapham speak of the wicked *Observer* and how it was trying to stir up discontent in Boston, urging the people to revolt against the mild rule of England. The comical little painted man looked so genial, so ready to welcome any-one, that Johnny stepped in.

He might have guessed he would waste his time. Of course the master would be off for dinner, but because he had liked the painted sign, he went in. He had not even stopped to con-sider whether or not a printer's work was something that he could do.

He saw the squat, buglike printing press, the trays of type, the strings on which printed sheets were hung to dry like clothes on a line. On a workbench was a smaller press for notifications, proclamations, broadsides, trade cards. Everything smelled of printers' ink.

A boy, larger than himself and probably a few years older, was standing at a counter talking with a stout marketwoman in a frayed red skirt. Her pig had strayed from her yard. She wished to advertise it. The boy wrote down what she said.

'Lost — a spotted sow from Whitebread Alley,' the boy repeated.

'She was the *dearest* pig,' said the woman — 'would come for a whistle like a dog. My children taught her to play "dead pig." We don't ever think to eat her — only her increase. We called her Myra.'

The boy did not write that down. He lifted his dark face, indolent dark eyes. The lashes flickered. He was interested.

'Was she hard to teach, ma'am?'

'Oh, no! Pigs are clever.'

'I never knew that. How do they compare with dogs?'

Then the old lady began to talk. She talked about pigs in general and her Myra in particular.

The printer's boy, unruffled, unhurried, heard her through. He was tall and powerfully built. There was something a little sluggish in his casual movements, in his voice — almost as though he was saving himself for emergencies, not wasting himself on every casual encounter.

The woman was delighted with so good a listener and his few intelligent questions. Johnny, standing at the door, forgot his own errand. He had no idea that either pigs or old market-women could be so interesting. It was the apprentice, standing at the counter in his leather apron and full white shirt, his thoughtful face framed in hair, black and straight as an Indian's, who had cast a spell over the old gossip and her subject.

Although the boy had nodded casually as Johnny came in, he did not speak to him until after the woman was gone and he had set up the few lines of type. There was nothing rude about this seeming neglect. It was almost as if they were friends of long standing. The strange boy had none of the bustling smartness of the usual Boston apprentice. Johnny had seen enough of them in the last month, apprentices who knew what you wanted and that you would not suit, and you were out on the street again in three minutes.

Having set the advertisement, the boy took a covered basket from under the counter, put it on a table, and drew up two stools.

'Why don't you sit down?' he said, 'and eat. My master's wife — she's my aunt — always sends over more than I can manage.'

Seemingly he had sized up everything with only half a glance from the lazy, dark eyes. He had known Johnny was hungry without once really looking at him and had also known that he was someone he himself liked. He was both friendly and aloof. Nonchalantly he took out his claspknife, cut hunks of bread from the long loaf. There were also cheese, apples, and ham.

The ham seemed to remind the printer's boy of the gossip and her pig.

'I grew up on a farm,' he said, 'but I never knew you could teach a pig tricks. Help yourself to more bread?'

Johnny hesitated. So far he had not taken his bad hand out of his pocket since entering the shop. Now he must, or go hungry. He took the claspknife in his left hand and stealthily drew forth the maimed hand to steady the loaf. It was hard to saw through the crusty loaf with a left hand, but he managed to do it. It took him a long time. The other boy said nothing. He did not, thank God, offer to help him. Of course he had seen the crippled hand, but at least he did not stare at it. Asked no questions. Seemingly he saw everything and said nothing. Because of this quality in him, Johnny said:

'I'm looking for some sort of work I think I could do well in . . . even with a bad hand.'

'That's quite a recent burn.' It was the first intelligent re-

mark any man, woman, or child had made about Johnny's
hand in any shop he had been in.

'I did it last July. I am ... I *was* apprenticed to a silversmith.
I burned it on hot silver.'

'I see. So everything you are trained for is out?'

'Yes. I wouldn't mind so much being a clockmaker or instrument-maker. But I can't and I *won't* be a butcher nor a soap-
boiler.'

'No.'

'I've *got* to do something I like, or ... or ...'

The dark boy put the question to him he had not been able
to ask himself.

'Or what?'

Johnny lifted his thin, fair face. His lips parted before he
spoke.

'I just don't know. I can't think.'

Apparently the printer's boy did not know either. All he
said was, 'More cheese?'

Then Johnny began to talk. He told all about the Laphams
and how he somehow couldn't seem even to thank Cilla for the
food she usually got to him. How cross and irritable he had
become. How rude to people who told him they were sorry for
him. And he admitted he had used no sense in looking for a
new job. He told about the burn, but with none of the belliger-
ent arrogance with which he had been answering the questions
kind people had put to him. As he talked to Rab (for the boy
had told him this was his name), for the first time since the
accident he felt able to stand aside from his problems — see
himself.

Mr. Lorne, Rab's uncle by marriage, came back. He was a
scholarly young man with a face as sharp and bright as a fox's.
Rab did not immediately spring into action to make a good show
of his industry before his master. He had none of the usual
'yes, sir,' 'no, sir,' 'please, sir.' He went on calmly eating bread
and cheese.

On Mr. Lorne's heels came two little boys in big aprons — the

Webb twins. Seemingly they went back to their master's house across Salt Lane for dinner, while the nephew ate out of a basket and minded the shop.

The Webbs were set to work. Mr. Lorne began to ink a pad. Johnny felt he must go. Rab walked with him to the door. He was still eating bread and cheese.

'I don't know how you'll make out,' said Rab. 'Of course you can get work — if you'll take it.'

'I know . . . unskilled work.'

'Yes, work you don't want.'

'But' — the dinner had raised Johnny's hopes — 'I feel sure I'll get something.'

Overhead the little man with the spyglass and the red breeches was swinging in the wind — observing Boston from a variety of angles.

Rab said: 'There is some work here you could do. Not the sort that teaches a boy a skilled trade. Just riding for us — delivering papers all over Boston and around. Nothing you'd want. But if you can't find anything else, you come back.'

'I'll come back all right — but not until I can tell you what a good job I've found myself.'

'You haven't any folks?'

'None at all.'

'I've got lots of relatives,' said Rab, 'but my parents are dead.'

'Oh.'

'Come again.'

'I'll come.'

It wasn't the food alone that so raised Johnny's hopes. It was Rab himself; an ease and confidence flowed out and supported those around him. The marketwoman had felt better about losing her Myra after she had talked with Rab. He was the first person to whom Johnny Tremain had confided his own story.

- 2 -

The coming of Mr. Percival Tweedie, journeyman silversmith of Baltimore, cast a longer and longer shadow over the Lapham household and conversation. While the terms of partnership were being drawn up, he stayed at a cheap lodging house on Fish Street. Johnny left right after breakfast and often did not return until dark. He did not meet Mr. Tweedie for a long time and he got tired of hearing about him. Mr. Tweedie was ready to sign the contract of partnership Mrs. Lapham had had drawn up — and Mr. Tweedie would not sign. When Mr. Tweedie came to the shop it was Dorcas he seemed to fancy — no, it was Madge. Although almost forty, he was still a bachelor — Mrs. Lapham had asked him about that.

Johnny already hated the very sound of his name, and then one morning, before breakfast, he met him. Mr. Tweedie was diffidently standing about in the shop, hoping Mrs. Lapham would ask him to breakfast. He was fingering a pocketbook sent in for a new clasp, and his stomach was rolling from hunger.

'Heh!' said Johnny rudely. The timid creature jumped like a shot rabbit and dropped the pocketbook.

'What are you doing here?' the boy demanded, pretending he had caught a thief.

Mr. Tweedie swallowed twice, his Adam's apple rising and falling with emotion, but said nothing.

'Are you a thief or are you that Tweedie man I've heard tell of?'

'I'm Tweedie.'

'I'm Johnny Tremain.'

'You don't say.'

'I'll tell Mrs. Lapham you're here — for breakfast.'

'I just happened by — just thought I'd come in.' He had a queer, squeaky voice. Johnny disliked him even more than he had expected. Such impotence, such timidity in a grown man irritated the boy.

'Oh, come out with it flat,' he said. 'You've been getting your dinners here free for two weeks and now you're feeling out for breakfast. I don't care, not me. But I'll warn the women to put on an extra plate.'

The man said nothing, but he looked at Johnny and the look of bleak hatred amazed the boy. He had not guessed Mr. Tweedie had that much gumption in him.

Mrs. Lapham came thumping down the stairs. It was her second trip to the foot of the attic ladder and she still wasn't sure Dove and Dusty were out of bed. Everything had gone wrong. Breakfast was late. Madge had a felon on her finger and wasn't good for anything and Dorcas was complaining because there was no butter for breakfast. She had slapped Dorcas, who had gone out back to cry. How easily, smoothly everything had gone in the old days before Johnny got hurt! Then the household went like clockwork and the shop had earned money for butter and butcher's meat once or twice a week. The sight of Johnny Tremain standing there in the lower hall doing nothing, good for nothing, irritated her.

'Hurry,' she snorted and waddled into the kitchen, Johnny on her heels. The fire was smoking and she knelt down to mend it. Johnny might have done that while she was upstairs.

Although Johnny was now looked upon as something of a black sheep and Mrs. Lapham was no longer telling him he would end up picking rags, but on the gallows, he thought it behooved him to tell her just what he thought of Mr. Tweedie.

'I can see why that Tweedie has never been a master smith. He hasn't the force of character. As a man he's no good — if he is a man, which I doubt. I think he is somebody's spinster aunt dressed up in men's clothes.'

Mrs. Lapham heaved herself to her knees and brushed back her streaming hair with a red forearm.

'You don't say!' Her voice showed her exasperation. She had found Mr. Tweedie herself. She was trying to nurse him along, to get the wary creature to sign her contract and marry one of her girls.

'Yep, I do say,' said Johnny. 'I've just been talking with him. He's no good and ——'

'He's here now?'

'Yep. In the shop. That squeak-pig is trying to horn in on breakfast.'

The doors were all open. Anyone in the shop could have heard Johnny's insults.

Slowly, like a great sow pulling out of a wallow, Mrs. Lapham got to her feet, glaring down at Johnny, her enormous bosom heaving.

'And I'm going to tell you what I think of that squeak-pig.' Without a word and before he could finish his remarks or dodge, Mrs. Lapham gave him a resounding cuff on the ear.

'Sometimes actions do speak louder than words,' she said, 'and this is one of them times. You get right out of here, Johnny Tremain. That tongue of yours isn't going to do any more damage in *my* house.'

- 3 -

Johnny grabbed his jacket (Cilla had not yet put food in it), pulled his tattered hat over his eyes, and stalked out.

Since his accident he had unconsciously taken to wearing his hat at a rakish angle. This, and the way he always kept his right hand thrust into his breeches pocket, gave him a slightly arrogant air. The arrogance had always been there, but formerly it had come out in pride in his work — not in the way he wore his hat and walked. He told no one what he did all day and Mrs. Lapham was convinced that he had taken to, or was about to take to, 'evil ways.' He did look, at times, both shabby and desperate; in other words, a potential criminal. Sometimes he looked so proud and fine people thought he must be a great gentleman's son in misfortune. One thing he did not look like any more was a smart, industrious Boston apprentice.

He walked down Fish Street to Ann, crossed Dock Square with Faneuil Hall on his left. It was market day. He picked his way about the farm carts, the piles of whitish green cabbages, baskets of yellow corn, rows of plump, pale, plucked turkeys, orange pumpkins, country cheeses — big as a baby's head. Some of the market folk, men and women, children and black slaves, called to him, seeing in the shabby, proud boy a possible rich customer, but others counted the pats of butter on their tables after he had passed by.

Without heeding anyone, he crossed Dock Square and in a moment's time stood beside the brick Town House at the head of King Street. The lower floor of the Town House was an open promenade and here every day the merchants gathered 'on 'change.' Not a merchant in sight. They did not rise as early as market folk. Suddenly Johnny had an idea. Although seemingly he had tried every shop in Boston in search of a new master, he had not tried the merchants. From where he sat on the steps of the Town House, he could look the brief length of King Street which quickly and imperceptibly turned into Long Wharf, running for half a mile into the sea. It was the only wharf in Boston larger than Hancock's. There was not another wharf in all America so large, so famous, so rich.

As at his own wharf, one side was built up solidly with counting houses, warehouses, sail lofts, stores. The other side was left open for the ships. Already sailors, porters, riggers, and such were at work. He waited — it seemed to him for a long time — and then the clerks began to arrive, counting-house doors were unlocked, warehouses were unchained.

At last the merchants came, some striding down King Street, rosy-faced, double-chinned, known and greeted by everyone, apparently knowing and greeting everyone in return. Some came in chaises, gigs. Some had sour, gimlet-eyed faces; some had not yet lost the rolling gait of sea captains. Johnny saw the same gray horse and gig, with the arms upon the door, that had carried John Hancock to the Laphams' last July, trot quickly down King Street onto Long Wharf. Although Mr.

Hancock had recently bought Hancock's Wharf, his principal place of business was on Long.

Mr. Hancock has on a cherry-red coat, Johnny thought. He drives the horse himself, but now he is getting out, telling that dressed-up doll of a black boy to put his horse up for him. Johnny decided he would start at the top of the merchants and work down, only, of course, skipping Merchant Lyte. He'd go first to John Hancock.

From where he sat he could see that a great ship was slowly warping in — no coaster this, no mere sugar boat from the Sugar Isles. A number of fashionably dressed young men, as well as the usual dockhands and porters, were crowding about to welcome her.

There was the heavy clatter of a great coach almost beside him and a coachman was bawling to lesser folk, 'Make way, make way.' Black horses in glittering, silver-mounted harnesses, the rumble and rattle of a ruby coach on cobbles, and on the door panel the familiar crest — a rising eye. Half-seen inside, Merchant Jonathan Lyte. Evidently he had just heard his ship was in and had come down from his mansion on Beacon Hill in a hurry. He was still struggling with the lace about his throat.

Johnny left his seat and strolled down the wharf to watch. No one had ever told him not to watch the Lytes, but he always felt guilty when he did. From afar he knew them all. He knew, for instance, that Mr. Lyte had a broken front tooth. He knew Mrs. Lyte was dead and two sons had been drowned as boys, and girls had died in infancy — this he could read upon the slate gravestones of Copp's Hill. He knew that besides the town house on Beacon Hill there was a country seat at Milton. And he knew that Lavinia Lyte had spent the last summer in London. Now she was back in Boston once more.

She was very tall for a woman, slender and graceful, and moved slowly down the gangplank with the stately self-consciousness which happened to be the fashionable gait for a lady at the moment. A hundred times before, Johnny had stopped on the streets of Boston, or before her house, to watch her:

he but one more gaping face in a crowd, she the accepted reigning belle. He admired her odd, strong beauty which, unlike her regal gait, was not of the fashionable type. To begin with, she was too tall, and golden curls, pink-and-white skin were the mode. She was a black-haired woman, and only for balls and such was she powdered and curled. In contrast, her skin was dead white. Her features were clear-cut enough to justify the poems written to her in London and even here in Boston, comparing her to a classic goddess.

There was only one flaw to her marble beauty. Between the low-sweeping black brows was a tiny perpendicular line. Once, and once only, the master hand that carved her face had let the chisel slip. This blemish was odd enough for a young lady still in her twenties. It boded no good for the peace of mind of those about her — nor for her own. Now she was all glitter and smiles, greeting the young gentlemen who had come to meet her. Johnny did not notice what she wore, but the mantua-makers, dressmakers, milliners, glovers, and jewelers all knew that whatever Lavinia Lyte brought back from London would set Boston styles for the winter.

'Oh, Papa! Papa!' she suddenly exclaimed. There was an urgency in her voice, a soft flash in her eyes none of the young men's faces had called forth. Like any country girl, merely glad to be home again, she flung herself into her father's arms.

Spiritually Johnny shrugged, determined to be neither overimpressed nor envious. That overdressed moppet. That lean beanpole — for Miss Lavinia was lean in comparison to Madge and Dorcas, who had always been held up to Johnny as the end-all of feminine beauty. Bad-tempered, too. I hope she kills herself overeating cakes and plum pudding, turkeys with stuffing and gravy, hot white rolls. His stomach was gnawing at him. He forgot Lavinia Lyte as he thought of the wonderful things it was her privilege to overeat if she wished.

Surely by now enough time had passed since John Hancock's arrival at his counting house so that he would be ready to talk to a likely boy looking for work. His hand might be good enough for a cabin boy.

Johnny found one does not step into a great merchant's
counting house and see the merchant as easily as one steps into
a shop and sees the master artisan. Although he had made up
his mind that he would begin his conversation with Mr. Hancock
by explaining he had a burned hand, he did not see any reason
why he should explain to the clerk who stopped him in the
outer office. All he said was that he wanted work.

The clerk asked him if he could read and write.

He said he could.

The thin, weak-eyed gentleman gave him a mortgage and told
him to read that. This he read well.

Then Mr. Hancock, who had been sitting alone over his little
hearth fire in the back office, came out. He had been attracted
by the quality of the boy's voice, for, although Johnny often
spoke in the rougher, slurring manner of Hancock's Wharf, in
reading he reverted to the cleaner speech his mother had
taught him.

Mr. Hancock did not recognize him as the apprentice of Mr.
Lapham who had rashly promised a sugar basin in time for his
Aunt Lydia's birthday. And then the old man had been forced
at the last to admit he could not do it.

'Add this, my lad,' he said, handing Johnny an invoice he held
in his hand.

Johnny added easily. He was given a few more simple sums
which he did in his head.

The clerk and merchant exchanged glances.

Mr. Hancock said: 'If your handwriting is as good as your
reading and ciphering, I promise you a place right here in my
counting house. I've been put to it to find just the right boy.
Your writing . . .'

'I've been taught to write.' But Johnny was suddenly frightened.

The clerk put a piece of paper before him and inked a pen.

'Write John Hancock, Esquire.'

Johnny stubbornly stared at the paper. At last he had found a
place where he wanted to be. And he knew that ever and again

boys who started working for great merchants became great merchants themselves. Surely, surely, if only he tried hard enough he could do it. He could write for the length of just 'John Hancock, Esquire.' His hand shot out of his pocket, grasped the pen. The letters were as clumsy as though written with a left hand.

The clerk laughed. 'Mr. Hancock, I've never seen worse writing.'

The merchant said, 'My boy, you must have been rattled. Surely you can do better than that.'

Johnny stared at his miserable scratches. 'God help me,' he whispered. 'It is the best I can do.'

'Why, the lad has a crippled hand — look, Mr. Hancock.'

Mr. Hancock quickly averted his fine eyes.

'Run away, boy, run away. You knew you could not do the work and yet you came and took up my valuable time and...'

'But I thought maybe you could ship me as a cabin boy.'

'And carry the captain's grog? And be brisk and useful to him? No, no, my captains want whole boys. So now — go away... please.'

Johnny wandered off. 'I burned my hand making you a silver basin... Now, it is "go away, please." '

He flung himself down in the shadow of a sail loft, for the late September day was warm as summer. He could hear the tap of shipwright's hammers, the creak of wooden wheels, a boatswain's whistle. Everywhere boys and men were at work. Only he was idle.

He saw picking his way delicately around barrels of molasses, bales, ox teams, a familiar, fantastic figure. It was Mr. Hancock's little black slave, Jehu. He was looking from side to side. When he saw Johnny, he went to him and said like a parrot, 'My master, Mr. John Hancock, Esquire, has commanded me to give this purse to the poor work-boy in the broken shoes who just left his counting house, and to tell him that he wishes him well.'

Johnny took the purse. It was heavy. That much copper would provide him with food for days. He opened it. It was not copper, but silver. John Hancock had not been able to look at the crippled hand — nor could he help but make this handsome present.

-4-

The thought of Lavinia Lyte gorging herself to death (if it pleased her) on fine foods had started the gastric juices in his stomach an hour ago. He had had no breakfast and for supper the night before only one salt alewife and a mug of milk. It was noontime and he craved food — not the mere coarse bread, cheese, ale, and apples which had always made up the large part of his diet, but rare and interesting things such as he had smelled cooking in rich people's houses and the best taverns, but had never tasted.

First he tormented his hunger by going from one tavern kitchen to the next to see which smelled the best. At the Bunch of Grapes a maid was basting a roast of beef. A spicy pudding was bubbling on the hearth. At the King's Coffee House a suckling pig was so crisp and brown it was fairly bursting. He almost drooled at this pig, but walked on. And everywhere he smelled chocolate and coffee. He had never in his life tasted either. He stopped in the kitchen of the Afric Queen. What he saw there made him feel he had swallowed a small live kitten, but he could almost enjoy these pangs, for in his pocket was Mr. Hancock's silver. Any minute he could assuage that kitten. And so to the Cromwell Head and back again to Union Street. His mind was made up. He would dine at the Afric Queen. For here he had seen maids roasting innumerable small squabs, each stuffed with fragrant dressing and wrapped in bacon. And he had seen pastries — apple, mince, pumpkin, plum tarts — coming out of the brick oven. The crust on them was an inch thick and so short and flaky it looked like scorched tissue paper.

'Well, kitten,' he said contentedly to his stomach as he took his seat humbly in the kitchen where grooms and such were fed while their betters ate in the dining rooms, 'you're going to have more than a saucer of milk today. How'd you like, say, five of those little squabs?'

But when he began to give his order to the serving maid, she giggled and ran off for the landlady.

'Now, boy,' this lady said to him firmly, 'you just show me the color of your money.'

Satisfied, she grunted, and told the maid to serve 'the little master.' This young girl was hardly older than Cilla. She could not help laughing at the things he ordered. The five little squabs, three of each kind of pastry, a wreath of jellied eels (because she said it was a specialty of the house), a tipsy parson — white bread tied into little knots, buttered and baked. And a pot of coffee and another of chocolate. When Johnny saw a dish being prepared in the kitchen for some diner in the other room, he would call for 'some of that,' and she giggled again and fetched it for him.

There was only one disappointment. The smell of coffee had always attracted him. He was disappointed at the bitter taste. The chocolate, however, was even better than he had dared to hope.

But when he came to pay, he was chagrined to find so much of his money had gone to fill and overfill his stomach. The kitten was no longer gnawing inside him, trying to get out. In fact, it was no longer a kitten. 'I feel as if I had swallowed a Newfoundland dog and it had died on me.'

What a fool he had been! He thought suddenly of Rab: that Rab wouldn't have let himself go so; and for the first time, standing in the cobbled stable yard behind the inn, he realized that the back of the little building he saw beyond the Afric Queen stables was the printing shop of the *Boston Observer* on Salt Lane. He wanted to cross through the back yards — go to see that Rab — but thought better of it. Not until he came as a friend and equal — not as a beggar. No.

He decided he would buy himself some shoes. His own

flapped as he walked. His toes showed, but he hadn't liked it
when Jehu had referred to him as 'a boy with broken shoes.'

As he left the cobbler's, his new shoes squeaking on his feet,
he saw a peddler pushing a barrow of limes up Cornhill.

'Fine lemons and limes — lemons and limes.'

There was nothing in the world Isannah so craved as limes
and Mrs. Lapham could not buy them for her. They were too
dear. But sometimes sailors from the Indies or storekeepers
would give her one — because she was so beautiful and would
hug and kiss anyone who gave her a lime.

Johnny filled the pockets of his jacket and breeches with limes.
Now for Cilla. He could not buy her a gray pony, a gold
necklace, nor a little sailboat. He went to a stationer's. There
he found a book with the most wonderful pictures of Calvinistic
martyrs, dying horrible but prayerful deaths. He glanced at the
text. With his help she would soon be able to read it. Next he
bought pastel crayons, but he passionately regretted all those
squabs. He had no money left to get her drawing paper.

His new shoes fitted to a nicety. If the Newfoundland dog was
a heavier tenant in his stomach than the kitten, it was more
restful. His pockets were full of fine gifts. He whistled as he
walked, and entered the Lapham kitchen ready to tell of his
adventure with Mr. Hancock.

The womenfolk had spent all day paring apples, threading
them on strings preparing to dry them for the winter. Even
Mrs. Lapham looked tired. The lazy apprentice bursting in,
happy for the first time in two months, irritated her. Then
she saw his new shoes.

'Johnny Tremain,' she cried, 'what have you been up to?'

'What?'

'You wicked, wicked boy! Oh, I declare, you are going to
bring disgrace on us all.'

He did not understand.

'Them shoes!' she roared. 'You never got them honestly.
You've taken to thieving. I'm going to tell your master. He'll
call a constable and then see if you darest not tell where you

stole them. You've just gone from worse to worse. You're going
to get whipped for this — set in the stocks. You're going to jail.
You'll end up on the gallows.'

He let her scold, shake her wattles at him. As she flounced
out of the room, Madge and Dorcas saw their chance to escape
for a moment. All afternoon Frizel, Junior, the leather-dresser,
had been standing outside on the street waiting for one or the
other to come out. Frizel, Junior, was an accepted suitor, but
no one knew whether it was Madge or Dorcas he was after.
Mrs. Lapham didn't know. The girls didn't know. Frizel,
Junior, himself did not seem to know. Both Madge and Dorcas
were now wild to get out and after him. It looked as though
whichever one was not Mrs. Frizel would end up Mrs. Tweedie.

Johnny stood before Cilla and Isannah, who had huddled
together in a corner of the settle like frightened little animals as
their mother accused Johnny of theft. He smiled and they
smiled. He was so happy about his gifts that he forgot his mis-
fortunes.

Cilla said happily, 'I know you didn't steal.'

'Of course not. Look, girl . . . I've got crayons for you.' He
put them on the table.

'For me?'

'And a book with pictures. Now, Cil, the printing is so easy
I think you can almost teach yourself to read.'

'Oh, Johnny, look, *look* at that funny little man. See, he's got
tiny little buttons on his coat. Oh, I never thought to own a
book with pictures.'

He began fishing limes out of his frayed pockets. Isannah
jumped about him like a puppy. 'Limes, limes!' she cried.
They began to fall on the floor, rolling in all directions. All three
children went down after them. Cilla was almost happier over
Isannah's pleasure than her own. Johnny was happiest of all.
For the first time he completely forgot his crippled hand. It
was all as if nothing had happened and he and Cilla and Isannah
were all one again.

He was pretending not to give the limes to the little girl. He

was going to put them back in his pockets. But she knew they
were for her. She wrapped herself about him, hugging him,
kissing the front of his shirt (this was as far as she could reach).
He started to pick her up in his arms, hold her over his head
until she said, 'Please pretty.'

Suddenly Isannah's delighted cries changed to hysterical
screams.

'Don't touch me! Don't touch me with that dreadful hand!'

Johnny stopped. It was the worst thing anyone had said to
him. He stood like stone, his hand thrust back into his pocket.
Cilla froze too — half under the kitchen table, a lime in her hand.

'Oh, Isannah! How could you?'

The nervous child went on screaming. 'Go away, Johnny,
go away! I hate your hand.' Cilla slapped her and she burst
into tears.

So he went away.

- 5 -

Now he was sure that what they all felt Isannah had been
young enough to say. He felt his heart was broken. Once again
he started to walk until he was so tired he could not think. The
long, late-September night had already begun before he reached
the town gates on the Neck. Beyond him, in the semi-darkness,
running across mud flats, was the one road which connected
Boston with the mainland. And here the gallows — on which
Mrs. Lapham promised him to end. He turned back from the
lonely place. The gallows and the graves of suicides frightened
him a little. He wandered about through the salt marshes at
the foot of the Common, circling until he came out on Beacon
Hill. There he sat in an orchard for quite a while. It was either
Mr. Lyte's or Mr. Hancock's, for the houses stood side by side.
He saw the glitter of candles throughout the great mansions,
guests coming and going, heard the music of a spinet. Isannah's

words rang in his ears. He who had struggled hard never to cry now wished that he could. Then he walked off into sparsely settled West Boston. Behind the pesthouse by lantern light men were digging a hurried grave. He left West Boston and, skirting dirty Mill Cove, came at last into his own North Boston. On Hull Street he heard the staves of the town watch and the feet of the watchmen clumping on cobbles. By law no apprentice was allowed out so late. He slipped into Copp's Hill graveyard to hide until they were gone.

'One o'clock and a warm fair night,' called the watch.

It was indeed warm and fair and no hardship to spend such a night out under the moon and stars. Around about him everywhere lay the dead worthies of Boston. Their slate stones stood shoulder to shoulder. This was the highest land in Boston, next only to Beacon Hill.

Here, close to Hull Street, his mother was buried in an unmarked grave. He had not forgotten where and flung himself down beside the spot. Then he began to cry. He had not been able to cry before. It was as if Isannah's words had broken down the last strength in him. He cried half for himself and half because he knew how sorry his mother would be for him if she knew. I can't do decent work. I can't ever be a silversmith — not even a watchmaker. My friends don't want me to touch them with my dreadful hand.

Seemingly neither the moon nor the stars above him nor the dead about him cared.

Then he lay face down, sobbing and saying over and over that God had turned away from him. But his frenzied weeping had given him some release. He must have slept.

He sat up suddenly wide awake. The moon had seemingly come close and closer to him. He could see the coats of arms, the winged death's heads, on the slate stones about him. He was so wide awake he felt someone must have called his name. His ears were straining to hear the next words. What was it his mother had said so long ago? If there was nothing left and God Himself had turned away his face, then, and only then,

Johnny was to go to Mr. Lyte. In his ears rang his mother's sweet remembered accents. Surely for one second, between sleeping and waking, he had seen her dear face, loving, gentle, intelligent, floating toward him through the moonlight on Copp's Hill.

He sat a long time with his arms hugging his knees. Now he knew what to do. This very day he would go to Merchant Lyte. When at last he lay down, he slept heavily, without a dream and without a worry.

IV. The Rising Eye

IT WAS PAST DAWN when he woke, his feeling of contentment still in him. He was no longer his own problem but Merchant Lyte's. Tomorrow at this time what would he be calling him? 'Uncle Jonathan?' 'Cousin Lyte?' Perhaps 'Grandpa,' and he laughed out loud.

Only imagine how Mrs. Lapham would come running, dropping nervous curtsies, when he drove up in that ruby coach! How Madge and Dorcas would stare! First thing he did would be to take Cilla for a drive. He'd not even invite Isannah. But how she would bawl when left behind! And then . . . his imagination jumped ahead.

At the Charlestown ferry slip he washed in the cold sea water, and because the sun was warm sunned himself as he did what he could to make his shabby clothes presentable. He combed his lank, fair hair with his fingers, cleaned his nails with his teeth. Of course now he could buy Cilla that pony and cart. And Grandpa Lapham . . . oh, he'd buy him a Bible with print an inch high in it. Mrs. Lapham? Not a thing, madam, not one thing.

Christ's Church said ten o'clock. He got up and started for Long Wharf where his great relative had his counting house. On his way he passed down Salt Lane. There was the comical little painted man observing Boston through his tiny spyglass. Johnny wanted to stop — tell that fellow — that Rab — of his great connections, but decided to wait until he was sure of his welcome into the Lyte family. Although half of him was leaping ahead imagining great things for himself, the other half was wary. It was quite possible he would get no welcome at all — and he knew it.

He walked half the length of Long Wharf until he saw carved over a door the familiar rising eye. The door was open, but he knocked. None of the three clerks sitting on their high stools with their backs to him, scratching in ledgers, looked up, so he stepped inside. Now that he had to speak, he found there was a barrier across his throat, something that he would have to struggle to get his voice over. He was more excited than he had realized. But he was scornful too. These three clerks would not even look up when he came in today, but tomorrow what would it be? 'Good morning, little master; I'll tell your uncle — cousin — grandfather that you are here, sir.'

Finally a well-fed, rosy youth, keeping one finger in his ledger, swung around and asked him what he wanted.

'It is a personal matter between myself and Mr. Lyte.'

'Well,' said the young man pleasantly, 'even if it is personal, you'd better tell me what it is.'

'It is a family matter. I cannot, in honor, tell anyone except Mr. Lyte.'

'Hum . . .'

One of the elderly clerks laughed in a mean way. 'Just another poor suitor for the hand of Miss Lavinia.'

The young clerk flushed. Johnny had seen enough of Madge and Dorcas and their suitors to know that the gibe about poor boys aspiring to Miss Lavinia had gone home.

'Tell him,' snickered the other ancient spider of a clerk, 'that Mr. Lyte is — ah — sensible of the great honor — ah — and regrets to say he has formed other plans for his daughter's future. Ah!' Evidently he mimicked Mr. Lyte.

The young clerk was scarlet. He flung down his pen. 'Can't you ever forget that?' he protested. 'Here, kid,' and turned to Johnny. 'Mr. Lyte's closeted behind that door with two of his sea captains. When they leave, you just walk in.'

Johnny sat modestly on a stool, his arrogant shabby hat in his good hand, and looked about him. The three backs were bent once more over the ledgers. The quill pens scratched. He heard the gritting of sand as they blotted their pages. There was a handsome half-model of a ship on the wall. Sea chests, doubtless full of charts, maps, invoices, were under the desks.

The door opened. Two ruddy men with swaying walks stepped out and Mr. Lyte himself was shaking hands, bidding them success on their voyaging, and God's mercy. As he turned to go back to his sanctuary, Johnny followed him.

Mr. Lyte sat himself in a red-leather armchair beside an open window. Through that window he could watch his *Western Star* graving in the graving dock. He would have been a handsome man, with his fine dark eyes, bushy black brows, contrasting smartly with the white tie-wig he wore, except for the color and quality of his flesh. It was as yellow as tallow. Seemingly it had melted and run down. The lids were heavy over the remarkable eyes. The melted flesh made pouches beneath them. It hung down along his jawbone, under his jutting chin.

'What is it?' he demanded. 'Who let you in? What do you want, and who, for Heaven's sake, are you?'

'Sir,' said Johnny, 'I'm Jonathan Lyte Tremain.'

There was a long pause. The merchant's glittering black eyes did not waver, nor the tallow cheeks redden. If the name meant anything to him, he did not show it.

'Well?'

'My mother, sir.' The boy's voice shook slightly. 'She told me . . . she always said . . .'

Mr. Lyte opened his jeweled snuffbox, took snuff, sneezed and blew his nose.

'I can go on from there, boy. Your mother on her deathbed told you you were related to the rich Boston merchant?'

Johnny was sure now Mr. Lyte knew of the relationship. 'Yes, sir, she did, but I didn't know you'd know.'

'*Know?* I didn't need to *know*. It is a very old story — a very old trick, and will you be gone — or shall I have you flung out?'

'I'll stay,' Johnny said stubbornly.

'Sewall.' The merchant did not raise his voice, but instantly the young clerk was on his threshold. 'Show him out, Sewall, and happens he lands in the water, you — ah! can baptize him with my name — ah . . . ha, ha!'

Mr. Lyte took up a handful of papers. The incident was over. Sewall looked at Johnny and Johnny at Sewall. The young man was as kind as his cherubic face suggested.

'I can prove to you one thing, Mr. Lyte. My name is Jonathan Lyte Tremain.'

'What of it? Any back-alley drabtail can name her child for the greatest men in the colony. There should be a law against it, but there is none.'

Johnny's temper began to go.

'You flatter yourself. What have you ever done except be rich? Why, I doubt even a monkey mother would name a monkey child after you.'

Mr. Lyte gave a long whistle. 'That was quite a mouthful. Sewall!'

'Yes, sir.'

'You just take this monkey child of a monkey mother out, and drown it.'

'Yes, sir.'

Sewall put a soft hand on the boy's shoulder, but Johnny fiercely shook himself free.

'I don't want your money,' he said, more proudly than accurately. 'Now that I've met you face to face, I don't much fancy you as kin.'

'Your manners, my boy, are a credit to your mother.'

'But facts are facts, and I've a cup with your arms on it to prove what I say is true.'

The merchant's unhealthy, brilliant eyes quivered and glittered.

'You've got a cup of mine?'

'No, of *mine*.'

'So . . . so you've got a cup. Will you describe it?'

Johnny described it as only a silversmith could.

'Why, Mr. Lyte, that must be...' Sewall began, but Mr. Lyte hushed him. Evidently not only Mr. Lyte, but his clerks had heard of this cup. Johnny was elated.

'My boy,' said the merchant, 'you have — ah — brought me great news. I must see your cup.'

'Any time you say, sir.'

'My long-lost cup returned to me by my long-lost little — ha-ha — whatever you are — kerchoo!' He had taken more snuff. 'Bring your cup to me tonight. You know my Beacon Hill house.'

'Yes, sir.'

'And we'll kill the fatted calf — you long-lost whatever-you-are. Come an hour after candles are lit. Prodigal Son, what? Got a cup, has he?'

- 2 -

Although Johnny might have been more cordially received by Merchant Lyte, he was satisfied enough with his welcome to build up air castles. He really knew they were air castles, for at bottom he was hard-headed, not easily taken in even by his own exuberant imagination. Still, as he trudged up Fish Street, turned in at the Laphams' door, in his mind he was in that ruby coach. Money, and a watch in his pocket.

He had hoped to slip to the attic and fetch away his cup without being noticed, but Mrs. Lapham saw him enter and called him into the kitchen. She said nothing about his shoes. Evidently the girls had told her his story and she had believed it.

'Johnny, you come set a moment. No, girls, you needn't leave. I want you to hear what I'm going to say.'

Johnny looked a little smug. Had he not (almost) arrived in the Lyte coach?

'Grandpa says as long as he lives you are to have a place to

sleep. But you've got to go back to the attic. Mr. Tweedie's to
have the birth and death room, and you can have a little somewhat to eat. I've agreed that's all right. I'll manage *somehow*.'

'Don't fret ... I'm going for good.'

'I'll believe that when I see it. Now, mind. I've two things to
say to you.'

The four girls were all sitting about, hands folded as though
they were at meeting.

'First. You shan't insult Mr. Tweedie — least, not until he
has signed the contract. No more talk of his being a spinster
aunt dressed up in men's clothes. And NO MORE SQUEAK-PIGS.
He's sensitive. You hurt his feelings horribly. He almost took
ship then and there back to Baltimore.'

'I'm sorry.'

'Secondly. There's to be no more talk of you and Cilla.
Don't you ever *dare* to lift your eyes to one of my girls again.'

'*Lift* my eyes? I can't see that far down into the dirt even to
know they are there.'

'Now, you saucebox, you hold that tongue of yours. You're
not to go hanging 'round Cilla — giving her presents — and
dear knows how you got the money. I've told her to keep shy
of you. Now I'm telling you. You mark my words...'

'Ma'am, I wouldn't marry that sniveling, goggle-eyed frog
of a girl even though you gave her to me on a golden platter.
Fact is, I don't like girls — nor' — with a black look at his
mistress — 'women either — and that goes for Mr. Tweedie too.'

He left to go upstairs for his cup.

When he came down, the more capable women of the household were out in the yard hanging up the wash. Cilla was paring
apples in that deft, absent-minded way she did such things.
Isannah was eating the parings. She'd be sick before nightfall.

Cilla lifted her pointed, translucent little face. Her hazel eyes,
under their veil of long lashes, had a greenish flash to them.
There never was a less goggle-eyed girl.

'Johnny's mad,' she said sweetly.

'His ears are red! He's mad!' Isannah chanted.

These words sounded wonderful to him. He was happy because once more they were insulting him. They were not pitying him or being afraid of him because he had had an accident.

'Goggle-eyed, sniveling frogs!'

With his silver cup in its flannel bag, he set off to kill time until he might take it to Mr. Lyte.

He spent a couple of hours dreaming of his rosy future. And the tears in Merchant Lyte's unhealthy, brilliant black eyes — the tremor in his pompous 'ah-ha-ha' manner of speech as he clutched his 'long-lost whatever-you-are' to his costly waistcoat. Even if he did not like women, Miss Lavinia, he decided, was to kiss him on the brow. Through this dreaming he felt enough confidence in his good fortune at last to stop in to see 'that Rab.' There had not been a day since the first meeting that he had not wanted to.

Rab showed no surprise either over his return or the strange story that he proceeded to pour out. It was nightfall and, as Johnny hoped, Uncle Lorne and the little Webbs were gone. Rab was waiting for the ink to dry on the *Observer* so he could fold it. He sat with his long legs stretched before him, his hands clasped behind his neck.

'Lyte's crooked, you know,' he said at last.

'I've heard that before.'

'He's sly. When the merchants agreed not to import any English goods until the Stamp Act was repealed, he was one of the first to sign — then imported secretly. Sold through another name. Made more money. Sam Adams spoke to him privately — scared him. He says he won't do that again. He's trying to ride two horses — Whig and Tory.'

Johnny's life with the Laphams had been so limited he knew little of the political strife which was turning Boston into two armed camps. The Whigs declaring that taxation without representation is tyranny. The Tories believing all differences could be settled with time, patience, and respect for government.

Rab obviously was a Whig. 'I can stomach some of the Tories,' he went on, 'men like Governor Hutchinson. They

honestly think we're better off to take anything from the British
Parliament — let them break us down, stamp in our faces, take
all we've got by taxes, and never protest. They say we American
colonies are too weak to get on without England's help and
guidance. But Governor Hutchinson's a good man. Of course
we'll destroy him. We've marked him down. Sam Adams is
already greasing the ways under him. But I can't stand men like
Lyte, who care nothing for anything except themselves and their
own fortune. Playing both ends against the middle.'

'I'd never have picked him for a relative. But beggars can't
be choosers — and happens I'm a beggar. It's on to time to get
ready to go to him.'

Understanding Johnny's unspoken desire not to appear too
meanly before the great gentleman, Rab went to the attic above
the shop where he slept and came down with a clean shirt of
finest white linen and a fawn-colored corduroy jacket with
silver buttons.

'It's too small for me. Ought to about fit you.'

It did.

Almost miraculously — for Johnny had not seen where it
came from — bread and cheese were on the counter. It was his
first food since yesterday's gorging.

With the straight, fair hair well brushed and tied behind with
taffeta, the handsome jacket, the frilled, immaculate shirt,
Johnny did cut a very presentable figure.

By the printing-shop clock the sun had been set for almost an
hour. Rab was folding newspapers.

'You can sleep here,' he said, 'if they don't offer you anything.
But . . . good luck, bold fellow.'

- 3 -

Standing on Beacon Hill, so far removed from the hurly-burly
of the wharves, shops, markets of town, Johnny hesitated. Should
he, as a poor out-of-work apprentice, go around back, or should

he, as a long-lost something-or-other, raise that gleaming brass knocker on the paneled front door? The silver buttons and Rab's 'bold fellow' heartened him. The knocker fell, and instantly a maid was bidding him enter, curtsying, asking his name.

'I'm Jonathan Lyte Tremain.'

The front hall was very large. From it rose a flight of stairs, taking their time in their rising, taking all the space they needed. Along the walls were portraits: Merchant Lyte in his handsome, healthy youth; Lavinia, painted long before in London, as regal a child as now she was a young woman. Time blackened old things, already a hundred years old. Was it their long dried blood which now ran red and living in Johnny's veins?

To the left was the drawing room. The tinkle of a spinet, low voices, laughter. Could it be they were laughing because the maid was announcing him? He wished he had called himself merely Johnny Tremain.

'Ah-ha-ha.' That was Merchant Lyte. 'Fetch him in, Jenny. Just a little family party. All want to see him, eh?'

Johnny's first impression was of dozens of wax candles lighting the long, dove-colored and lavender-and-yellow room. They were reflected in mirrors, silver, gleaming floors and mahogany. A dozen people were gathered together in the far end of the room.

Johnny stood a moment, anxious to do nothing wrong, conscious that the new shoes he had been so proud of did not much resemble the little black buckled pumps on the gentlemen.

'Well,' said Mr. Lyte, rising, but not approaching him. 'So ... here we are?'

'Yes, sir.'

'Lavinia, Cousin Talbot, Aunt Best, how do you like his looks?'

Aunt Best, a horrifyingly ugly, cross old woman with two gold-headed canes, vowed through her whiskers and toothless gums that he looked just as bad as she had expected.

Lavinia turned from the spinet. She had on a stiff, turquoise-blue dress that suited her marvelously. She looked at the boy

with her head tipped sidewise as Johnny had seen other ladies
look at silver teapots before they bought.

'At least, Papa, he's a deal handsomer than most of my relatives. Isn't he, Cousin Sewall?' It was the rosy clerk, lovelorn
Sewall, who was turning her music for her.

'Yes, daughter.' Mr. Lyte's eyes flickered over Johnny.
'Quite the little gentleman — from the waist up. Silver buttons,
eh? Ruffled shirt?'

His eyes slid over his 'little family party.' He addressed them
in so low a voice he seemed to ignore Johnny standing at the
far upper end of the long room.

He had been expecting some such apparition from the past
ever since last August. In spite of family efforts to keep certain
things dark, he had reason to believe certain things were well
known, even among the — ah — lower classes. Then he called
to Johnny.

'Now, boy, you brought your cup?'

'It is here — in this bag.'

'Very good. Will you — and all of you — please to step into
the dining room?' This took some time, for Aunt Best had to be
pulled in front and pushed from behind before she was balanced
on her two gold-headed canes. She scolded, muttered, and shook
her whiskers at everyone, including her famous nephew.

Only Lavinia, still at the spinet, and Cousin Sewall bending
over her, did not go into the dining room.

There on the sideboard were three standing cups. They were
identical with Johnny's. Silently he took his from its bag, set it
with the other three, then stood back to look at the silken, be-
jeweled, perfumed folk crowding about him.

Mr. Lyte took up the cup, studied it, compared it with one of
his own. Silently he handed it to a plainly dressed, thick-set
gentleman who thus far had said nothing.

'I think,' said Mr. Lyte quietly, 'all of you ladies and gentlemen will agree that this cup our — ah, cousin, is it? — has
brought back tonight is one of this set?'

There was a murmur of assent. Johnny could hear the tiny
tinkle, seemingly far away, of Miss Lavinia's spinet.

'It is perfectly obvious that this cup now stands where it belongs. The question is how was it ever separated from its fellows?'

Johnny felt that everyone there except himself knew the answer to this question.

'In fact,' the merchant's voice was smooth as oil, 'I declare this to be the very cup which was stolen from me by thieves. They broke through yonder window on the twenty-third of last August. Sheriff, I order you to arrest this boy for burglary.'

The thick-set plain man whom Johnny had already noticed, put a heavy hand on his shoulder. His formal words flowed over him.

'Johnny Tremain, alias Jonathan Lyte Tremain ... apprentice to Ephraim Lapham ... name of King and Bay Colony ... standing cup ... taken away the twenty-third day ... month ... year of our Lord one thousand seven hundred and seventy-three.'

'This is not true,' Johnny said.

'You can explain to the Judge.'

'Very well, I can and will.' The full horror of the accusation (for a boy might be hanged for stealing a silver cup) froze him into seeming nonchalance. This coolness made a bad impression. Aunt Best was poking at him with one of her canes. She hoped she'd live long enough to see him hanged. He was a perfect little viper — and he looked it. A florid woman was flapping a pink feather fan. She thought he had one of those falsely innocent little faces that are such an aid to evil boys.

'No,' someone else was saying, 'he has a shifty eye.'

Aunt Best croaked, 'Look at those silver buttons on his coat. I'm sure he stole them.'

Mr. Lyte said, 'Boy, where did you get that coat?'

'It was lent me.'

'Lent you? By whom, pray?'

'A printer's boy. I don't know his last name. Down at the *Observer* office ... He's called Rab.'

'That coat is worth money. Do you think someone whose last name you admit you don't know would *lend* you a coat?'

'It doesn't sound likely — but happens it's true.'

'Sheriff, look into this.'

'I certainly will, Mr. Lyte.'

'I sent Sewall over to the Laphams — a very respectable, humble, pious, poor sort of folk. Mrs. Lapham swore this boy never owned a thing but the clothes he stood in. As for his name, she showed Sewall the papers of his indenture, signed by his dead mother. She put him down as Johnny Tremain, no Jonathan Lyte about it. And Mrs. Lapham believed that lately he had taken to evil ways — stealing shoes and little things. She swore he never owned a cup. And Mr. Tweedie, a partner of Mr. Lapham, said the boy was a notorious liar, and of most evil report.'

The sheriff was taking out handcuffs, snapping them on Johnny's wrist and his own.

"Soon's I get this scamp locked up, I'll be back for that bowl of punch you promised, Mr. Lyte,' he called cheerfully as he left. The last sound Johnny heard was the fairy tinkle of the spinet.

The chain clanked. The sheriff said nothing until they had reached the stone jail in Prison Lane. Then, as the jailer was writing down Johnny's name in his book, the sheriff said kindly:

'Now, boy, you've got some rights. Who do you want notified? Got any kin except the Lytes, eh? How about old Mr. Lapham?'

'He's my master no more. He dismissed me months ago.'

'Relatives? Parents?'

'I've nothing. But will you please tell that boy down at the *Observer*? He's a tall boy, and dark — all I know is that his name is Rab.'

'The one you stole the coat off, hey? I was going to look him up tonight.'

- 4 -

Oddly enough, Johnny slept well on his straw pallet in the jail. The night before, lying and weeping among the graves of Copp's Hill, he had reached bottom. He could not go lower than that. No matter what happened, he could not help but now go up. He knew Isannah's childish squeals were nothing compared to the serious charge Mr. Lyte had brought against him, but the squeals had just about broken his heart. The accusation of burglary he could take. He felt tough enough and hard enough to take anything. But he could not help but think of the gallows, just beyond the town gates, how they had loomed up at him through the dark of the night like a warning.

Before he had finished his breakfast of corn gruel, Rab arrived. Johnny had known he would come. He brought blankets, books, food. Seemingly by the nonchalance of his manner, nothing was more usual than to find one's friends in jail. About his muscular, brown throat Johnny could see a medal hung upon a string. On it was engraved a Tree of Liberty. So Rab was one of the semi-secret famous Sons of Liberty, those carefully organized 'mobs' who often took justice into their own hands. They frightened royal officers out of Boston, stopped British admirals from impressing Yankee seamen, as they were impressed in England. They could at will paralyze trade, courts, government. Many a night Johnny had heard their whistles, conch shells, and cries of 'town-born, turn out,' the running of their feet. And next day had seen the effigies they had hung, the Tory fences they had torn down or windows broken, and heard that Royal Commissioner So-and-So had been frightened out of Boston. Or such-and-such a merchant had wept when haled before the Liberty Tree and sworn never to do trade with England until all grievances had been righted. The Laphams had hated such lawless seizure of government by the Sons of Liberty. Johnny had not thought much about it. Seeing the medal at Rab's throat made him think it might be fun to be out with them.

The medal did its work, for both the turnkey and the jailer
were also 'Sons.' Johnny was given a neat, private room on the
ground floor. Such rooms were usually reserved for gentlemen
jailed for debt.

Here he told Rab his entire story. Rab had already found out
that the case would come up on the following Tuesday, before
Mr. Justice Dana. If Mr. Justice thought there was not sufficient evidence to hold him for a higher court and a jury trial,
he would immediately release him. Then he asked if Johnny
had shown his cup to any living soul sometime before August
twenty-third. Such a witness would prove that Johnny had
owned a cup, before Mr. Lyte's had been stolen.

'Why, of course — Cilla Lapham. That was July. Come to
think, it was the very day Mr. Hancock ordered his sugar basin.
It was the second day of July — that was a Tuesday.'

'That's all you'll need. Mr. Lyte was a fool to bring so flimsy
a charge against you.'

'What do you suppose he meant when he said he had expected
something like me turning up as soon as that cup was stolen?'

'I don't know what goes on in that clever, bad head, but perhaps he thinks you are an impostor and stole the cup first to
back up some claim of kinship. Of course Cilla will come to
court for you?'

'She will. If her mother will let her.'

'Would Mrs. Lapham give you a good character?'

'No. She thinks these days I'm bad enough to steal a wig off a
parson's head.'

Next day Rab was back at the same time. He was a little
perturbed. Mr. Lyte himself had been to the Laphams (in the
ruby coach) and ordered a dozen silver spoons, a tea caddy, and,
if all went well, would order a silver tankard a foot high.

'A bribe?'

'Cilla says he paid in advance. Then it was Mrs. Lapham said
she would not have her girl mixed up in such a disgraceful case.
She promised Cilla would spend next Tuesday under lock and
key.'

'I could hang first?'

'And she is determined to please that Mr. Tweedie too. If he won't sign that contract and get right to work, she can't get Mr. Lyte's silver made. Poor old Mr. Lapham won't do anything but read his Bible. Says he hasn't long to prepare to meet his Maker. By the way, Mr. Tweedie just about hates you. Says you called him a squeak-pig. He didn't like it.'

'Of course, I called him a squeak-pig. Don't see why he cares.'

'Well — you go around calling people squeak-pigs and you've just about got to take it when they hit back. Not with their tongues — mostly they're not quick enough — but like this. Tweedie saw his chance to get back at you. He says if Mrs. Lapham lets Cilla testify for you, he'll take a ship back to Baltimore. Says he's sensitive and a great artist and he can't be upset by thieves and brawlers. Well . . . never mind. But I don't see the point of going around and . . .'

'Oh, forget those squeak-pigs, for Heaven's sake.' Johnny was sulky.

'Now for a lawyer. I've talked to Josiah Quincy. He often writes for the *Observer*. He says if you want him, he's ready.'

'Josiah Quincy? But . . . Rab, you tell him not to . . .'

'You don't want him? He's the best young lawyer in Boston.'

'I could never pay him.'

'You don't understand. He'll give you his time for nothing. He's coming to see you this afternoon. And I'm meeting Cilla, sort of behind her mother's back, to make plans.'

'It all depends on Cilla, doesn't it?'

'Well . . . pretty much.'

'And Mrs. Lapham and the squeak — I mean Tweedie — say they'll lock her up?'

'Lock her up so I can't get her out? Boy, I could get her out of this jail. Get her out of the Tower of London. And that girl would testify for you, even if it cost her her life. What's her real name?'

'Priscilla.'

'Well, may Priscilla be on my side if ever I'm accused of anything. What about the little girl — is she really as bright as she looks?'

'No, I don't think so. She's just sort of a parrot. She's always going around repeating what Cilla or anyone else says to her as if she had thought it all up herself.'

-5-

Mr. Justice Dana was a stout and florid man, dressed in a black silk robe and a great woolly white wig.

Johnny sat close to Mr. Quincy, watching the Justice's nervous, taut hands, listening to his 'What have we heres' and quick questions to the men and women shoved up before him. Some people he dismissed, some he ordered fined, or whipped, or set in the stocks, or held for a higher court. Johnny knew when his own case would soon be called because he heard the Justice tell a beadle to run down to Long Wharf and tell Merchant Lyte to present himself in half an hour.

Once again Johnny squirmed about, studying every face in the courtroom. Rab and Cilla were not there and he was frightened.

Mr. Quincy whispered to him.

'Rab said he'd get her here by eleven. Rab's never slipped yet.'

Johnny liked his young lawyer. A frail man, flushed with fever. His cough was prophetic of an early death. That was how Johnny's mother had died — burned up by fever, coughing herself to death. The man had a mobile, passionate face, handsome except for one wall eye.

Mr. Lyte arrived, escorted by his poor relative and clerk, Sewall. He entered as though he owned the court, calling a cheery good morning to Mr. Justice, interrupting the mumbled explanation of a shabby bakeress accused of selling mouldy bread. Next there was a rattle of light gig wheels, a jingle of horse gear, and to the intense pleasure of everyone Miss Lavinia Lyte entered and, as modestly as she was able, took a seat near the door.

Even the Justice straightened the bands at his throat. Sewall blushed. The bakeress forgot what she was saying as she turned to gape at the beautiful, dark woman, darkly dressed. Restless, easily bored, Miss Lyte often did unexpected things.

'Jonathan Lyte *versus* Johnny Tremain, alias Jonathan Lyte Tremain.'

Mr. Quincy gave him a secret pat on the knee. Johnny knew he must now step forward, take his oath on the Bible to tell the truth, the whole truth — so help him God. He was frightened, for as he stepped forward he was conscious that these might be the first steps toward those gallows — waiting in the dark beyond the town gates.

Next Mr. Lyte was called and was taking the same oath. Mr. Quincy's one good eye caught Johnny's. He was forming words on his lips. The clock had indeed struck eleven and there, standing in the doorway, were Rab and Cilla. Rab, enigmatical, dark, capable, looked as always. Cilla had on a hood that half-covered her face.

Mr. Lyte was talking as informally as though he and Mr. Dana were alone together, sitting at a tavern, cracking walnuts, drinking Madeira. He told how his great-grandfather, Jonathan Lyte, Mayor of Causeway, Kent, England, had had six identical cups made — one for each of his sons. Four of these cups had come to this country and these he himself had owned until last August. On the night of the twenty-third, a thief or thieves had broken a pane out of his dining-room window. The space was too small to admit a grown man, so it was a half-grown boy who had slipped in and taken only one of the famous cups.

Then he snapped his fingers at Sewall, who stepped forward and set four silver cups on the table before the Justice.

'This is the stolen cup,' Mr. Lyte said confidently. 'I've tied a red ribbon on it.' Then he went on to tell, with considerable humor and a bright sparkle in his slippery black eyes, about

Johnny's visit to his shop, his claims of kinship, and how he had
lured him to his house with the stolen cup.

The Justice said: 'Mr. Lyte, could it not be possible that this
boy is related to you? Could his story be true?'

No, no, it was impossible. Would Mr. Justice Dana be so good
as to glance at this indenture — which the boy's erstwhile
master, Mr. Lapham, had been so kind as to lend him? The
name was put down as Johnny Tremain — nothing about Lyte.
Undoubtedly older heads than this boy's had egged him on to
this wretched, scurvy trick, but Mr. Lyte had no wish to go into
the matter beyond the recovery of his own property. He did not
wish to suggest in any way that the Laphams had any part in the
imposture — they were very humble, honest, pious folk. He believed that the case of the theft, all that interested him at the
moment, was 'dead open and shut against the boy.' And might
he ask the death penalty? There was too much thieving going on
in Boston. Poor apprentices were getting out of hand. The gallows had been too long empty.

'That's for the court to say,' said the Justice sourly. He took
snuff and Mr. Lyte took snuff. They sneezed together.

Mr. Quincy led Johnny on to tell his own story. The boy
spoke confidently, now that Rab and Cilla were there. He had
never had an audience before and he felt the courtroom hanging
on his words, believing him. He spoke better and better. He
told how his mother had given him the cup, the little that she
had told him. She had bidden him not to part with the cup —
ever. Nor ever go to the Lytes unless he had come to the end of
everything. Then he spoke simply and easily of his accident, his
hunt for work, his despair — and arrest. There was a murmur
almost of applause.

'Johnny,' said Mr. Quincy, 'did you obey your mother —
never show your cup to anyone?'

'Once I disobeyed. It was the second day of last July. I forgot
— or didn't heed. I told my master's daughter, Priscilla Lapham, what my mother said was my true name, and about the cup.
She wanted to see it. It was just dawn — that is, the dawn of the
third of July. Tuesday it was.'

Cilla was called. Johnny had always thought her a shy girl, but she stood up straight before the Judge, speaking in her clear, low voice. He was proud of her. And he had always thought her a skinny, plain girl. She looked at the moment just about beautiful to him.

As she finished, there was a sensation in the courtroom that outweighed the arrival of Mr. Lyte and even his handsome daughter. Isannah, her bright curls in wild array, flew into the courtroom, seeming, like a mouse, to run without feet. She stopped for no oath, no formalities, but flung herself upon Mr. Justice Dana, telling over again Cilla's story. Johnny knew she had been sound asleep when he had told Cilla. She had even been in bed when he had actually shown the cup to her older sister. He was amazed at the vividness of her jumbled recital and touched by the virtues she attributed to himself. Yet she was making it all up.

In vain Mr. Justice Dana's 'What have we here?' and 'I cannot accept this as testimony,' and Cilla's attempts to quiet her. She was so enchanting, so seemingly come from another world, she had her say.

'Bless me!' said Mr. Justice, blowing his nose. 'And how old might you be?'

'Eight, sir, going on for nine.'

'There now — be a good girl — here, you take this piece of licorice I have in my pocket and sit down quietly and eat it. There!'

Almost immediately he dismissed the case. There was not the slightest evidence, the Justice was saying, that the accused had stolen a cup, nor that the cup with the red ribbon, now illegally in the possession of Mr. Lyte, was the same one as was stolen from his house last August. Evidence was against that. For these young Lapham misses had proved to his satisfaction (and might he point out to Mr. Lyte his own testimony about the high character of honesty and piety the Laphams enjoyed?) that, unlikely as it might seem, the apprentice had possession of a silver cup, undoubtedly one of the original six ordered by the Mayor of

Causeway, Kent. He bade Johnny Tremain take the one with
the red ribbon. It was his own. If he liked, he might even bring
a suit against Mr. Lyte. Didn't recommend it — Mr. Lyte was
too powerful.

Johnny took the cup. In a moment he and Mr. Quincy, Rab
and Cilla, were standing in the sunshine of the street outside the
courthouse. They were so happy they could only laugh. The
lawyer said now they would all go together, as his guests, to a
tavern, to eat at their leisure, and drink a health to Johnny from
the cup. But where was Isannah?

She was standing with a tiny hand in one of Miss Lyte's gloved
ones, gazing up at her in adoration.

Cilla called her crossly. Miss Lyte stepped up into her high
gig. It was a long step, but she was a lithe, long-legged woman.

'She said,' panted Isannah, 'she had never seen anything like
me . . . not even in some lane in London.'

'Drury Lane,' said young Mr. Quincy dryly. 'I was thinking of
that myself.'

'Rab,' said the little girl, 'was I really all right?'

'Just about perfect. Only some of it you put in the first person,
so it wasn't quite the truth, but . . . you'll never starve.'

Then she tried to kiss Johnny, but he thought it beneath his
dignity to be kissed on the street.

'You're too mussed up with licorice,' he said.

She bent and kissed his burned hand.

He said nothing. He was suddenly afraid he might cry.

V. *The Boston Observer*

THEY WENT to the Afric Queen and ate in the dining room. This time no one asked to see the color of Mr. Quincy's money. The party even grew a little noisy. Isannah, Johnny, and Mr. Quincy himself were the most hilarious. Many of the leading Whigs dined daily at the Queen, and one man after another stopped at their table to laugh over Merchant Lyte's public discomfiture that morning in court. Hadn't Quincy practically caught the old fox thieving a silver cup from an apprentice? Mr. Quincy, flushed and happy, agreed to all this, but more seriously he warned Johnny to watch out for himself. Mr. Lyte was very proud. That pride had been hurt. From now on he was Johnny's enemy. But all enjoyed themselves, although Isannah drank herself sick and silly on sillabubs.

Johnny was disappointed when Rab told exactly how he had got Cilla to court that day. It was not half so exciting a story as Johnny had expected. Rab had simply shown Mrs. Lapham a letter signed by Governor Hutchinson and stamped with the Great Seal of the Colony. It had been sent to Mr. Lorne, commanding him and the other printers of Boston to quit their seditious, rebellious publications — or else. Mrs. Lapham could not read. All Rab had done was to take Cilla by the arm, unfurl the letter at Mrs. Lapham, point to the seal and say, 'Governor's orders.' He had not given her time to call the well-educated Mr. Tweedie out of the shop. Rab and Cilla ran hell-for-leather to the courthouse. He had already schooled Isannah and hidden her near-by in case he was unable to produce Cilla. Both girls, he thought, had done marvelously.

'That's what Miss Lyte said,' the little girl agreed eagerly. 'At least she said *I* was wonderful and . . .'

'Oh, forget it,' said Johnny rudely. That Isannah was just about getting above herself.

During dinner it seemed to Rab that Johnny planned to go back to the Laphams to sleep, and to Cilla that he was moving in with Rab. But Johnny decided to sponge on neither — not until he had a job, and something a lot better than delivering papers for Uncle Lorne. He had noticed the number of boys who came and went about the Queen's stable.

The wind was howling up from the sea, beating the waves against the wharves. It was a fine fall, the days crisp and full of sparkle, but the nights, from now on, would be too cold in the open, although warm enough hidden away in the stable, with hay or a horse blanket to cover one and the warm animals giving off heat.

He slept in the stable that night and on the next day did find a sea captain who would — in spite of the bad hand — take him on as a cabin boy. Johnny did not like the captain, the ship, nor the voyage. It was going to Halifax and the cold turn the weather had taken and his insufficient clothing made him desire a trip to the tropic Sugar Isles above all else. But all seemed settled until the shipmaster casually told him he must furnish his own blankets, oilskins, sea boots, warm pea jacket. Johnny had no money to buy such things.

Having no safe place now to leave his cup, he had tied the strings of the flannel bag to his belt. It struck at him as he walked. The luckiest thing he had ever done was to disobey his mother and show this cup to Cilla last July. Now he would disobey her again and sell it.

There were many silversmiths who would have bought it, but the cup was so old-fashioned he could not expect from them more than its value in old silver. However, Mr. Lyte, owning

the matching cups, would pay a very good price. So once more
he went to that merchant's counting house on Long Wharf.

It was the same as before, except 'Cousin Sewall' was not
there. The grasshoppery old clerks were bent over their ledgers.
Neither moved as Johnny slipped quietly past them and entered
the inner office.

Mr. Lyte looked up from his papers. There was a glimmer
almost of hatred in the sliding black eyes as he recognized
Johnny. Mr. Justice had humiliated him publicly, and the
story had gone quickly around the wharves, among his friends.

He spoke very quietly. 'Well?'

'Look. I have no money. No food. Only the clothes I stand
in. I've no choice. This cup is worth about four pounds if I sold
it for old silver. I'm a silversmith and I know. But to you, because it matches your others, it is worth about four times as
much. Give me twenty pounds and you can have it.'

Through the melted tallow on his face there was a faint flush
of blood. Although his voice was suave enough, Johnny knew he
was furious.

'I've never yet bought stolen goods. I'm not going to begin
now — not even with my own.'

Johnny put the cup back in its bag, but before he could tie the
strings to his belt Mr. Lyte's long fingers had reached out and
taken it.

'If you will give me back my property,' Johnny said politely,
'I'll take it to Mr. Revere or Mr. Burt. Four pounds is all I
really need.'

'Now wait a moment, young man. You *know* you stole it.
Make a clean breast of the matter and I will not be too hard on
you. Justice Dana was a fool to be taken in by those lying girls.'

'I didn't steal it. That was settled for all time, in court.'

Once on his feet Mr. Lyte moved quickly enough. He was at
the door, blocking Johnny's escape.

'Hadden and Barton,' he said.

The old clerks came scurrying in, their pens in their hands.

'Sewall's still down the wharf seeing about molasses? Very

well. We can do what's to be done better without that puppy. Now Hadden and Barton . . . here's a boy . . . that Johnny Tremain. You've heard tell . . .?'

'Yes, sir.'

'Shut and lock that door. He's not so sunk in poverty and vice but to have a glimmer of conscience.'

'No, sir.'

'And so two days after Mr. Dana found him innocent of stealing my cup he comes to me privately, confesses the theft, and wishes to return it to me.'

'Indeed! Very noble of him, sir.'

'*Mr*. Hadden and *Mr*. Barton, you are witnesses of his repentance and *voluntary* return of my stolen property.'

'Yes, sir.'

'Give me my twenty pounds.' Johnny was breathing hard.

'You thick-witted, little wharf-rat. Go whistle for it. I've two respectable witnesses who will go into court and swear that whatever I say is true. Do you think any court in Boston, even Dana's, would listen to you and your wretched girls if I and my clerks said contrary-wise? You daring to suggest you are my kin!'

Johnny saw he was trapped. 'I'll get that cup back,' he said through white lips. 'You thief . . .'

'Hadden, look in the street. See if Captain Bull is still about. Fetch him.'

'If anyone is hung for stealing cups, it will not be me. Wharf-rat, am I? You gallows bird.'

'Threatening my life, is he? Now I'm not going to be too hard on you, Ah-ha-ha-ha. As long as you had the decency to admit your theft. Having a bad time getting work since you burned your hand, eh? Well, my Captain Bull is taking the *Unicorn* to Guadalupe on ebb tide. Maybe you'd like to settle in Guadalupe? Boston is getting a little crowded. More opportunity in Guadalupe for *lying, thieving, scurvy knaves!*'

Hadden came back with Captain Bull. Johnny gave the captain one startled glance. He was an enormously powerful man,

with a neck as big as Johnny's waist and huge hands hanging
down to his knees. Each hand looked as large as a bunch of
bananas. The courtly bow he attempted at his employer only
made him seem more the baboon, but this formality gave Johnny
one split second. He shot out of the inner office before Captain
Bull had recovered from his bow. Hadden flung up his bony
arms trying to stop him, but went down like a bunch of fagots.

Johnny kept on running up Long Wharf and the short length
of King Street. He dove down Crooked Lane into Dock Square,
knocked over a basket of feathers a woman was selling, for a
moment was mixed up in a drove of squealing pigs, but he knew
where he was going and shot down Union Street. Salt Lane at
last, and the little man observing Boston so genially through his
spyglass. Then he stopped, looked behind him. The street was
empty. No Captain Bull. Baboons could not run that fast.

Rab was not in the shop. Only Uncle Lorne.

'Do you still want a horse boy?' He was breathing so hard he
could hardly speak.

'Why, yes,' said startled Mr. Lorne, 'sometime — but there's
no such a hurry. We've been hiring a boy from the Afric Queen
for a month and . . .'

'Will I do?'

Mr. Lorne went to the window opening on the shop's back
yard. Rab was out there brewing up a kettle of printer's ink.
The Webb twins were learning how and fetching fagots for him.

'Rab, *Rab*,' his uncle called to him, 'here's that Johnny back
again. Will he do for a rider?'

'Yes.' Rab's voice, cool, haunting, drifted back on a cloud of
evil-smelling black smoke from the yard.

'Very well, Johnny. Of course you know how to ride?'

'I've never been on a horse in my life.'

'Well, I'm afraid now, really . . .'

'I can learn.'

'*Rab!*'

'What?'

'*Can that Johnny Tremain learn to ride a horse?*'

'Yes.'

'All right, boy. You sit down and catch your breath and I'll
explain. This isn't a full-time job and I can't do more than sleep
you, bait you, and clothe you. But you'll have the first four days
of the week to pick up money for yourself, or to go on with your
learning (if any). I've got a fine library. If Rab says so, you can
sleep in the loft above this shop with him. If he'd rather go on
alone, my wife will put you up across the way. The *Observer* is
out every Thursday and the papers are delivered to the Boston
subscribers on that day. You can do it faster on horseback, but
on foot if you'd rather. That takes most of the day. Then next
day, Friday, you start about five in the morning, and you ride
through Dorchester, Roxbury, Brookline, Milton, and so on —
Rab will draw you a map — leaving a certain number of papers
at various inns. The subscribers go fetch them themselves. So
late Friday or early Saturday you cross the Charles and go
through Cambridge, Watertown, Waltham, Lexington, and so
on, and last is Charlestown. From there you cross back into
Boston on the ferry Saturday night.'

Rab came in with a kettleful of the warm, black, syrupy ink.
There was not a smootch on his white shirt or leather apron. The
Webbs were black as imps from Hell.

'Rab,' said his uncle, 'where's Johnny to sleep?'

'With me, of course.'

'Well, you show him where. But first take him over to the
Queen's stables and show him that horse you bought. If ever
you made a bad bargain, it was when you gave money for that
Goblin. But you take the afternoon off and give Johnny a lesson
in equitation — show him how to fall off without getting hurt.
He'll need it if he's going to ride that devil . . .'

Johnny's new life had begun.

- 2 -

'What's the matter with Goblin?' Johnny asked, a little nervously. 'Mr. Lorne doesn't seem to hold by him much.'

'Well,' said Rab mildly, 'if you can ride Goblin you can really ride. After him anything will seem easy. But that's a good way to learn. Now remember, Johnny, there's not such a lot to riding except getting along with your horse. Horses are timid animals at heart, but Goblin's the most timid of all.'

'Has he been treated badly?'

'Yes — whipped because he's so timid. I got interested in him out in Lexington where my folks live. He had four owners in one year. Each time he was sold, he went for half price. The last owner practically gave him to me. He's not mean, nor a bully. He's as sweet and gentle an animal as you'll ever find. A piece of paper blowing in the street might make any horse shy — and he's ashamed of himself next moment. But Goblin doesn't ever stop to see what it is. He thinks maybe it's a little white dog about to bite his heels and he jumps out of his skin and *leaves*. Sometimes it takes half an hour to quiet him again. As for clothes on the line, they aren't just shirts and petticoats. He thinks they are white hippogriffs big enough to carry horses off in their talons. From his point of view the only sensible thing is to get moving, and he moves pretty fast. Now what you've got to do is to get his confidence so completely he'll know you'll never let anything hurt him — you can't do that by whipping him. Then he'll go through Hell, a laundry yard from his point of view, for you.'

'But I don't know how to ride.'

'It's about like dancing ... keeping rhythm. You'll learn right off. Of course you'll be scared, but just remember this: no matter how scared you are, he's more so.' They were entering the Afric Queen's stable.

'The horse boy who has been riding him for us has made him worse and worse. If I had time I could get his confidence and cure him — somewhat. Nobody could make him safe and steady. Now you just look at him. Isn't he a beauty?'

Rab had gone into one of the many stalls and backed out a tall, slender horse, so pale he was almost white, but flecked all over with tiny brown marks. The mane and tail were a rich, blackish mahogany. His eyes were glassy blue.

Rab said: 'I never saw a horse his color before. His sire was Yankee Hero, a white horse, fastest horse I ever saw run. Narragansett breed. We could no more afford to own one of Yankee Hero's sons than we could the Lytes' coach unless there was *some* little thing wrong with him. Eh, Goblin?'

The beautiful, wild, timid thing breathed softly, caressingly at Rab, but at the same time the queer, crystalline eyes watched Johnny as though sure that this was a boy who ate horses.

'Now you put on a bridle like this — see? And when winter comes, don't ever put a cold bit in a horse's mouth. Breathe on it first. The saddle blanket — steady, steady, Goblin — it won't hurt you. And then the saddle. Now you lead him out in the yard. You hold the reins like this — left hand *always* and the thumb on the upper side, but down on the reins. And you put your left foot in the stirrup. If you get on from the right side and get kicked, it serves you right. There, see how easy? On and off just like that. You hold him a second.'

Rab went into the tavern, and when he came back he had permission to take out the landlady's genteel nag. With Johnny on the nag and Rab on Goblin, they went to the Common. Here were acres upon acres of meadow and cow pasture, hard ground cleared for the drilling of militia. The sun and the wind swept through them. Trees were turned to scarlet, gold, beefy red: blueberry bushes to crimson. Through one patch a white cow was plodding, seemingly up to her belly in blood. The cold, wild air was like wine in the veins. And across the vast, blue sky, white clouds hurried before the wind like sheep before invisible wolves.

'Easy, easy,' cried Rab. 'Easy does it.' Goblin had been cavorting, blowing through his nostrils, begging to be let out. Rab kept him at a close canter. The landlady's sorrel flung himself after him. Now and then Rab would glance behind to see how Johnny was making out.

'Not so stiff... give more. I said keep your *thumb* up.' Then
they would stop a moment, Rab making Johnny mount and dismount. 'Trot him from that stump yonder, back again to me.'

Once again both in the saddle, and he was setting a faster pace.
The two horses tore across the packed earth of the drill ground,
and for the first time in his life Johnny heard that wonderful
music — galloping hoofs on hard earth.

At the end, when Goblin had got most of the play out of him,
they changed horses. Actually Goblin's gaits were so smooth he
seemed easier than the sorrel.

Johnny felt he had learned a lot in his first lesson. A few more
and he would have had no fear of Goblin. But there were no
more lessons. Rab was too busy. He was teaching Johnny to
ride as he did everything else — with a minimum expenditure
of his own energy. Every day Johnny led Goblin to the Common,
for it was quite a long time before he dared ride him through the
narrow, crowded streets. And he sat in his manger and talked to
him.

The idea that Goblin was more scared than he gave him great
confidence and so did Rab's belief in him and his powers to learn.
He had always been quick on his feet, rhythmic and easy in his
motions. He had no idea that learning to ride by himself, with a
notoriously bad horse for one instructor and a boy who never left
his printing press for the other, he was doing an almost impossible
thing. But one day he overheard Uncle Lorne say to Rab, 'I
don't see how Johnny has done it, but he is riding real good now.'

'He's doing all right.'

'Not scared a bit of Goblin. God knows *I* am.'

'Johnny Tremain is a bold fellow. I knew he could learn — if
he didn't get killed first. It was sink or swim for him — and happens he's swimming.'

This praise went to Johnny's head, but patterning his manners
on Rab's he tried not to show it.

For the first week Uncle Lorne did hire the landlady's gentle
nag for Johnny. Even with the lists and maps Rab made for him,
those three days of delivering papers, first through Boston, then

circling out through the surrounding towns and returning Saturday night by ferry from Charlestown were confusing enough.

Soon, however, these three days of riding became a delight to him. He was a town boy, knowing little of country ways. The ships in the harbor he knew. The wharves and the world of shops and trade. Now he reveled in broad harvest fields, orange pumpkins, shocked corn, frost-touched grapes. And the towns clustering around Boston interested him.

He liked to make a handsome entrance. Even if he and Goblin had dawdled a bit on country roads, they both liked arriving at the inns at a gallop. Then Johnny would bustle in with his newspapers and often find the subscribers already sitting about the taproom waiting for him. Because he came from Boston and rode for the *Observer*, he was often questioned about the political thinking at the capital. By reading the papers, talking to Rab and Uncle Lorne, listening to the leaders of opposition about Boston, he quickly became well informed. In only a few weeks he changed from knowing little enough about the political excitement, and caring less, to being an ardent Whig.

He also enjoyed the showy, queer beauty of his horse. When people on the streets or at the taverns complimented him on his mount, there would come the same fatuous expression on his face he had often ridiculed on Cilla's when people stopped her and said how angelic Isannah was, but he did not know it.

At first he fell off fairly often and it would take him half an hour to catch the wary animal, but once a farmer's wife gave him his hat full of bad apples and he lured Goblin easily. After that he always stuffed his pockets with windfalls. If Goblin would approach something he feared, Johnny rewarded him with a specked apple, but when he did fall off, he would come home smelling like a cider press.

The boys shared the loft above the printing shop. It was reached only by a ladder, but was large, comfortable, and had a big fireplace. There was one odd thing about this attic and that was the number of chairs stored there. He started to ask Rab why this was, but thought better of it, and at last Rab told him.

It was here in the attic, ever and anon, 'The Boston Observers' met. It was a secret club, as powerful as any in Boston, and here in the last few years had been hatched much 'treason,' as the Tories called it. Rab did not even tell Johnny to keep his mouth shut. He knew he would.

Breakfast they made for themselves. Dinner was sent over by Mrs. Lorne. Supper they either got for themselves or ate at Aunt and Uncle's. Rab's aunt was a plump, red-headed, white-skinned woman. She must have been a variation of a well-known family pattern, for Johnny often heard people say, as they looked at Rab, 'That boy is a regular Silsbee from Lexington.' If he was, then she was not. But her eight-months-old son was. He was the longest baby Johnny had ever seen, had the straightest black hair, cried the least and ate the fastest. Never fussed, and watched the world through enigmatical, questioning, dark eyes. Even Uncle Lorne, who might have preferred that his only child should have repeated the fox-like, scholarly brightness of his own face, admitted, as he looked thoughtfully at his baby, 'That child of yours, Jenifer, is a regular Silsbee of Lexington.'

Johnny became absorbed in Goblin. He was afraid the stable boys at the Afric Queen struck at him, bullied him because he was timid, so he took upon himself the feeding and care of the animal. This saved Mr. Lorne a few pennies a week on the board bill, and he generously gave the money to Johnny. The landlord at the Queen liked the boy. When guests wished a letter delivered faster than the dawdling post riders, he would recommend Johnny. So once that fall he rode as far as Worcester, and again to Plymouth. This money was divided between the owner of the horse and the rider, and Johnny bought himself spurs, boots, and a fur-lined surtout, all second hand.

Although Johnny held the reins in his left hand, as Rab had taught him, many times as the horse was off on a wild tear and he was struggling to get him once more under control, he was forced to use his crippled hand. He could not keep it proudly in his pocket while careening about on a horse like Goblin. Although too badly injured ever to be skillful again, it was no longer in

danger of atrophying — as it had been in Johnny's pocket. As a
silversmith he had already learned to use his left hand a certain
amount. Rab never said to him, 'Now, Johnny, you've got to
learn to write with your left hand,' but he would give him things
to copy, take it for granted that he could — and he did.

For the first four days of every week Johnny was his own
master. He spent his time exercising his horse, unless he got an
order to ride express for the Afric Queen, in learning to write with
his left hand, and an orgy of reading. Mr. Lorne had a fine library. It was as if Johnny had been starved before and never
known it. He read anything — everything. Bound back copies
of the *Observer*, *Paradise Lost*, *Robinson Crusoe* — once more, for
that was one of the books Rab had brought him to read in jail —
Tom Jones and Locke's *Essays on Human Understanding*, Hutchinson's *History of Massachusetts Bay*, *Chemical Essays*, *Spectator Papers*,
books on midwifery, and manners for young ladies, Pope's *Iliad*.
It was a world of which he never had guessed while living with
the Laphams, and now he remembered with gratitude how his
mother had struggled to teach him so that this world might not be
forever closed to him. How she had made him read to her, when
he would rather have been playing. Poor woman! Her books
had been few and mostly dull.

So he sat for hours in the Lornes' sunny parlor, the books about
him stretching to the ceiling. Mrs. Lorne never called to him to
help her in the kitchen. She, Uncle Lorne, and Rab all took it
for granted that Johnny ought to read. Mrs. Lapham could not
have borne the sight of so 'idle' a boy. But Aunt Lorne never
interrupted him except to come in now and then with a plate of
hot gingerbread or seed cakes, and once in a long time ask him if
he would mind baby as she went out marketing or visiting.

'I'll just put baby in his cradle here, and if he doesn't go right
to sleep you rock him a little with your foot.' The first time he
read *Tom Jones*, he got so excited he absent-mindedly rocked
baby for half an hour, but even this did not upset that regular
Silsbee of Lexington. The baby gulped a little, but took it philo-
sophically — just like Rab. Secretly, and only when alone,

Johnny began calling him 'Rabbit.' It was easy for him to love, and he loved the baby. He would have died before he would have let anyone guess he was so simple, but Aunt Lorne knew. Sometimes she would come into the kitchen quietly and hear Johnny holding long, one-sided conversations with Rabbit. When she came into the room where he was with the child, he would merely say scornfully, 'Aunt Lorne, I think it is wet,' and pretend to be lost in his book.

Then she would feel so fond of the lonely boy, who never knew he was lonely, and so amused at his pretense of scorn for something he in his heart loved, she could not help but kiss him. She always kissed him where his hair began to grow in the middle of his forehead. He had never known until she told him that he had a widow's peak, which she assured him was a great mark of beauty. 'Why, I'd give anything for a widow's peak,' she would say, 'I'd give a plate of cookies,' and off she would waddle — for she was tiny-footed and too plump — and come back with the cookies.

Johnny thought Rab was lucky to have an aunt like that.

- 3 -

This was Johnny's new life. He liked it, but was at first a little homesick for the Laphams. He had never been so glad in his life as that Thursday, a few weeks after he had begun delivering newspapers, when he saw Cilla and Isannah standing by the town pump in North Square. He had left his last paper for the day with Paul Revere and was starting back to put up his horse at the Afric Queen. He had felt he could never again go to the Laphams'. Mrs. Lapham and her Mr. Tweedie had been too ready to let him hang. He'd just about kill Dove if ever he met him.

'Cilla!' he cried. She looked at him and her eyes shone.

Goblin stretched his muzzle toward the empty drinking trough.

'I'll pump him fresh water.' Cilla pumped and the horse drank gratefully.

'Cilla, do you come over often to fetch water?' It hurt him that the heavy yoke and the two buckets which he had worn so often, to his humiliation, had somehow descended upon her thin shoulders.

'Mr. Tweedie won't have it that Dove and Dusty stop their work. Before breakfast they are supposed to bring in all we need for the day. When we run short, he says we girls are to go. He's upset everything, Johnny.'

'I didn't know he had that much gumption.'

'Ma abets him. And Ma says it's not suitable for grown women like Madge and Dorcas to be carrying buckets through the streets. So I'm the one.'

'If you'll lead my horse,' said Johnny, 'I'll carry the water as far as Fish Street. I'm not going into that house for a long time yet — but I'll go pretty near. Close enough to spit at them all.'

'Still mad?'

'Sure. Of course I am. Why not?'

Isannah had wandered off because a passing clergyman had seen the sunlight on her hair and was asking her to say the shorter catechism as proof that she was as pious as she was beautiful. And he was giving her a poke of sweetmeats he had bought for his wife.

'Look you, Cil,' said Johnny. 'Every Thursday, see? I'll leave Mr. Revere's paper and I'll be here to help you, just about the same time as today.'

'I can carry the water myself,' said Cilla stiffly.

'No, it's not just that, but . . . I've been wanting to see you. And Isannah too. I didn't know how to manage.'

They were stopping on Fish Street. It was not close enough for Johnny to spit at his old residence, but as close as he cared to go.

'Don't you go promising, Johnny,' she said. She was stroking Goblin's face. 'I think your horse is the most beautiful horse I ever saw. I think he likes me already.'

'Yes, I know. But I'm going to be here every Thursday. And

Sunday afternoon, too. If there's water to carry, I'll carry it, but it's more important that we talk. Couldn't you sneak off and meet me up by the pump?'

'Yes, I could.'

'Well, *will* you?' She was a 'sot' and stubborn girl.

'I don't know — but if you want me and Isannah very much, I can say ... maybe ...'

Isannah flew up to join them. She had just eaten every one of her sweetmeats and was now exclaiming over the beauty of the paper poke, suggesting, at least, that that was all the kind clergyman had given her — an empty paper poke — but Johnny could smell chocolate and peppermint on her. Cilla shouldn't let her get away with such selfishness and gluttony.

Although 'maybe' was all Cilla promised, Johnny promised much more.

'Every Thursday and every Sunday afternoon.' Those were his last words and he thought he meant them. He thought six months, a year, six years from now, the girls would be as dear to him as they were at that moment.

Back once more in Goblin's saddle, he turned to watch them, Cilla bent under the heavy load, Isannah skipping about and for no particular reason chanting the shorter catechism once more. But maybe she had reason — maybe another clergyman was in the offing.

There was a lump in Johnny's throat.

- 4 -

So far in his new life there had been one, and only one, slight disappointment. Rab was so self-contained. It was as if nothing could come in from the outside to upset him. He owned himself. By temperament Johnny was expansive, easily influenced. Although Rab would have been exactly the same if he had been the son of the wealthiest merchant or the poorest tinker in Boston,

Johnny would not. When he had been the prize apprentice of Hancock's Wharf, the envy of all the other masters, the principal bread-winner of the Laphams (and he knew it), he had been quite a different boy from the arrogant, shabby young tramp of late summer and early fall. Those marketwomen who had counted their pats of butter after he brushed past their stands, Mrs. Lapham with her prophecies that he would end on the gallows, had not been so far wrong. For a little while it had been touch-and-go with him. If pushed a little farther, he might have taken to crime — because that was what was expected of him. But no matter what happened to Rab, good or bad fortune, good or bad reputation, he would never change. Johnny felt he knew him but little more than at their first meeting, but he admired him more and more all the time. Rab did not criticize him, but he had a way of asking him why he did certain things which had a great influence upon Johnny.

Once, as they sat in the attic toasting cheese and muffins by their hearth, the older boy asked why he went about calling people 'squeak-pigs' and things like that. Johnny was always ready to do his share, or more than his share, in fanning up friendship — or enmity. Sometimes it seemed to Rab he did not much care which.

'Why do you go out of your way to make bad feeling?

Johnny hung his head. He could not think why.

'And take Merchant Lyte. Everybody along Long Wharf knows you called him a gallows bird. He's not used to it.' Was it fun, he wondered — going about letting everybody who got in your way have it?

After that Johnny began to watch himself. For the first time he learned to think before he spoke. He counted ten that day he delivered a paper at Sam Adams's big shabby house down on Purchase Street and the black girl flung dishwater out of the kitchen door without looking, and soaked him. If he had not counted ten, he would have told her what he thought of her, black folk in general, and thrown in a few cutting remarks about her master — the most powerful man in Boston. But counting ten had its rewards. Sukey apologized handsomely. In the past he had never given anyone time to apologize. Her 'oh, little master, I'se so sorry! Now you just step right into de kitchen and I'll dry up dem close — and you can eat an apple pie as I dries,' pleased him. And in the kitchen sat Sam Adams himself, inkhorn and papers before him. He had a kind face, furrowed, quizzical, crooked-browed. As Sukey dried and Johnny ate his pie, Mr. Adams watched him, noted him, marked him, said little. But ever after when Johnny came to Sam Adams's house, he was invited in and the great leader of the gathering rebellion would talk with him in that man-to-man fashion which won so many hearts. He also began to employ him and Goblin to do express riding for the Boston Committee of Correspondence. All this because Johnny had counted ten. Rab was right. There was no point in going off 'half-cocked.'

Twice that fall he saw Rab moved out of his customary reserve. Johnny always spent Friday night with Rab's folks at Lexington. There were hundreds of fine acres called 'Silsbee's Cove.' Old Grandsire, who had brought Rab up, lived in the big house, but he had sons, grandsons, nephews, close about him. Grandsire, Major Silsbee, was confined mostly to his chair. An old wound he had received fighting twenty years ago in the French and Indian Wars had stiffened up on him.

At the end of harvest the Silsbees had a dance in Grandsire's big barn. There were at least twenty Silsbees there and both Johnny and Rab came out from Boston. The tall, powerfully built, silent Silsbee men were easy to pick out from among the neighbors and friends invited, but Grandsire and Rab were more completely Silsbees than anyone else.

At this country dance Johnny for the first time saw Rab move suddenly into action. He flung himself into the dancing. Johnny thought in amazement how nonchalant and even sluggish Rab could seem about the printing shop, and yet he did his work with a machine-like perfection. Now he saw the dark eyes glowing and the white teeth flash. It was amazing that an old fiddle in Grandsire's hands and the old voice calling, 'Gents 'round the Ladies

— Ladies 'round the Gents' could work such a change in him. He had stepped out of his imperturbable usual self. Here was a Rab Johnny had always known existed, but had never before seen. All the Lindas and Betsys, Pollys, Peggys, and Sallys of Lexington were clamoring to stand up with him. He loved to dance, and seemingly all the girls loved him and he all the girls. Johnny, two years younger, noticed with disapproval.

One other thing happened at that barn dance that made a great impression on Johnny. He forgot entirely about his hand. Although in the reels and jigs they danced, every moment a different girl was clinging to it, none of them seemed to notice. Johnny spoke of this fact to Rab as they undressed at Grandsire's. The Boston girls (he was thinking of Isannah's words — such cruel words he had never even told Rab) had said his hand disgusted them. He wasn't to touch them with it.

'It is you who put the idea in their heads,' said Rab, pulling off his shirt. 'You know you usually go about with that hand in your pocket, looking as if you had an imp of Hell hidden away, and then someone asks you and you pull it out with a slow flourish, as if you said, "This is the most disgusting thing you ever saw." No wonder you scare everybody. Tonight happens you just forgot.'

The other time he saw Rab moved out of himself was a few days later. The Webb twins were timid, weakly little fellows, natural butts for any bullies. They never seemed to need any company except each other and their cat. Mrs. Lorne one day sent them to the butcher for stew meat, and they, thinking it was an errand a cat might enjoy, carried her with them. The butcher's boy was a well-known tyrant. He grabbed the Webbs' cat, trussed her, hung her up by her heels to a hook, and began to sharpen his knife. He was going to butcher her, skin her, and give the carcass to the Webbs for stew meat. The butcher sat by and roared with laughter at the frantic children's tears and cries.

Rab heard the terrified screams of the little boys. He rescued the cat, who was the first to get home, with the Webbs on her heels. Next he began on the butcher's boy. By then Johnny had arrived. Together they took on the butcher, his oldest son, the butcher's wife, armed with boiling water she had prepared for scalding pigs, her mother, and a passer-by. Yet before the constable had arrived, Rab was out of it, back cleaning his press, and he had got Johnny out of it, too. Johnny had a black eye, a lame shoulder, a torn shirt, a bite in his wrist — that was the butcher's wife's mother; she had good teeth for seventy. Rab had nothing except an uncommonly high color in his face and a look of intense pleasure. It was strange that a boy who could fight like that and enjoy it so intensely never quarreled, never fought, and he had almost nothing to say about this really Homeric battle. But for days afterward Johnny would see a look of dreamy content in his eyes, a slow smile form absent-mindedly on his lips. Rab was thinking of the fun he and Johnny had had at the butcher's shop. All he would say was, 'We certainly made hash of *that* shop.' The boy was a born fighter — ferocious, utterly fearless, quick and powerful — but he didn't fight often and he hadn't much to say afterward.

Seemingly Silsbees were like that. Johnny had already seen a pack of them out at Lexington, and there over at the Lornes was Rabbit repeating the old pattern. One day Aunt Lorne came in as Johnny sat reading, with the baby in her arms.

For once she looked a little discouraged. 'My land, I don't know what's wrong with baby. There's something — and he won't tell me ——'

'Isn't he pretty young to tell much?'

'Oh, no, no. Other babies can tell you whether it's gas or a pin, or milk souring on them. But he's a real Silsbee, and they never do, you know.'

'Aren't you a Silsbee too?'

'Me? Oh, no. Thank Heaven, it skipped me. Look at my red hair — and my build. I'm just like Mother — a mere Wheeler. I can say what hurts me — sometimes before I'm hurt. Those Silsbees — they just about can't. They don't tell anything, but they are about the best men ever lived. If you'll just learn to take 'em or leave 'em.'

Johnny was learning to 'take or leave' Rab.

VI. *Salt-Water Tea*

ON SUNDAYS the boys might relax a little, breakfast when they pleased, only they must turn up clean and shining in time to go to church with Aunt and Uncle and listen to the inflammatory Reverend Sam Cooper. Doctor Cooper was putting more politics than gospel into his sermons that fall and more fear of 'taxation without representation' than God into his congregation.

England had, by the fall of 1773, gone far in adjusting the grievances of her American colonies. But she insisted upon a small tax on tea. Little money would be collected by this tax. It worked no hardship on the people's pocketbooks: only three-pence the pound. The stubborn colonists, who were insisting they would not be taxed unless they could vote for the men who taxed them, would hardly realize that the tax had been paid by the East India Company in London before the tea was shipped over here. After all, thought Parliament, the Americans were yokels and farmers — not political thinkers. And the East India tea, even after that tax was paid, would be better and cheaper than any the Americans ever had had. Weren't the Americans, after all, human beings? Wouldn't they care more for their pocketbooks than their principles?

Shivering — for the last week in November was bitterly cold – Johnny built up the fire in the attic. From the back window he could see that the roofs of the Afric Queen were white with frost.

A sharp rat-tat on the shop door below woke Rab.

'What time's it?' he grumbled, as people do who think they are disturbed too early Sunday morning.

'Seven and past. I'll see what's up.'

It was Sam Adams himself. When either cold or excited, his palsy increased. His head and hands were shaking. But his strong, seamed face, which always looked cheerful, today looked radiant. Sam Adams was so pleased that Johnny, a little naively, thought he must have word that Parliament had backed down again. The expected tea ships had not sailed.

'Look you, Johnny. I know it's Lord's Day, but there's a placard I must have printed and posted secretly tonight. The Sons of Liberty will take care of the posting, but Mr. Lorne must see to the printing. Could you run across and ask him to step over? And Rab — where's he?'

Rab was coming down the ladder.

'What's up?' said Rab sleepily.

'The first of the tea ships, the *Dartmouth*, is entering the harbor. She'll be at Castle Island by nightfall.'

'So they dared send them?'

'Yes.'

'And the first has come?'

'Yes. God give us strength to resist. That tea cannot be allowed to land.'

When Johnny got back with Mr. Lorne, Rab had Mr. Adams's text in his hands, reading it as a printer reads, thinking first of spacing and capitals, not of the meaning.

'I can set that in no time. Two hundred copies? They'll be fairly dry by nightfall.'

'Ah, Mr. Lorne,' said Adams, shaking hands, 'without you printers the cause of liberty would be lost forever.'

'Without you' — Mr. Lorne's voice shook with emotion — 'there would not have been any belief in liberty to lose. I will, as always, do anything — everything you wish.'

'I got word before dawn. It's the *Dartmouth* and she will be as far as Castle Island by nightfall. If that tea is landed — if that tax is paid — everything is lost. The selectmen will meet all day today and I am calling a mass meeting for tomorrow. This is the placard I will put up.'

He took it from Rab's hands and read:

Friends! Brethren! Countrymen! That worst of Plagues, the detested tea shipped for this Port by the East India Company, is now arrived in the Harbour: the hour of destruction, of manly opposition to the machinations of Tyranny, stares you in the Face; Every Friend to his Country, to Himself, and to Posterity, is now called upon to meet at Faneuil Hall, at nine o'clock this day [that, of course, is tomorrow Monday], at which time the bells will ring to make united and successful resistance to this last, worst and most destructive measure of Administration. . . . Boston, Nov. 29, 1773.

Then he said quietly: 'Up to the last moment — up to the eleventh hour, we will beg the Governor's permission for the ships' return to London with their cargo. We have twenty days.'

Johnny knew that by law any cargo that was not unloaded within twenty days might be seized by the custom-house and sold at auction.

'Mr. Lorne, needless to say the Observers will meet tonight. There are *private* decisions to be made before the mass meeting tomorrow at nine.'

Johnny pricked up his ears. Ever since he had come to Mr. Lorne's (and Rab said he might be trusted with anything — possibly with men's lives) he had now and then summoned the members of the Observers' Club. They were so close to treason they kept no list of members. Rab made Johnny memorize the twenty-two names. They met in Rab and Johnny's attic.

'Johnny,' said Mr. Lorne, anxious and overanxious to please Mr. Adams, 'start right out.'

'No, sir, if you please. Noon will be better. That will give the members time to get home from church. And as usual, Johnny, make no stir. Simply say, "Mr. So and So owes eight shillings for his newspaper."'

Johnny nodded. That meant the meeting would be tonight
at eight o'clock. If he said one pound eight shillings, it would
mean the next night at eight. Two pounds, three and six would
mean the day after at three-thirty. It gave him a feeling of excitement and pleasure to be even on the fringes of great, secret,
dangerous events.

Today he could not make his rounds on horseback. A constable might stop him and ask embarrassing questions. There
was a law against riding out on Sunday for either business or
pleasure.

The Reverend Samuel Cooper he 'dunned' as he was shaking
hands with his parishioners at the end of the service. He nodded
as Johnny told him that eight shillings were due on the paper, but
a fashionable woman standing by said it was a fair scandal for
boys to be intruding into God's house and dunning a clergyman,
and if collecting bills wasn't work, what was? She would call a
constable and have the 'impertinent imp' whipped for Sabbath-
breaking. Mr. Cooper had to cough so he could pretend not to
be laughing, and he winked at Johnny in spite of the dignity of
his black clericals, white bands, and great woolly wig.

'I'll tell my brother William, too, eh?' he offered. 'Brother
William and I will both pay you tonight.'

Johnny found four more of the members also at this meeting
and then headed for Beacon Hill. At all the great mansions he
commonly went to the back door, either to leave newspapers or
to 'collect bills.' A skinny, slippery-looking old black slave in the
kitchen told him Mr. Hancock was in bed with a headache. No,
she would *not* permit Johnny to go to his bedchamber. So the boy
went to the front door, rang the bell, hoping some other less ob-
durate servant might let him in. Maybe little Jehu. The old slave
guessed what he was up to and got there first.

Might he not send a note up to Mr. Hancock? They wrangled
a little and at last she said yes he might. She was preparing a cat-
nip tea to send to the master. He could write a note and ｝ut it on
the tray. In the kitchen he wrote his note — 'Mr. Hancock owes
the *Boston Observer* eight shillings,' folded it, and on the outside

wrote, 'John Hancock, Esquire.' Was it only two months before
he had tried to write those very words and failed so miserably?

The cook was squatting at the hearth toasting thin toast.
Johnny lifted the teapot to set his note under it. That teapot . . .
its handle was in the shape of a winged woman! Beside it was the
creamer that he had loved so much. Even now he could shut his
eyes and feel it in his hands. Ah . . . a sugar basin to match! Mr.
Hancock had indeed found a smith to make it after Mr. Lapham
failed so lamentably. Behind the cook's back Johnny lifted it in
trembling hands. The handles were wrong. Done exactly as
Johnny had started to do them before he talked with Mr. Revere.

He thought with longing, but contentment, of that other
basin . . . the one that had been exactly right and never completed. This one he held in his hands was nothing, trash. But
how beautiful . . . how perfect, had been the other one! 'If I
had to hurt my hand, I'm glad it was while doing something
worth while — not merely mending an old spoon.'

The cook's wiry black fingers were in his hair.

'You no-account! Don't you never think to go stealing sugar
in this house. Mr. Hancock is that generous I'd have given you
a piece if you had asked politely.'

Next to the Hancock house was the Lytes'. Mr. Lyte, in his
effort to play both ends against the middle, did take the *Observer*
and every Thursday Johnny habitually crossed from one stable
yard to the other. There was no reason he should do so today.
But it was as he told Cilla — he just about couldn't help watching the Lytes. What did they do on Sundays? Would the
merchant be home today? He might have asked Captain Bull to
dine with him. Would he see Miss Lavinia — or only the fat
cook, the scullery maids, Aunt Best, or the stable men?

The cobbled stable yard was deserted. He did not hear the
usual chatter from the kitchen. He glanced at the dining-room
window — the one Mr. Lyte thought he broke the night the
cup was stolen. Doubtless now that cup Mr. Lyte had actually
stolen from him stood with the other three on the sideboard.
His jaw clenched. Sometime, someday, he would get it back,
and not by snitching it either.

A horse came clattering into the stable yard. Contrary to law and decent propriety, Miss Lavinia had been out for a gallop on the Common. Her black horse was wet and foaming. The young woman sat her side-saddle superbly. Her dark green London habit almost swept the ground. He knew that she had recognized him as the boy who had 'stolen the cup,' the very first time she had met him delivering papers at her house, but she pretended not to. Now she glanced at him and the chisel mark between the sweeping black brows deepened.

'Williams!' she cried. 'Dolbear!'

There was no groom at the stable to help her dismount. The black horse reared. Johnny smiled. He knew enough about equitation to realize she was showing off. Johnny could make Goblin rear like that any time he pleased. It amused him that she pretended such contempt for him and yet condescended to show off her skill before him.

'Well, *you* then!' she cried to him. With her nervous horse and long skirts it was impossible for her to dismount from a side-saddle without help. He gave her the help. She did not thank him. It was as if she knew that proximity to such famous beauty was reward enough for any boy or man in Boston. If anyone thanked, obviously it should be Johnny. He thought she was the most disagreeable woman he had ever seen, and yet the fact was he had slipped thus into the Lytes' yard in the hope of seeing her — even risking Captain Bull and that threatened trip to Guadalupe. He liked to tell Rab how awful she was — and then would sneak back to take another look.

Near-by was William Molineaux's house. Its seedy appearance advertised to the whole world that its owner was close to bankruptcy. Mr. Molineaux was standing in his orchard, shaking his cane at a couple of small boys he had treed in an apple tree. He had a terrible temper, which he thoroughly enjoyed. Although Johnny told him three times about those eight shillings, he was not sure whether the idea had penetrated the wild Irishman's thick skull or not. Nor did he care.

His good friend, Josiah Quincy, plump little John Adams, and

James Otis he found together at the Quincy house. They were
still sitting over their port and cracking nuts. James Otis did
not even look up when Johnny entered. He was hunched up in
his chair, his thick-skulled, heavy head hung forward. He was
busy drawing a row of little people on the paper before him.
Quincy, having already heard about the meeting that night,
put a finger to his lips and shook his head, at the same time
glancing at the heavy, lonely figure of Otis. Johnny guessed
that neither he nor John Adams wanted Otis notified of the
meeting, although he was a member.

For four years Otis had been crazy and sane, turn and turn
about, on again and off again. He was the most brilliant man
of them all, thought in the largest terms, not ever merely of
Boston; was passionate in his demand for the rights of Englishmen everywhere — over here and in Old England too. Now
he was not even listening to what was going on about him. His
heavy head was swinging back and forth. John Adams and Josiah
Quincy were watching him so intently their heads were also
moving a little. Johnny stole out and closed the door softly
after him. He guessed that in a day or two he'd hear it whispered,
James Otis had got into a mad freak and fired guns from the
windows of his house: James Otis had been seen leaving Boston
in a closed chaise with a doctor and in a straitjacket.

Next he went to Doctor Church. Here was a queer man
surely. He was still in his bedgown and slippers, with paper,
inkhorn, and pens about him, writing poetry. Johnny did not
care for Molineaux because he bellowed and roared so loudly.
But he disliked Doctor Church. He did not know one thing
against him, but he felt the man was crooked, and he knew that
Paul Revere and Joseph Warren felt as he felt about Church.

Doctor Warren was in Roxbury tending a sick woman. His
wife bade Johnny come back at five.

- *2* -

Johnny had saved Paul Revere for the last because he lived at North Square and, being a Sunday, he knew that Cilla and Isannah would be waiting for him by the town pump. Guiltily he remembered he had not bothered to meet them last Thursday, nor the Sunday before, nor the Thursday before that.

He glanced about. The girls were not there, and secretly he was relieved. He went on to Mr. Revere's. The silversmith was busy drawing a political cartoon concerning tea and tyranny. He did not draw well — not the way he made silver. As he drew, his children crowded about him, standing on the rungs of his chair, breathing down his neck, dropping crumbs of ginger-bread into his hair; but Paul Revere took all this confusion as he took everything else, without any fussing.

'I believe I owe you eight shillings?' he said, with a wide smile on his dark, ruddy face. The eyes gleamed.

Now there was only Doctor Warren left; then he'd go back and help Rab set out all those chairs in the attic, get ready for the meeting that night. But Cilla and Isannah were standing by the pump. Cilla looked little and forlorn. The delicate face was pale. Things were not going too well for the Laphams. Cilla was a little shabby. The sight of her touched Johnny's heart. He pitied her — and yet he wished she had not come. Now it seemed years ago, not months, that he had lived at the Laphams', and then surely Cilla and Isannah were the only friends he had. But he had on going to the *Observer* entered a new, vast, and exciting world. He had made new friends. He was absorbed in the excitement over the tea, over the secret meeting tonight. Of all of these things and people Cilla knew nothing, nor could he tell her, yet he tried to show interest in what she had to tell him. Once he would have been very inter-ested. Now he felt like a hypocrite, and because he was uncom-fortable he blamed it in some way on Cilla.

Had Mr. Tweedie decided whether he would marry Madge or Dorcas?

Cilla hoped he would choose Madge. Dorcas was just about crazy over Frizel, Junior. She said she would elope with him if Ma tried to make her marry Tweedie.

How was Dove?

Just like always.

Dusty?

Hadn't he heard? Dusty had run away to sea.

Old master?

No, he had not even stepped inside his shop since he had signed with Mr. Tweedie. He said he hadn't long to live and he was going to spend all his time preparing to meet his Maker.

But Johnny wasn't really interested in all this news. He was absorbed with the meeting this night — the tea ships. It bothered him a little that Cilla was so faithful. There had been many and many a Sunday when he did not get to North Square. He was too busy with Rab and his new world. But he knew that Cilla, usually as today toting Isannah along with her, never failed. She said she understood he could not always keep his schedule, but if he had tried harder he could certainly have done a lot better. That very feminine faithfulness of the girl irritated him, but he had not admitted this to himself. She took it for granted that Johnny had not changed, and he had changed much. If, the winter of seventy-three, Johnny Tremain had a romantic attachment to anyone, it was to that black-haired and, as far as he knew, black-hearted, bad-tempered, disagreeable, conceivable 'cousin' of his Miss Lavinia Lyte. Certainly not Priscilla Lapham.

Isannah especially got on his nerves. She was showing off more and more all the time. She knew that if she kept her hood off someone would come along and say how pretty she was. Even now an elderly clergyman was approaching, opening his mouth.

Johnny did not stop to hear. He left.

Doctor Warren was back from Roxbury. He was sitting in his surgery, still in his riding boots and spurs.

'Eight shillings, sir,' said Johnny.

'I guessed we'd meet tonight. I'll be there . . . but wait a moment. I promised this article to Mr. Lorne this morning — got held up. Woman fell out of an apple tree. Broken thigh . . .' He went on writing.

He was a fine-looking young man, with fresh skin and thick blond hair and very bright blue eyes.

Even a horse boy merely entering that surgery would feel confidence in him and his skill. Johnny took off the red mittens Aunt Lorne had knit for him and stretched his hands toward the fire blazing on the hearth.

The pen stopped scratching. Doctor Warren had stopped writing, and, although his back was to him, Johnny knew those clean, clear blue eyes were staring at him. They were staring at his crippled hand.

Instantly Johnny thrust it back into his breeches pocket. He straightened himself unconsciously, preparing to be either sullen or arrogant.

'My boy,' came the doctor's gentle voice, 'let me see your hand.'

Johnny did not face him. He said nothing.

'You don't want me to look at it?'

As long as it might take to count ten, there was complete silence. Then the boy said, 'No, sir — thank you.'

'Was it God's will it should be so?' Doctor Warren meant was it crippled from birth. If so, it would be harder for him to help.

'Yes,' said Johnny, thinking of how he had ruined it upon a Lord's Day.

'God's will be done,' said the young doctor.

He went back to his writing.

- *3* -

Outside, Johnny could hear shouting, yelling, whistles, the running of feet. With the coming of night, the Sons of Liberty were abroad, tacking up Mr. Adams's placards. Tonight Rab

was not out with them, although he had been off once or twice
of late helping to frighten the tea consignees out of Boston to the
protection of a handful of British soldiers stationed on Castle
Island. Johnny was too young to be a 'Son.' But when the
Observers met, the boys always stayed in the room below to run
errands for them, and it was always Rab who mixed the fragrant
punch with which the meetings ended.

All over Boston was a feeling of excitement. Everyone knew
that the *Dartmouth* was but a few miles away. Great events were
brewing. Johnny went to the door to see what the clamor was.
A courageous Tory was chasing the men whom he had found
tacking a placard on his property. They had let him chase them
thus far to dark Salt Lane and now had turned on him. Such
street brawling made Johnny feel sick. He closed the door, sat
down beside Rab, and began slicing lemons, oranges, and limes.

'Rab...'

'Yes?'

'What will they decide ... those men upstairs?'

'You heard Sam Adams. If *possible*, the ships will sail home
again with their tea. We've got twenty days.'

'But if the Governor won't agree?'

'He won't. You don't know Hutchinson. I do. And you saw
how happy Sam was this morning? He knows the Governor a
lot better than I do.'

'And then ... and what next, Rab?'

Johnny heard blows and oaths from the street outside. His
hands shook. He put down the knife so Rab wouldn't know.
They were doing something — something awful, to the Tory.

'As soon as we go upstairs with our punch, we'll know. Look
at Sam Adams. If he looks as pleased as an old dog fox with a
fat pullet in his mouth, we'll know they've agreed to violence
if everything else fails. He doesn't care much any more about
our patching up our differences with England. He'd just about
welcome a war.'

'But the King's warships are in the harbor. They'll protect
the tea. They'll fight.'

'We can fight, too.' Rab was putting the last delicate touches to his kettleful of brew, for tonight the punch would be hot. He was grating nutmegs, cautiously sprinkling in cloves, and breaking up cinnamon bark.

'Taste it, Johnny. That Madeira Mr. Hancock brought with him is first-class.'

But Johnny heard a low moaning in the street, close to the shut door. That Tory, who had been so brave — and foolish — as to follow the Sons of Liberty down a black alley was alone now — was sobbing, not from pain but from humiliation. Johnny declined to taste the punch.

Mr. Lorne called down the ladder.

'Boys, ready with your punch?'

'They made up their minds fast tonight,' said Rab. 'I rather thought they would.'

Johnny carried a handful of pewter cups and the big wooden bowl. Rab followed with two pitchers of his spicy brew.

The attic where the boys commonly slept looked strange enough with those chairs pulled out and arranged for the meeting. John Hancock sat in the moderator's chair. His face looked white and drawn. Probably his head still ached. Beside him was Sam Adams leaning toward him, whispering and whispering. Johnny thought how the Tories were saying that Sam Adams seduced John Hancock, even as the Devil had seduced Eve — by a constant whispering in his ear.

Adams turned his face as Johnny set down the wooden bowl on the baize-covered box before the moderator. Johnny had never seen an old dog fox with a fat pullet in his mouth, but he recognized the expression when he saw it. Rab poured the punch and instantly the tense silence was broken. The men were on their feet, crowding up about the bowl. Rab and Johnny were well known. Here was Paul Revere clinking his cup with Rab, and John Hancock was telling Johnny how far too well his old slave woman guarded his privacy. Actually three men had come to the house to tell him the first of the tea ships had been sighted, but he had not known anything was afoot until he got Johnny's 'bill' on his tray. Then he guessed what had happened.

'Here's to December the sixteenth.'

'Hear! Hear!'

, They drank to that last day, the day on which the tea must be destroyed — unless it was allowed to return to England. And Johnny saw that Sam Adams had carried them all with him. They did not honestly want the tea returned and a peaceful settlement made. They wanted grievances and more grievances... well, yes, armed warfare. Things were in such a state they did not honestly believe there could be any permanent, friendly settlement with the mother country.

Johnny looked about through the haze of tobacco smoke. There was Doctor Warren. He was talking with Uncle Lorne and John Adams about that article he had written for the newspaper. Suddenly he lifted his head, smiled, almost laughed.

Johnny did not know why Warren smiled. Why had Johnny been such a fool... why couldn't he have shown his hand to the doctor? He bit into his lower lip. After his rudeness to Doctor Warren, he did not see how he ever could go to him and say, 'I've changed my mind. I want you to look at it. I think you are the only person in the world who can help me.' So when Doctor Warren, a little later, looked toward Johnny ready to smile, forgive his discourtesy, the boy looked away. He was so embarrassed he was rude again.

Sam Adams was standing at the far end of the room and Mr. Hancock still sat, his head in his hands. Adams clapped slightly and instantly conversation stopped.

'Gentlemen,' he said, 'tonight we have made our decision — and know the method by which the detested tea can be destroyed, if the ships are not allowed to return. Here we have with us two of exactly — ah — the sort of boys or young men we intend to use for our great purpose. Two boys in whom we have implicit trust. If it is the wish of the assembled club members, I suggest we approach them with our proposition tonight... enlist their aid. Twenty days will be up before we know. We'd best get on with our plans.'

The members once more took their seats, but the pewter cups of punch were passing from hand to hand. Only Will Molineaux was too restless to sit. He was muttering to himself. Ben Church sat alone. He often did. No one really liked him.

All agreed the boys were to be told.

'First,' Adams said to the boys, 'raise your right hands. Swear by the great name of God Himself never, for as long as you live, to divulge to anyone the secret matters now trusted to you. Do you so swear?'

The boys swore.

Hancock was not looking at them. He sat with his aching head in his hands.

'There's no chance — not one — those ships will be allowed to return. The mass meetings which will be held almost daily demanding the return of the tea are to arouse public opinion and to persuade the world we did not turn to violence until every other course had been blocked to us. When the twenty days are up, on the night of the sixteenth of December, those ships are going to be boarded. That tea will be dumped in Boston Harbor. For each ship, the *Dartmouth*, the *Eleanor*, and the brig, the *Beaver*, we will need thirty stout, honest, fearless men and boys. Will you be one, Rab?'

He did not say Rab and Johnny, as the younger boy noticed. Was this because he thought Johnny too cripple-handed for chopping open sea chests — or merely because he knew Rab better and he was older?

'Of course, sir.'

'How many other boys could you find for the night's work? Strong and trustworthy boys — for if one ounce of tea is stolen, the whole thing becomes a robbery — not a protest?'

Rab thought.

'Eight or ten tonight, but give me a little time so I can feel about a bit and I can furnish fifteen or twenty.'

'Boys who can keep their mouths shut?'

'Yes.'

Paul Revere said, 'I can furnish twenty or more from about North Square.'

'Not one is to be told in advance just what the work will be, nor who the others are, nor the names of the men who instigated this tea party — that is, the gentlemen gathered here tonight. Simply, as they love their country and liberty and hate tyranny, they are to gather in this shop on the night of December sixteenth, carrying with them such disguises as they can think of, and each armed with an axe or hatchet.'

'It will be as you say.'

The discussion became more general. Each of these three groups must have a leader, men who could keep discipline.

'I'll go, for one,' said Paul Revere.

Doctor Warren warned him. 'Look here, Paul, it has been decided this work must be done by apprentices, strangers — folk little known about Boston. The East India Company may bring suit. If you are recognized . . .'

'I'll risk it.'

Uncle Lorne was motioning to the boys to leave the conspirators. They did not want to leave, but they did.

- 4 -

Both the boys were in their truckle beds. The loft still smelled of tobacco and the spices of the punch.

Johnny moved restlessly on his bed.

'Rab?'

'Uh?'

'Rab . . . those boys you promised. Am I one?'

'Of course.'

'But my hand . . . What will we have to do?'

'Chop open tea chests. Dump tea in the harbor.'

'Rab?'

'Hummmmm?'

'How can I ever . . . chop?'

'You've twenty days to practice in. Logs in back yard need splitting.'

'Rab...'

But the older boy was asleep.

Johnny was so wide awake he couldn't close his eyes. Old Meeting struck midnight. He settled himself again. Surely if he tried hard enough he could sleep. He was thinking of those tea ships, the *Dartmouth*, the *Eleanor*, the *Beaver*, great white sails spread softly, sweeping on and on through the night to Boston. Nearer, nearer. He was almost asleep, twitched, and was wide awake. He would not think of the tea ships, but of those logs in the back yard he would practice on. He thought of Doctor Warren. Oh, why had he not let him see his hand? Cilla, waiting and waiting for him at North Square — and then he got there only about when it pleased him. He loved Cilla. She and Rab were the best friends he had ever had. Why was he mean to her? He couldn't think. He would take an axe in his left hand and chop, chop, chop... so he fell asleep.

Something large and white was looming up over him — about to run him down. He struggled awake, sat up, and found he was sweating. It was the great sails of the tea ships.

From the bed next to him he heard the soft, slow breathing of the older boy. So much more involved than Johnny in the brewing storm, Rab had been able to drop off immediately. Somehow Johnny must draw into himself something of Rab's calm, his nerveless strength. He began to breathe in unison with the sleeping boy — so slowly, so softly. He fell into a heavy sleep.

- 5 -

Next morning Johnny was up and out in the back yard early. At first it seemed impossible to hold an axe in a left hand, steady it with his bad right. He gritted his teeth and persevered. Rab said nothing of his struggles. He merely set type, pulled proofs as usual. But often he was gone from home, and Johnny knew he was 'feeling about' for those fifteen to twenty boys he had promised. Would the others go and Johnny be left behind? He could not bear the thought, and Rab had promised him that in twenty days he might learn to chop. Having finished the logs in Mr. Lorne's back yard, he began chopping (free gratis) for the Afric Queen.

Almost every day and sometimes all day, the mass meetings at Old South Church went on. Tempers grew higher and higher. Boston was swept with a passion it had not known since the Boston Massacre three years before. Riding this wild storm was Sam Adams and his trusty henchmen, directing it, building up the anger until, although the matter was not publicly mentioned, they would all see the only thing left for them to do was to destroy the tea.

Sometimes Rab and Johnny went to these meetings. It happened they were there when the sheriff arrived and bade the meeting forthwith to disperse. He said it was lawless and treasonable. This proclamation from Governor Hutchinson was met with howls and hisses. They voted to disobey the order.

Sometimes the boys slipped over to Griffin's Wharf. By the eighth of December the *Eleanor* had joined the *Dartmouth*. These were strange ships. They had unloaded their cargoes — except the tea. The Town of Boston had ordered them not to unload the tea and the law stated they could not leave until they had unloaded. Nor would the Governor give them a pass to return to England. At Castle Island the British Colonel Leslie had orders to fire upon them if they attempted to sneak out of the harbor. The *Active* and the *Kingfisher*, British men-of-war, stood by ready to blast them out of the water if they obeyed the Town and returned to London with the tea. The ships were held at Griffin's Wharf as though under an enchantment.

Here was none of the usual hustle and bustle. Few of the crew were in sight, but hundreds of spectators gathered every day merely to stare at them. Johnny saw Rotch, the twenty-three-year-old Quaker who owned the *Dartmouth*, running about in despair. The Governor would not let him leave. The Town would not let him unload. Between them he was a ruined man.

He feared a mob would burn his ship. There was no mob, and night and day armed citizens guarded the ships. They would see to it that no tea was smuggled ashore and that no harm was done to the ships. Back and forth paced the guard. Many of their faces were familiar to Johnny. One day even John Hancock took his turn with a musket on his shoulder, and the next night he saw Paul Revere.

Then on the fifteenth, the third of the tea ships arrived. This was the brig, the *Beaver*.

- 6 -

The next day, the sixteenth, Johnny woke to hear the rain drumming sadly on the roof, and soon enough once more he heard all the bells of Boston cling-clanging, bidding the inhabitants come once more, and for the last time, to Old South to demand the peaceful return of the ships to England.

By nightfall, when the boys Rab had selected began silently to congregate in the office of the *Observer*, behind locked doors, the rain stopped. Many of them Johnny knew. When they started to assume their disguises, smootch their faces with soot, paint them with red paint, pull on nightcaps, old frocks, torn jackets, blankets with holes cut for their arms, they began giggling and laughing at each other. Rab could silence them with one look, however. No one passing outside the shop must guess that toward twenty boys were at that moment dressing themselves as 'Indians.'

Johnny had taken some pains with his costume. He had sewed for hours on the red blanket Mrs. Lorne had let him cut up and he had a fine mop of feathers standing upright in the old knitted cap he would wear on his head, but when he started to put on his disguise, Rab said no, wait a minute.

Then he divided the boys into three groups. Beside each ship at the wharf they would find a band of men. 'You,' he said to one group of boys, 'will join the boarding party for the *Dartmouth*. You for the *Eleanor*. You for the *Beaver*.' Each boy was to speak softly to the leader and say, 'Me Know You,' for that was the countersign. They would know the three leaders because each of them would wear a white handkerchief about the neck and a red string about the right wrist. Then he turned to Johnny.

'You can run faster than any of us. Somehow get to Old South Church. Mr. Rotch will be back from begging once more the Governor's permission for the ships to sail within a half-hour. Now, Johnny, you are to listen to what Sam Adams says next. Look you. If Mr. Adams then says, "Now may God help my country," come back here. Then we will take off our disguises and each go home and say nothing. But if he says, "This meeting can do nothing more to save the country," you are to get out of that crowd as fast as you can, and as soon as you get into Cornhill begin to blow upon this silver whistle. Run as fast as you are able back here to me and keep on blowing. I'll have boys posted in dark corners, close enough to the church, but outside the crowd. Maybe we'll hear you the first time you blow.'

About Old South, standing in the streets, inside the church, waiting for Rotch to return with the very last appeal that could be made to the Governor, was the greatest crowd Boston had ever seen — thousands upon thousands. There was not a chance, not one, Johnny could ever squirm or wriggle his way inside, but he pushed and shoved until he stood close to one of the doors. Farther than this he could not go — unless he walked on people's heads. It was dark already.

Josiah Quincy's voice rang out from within. 'I see the clouds roll and the lightning play, and to that God who rides the whirlwind and directs the storm, I commit my country . . .'

The words thrilled Johnny, but this was not what he was waiting for, and it was not Sam Adams speaking. He was bothered with only one thing. Quincy had a beautiful carrying voice. It was one thing to hear him and another Sam Adams, who did not speak well at all.

The crowd made way for a chaise. 'Rotch is back! Make

way for Rotch!' Mr. Rotch passed close to Johnny. He was so young he looked almost ready to cry. This was proof enough that the Governor had still refused. Such a turmoil followed Rotch's entry, Johnny could not hear any one particular voice. What chance had he of hearing Sam Adams's words? He had his whistle in his hand, but he was so jammed into the crowd about the door that he did not believe he would be able to get his hand to his mouth.

'Silence.' That was Quincy again. 'Silence, silence, Mr. Adams will speak.' Johnny twisted and turned and brought the whistle to his lips.

And suddenly there was silence. Johnny guessed there were many in that crowd who, like himself, were hanging on those words. Seemingly Mr. Adams was calmly accepting defeat, dismissing the meeting, for now he was saying,

'This meeting can do nothing more to save the country.'

Johnny gave his first shrill blast on his whistle, and he heard whistles and cries seemingly in all directions, Indian war whoops, and 'Boston Harbor a teapot tonight!' 'Hurrah for Griffin's Wharf!' 'Salt-water tea!' 'Hi, Mohawks, get your axes and pay no taxes!'

Johnny was only afraid all would be over before Rab and his henchmen could get to the wharf. Still shrilling on the whistle, he fought and floundered against the tide of the crowd. It was sweeping toward Griffin's Wharf, he struggling to get back to Salt Lane. Now he was afraid the others would have gone on without him. After all, Rab might have decided that Johnny's legs and ears were better than his hands — and deliberately let him do the work that best suited him. Johnny pushed open the door.

Rab was alone. He had Johnny's blanket coat, his ridiculous befeathered knitted cap in his hands.

'Quick!' he said, and smoothed his face with soot, drew a red line across his mouth running from ear to ear. Johnny saw Rab's eyes through the mask of soot. They were glowing with that dark excitement he had seen but twice before. His lips were parted. His teeth looked sharp and white as an animal's. In spite of his calm demeanor, calm voice, he was charged and surcharged with a will to action, a readiness to take and enjoy any desperate chance. Rab had come terrifyingly alive.

They flung themselves out of the shop.

'Roundabout!' cried Rab. He meant they would get to the wharf by back alleys.

'Come, follow me. *Now* we're really going to run.'

He flew up Salt Lane in the opposite direction from the waterfront. Now they were flinging themselves down back alleys (faster and faster). Once they had a glimpse of a blacksmith shop and other 'Indians' clamoring for soot for their faces. Now slipping over a back-yard fence, now at last on the waterfront, Sea Street, Flounder Alley. They were running so fast it seemed more like a dream of flying than reality.

The day had started with rain and then there had been clouds, but as they reached Griffin's Wharf the moon, full and white, broke free of the clouds. The three ships, the silent hundreds gathering upon the wharf, all were dipped in the pure white light. The crowds were becoming thousands, and there was not one there but guessed what was to be done, and all approved.

Rab was grunting out of the side of his mouth to a thick-set, active-looking man, whom Johnny would have known anywhere, by his walk and the confident lift of his head, was Mr. Revere. 'Me Know You.'

'Me Know You,' Johnny repeated this countersign and took his place behind Mr. Revere. The other boys, held up by the crowd, began arriving, and more men and boys. But Johnny guessed that many who were now quietly joining one of those three groups were acting on the spur of the moment, seeing what was up. They had blacked their faces, seized axes, and come along. They were behaving as quietly and were as obedient to their leaders as those who had been so carefully picked for this work of destruction.

There was a boatswain's whistle, and in silence one group boarded the *Dartmouth*. The *Eleanor* and the *Beaver* had to be warped in to the wharf. Johnny was close to Mr. Revere's heels. He heard him calling for the captain, promising him, in the jargon everyone talked that night, that not one thing should be damaged on the ship except only the tea, but the captain and all his crew had best stay in the cabin until the work was over.

Captain Hall shrugged and did as he was told, leaving his cabin boy to hand over the keys to the hold. The boy was grinning with pleasure. The 'tea party' was not unexpected.

'I'll show you,' the boy volunteered, 'how to work them hoists. I'll fetch lanterns, mister.'

The winches rattled and the heavy chests began to appear — one hundred and fifty of them. As some men worked in the hold, others broke open the chests and flung the tea into the harbor. But one thing made them unexpected difficulty. The tea inside the chests was wrapped in heavy canvas. The axes went through the wood easily enough — the canvas made endless trouble. Johnny had never worked so hard in his life.

He had noticed a stout boy with a blackened face working near him. The boy looked familiar, but when he saw his white, fat hands, Johnny knew who he was and kept a sharp eye on him. It was Dove. He was not one of the original 'Indians,' but a volunteer. He had on an enormous pair of breeches tied at each knee with rope. Even as Johnny upended a chest and helped get the tea over the rail, he kept an eye on Dove. The boy was secretly scooping tea into his breeches. This theft would come to several hundred dollars in value, but more important it would ruin the high moral tone of the party. Johnny whispered to Rab, who put down the axe he had been wielding with such passion and grabbed Dove. It wasn't much of a scuffle. Soon Dove was whining and admitting that a little of the tea had happened to 'splash' into his breeches. Johnny got them off and kicked them and the many pounds of tea they held into the harbor.

'He swim good,' he grunted at Rab, for everyone was talking 'Indian' that night.

Rab picked up the fat Dove as though he were a rag baby and

flung him into the harbor. The tea was thicker than any sea-weed and its fragrance was everywhere.

Not a quarter of a mile away, quite visible in the moonlight, rode the *Active* and the *Kingfisher*. Any moment the tea party might be interrupted by British marines. There was no landing party. Governor Hutchinson had been wise in not sending for their help.

The work on the *Dartmouth* and the *Eleanor* finished about the same time. The *Beaver* took longer, for she had not had time to unload the rest of her cargo, and great care was taken not to injure it. Just as Johnny was about to go over to see if he could help on the *Beaver*, Mr. Revere whispered to him. 'Go get brooms. Cleam um' deck.'

Johnny and a parcel of boys ʋrushed the deck until it was clean as a parlor floor. Then Mr. Revere called the captain to come up and inspect. The tea was utterly gone, but Captain Hall agreed that beyond that there had not been the slightest damage.

It was close upon dawn when the work on all three ships was done. And yet the great, silent audience on the wharf, men, women, and children, had not gone home. As the three groups came off the ships, they formed in fours along the wharf, their axes on their shoulders. Then a hurrah went up and a fife began to play. This was almost the first sound Johnny had heard since the tea party started — except only the crash of axes into sea chests, the squeak of hoists, and a few grunted orders.

Standing quietly in the crowd, he saw Sam Adams, pretending to be a most innocent bystander. It looked to Johnny as if the dog fox had eaten a couple of fat pullets, and had a third in his mouth.

As they started marching back to the center of town, they passed the Coffin House at the head of Griffin's Wharf. A window opened.

'Well, boys,' said a voice, so cold one hardly knew whether he spoke in anger or not, 'you've had a fine, pleasant evening for your Indian caper, haven't you? But mind . . . you've got to pay the fiddler yet.'

It was the British Admiral Montague.

'Come on down here,' someone yelled, 'and we'll settle that score tonight.'

The Admiral pulled in his head and slapped down the window.

Johnny and Rab knew, and men like the Observers knew, but best of all Sam Adams knew, that the fiddler would have to be paid. England, unable to find the individuals who had destroyed this valuable property, would punish the whole Town of Boston — make every man, woman, and child, Tories and Whigs alike, suffer until this tea was paid for. Nor was she likely to back down on her claim that she might tax the colonists any way she pleased.

Next day, all over Boston, boys and men, some of them with a little paint still showing behind their ears, were so lame they could scarce move their fingers, but none of them — not one — told what it was that had lamed them so. They would stand about and wonder who 'those Mohawks' might have been, or what the British Parliament might do next, but never say what they themselves had been doing, for each was sworn to secrecy.

Only Paul Revere showed no signs of the hard physical strain he had been under all the night before. Not long after dawn he had started on horseback for New York and Philadelphia with an account of the Tea Party. He could chop open tea chests all night, and ride all day.

VII. The Fiddler's Bill

But when that bill came — the fiddler's bill — that bill for the tea, it was so much heavier than anyone expected, Boston was thrown into a paroxysm of anger and despair. There had been many a moderate man who had thought the Tea Party a bit lawless and was now ready to vote payment for the tea. But when these men heard how cruelly the Town was to be punished, they swore it would never be paid for. And those other thirteen colonies. Up to this time many of them had had little interest in Boston's struggles. Now they were united as never before. The punishment united the often jealous, often indifferent, separate colonies, as the Tea Party itself had not.

Sam Adams was so happy his hands shook worse than ever.

For it had been voted in far-off London that the port of Boston should be closed — not one ship might enter, not one ship might leave, the port, except only His Majesty's warships and transports, until the tea was paid for. Boston was to be starved into submission.

On that day, that first of June, 1774, Johnny and Rab, like almost all the other citizens, did no work, but wandered from place to place over the town. People were standing in angry knots talking, gesticulating, swearing that yes, they would starve, they would go down to ruin rather than give in now. Even many of the Tories were talking like that, for the punishment fell equally heavily upon the King's most loyal subjects in Boston

and on the very 'Indians' who had tossed the tea overboard.
This closing of the port of Boston was indeed tyranny; this was
oppression; this was the last straw upon the back of many a
moderate man.

The boys strolled the waterfront. Here on Long Wharf, merchants' counting houses were closed and shuttered, sail lofts deserted, the riggers and porters stood idle. Overnight, hundreds
of such, and sailors and ropemakers, wharfingers and dock hands,
had been thrown out of work. The great ships of Boston which
had been bringing wealth for over a hundred years were idle
at their berths. Not one might come and go.

At first it was the men of the ships and wharves that were
thrown out of work and could not get food for their families.
The paralysis that started there would soon spread out and in-
clude everybody. For who now could buy new clothes? The
clothiers and tailors would close shop. Not one man in Boston
could afford a silver basin. The silversmiths would not last long.
Nobody could pay rent. The wealthy landowners were headed
for bankruptcy.

'So,' said Rab cheerfully, 'looks like we'd all starve together.'

They stood at the very end of Long Wharf which ran a half-
mile out into the harbor. They could see the *Captain*, British
flagship, stationed between Long and Hancock's Wharf, and
over by Governor's Island, the *Lively*, and beyond, the *Mercury*,
the *Magdalen*, the *Tartar*. His Majesty's fleet surrounded Boston,
enforcing the Port Act.

'Uncle Lorne is upset. He says the printers will not be able to
go on with the newspapers. He won't be able to collect subscriptions, or get any advertising. He won't be able to buy paper nor
ink.'

'He's sending the Webb twins home?'

'Yes. Back to Chelmsford. But he and I can manage. The
Observer is to be half-size. He won't give up. He'll keep on
printing, printing and printing about our wrongs — and our
rights — until he drops dead at his press — or gets hanged.'

There had been a good deal of talk about hanging. Governor

Hutchinson was ordered to England. General Gage from now on would be in charge. Regiment upon regiment of the finest British troops were arriving. They were planning to put down sedition all right. And everyone knew that Gage had the right to send any man whom he believed a leader in this revolt against England to London and the parody of a trial, certain death on the gallows. Or, if he wished, Gage might erect his gallows over here.

Sam Adams and Hancock, Doctor Warren, perhaps still James Otis, would be the first to go. Certainly all the other members of the Observers, if ever their names were known, would follow, and so would all the Whig printers of Boston. No wonder Uncle Lorne was a little nervous. By nature, he was a timid man, yet timid or bold he would go on printing, begging the people of Massachusetts to wake up and resist this tyranny before it was too late. He would print until he had not a sheet of paper left to print on, or until the very day the gallows was set up for him.

As yet, only the British men-of-war had arrived. But the transports were on the seas. Soon it seemed that almost every day another transport put in. There was the rattle of drums, with the shouts of officers, and off the ships poured a flood, scarlet as a tide of blood. Boston was inundated with British soldiers, and now every third person one met in the street wore the handsome uniform of King George the Third.

There wasn't much work to do. Rab by himself could set the entire newspaper in a day. The subscriptions had dropped, partly because many people could not afford a paper, and partly because so many Whig families were leaving Boston for the country. Johnny could deliver the Boston papers in a morning — instead of taking all day. June was ending and the boys stood about the Common watching the soldiers of the First Brigade camped there under Earl Percy. Row upon row of identical tents, cook fires, tethered horses of officers, camp followers, stacked muskets, the quick, smart pacing of sentries. All was neat and orderly.

Muskets. It was the muskets which interested Rab the most. Already on every village green throughout New England, men and boys were drilling in defiance of the King's orders. They said they were afraid of an attack from the French. These men had no uniforms. They came from the fields and farms in the very clothes they used for plowing. That was all right. But the weapons they brought to their drilling were not. Many had ancient flintlocks, old squirrel guns, handed down for generations. Rab, for instance, all that spring had been going to Lexington once or twice a week to drill with his fellow townsmen. But he could not beg nor buy a decent gun. He drilled with an old fowling piece his grandsire had given him to shoot ducks on the Concord River. Never had Johnny seen Rab so bothered about anything as he was over his inability to get himself a good modern gun.

'I don't mind their shooting at me,' he would say to Johnny, 'and I don't mind shooting at them ... but God give me a gun in my hands that can do better than knock over a rabbit at ten feet.'

The British soldiers went about their business as though oblivious of the many hostile, curious eyes watching them. They were confident that these provincials, these yokels now gaping at their equipment, gauging the manner of fighting men they were, would be so impressed they would never stand up and fight them. Rab, so concerned over a gun as he was, did an uncharacteristic, foolish thing. The two boys were standing close to a stack of muskets. As Rab explained to Johnny their good points, he put out a hand and touched the lock on one.

Without even showing bad temper, almost impartially, a mounted officer sitting his horse close by chatting with a couple of Boston's Tory girls, swung about and struck Rab a heavy blow on the side of his head with the flat of his sword. Then he went on flirting with the girls as though nothing had happened. Rab never knew what hit him.

Now a sergeant came bawling, 'Spectators are not to intrude. Get back behind them ropes! Get back all of you! Get back!'

Johnny stayed where he was beside the unconscious Rab. Yet, after this act of sudden violence, the boys were well treated. Johnny was not run through because he stayed with his friend, did not obey the sergeant. A gray, older man, a medical officer, approached, called for water, sponged Rab's face for him, and said he was coming to. Johnny was not to worry.

'What was he doing?'

'Just looking at a gun.'

'Touching it?'

'Well . . . yes.'

'And only got hit over the head? He got off easy. Filching a soldier's arms is a serious misdemeanor. Wonder Lieutenant Bragg didn't kill him.'

Rab said thickly. 'I hadn't thought to filch it! Not bad idea. Guess I'll . . . guess I'll . . .' He was still groggy from the blow. 'If ever I get a chance I'll . . .'

The medical man only laughed at him.

'Now, boys,' he said seriously, 'you forget talk like that. You remember that *we* don't like being here in Boston any better than you like having us. I'd rather be with my wife and children in Bath. We're both in a tight spot. But if we keep our tempers and you keep your tempers, why, we can fix up things between us somehow. We're all one people, you know.'

As he talked, Johnny had an experience he was to have many more times. The troops would do something he considered unforgivable (like nearly braining Rab for merely touching a gun) and then the next moment be so civil and friendly he could not help but like them — at least some of them, as individuals. The medical man, noticing Johnny's riding boots and spurs, was saying, 'I've a cousin lives over in Cambridge. Haven't had a chance to send him a letter. Do either of you know a boy with a good horse who'd ride for me?'

Rab was mouthing 'yes' at Johnny.

'I've got a good horse.'

'Come to me at one o' the clock sharp this noon. I'm quartered on Mr. Shaw, North Square.'

On the way home Rab said: 'If you can get started carrying messages for him, others may follow. Might be we could learn things Sam Adams and Doctor Warren and Paul Revere would like to know. They wouldn't dare send their own orderlies — fearful somebody might kill them.'

'I'd thought of that myself.'

But at one o'clock, as he stood beside Goblin in North Square receiving money and the letter from the medical captain (also a pleasant smile), one thing upset him. Paul Revere's house was almost next door. There was a girl there about his age. She was standing before her house, almost bent horizontal at the hips. She was sticking out at him the longest, reddest tongue he had ever seen. And as he mounted and swung about to leave the British officer, he heard her shrilling in a horrible sing-song, 'He loves the Brit-ish. He loves the Brit-ish.'

But that night, on his return, when he went to tell Mr. Revere there was no question but that Mr. Shurtleif of Cambridge, always considered a lukewarm Whig, was in reality a leader of Tories in Middlesex County, he saw little Miss Revere again. 'Father says,' she apologized handsomely, 'that I'm not to believe everything I see and . . .'

'Believe anything you like.' Johnny was feeling good. He had charged the medical man three times the price he would have dared charge a Yankee, and by what Mr. Shurtleif had said to his wife on reading this letter he had found out something worth — not much — but at least worth knowing.

'I *like* to see you stick out your tongue,' he went on. 'It is so long and red I thought at first it was a hound-dog dressed up in pink petticoats. I never guessed it was a young lady.'

- 2 -

Now Johnny no longer kept half of the money he and Goblin earned carrying letters. He charged the British officers such a figure (and they never complained), he was bringing in a considerable sum and he gave it all to Aunt Lorne to buy food for her family, of which he was one. At first she wouldn't take it, then she cried and kissed him on the little peak of hair that turned down upon his forehead, and did take it.

No gallows was set up to hang 'rebels.' General Gage was doing his best to make friends with the people of Boston. He did not stop the flood of treasonable oratory which poured forth from men like Warren and Quincy. He did not prohibit the publication of such inflammatory presses as the *Observer*. The Whigs had their say. The papers were allowed to print outrageous things about himself and his troops. He was not brilliant, but he was no tyrant. In time he confidently expected all the trouble would smooth out by itself . . . if only the soldiers and the inhabitants did not get to quarreling.

Nor did Boston starve. From one end of the Atlantic seaboard to the other, towns and even villages sent great shipments of food. Rice from South Carolina or quintals of fish from Marblehead; money even from London, for there was much sympathy in England for Boston. Flour, corn, beef, sheep, all day were passing through the town gates upon the Neck, in carts and wagons. This was the only road connecting Boston with the mainland. Formerly almost everything she used came to her on her hundreds of famous ships. Now the ships were lying like dead birds along her wharves. So July was ending.

Johnny had not seen Priscilla Lapham for three weeks. His schedule was now so much upset he never did know when he would be in North Square on a Thursday. And every Sunday of late he had gone out to Lexington to watch the Minute Men drilling, a little secretly, behind Grandsire Silsbee's great barn. It might be Sabbath-breaking, but these men were so sure they were doing God's will in preparing to resist tyranny they did not care. Johnny could only stand and watch. True enough, there were boys no older than he drilling there, but his crippled hand made it impossible for him to pull a trigger. This incapacity fretted him badly and he would sometimes take it out on

Rab... The militia troops didn't look like much. They had funny-looking guns. They were funny-looking men and... Rab let him talk. He knew why Johnny was criticizing. It was because he could not be one himself.

So he had not seen Cilla since late in June.

Thus far she had never once come to the *Observer's* office in Salt Lane. It was as if she recognized it as that other world into which Johnny Tremain had disappeared and knew that she could not follow him. So Johnny was surprised one afternoon, riding back from Plymouth where he had delivered a letter for Major Pitcairn, to find her sitting in the shop with Rab. She did not look at all forlorn, in her fresh lavender muslin frock, her neat white stockings and black pumps. Her head was tipped back and she was laughing. She had been drawing a picture and Rab was telling her what to draw. For once — for the first time since Johnny had left the Laphams — Isannah was not with her. Johnny was so glad to see her, he wondered could it have been that it was Isannah always hanging onto her, always showing off, that had irritated him — made him not care whether he kept his rendezvous with the girls or not?

As he came in, booted and spurred, sunburned and hatless, Cilla glanced at him. Her eyes were happy, filled to the brim with happiness. She had been having such a good time with Rab; and unconsciously and unreasonably Johnny stiffened. He couldn't see why she and Rab should have been having such a good time.

They were explaining. Rab had wanted a picture of Boston being strangled to death by a British grenadier. It was for the newspaper and — she, Cilla, having chanced in, had drawn it beautifully — now Johnny would have to cut a block of it for printing.

'I can do it — not very well, of course, but I can. You certainly can draw better and better.'

'Mr. Tweedie can draw. He's giving me lessons. And Rab posed for the British grenadier. Look, I've pictures of him here.'

'Those Rab? They look more like woodchucks than Rab to

me,' he said. But Cilla knew he thought they were fine pictures and was proud of her.

She was so pretty Johnny could hardly think where all this prettiness came from, and sourly he thought it came from Rab. He had a way of lighting people up, showing them at their best. No, partly at least it was because of that lavender dress, and her face had color in it because she was eating enough. When the troops came and times were so hard, Cilla had always given a large share of her food to Isannah and had grown to look more peaked and worried every week. Now she looked fine.

'Sit there, like that, Johnny. I'm going to draw you too. You're easier than Rab.'

'Why'm I easier than Rab?'

'Because,' she said, intentionally hurting his feelings, 'you're just a child yet — Rab's grown up. There! You don't mind if I make you look a little like a raccoon, do you?'

'I'll draw a bushy tail for you, Cilla,' Rab said.

Johnny fidgeted, as people do who are having their pictures drawn, crazy to see what somebody else thinks they look like. It wasn't much of a picture. Between them they had drawn a funny, half-raccoon, half-boy. Somehow it did look like Johnny, and they all laughed.

'Four o'clock! I must be getting back. I was told to pick up a pair of gloves on Queen Street and be back at five.'

She got up, tied a flowered bonnet on her head, and started for the door.

'Wait . . . Cilla, you haven't told me any news.' He had forgotten how recently her news had bored him.

'That's right. I've just told Rab. Johnny, I won't be able to meet you regularly any more. Things have changed.'

'How so? Your mother mad?'

'No . . . that is, yes, she is mad, but about something else. She's mad because Dorcas really did have the guts to run off and marry Frizel, Junior, just as soon as Mr. Tweedie declared for her.'

'Dorcas isn't going to get much of that elegance she was always out after from Frizel, Junior.'

'No, but she doesn't care.' The young girl's voice softened. 'She says when you really are in love, you don't care much about anything — except him.'

Johnny, remembering the gawky, callow, but upstanding young leather-dresser of Fish Street, was surprised that anyone could value him so highly.

'She ran off with Frizel, Junior, just as soon as Mr. Tweedie came out and said he preferred her to Madge. But what put Ma right through the roof was when he said he was in no hurry. He didn't mind passing up Madge and waiting for me.'

'*You!*' cried Johnny hotly; 'that old man — if he is a man! Why, he must be about forty. Cilla, you're lying to me if you say anybody's talking of marrying you.'

'I was fifteen last month. And you were fifteen way back in January.'

'I'd not stopped to think. Rab, did you hear that? I'm only a year younger than you are now.'

Rab grinned. 'I was seventeen last week.' Johnny thought that was like Rab — slipping off by himself, getting ahead of you and then grinning at you out of the corner of his mouth.

'Mother didn't like it — Mr. Tweedie stalling like that. Then one thing happened after another.'

'For instance?'

'Ever since — well, last fall — the Lytes have been giving us work to do. Mr. Tweedie is clever — although so queer. A couple of weeks ago Miss Lyte came in. She wanted her arms, that old rising sun, engraved on the top of her riding whip. So she stands about and I stand about and Mr. Tweedie and Ma. The shop door was open into the back yard ... and Isannah was standing about too, in the back yard.'

'I'll bet she was.'

'Yes, Miss Lavinia just about had a fit.'

'What was Isannah doing? Throwing up?'

'I had just washed her hair,' Cilla said dreamily, 'and the sun was on it.'

'Oh, I see,' said Johnny sourly.

'And Isannah was walking back and forth reciting some poetry to herself. Acting it out. Something about Captain Kidd and how he sailed. Old Stumpy Joe, the one-legged sailor-man, taught it to her. Miss Lavinia stood there watching Isannah, and she looked more like something cut out of stone than a human being.'

'She can't help it,' said Johnny, who liked to run her down. 'She was born that way. Go on.'

'She just turned her head like that and said to Ma through her teeth — like this, "Ma'am, I'm taking that child with me." Ma first said she wouldn't, and then she said she couldn't stand between Isannah and such an opportunity. And Isannah said she wouldn't go without me. So it was fixed this way. I'm signed up to work in the kitchen, or help Miss Lavinia dress, or anything, for a year, and Isannah is thrown in for nothing — because she is so young and has a delicate stomach. We are both living with the Lytes.'

'Do you like her?'

'Sometimes — well, yes.'

'Well, I think she's disagreeable.' He hoped Cilla would contradict him, but she did not.

'So now I'll be going back. She only gave me the afternoon off. I thought I'd tell you not to look for me around North Square any more.'

Johnny felt guilty. 'I do leave a paper at the Lytes' every Thursday . . .'

Cilla said nothing, but looked at him out of the corners of her eyes.

'Couldn't I see you sometime — maybe?'

'I don't know. You might ask Mrs. Bessie, the cook. She's sort of a friend of mine. So good-bye, I'll be going on.'

Cilla had changed so much Johnny felt confused. One thing was certain. She wasn't going to hang around and wait for him either on street corners or at back doors — and then not have him show up.

'Good-bye, Cilla, I'll see you soon.'

But Rab did not say good-bye. He did not even ask her if he might walk home with her to Beacon Hill. He simply went, and Johnny was mad. If anyone walked home with Cilla, it should be himself, or Rab might have said, 'Come on, Johnny, we'll both walk over to the Lytes' with Cilla.' But he'd forgive Rab for intruding himself. He'd cook him up a mess of eggs for supper. It would take about fifteen minutes to go to the Lytes', fifteen minutes to get back. He built the fire and cooked the eggs. He cooked them and cooked them. At last, in disgust, he took them off and ate them, every now and then going down to consult the shop clock. Rab was gone for exactly one hour and forty-seven minutes. Nor did he miss the eggs Johnny had eaten. He had been very well fed by Mrs. Bessie in the Lyte kitchen, and he thought Cilla was a grand kid.

He had had a good time. You could see it in his eyes, and whenever he looked at Johnny's long face he looked ready to laugh.

- 3 -

Now the only regularity in Johnny's life was the great effort he made to see Cilla every Thursday and the care he gave to Goblin. But when he went to the Afric Queen, he was going into enemy territory. The tavern had been taken over bodily by British officers, chief among whom was Colonel Francis Smith. Goblin was the only horse in the stable that did not belong to a British officer, for the landlord had sent his to the country, fearing they would either be commandeered by the occupying troops or that he could not get hay for them. About the stables, British orderlies, officers, servants, and small British horse boys, the servants of the servants, were always congregating. Johnny paid little heed to them. They all knew that he rode for the *Observer* — but they also knew that he often rode for their own officers.

Sometimes they picked on him. And once, when things got too bad and he felt he had to fight it out with the worst bully, the other boys, all his enemies, stood about demanding fair play, saying, 'Well fought, Yankee,' and 'That's neat,' when he beat the bully. He had rather thought the whole gang would be on him the second he got the bully down; instead they merely respected him. So he made out better than he could have expected, until one day he found that Colonel Smith had a new horse boy. The one he had brought over with him had run away, so he had told his orderly-officer to find a new one — and that boy was Dove. Johnny saw him grinning sheepishly at him, hoping they might be friends — they, the only two local boys at the stable.

'You . . .' Johnny muttered out of the corner of his mouth, 'you trash, you milk pudding, you cottage cheese, slug . . . so you're not above going to work for *them*, are you?'

'Honest, Johnny, I gotter eat. Old Tweedie fired me.'

An orderly stuck his head in the stable. 'Boy,' he said to Johnny, 'Colonel Smith has a letter to go to Milton. Please go to the parlor and see him or Lieutenant Stranger about it.'

A slow, gat-toothed grin spread over Dove's face.

'Looks like you work for them, too?'

'Looks like,' said Johnny fiercely.

He saw the Colonel, went home for his boots and spurs, then took out Goblin and saddled him. One of the English boys had got Dove down and was twisting his arm, making him swear allegiance to his Britannic Majesty, gracious George the Third. Dove was swearing fast enough and protesting that was the way he really felt. All rebels should be hung. Johnny had a queer feeling at the pit of his stomach. He wanted to go to his rescue. He had to make himself remember that he hated Dove.

'But that fellow over there' — Dove was pointing to Johnny — 'is really on the other side and . . .' Johnny left Dove to his fate.

It was a crisp, fresh day for summer, the first respite after a week of unendurable heat. Goblin felt fine. He came sidling out of the stable, dancing and playing. Johnny let him move about — get the kinks out of him. He loved the horse. He loved the admiration he saw on every face — grooms dropping curry-combs, officers looking out of windows and talking to each other and nodding toward Goblin, chambermaids, rich Tory gentle-men — all stopped to stare when Goblin played.

Although he mostly kept his eyes on Goblin's wickedly flat-tened ears (it is the only way you can tell which way a horse will jump next), he did notice a thick, red face at the parlor window, Colonel Smith, and he heard his booming voice.

'Boy . . . one moment.' Doubtless he had changed his mind about that letter for Milton.

Lieutenant Stranger, his orderly-officer, was coming out of the parlor. He had on no hat, his spurs were in his hand. He was a dark, young fellow, not much older than Rab, and some-thing in both his color and carriage had always made Johnny think of Rab.

'That's quite a horse you have there.'

'He's all right.'

'Well, we sort of hate to see a damned Yankee on top of a good horse like that. How much will you take?'

'He belongs to my master, Mr. Lorne.'

'Colonel Smith,' he called to the stiff, red face at the window, 'this horse belongs to Lorne, the printer. *Boston Observer*, you know. We can commandeer him all right.'

'You fix a proper price.'

'So, boy, how much will your master take for him?'

'He's not for sale.'

'Oh, he isn't, is he? You know damned little about the rights of His Majesty's armed forces. You get off and I'll try him around the block and see how I think he would suit Colonel Smith.' He knelt and buckled on his spurs.

The handsome black washerwoman of the inn, Lydia, came out carrying a hamper of wet clothes. Johnny had an idea.

'All right, Lieutenant Stranger,' he said politely.

'Put the stirrups down a couple of notches. Now, hand me my gloves. I'll be back in ten minutes.'

Goblin was watching out of the corner of his crystalline blue eyes. Not for months had anyone but Johnny Tremain been on his back.

But the Lieutenant mounted confidently, picked up the reins and held them exactly as Goblin liked. The horse moved quietly out of the inn yard. Colonel Smith's face disappeared from the parlor window.

'Lydia,' said Johnny, as he strolled over to the washerwoman, 'I'll help you with those clothes.'

She gave him a dazzling smile. 'Mah land, Johnny-boy, I could do with a bit of help. Them Britishers expect a clean sheet every week and seems like a clean shirt every day.'

Johnny gravely pinned a couple of shirts on the line, his mouth, like Lydia's, full of wooden clothespins. The ruffled shirts began snapping smartly in the breeze.

'Sheets?'

'We've got seventeen officers staying with us. We got sheets by the dozen.'

'Look, Lydia, you lend me a sheet for just a few moments. If I get it dirty, I'll wash it, and besides, I'll hang up every sheet in your basket.'

'Boy, I don't know what you're up to. And I suspect no good.'

'You'll do as I say?'

'If it's that Lieutenant Stranger what's took your horse away from you, I'll do plenty.'

'He wants to commandeer Goblin for his Colonel.'

'Whee! Don't know commandeer, but it sounds dreadful cruel to me.'

'It is a way you cook things,' said Johnny soberly.

'My land, boy, don't you let them cook that pretty horse of yours.'

'I'll cook them first. Now, look. We've got to stand fairly near to the driveway, like this. You get on that end of the sheet and I on this and we'll let her fill up with wind... Wait, he's coming back. So... now let go, Lydia, quick! Let go!'

The sheet bellied out like a sail when Lydia let go. Goblin, quickly recognizing Stranger's skill and good-will, had behaved admirably. The Lieutenant thought he'd advise his Colonel to pay a pretty fancy price for such a choice beast. Colonel Smith, a timid horseman, liked showy mounts. This one was showy all right, with his strange, pale coat and mane and tail like mahogany. He was young and high-strung. Stranger believed he himself would have to ride him for the next month to get him gentle enough for his superior. But his gaits were like dancing. Let me see, he was thinking . . . I'll offer Lorne . . .

And then the whole earth blew up from under him and hit him a terrific blow on his seat. There was a splash as well. He had landed in a mud puddle. The horse was disappearing into the stable. He got up, ruefully looked at his white breeches, shrugged, and walked over to where Johnny was diligently pinning up sheets. Both he and Lydia had their backs discreetly turned.

'Well?' he said to Johnny belligerently.

'Yes, sir?'

'I'd already noticed your horse worries a bit over blown paper in the streets — things like that. I suppose you know that, too?'

'Yes, sir.'

'Take those damned clothespins out of your mouth and turn around and answer me.'

Once the clothespins were out of his mouth, it was hard not to laugh.

'Answer you what, sir?'

'You flapped that sheet on purpose — just for the fun of seeing me sit in a puddle and . . .'

'And to keep my horse out of the army.'

'Oh, *you* . . .' said Stranger, pretending to be angry, but Johnny knew that at heart he was not.

Colonel Smith's great red face once more appeared.

'How'd he ride, Lieutenant? Gad, sir, what? Where's the horse, sir? What have you been mucking about in?'

'Mud puddles, sir. I fell off.' He made no effort to excuse himself.

'Beast vicious, eh?'

'No, sir. Just a mite jumpy. No good for army work nor even just hacking about Boston.'

'But that damned boy — how does he manage?'

'It's his horse, sir.'

'Thanks, Lieutenant, you can look elsewhere for me.' The head went in.

Stranger was stretching himself lightly.

'I'll drink my beer standing up for a few days,' he said to no one in particular. Then, as an afterthought, 'Beer . . . Hi, kitchen,' he yelled, in the arrogant way Johnny noticed the young officers always called for service. 'Two tankards of beer — out here in the yard.'

He turned to Johnny. 'What's your horse's name?'

'Goblin.'

'We'll drink to Goblin. Pot-boy, give that tankard to this young man. You know, of course, there's no real cure for a horse that shies as badly as that?'

'I've been told he'll never be gentle.'

'If he was as good as he looks, I'd hate to guess what he'd be worth. As it is, I'd not give fifteen shillings for him — except' — and he smiled suddenly — 'for myself to ride. Have you schooled him in jumping?'

'No, we're not fancy riders over here.'

'At the foot of the Common you'll find a series of hurdles we've put up. If happens you are over there sometime when I am, I'll show you a bit.'

'Thank you, sir.'

'Does he still throw you sometimes?'

'Sometimes. I'd have gone off fast enough when that sheet let loose.'

'That sheet! Ha, ha. That was a trick. That was good. That was fine. Hi, you black wench . . . you finish this beer for me and take the tankards back to the kitchen.' And off he stalked, still chuckling to himself.

Beginning with that day when Goblin had tumbled Lieutenant

Stranger in the mud, Johnny had no more trouble with the British stable boys. When it became hard for him to get the oats and hay for Goblin, they told him he might use theirs.

But Dove, who was always swearing allegiance to England, and Johnny knew that he honestly was a Tory, was the butt of all their jokes. Dove clung to Johnny like a drowning man and Johnny did protect him. He could not help himself. So Dove began oozing into his life. He spent most of his free time at the *Observer's* office and was always complaining, always gorging himself on the scarce food, and bored both Johnny and Rab. But Rab said, and Johnny knew this was true, sometime the British would not stay tamely shut up in Boston. Sometime they'd strike out and seize the military supplies they knew the provincials were collecting. A colonel's horse boy might very well know a day or so, or even a few hours, before a colonel marched. It was up to Johnny to keep in touch with Dove. It was all right for Rab to talk. Rab was training with the armed forces. But what could Johnny do? Not much, it seemed to him, except be bored to death for his country.

-4-

As he came back from Milton, riding the long lonely stretch of the Neck, with the gallows and the town gates still before him, Johnny realized how long ago it was that he had burned his hand, and how he had hated Dove when he found out the part he had played in that accident. How he had sworn to get even with him (the lying hypocrite — telling old Mr. Lapham that all he had meant to do was to teach a pious lesson). Now, as he saw Dove daily about the Afric Queen, he could hardly remember this feeling of hatred, his oaths of vengeance. Seemingly hatred and desire for revenge do not last long. He had made new friends. The old world of the Lapham shop and house was gone. Yet he remembered old Mr. Lapham, who had died that spring, with more affection than when he had been serving under him. Even Mrs. Lapham now did not seem so bad. Poor woman, how she had struggled and worked for that good, plentiful food, the clean shirts her boys had worn, the scrubbed floors, polished brass! No, she had never been the ogress he had thought her a year ago. There never had been a single day when she had not been the first up in the morning. He, like a child, had thought this was because she liked to get up. Now he realized that there must have been many a day when she was as anxious to lie abed as Dove himself. He remembered when there was no money to buy meat and how she would go from stall to stall until she found a butcher who would accept payment by a new clasp on his pocketbook, or a fishwife who would exchange a basket of salt herrings for a black mourning ring. Her bartering and bickering had then seemed small-minded to him; now he was enough older to realize how valiantly she had fought for those under her care.

True, Madge would make another of those big-fisted, hearty women — but women can be worse than that. He thought with some pity of Dorcas and her craving for elegance. Was she never — no, not once — to eat off china — always nothing but pewter? Poor girl — she'd not live too high with Frizel, Junior. But Johnny wished her well.

Priscilla Lapham. Ever since Rab had taken her home and left Johnny to eat six fried eggs by himself, he had felt differently about Cilla. She had been his best friend during the years he worked at the Laphams'. And then for some months she had been a drag on him. He had not bothered much with her. Overnight that had changed. He was always looking forward to Thursdays and the seed cakes and the half-hour sitting out under the fruit trees with Cilla. And sometimes he would see Miss Lavinia Lyte. Then Johnny would hold his breath a moment and enjoy the chill that went up his spine.

His feelings for Isannah had changed too — and not for the better. It would break Cilla's heart if the little girl did not live up to her lovely face. But Johnny had not liked it that last

Thursday when he had been sitting on the back stoop with Cilla and Miss Lavinia had driven up in her smart whiskey with a redcoat beside her and Isannah wedged in between. It could not be possible Isannah had not seen him. But she had glanced at him — and then looked away.

Johnny rode through the town gates, telling his business to the British sentries there, then went first to report to Paul Revere. A family of Tories in Milton wished to move into Boston and had written Colonel Smith about this move. Although a great many of the Whig families were moving out of the town, a great many Tories, frightened by the rough treatment they were getting in the inland towns, were moving in to be under the protection of the British troops. Then — as he had been thinking about the Laphams all the way over from Roxbury — Johnny decided to stop in and see them. He had not been in this house once since Mrs. Lapham and Mr. Tweedie had been so ready to cast him off for the sake of Mr. Lyte's patronage.

The squeak-pig was alone in the shop. He had not so much as one boy to help him with his fires or to sweep his shop. He liked to work alone. Johnny saw that he was mending the silver hilt of a British officer's sword.

'What are you doing here?' he muttered crossly at Johnny.

Johnny took off his spurs and showed the silversmith a broken rowel. 'I want you to fix that for me, this afternoon — Mr. Silversmith.'

'Yes, sir . . . yes, indeed.' Once Johnny was a patron, the past was forgiven him. 'If you'll take a chair, it shall be mended in fifteen minutes.'

Johnny couldn't help it. He said proudly. 'In ten minutes, Mr. Silversmith.'

'In ten minutes, sir.'

He walked into the kitchen. There was nobody about, but he could smell bread rising. He looked in the birth and death room. It was once more used for storage. It seemed strange beyond belief that he had ever lain so long in the room. And in a way he had died in that room; at least something had happened and the bright little silversmith's apprentice was no more. He stood here again at the threshold, but now he was somebody else.

Then he went outside to the little back yard with the coal house, the privy, and the old willow. Underneath the willow sat a British sergeant of marines with Madge Lapham in his arms.

He had rather guessed the Laphams would side with the Tories, but this was fraternizing with the troops at a great rate.

The sergeant was not half as big as Madge, but he was holding her in his lap. It is hard to hold even a small child very long in such a position. Johnny thought the sergeant must be very tough. They heard his feet and both looked up at him. Johnny laughed, as did the sergeant and Madge. She said, 'Just so it isn't Mother,' and she twisted and yearned down into her small lover's eyes. The bigger they come, thought Johnny, the harder they fall. Madge certainly likes that sergeant.

'Sergeant, dear,' she said, 'I'd like to make you acquainted with an old friend of the family — but, Johnny, how you have grown! I don't know whether to introduce you as Johnny or Mr. Tremain.'

Johnny had grown. Much of the last year had been spent out-of-doors and on horseback, and now he was always out in the sun and wind.

'Just Johnny.'

'Sergeant Gale, dear, this is Johnny Tremain.'

They both agreed they were glad to meet. Gale, whose legs must have been badly cramped, picked up Madge as though she were a pet cat and sat her down beside him. The little man must be prodigiously strong, thought Johnny, and he liked his ugly, lined face. He looked just about as tough as they come, even in the marines. Madge, whom he had always liked the least of the Lapham girls, was rosy, glowing and beaming. He had always heard that love was a wonderful thing. If it could make Madge Lapham so pleasant, he was ready to agree.

'Sit down, Johnny, and tell us about yourself.'

'There's not much to say. I'm making out.'

'Isn't Isannah in luck? Taken right into the family like a little sister.'

'Like a pet poodle dog,' Johnny said firmly.

'My! you haven't changed much. You always were sort of jumping on other people.'

'I still jump. How's Mrs. L.?'

'Don't mention her,' said Sergeant Gale.

'Ma says I've got to marry Mr. Tweedie. He doesn't want to and I don't want to. Oh, Johnny, you're too young to understand and I guess Ma's so old she's forgotten. I can't, can't marry Mr. Tweedie — not since I met Sergeant Gale.'

'I'll say not,' said the marine. 'Madge — in case you've been wondering — is going to marry me... aren't you, you toothsome, plump, suet pudding?'

The skinny little red rascal evidently liked his ladies plump.

Johnny went back to the shop, paid Mr. Tweedie for his work, and buckled on his spurs. He had enjoyed his visit to the Laphams. Mr. Tweedie had bowed to him, called him 'sir,' and rubbed his hands in gratitude for even this small favor. Madge, so pleasant, and the smell of Ma's good bread rising.

Goblin, tied to the head of the wharf, was pawing, turning toward him and nickering. As he settled himself in the saddle and the horse moved off down Fish Street, he thought it had been a nice visit — but he would not go again. That was all over.

- ʃ -

Mrs. Bessie, that 'monstrous fine woman' who cooked for the Lytes, always had an eye out Thursday afternoons for Johnny, and she usually could manage that Cilla was free then, for she was housekeeper as well as cook. This Thursday, as Johnny drew up, she shook her head.

'You come in, Johnny, but I guess today you'll have to put

up with just me. Your little sweetheart' — Johnny's stomach
turned over — 'will be needed in the parlor. We've got nine
or ten of those British officers in there and Miss Lavinia wants to
put on a good show for them.'

Johnny had often noticed before how disrespectfully Mrs.
Bessie spoke of Lavinia. And she was always telling Cilla that
she needn't jump so fast when the bell rang for her. 'Let her
blow her own nose for once,' she'd say. Johnny knew that it was
no good omen that the old woman had no loyalty toward her
mistress, whom she had known since her motherless infancy.
In his heart he knew there was something unlikable about
Lavinia Lyte. Mrs. Bessie knew what it was. And Cilla now
knew. But she wouldn't tell him. Now, when he wanted to talk
about Miss Lyte, she would veil her eyes and look at him from
out of the corners, and say nothing. But he knew Cilla knew.

'All they in the parlor are fixing up to go to a ball at the
Province House General Gage is giving tonight — masquerade.
Miss Lavinia is going like the black Queen of Spades and all
her special admirers are going as kings or knaves or jokers out
of the pack. Isannah's going too.'

'Isannah?'

'Yep. Where Miss goes these days, that child goes too. Izzy'
— no one had ever before called the little girl this — 'goes
dressed as a two-spot, holding up Miss Lavinia's train.'

Cilla shot into the kitchen looking bright and excited.

'Johnny, I thought you might be here. They are trying to
make a scepter for the Queen of Spades out of tin. I told them
you could do it. Miss Lavinia said show him in.'

The elegant dove-gray, lavender-and-yellow drawing room
was in what Mrs. Lapham would call 'a state.' The officers
seemed to have counted on their lady's help with their costumes,
but they had also brought with them a military tailor who was
sitting cross-legged on the floor, stitching at a black-and-yellow
striped jerkin for a knave.

Miss Lavinia looked half in and half out of her costume as
Queen of Spades. For a moment Johnny was confused. It was

not because she had less clothing on than he was accustomed to,
but because she was so beautiful. He had never seen her so
happy, so animated before. She was laughing hilariously, as
she attempted to fasten two flat surfaces of cardboard painted
with two spots onto Isannah. But Isannah had on nothing but
her undershift, her little pink legs bare to the middle thigh.
Ma would die if she saw her daughter like this. Johnny did not
care about that, but he could not bear to think of poor old Mr.
Lapham turning over in his grave. Johnny paid no attention
to the hilarious Miss Lyte. He went up to Isannah.

'Look here, girl. You go upstairs and you put some clothes on.'

Isannah stared at him, her beautiful, soft, brown eyes so
blank she looked almost blind.

'You know your grandpa is just about flopping over and over
in his grave. You weren't brought up to act like this.'

Isannah said, 'I'm too young to be lascivious.' She was evidently repeating what she had heard some adult say. Johnny
slapped her. Not for himself, but for her grandpa. She went
down in a heap, upended over a pile of finery brought down
from the attic. While standing up, it was possible she did not
have on quite enough clothes for mixed company, but upended
she did not look to have on any. Then everyone began to laugh.
Lavinia was wiping her eyes. Lieutenant Stranger — for it was
he who picked the child up — was reduced to painful gasps . . .
'Oh . . . oh . . . oh . . .' There was a major in a corner who was
vowing he was going to die. Only the military tailor never
lifted his eyes, but went on with his stitching.

'Oh, Johnny,' Miss Lavinia managed at last, for the first time
calling him by name. 'Will ou come to the ball and slap all
the ladies you think are underdressed? Oh . . . lah! I've burst
a stay string. Give me . . . Cilla, fetch . . .'

Cilla evidently knew what would be wanted. She came running with smelling salts, but she got it too close to her mistress's
nose. Miss Lavinia was gagging.

'Oh, you stupid, stupid girl! You've half-killed me. There,
take it away.'

Isannah ran up and hid her flushed face in Miss Lavinia's lap. She was half-frightened at the attention she had been receiving and half-squirming with delight at being the center of so many eyes. As Miss Lavinia was scolding one sister for a clumsy servant, she was fondling the flying, soft yellow hair of the other.

Suddenly Johnny saw red. He hated Miss Lavinia and the giggling officers and Isannah. He had already guessed that the two sisters were treated very differently, but he had not before actually seen the situation with his own two eyes.

Cilla had backed out of the picture, standing aside ready to serve if called upon, or ready to be of no more importance than a piece of furniture if not spoken to. Johnny went to her.

'Cilla,' he said, 'don't you stay here any more. I don't want you to. These people are nothing — just a pack of playing cards — tear them up and get out. And that goes for the whole collection of them — Miss Lavinia and Izzy too.'

Miss Lyte had regained her composure.

'I will not have Isannah called "Izzy" by my servants.'

'I'm not your servant, and if she acts like an Izzy, she gets called Izzy. But as I was saying, Cilla . . .'

'I will not have my servants intruding their personal affairs into my drawing room. Priscilla, if you are not satisfied here, I can arrange for your return to your mother, but you are not ever to bring in street boys, horse boys, riffraff . . .'

'You told me to fetch him in.'

'I did *not* tell you to fetch him in.'

'Yes, you did.'

'I said a clever metalworker and you came back with this boy . . . this saucebox, who couldn't do the work anyway, because he . . .'

Johnny waited grimly for her to finish her sentence. If she dared say what was in her mind — because he has a crippled hand — he was going over and take her by her long throat and shake her — even if she did look pretty well defended by His

Majesty's forces. Her eyes wavered and she did not finish her sentence.

'Now, Cilla, I want you to go to your room and lie down. You are too tired. If you had not been, you would never have been so impudent as to contradict me.'

'Yes, Miss Lyte.'

'And you' — she turned to Johnny — 'get back to the gutter or wherever boys like you keep themselves.'

'Yes, Miss Lyte,' he said, mimicking Cilla.

Mrs. Bessie said nothing, but she evidently knew what had been going on in the drawing room.

'There, Johnny,' she said mildly, 'you sit. This is not real tea, but I've put just a mite of brandy in it and it's good and hot.'

'Miss Lavinia is just about making a monkey out of Isannah,' he said at last.

'Nobody can make a monkey out of anyone who isn't a monkey to start with.'

'Is Cilla happy here?'

'Oh, happy enough. What do you expect? She knows she's lost Isannah. At first she used to cry, but now she accepts it. It's exciting for her and there's always a flurry and goings-on. The ball tonight — and next week we move out to Milton for the rest of the summer. We won't stay long.'

'Why?'

'Because the Sons of Liberty there are out to get Mr. Lyte. That's why they haven't yet been rough with Tories out there. Hope to tempt him to move out, same as usual. They are going to get him and tar and feather him. They are going to ride Miss Lavinia out of town on a rail. They are going to smash his great country house down — once he's inside.'

'But the girls . . . won't they get hurt?'

'I'll be there. It's my secret, so I suppose I can tell you, but I'd take it kindly if you'll keep your mouth shut. If there were Daughters of Liberty, I'd be one. You ask Sam Adams about me. I've been helping him secretly for years.'

Johnny had taken it for granted that an old servant in a Tory house would also be a Tory. They usually were. He looked at Mrs. Bessie with admiration.

'The Lytes will stay in Milton about a month,' she whispered. 'You mark my words.'

VIII. *A World to Come*

IT WAS by chance Johnny saw the Lytes' ruby coach trundling slowly down Orange Street, heading for Milton and a little country air. The bright sun glittered on the gold eye, rising on the coach door, on the black sheen of the strong horses. He half-wanted to stop the coach — Don't you go to Milton, Miss Lyte, they are lying in wait for you out there. He could not bear to think of her tossed about by rough men, ridden on a rail. He could see her profile through the window. Cilla sat facing her. Isannah, as befitted her higher station in the household, sat next to Miss Lyte. Only Isannah was staring about, observing the 'lower classes' milling about in the street. She looked straight at Johnny and he at her. Neither gave any sign of recognition.

It was not by chance Johnny next saw that ruby coach. Late in August, word was spread through Boston that Merchant Lyte 'had got it' or was 'going to get it' out in Milton. If driven from their country house, there was but one safe refuge for them — behind the British lines in Boston.

Toward evening, Johnny began to hang about the gate. The farm carts, carrying food and fuel to Boston, were still coming in over the mud flats connecting the town with the mainland. These the British guard at the gate (nearly two hundred men were kept stationed there night and day) let pass, but when night really fell, the gates were closed and most of the soldiers

returned to the barracks. There were a few sentries on duty
and a handful of men, with a corporal, in the guardhouse.
Johnny settled down to wait. He had been dozing, but woke
quickly, hearing the sentries yell and the corporal commanding
the gates to be opened.

Then, coming closer through the still summer night, the clatter
of hoofs, the rumble of a coach, was a sickening, hair-raising
howl ... the howling of a human wolf pack. The corporal had
not had time to get his tunic on, but he recognized the situation
— another of His Majesty's loyal supporters fleeing to Boston
with the mob at its heels.

'Torches only,' he was crying to his men. 'No muskets.
Death to any man who fires!'

The unarmed soldiers ran out to meet the coach with great
flaring torches in their hands. The mob already had stopped,
was drifting back from whence it came. Through the canopy
of shaking orange light and through the smell of burning pitch,
black horses, whitened with lather and dragging a heavy ruby
coach, slowly crawled to the safety of the gates. The gates shut
behind them. The coach seemed disabled, the horses were almost
spent. A torch flared up onto the coachman's face. It was
twisted with fear.

'Mr. Lyte yourself, sir,' the young corporal was saying, as
he opened the door of the coach, 'let me assist you, sir. You've
lost a wheel off your coach. Please to come into the guardhouse
while you wait for another vehicle.'

Mr. Lyte, helped by the corporal, but even more by Miss
Lavinia, did crawl from the coach. He tried to smile, but his
lips drew back from long, yellow teeth. Johnny had seen the
identical expression on the face of a dead woodchuck. He was a
desperately sick man.

Lavinia's face showed no fear — only concern over her father's
condition. Now she was telling the corporal that a doctor must
be fetched — and she wanted Doctor Warren.

'I know he's a rebel — but do get him for me. He's the best
doctor we have in town, and Papa — Papa must have the best.'

Her father safely inside the guardhouse, Miss Lavinia came into the street a moment, gazing blankly at the disabled coach and at the men carrying from it, into the guardhouse, such of their most precious possessions as they had had time to rescue from Milton. For the first time Johnny saw Cilla. She had been sitting on the box with the coachman. Now she went to Miss Lyte.

'Somehow,' she said, 'the silver got left behind.'

'The silver?' Miss Lyte did not seem to be able to take in anything but her father's sickness.

'You told me to pack it up, but just as I had begun we heard the mob coming and then Mr. Lyte had a fit...'

'Oh, yes... I remember... all that silver... well...'

She was standing there in the street, watching for the sight of Doctor Warren's chaise. Isannah, very good and quiet, was snuggled close to her, her hand in that of her patroness.

'Oh, never mind, child,' she said, with absent-minded kindness. 'At least we are all safe, and if only Papa is well and...'

'I'm going back to Milton, Miss, to get that silver before the riffraff steal it.'

'Most like they have it already.'

Doctor Warren's chaise was drawing up beside the guardhouse. He was getting out. Miss Lavinia had no more thought of her silver.

Johnny went up to Cilla.

'Look, Cil,' he said, 'I'm here.'

'It was so mixed up at the end.' The girl seemed to be trying to explain her error more to herself than to Johnny. 'Mr. Lyte turned purple and fell. The mob was getting closer. It came earlier than Mrs. Bessie warned us.'

'Mrs. Bessie?'

'Yes. She found out some way in the village.'

Johnny liked the old woman all the better that in the end she had been unable to see a considerate master, whom she had served for thirty years, a young woman whom she had taken care of since she was a baby, humiliated, tossed about, torn by

a mob. Sam Adams might respect her the less for this weakness.
Johnny respected her the more.

'Johnny — I've got to get back to Milton. I'm going to save
that silver. It was my fault.'

'But Miss Lavinia didn't seem to care. She didn't scold you.'

'If she had, I wouldn't go.'

'She thinks it has been stolen already.'

'No. After smashing the gates and some windows, the mob
left the house to chase us. We didn't dare leave by the front
drive. We started out through the haying fields, but they
heard us and caught up, and we were getting away all right
until just on the Neck a wheel came off the coach. It was terrible.
I've got to go back, though — and now.'

'I'll go with you. But looks like we'll need a horse and chaise.
It's seven miles.'

Doctor Warren was standing on the guardhouse steps, telling
Miss Lyte that her father must be allowed to finish the night
out on the bed the soldiers had made up for him. He was not
to be moved, and never again must he be so upset over anything.
From now on, as long as he lived, as she loved him, he was
never to be angered or worried. The handsome girl was nodding,
promising these impossible things. She went back to her father,
still clutching Isannah by the hand, and Johnny went to the
doctor.

Obviously, Doctor Warren did not want to lend his horse and
chaise. He did not care what happened to the Lyte silver, but
he was a generous man. He let Johnny have his rig and also
wrote him a pass which would prevent any molestation from the
Whig mobs and told Cilla to get a similar pass from the British
soldiers. Then they would be safe from either side. So at last
the gates once more swung slowly, heavily, in. Beyond was
darkness and a dreary waste of land and sea. The Doctor's little
rabbit-eared mare flung herself forward. It would not take
such a fast pacer long to get to Milton.

- 2 -

Although once or twice the light chaise slurred as it caught in great ruts made by the disabled Lyte coach, there was no other sign of the late violence. The mob was utterly gone. It was not until they reached Roxbury that they knew the time. The village clock struck two. Thus far they had not met one single human being. But here were a few turbulent fellows hanging about an inn door, and in Milton itself they were signaled to stop by a group whose faces they never did see. But Doctor Warren's chaise and horse were recognized.

'Go ahead, Warren . . . Good luck, Warren.'

They went up the steep road from Milton. It was here Mr. Lyte had his country seat. Then Johnny got out, struck tinder, and lighted the lantern he had found in the chaise. He stood by the entrance gates. Yes, Cilla was right. They had smashed the arms carved upon the gates. The poor people of Milton had had enough of that rising eye. Johnny wasn't sure but he had as well.

He walked ahead and Cilla drove the horse. Thus half-seen, and in the dark, things did not look too bad. Cilla had a key to the back door which showed hatchet marks, but was not broken down. They went into the dining room and from the lantern Cilla lit the candles in the two candelabra on the table, twenty candles in all, and the room filled with light.

Fear had overcome the Lytes as they had sat down to eat. Bread broken and never eaten. The roast of beef, with Yorkshire pudding sticking in the cold gravy. A bowl of salad was still fresh. Wine in the slender goblets. Already the great house did not seem to have been abandoned for a few hours only but for years. It was as if a witchcraft had been worked upon it. Johnny saw that Cilla had started to get the silver together.

'Where's Mrs. Bessie?'

'She left earlier than we did, in a farm cart. But — you know — she'll be all right.'

Cilla went to work packing the silver, and she built up a little

fire on the kitchen hearth so she might have hot water to wash
the dishes. Neat by nature, she would leave the house tidy.

Johnny took the lantern he had left on the kitchen table and
walked through the silent house. He could see that every window
in the lower floor had been broken, but no one had entered.
He went upstairs. Lavinia's room; and strewed about it things he
had never seen before — stays, kerchiefs, patchboxes, ribbons,
fripperies. It smelled faintly of lavender.

He went to Mr. Lyte's room. The great four-poster soared to
the ceiling. A damask dressing gown — and Mr. Lyte's best
wig on a wig rest. Off the big chamber and one step down was a
smaller room designed as a dressing room. Mr. Lyte seemingly
had used this as an office. Here was his desk, and above it a
painting of his favorite ship, the *Unicorn*. And here, judging by
the tipped-over chair and the rumpled rugs, Mr. Lyte had had
his all but fatal fit. It had caught him as he had been packing
his more important papers — papers he wished no one to see.
Johnny picked up what looked like a leather-bound book. It
had been hollowed out, turned into a box. In a bookcase no
one would suspect it. He glanced at the papers within. Every
one of them, he saw, Sam Adams would be thankful to get.
These he put in his pocket. Other books were scattered on the
floor. Johnny picked up a heavy Bible, hoping that this, too,
would prove to be a box. He put it on the desk and opened it.
There were sheets of paper between the Old and New Testa-
ments. Here a man might write his genealogy.

So . . . the first Jonathan Lyte had been born in Kent in
sixteen-something . . . and he had married a Matilda something.
Had come to Boston and had four sons and three daughters.
And they (all seven) had sons and daughters, and so on. Now
he was coming to the generation in which he might expect to
find his own mother. Here, indeed, was Merchant Lyte himself
and his daughter Lavinia, the two sons who had drowned at
Guadalupe, the girls dead in infancy. He even found that Aunt
Bert (who had stayed on at Boston with her own servant).
He found one Lavinia Lyte after another. One married an

Endicott and one an Otis. Neither was the right age for his mother.

Scratched out in such a way he had at first thought it was a mere decoration on the elaborately written page, there was another name. It was Lavinia Lyte. He held the lantern closer. Born 1740. Married to Doctor Charles Latour, both of whom had died of plague in Marseilles shortly before his own birth. His mother had told him he had been born in France and that his father had died before his own birth. But why Doctor Charles Latour? And why had his mother's name been scratched off the family record? But nevertheless, this was the spot — the very spot where he might hang his own few meager leaves to the Lyte tree.

Although in his day-dreaming he had often pictured himself a nephew, grandnephew, or even a grandson, of Merchant Lyte, he had never once believed the relationship was that close. Now he checked over the generations. His grandfather, Roger Lyte (dead now for twenty years and builder of this very house), had been the younger brother of Jonathan Lyte. Johnny himself was the merchant's grandnephew.

He took his knife from his pocket and cut the pages from the family Bible. Sometime they might be of use to him.

Cilla was calling him. She wanted him to help her carry the heavy boxes and hampers of silver to the chaise. On the sideboard, as yet unpacked, stood the four standing cups of the Lytes.

'Which one is yours, Johnny?'

He looked them over carefully. Only a silversmith could have told them apart. The base of one had been ever so little bent and straightened again.

'This is my cup.'

'Take it now.'

'No.' He set it down and turned restlessly to Cilla. He could not say to anyone what went through his mind — not to Cilla, not even to himself. He acted and spoke blindly.

'It's no good to me. We've . . . moved on to other things.'

'But it isn't stealing to take back what Mr. Lyte stole from you.'

'I don't want it.'

'What?'

'No. I'm better off without it. I want nothing of them. Neither their blood nor their silver . . . I'll carry that hamper for you, Cil. Mr. Lyte can have the old cup.'

'But your mother?'

'She didn't like it either.'

He came back when he had left the hamper and stopped by the kitchen hearth. Cilla had built up a little fire of fagots to heat water. He put his two hands on the mantelpiece and his forehead on his hands. He stood like that a long time. His grandfather had built this great house. His mother had played on the floor of this kitchen. Was it here his father had come — his father, the French doctor? . . . Doctor Latour the Bible had it. Here was mystery surely. Why not Doctor Tremain? And why had the Bible said both he and Lavinia Lyte died of plague in Marseilles: 1758 — three months before he himself had been born? Does it matter? Does it — or doesn't it? No. He answered his own question aloud, and took from his pocket the heavy pages he had cut from the Bible, all written over with the names of his genealogy. He could not think now why he had ever cut them out. Slowly, tearing each sheet to ribbons, he fed them to the fire upon the hearth.

Then Cilla was asking him to close and fasten all the heavy shutters through the house. This would protect the interior a little, in spite of broken window-panes. His footsteps echoed through the vast, silent reaches of the house. One after another the heavy shutters slammed to and he bolted them. A protest of unused hinges and then a bang, and he went on to the next. The echo of his own footsteps.

'My grandfather built this house . . .'

'My mother knew it and loved it . . .'

'My father dead before ever I was born . . .'

Now, for as long as it stood, this would be a haunted house. He felt the ghosts waiting in darkness until he and Cilla were gone before they stepped forth to take possession. Merchant

Lyte — soon enough he too would be back here. Miss Lavinia? She might live to be a hundred, but the time would come when, wilt she or not, she must return to this house. This haunted house, with its thin wreath of wraiths and his mother's among them. He had seen her face, heard her voice so clearly that night he had lain by her grave on Copp's Hill. He thought of her with love and a tender understanding (an understanding he had been too young to give when she had died), but he left the haunted chambers, echoing halls, and went gladly to the kitchen where Cilla was. For the dead should not look at the living — nor the living too long upon the dead.

Cilla, unaware of his emotions, looked about her with satisfaction. She had finished her work.

'Now it will be in good order when the Lytes come back.'

Johnny felt sad. He went to her and put his arms about her and his thin cheek against her hair.

'Cilla, they won't ever come back.'

'Never?'

'No. This is the end. The end of one thing — the beginning of something else. They won't come back because there is going to be a war — civil war. And we'll win. First folk like them get routed out of Milton — then out of Boston. And the cards are going to be reshuffled. Dealt again . . . Shall I shutter the kitchen too?'

'Yes.'

Each time a shutter groaned, protested, and then came to with a bang, it seemed to say, 'This is the end,' and the words echoed through the house: This is the end. This is the end.

'My mother played on the floor of this kitchen. My grandfather was but a young man when he built this house, and I, a grandson, have better right to it doubtless than an elder brother.'

The house was still filled with midnight and ghosts, but as they closed and locked the heavy kitchen door behind them they saw it was close upon dawn.

'It is like a funeral,' Cilla whispered, 'only worse.'

So he knew that much of what he had been feeling, Cilla had also felt.

Along down Old Country Road, marching through the meager, half-light of the new day, came a company of Minute Men up and out early, drilling for coming battles before it was yet the hour to get to their chores. Left, right, left, right, left . . . they did not march too well. A boy no bigger than Dusty Miller had put a fife to his lips, was trying to blow it. He made awkward little tootles. The men marched on past the defaced gates of the Lytes' country seat, never turning to look at them or Doctor Warren's chaise with Cilla and Johnny under the hood.

Oh, God help them, thought Johnny. They haven't seen those British troops in Boston. I have. They haven't seen the gold lace on the generals, those muskets — all so alike, and everyone has a bayonet. They haven't seen . . .

The chaise overtook and passed the marching farmers.

- 3 -

That musket which Rab did not have bothered Johnny. However, the soldiers never carried them while loitering about alehouses and wharves, or the stables of the Afric Queen. They stood guard with them. They drilled with them. They practiced marksmanship (very badly, Rab said), and now and then over at the foot of the Common they executed a deserter with them, but never, not once, as far as Johnny could make out, did they leave them about. Drilling, shooting, marching over, they stacked them at their barracks and there was always at least a sergeant guarding these stacked guns.

Johnny and Rab dropped their voices, even in the privacy of their attic, when they discussed these muskets. The Yankee gunsmiths were working from dawn to dusk preparing guns, making new ones, but as long as Rab had a weapon and was, after all, little more than a boy, he believed he had no chance for a modern gun unless he got it for himself from the British.

'How soon,' Johnny whispered, 'before they march out ... and the war begins?'

'God knows,' Rab murmured. 'God and General Gage. Maybe not until next spring. Armies always move in the spring. But before then I must have a good gun in my hands. A man can stand up to anything with a good weapon in his hands. Without it, he's but a dumb beast.'

Johnny had never seen Rab so blocked by anything. Apparently he went through every situation without friction, like a knife going through cheese. Now he was blocked and it made him restless, possibly less canny. One day he told Johnny that he had a contract with a farmer from Medway who was making a business of buying muskets from the British privates and selling them to Minute Men. Rab did not like to ask his aunt for so large a sum. She had little enough to buy food. But she had said, 'Weapons before food.'

One morning Johnny knew Rab was meeting the farmer at market. He knew that the soldier, returning from guard duty, was going, absent-mindedly, to leave his musket on a pile of straw. It had all been worked out. But when he heard yells and shouts from the market-place and the rattle of British drums calling up reserves, he tore over to Dock Square. He had a feeling that the turmoil was over Rab's gun. He was right.

A solid block of redcoats faced out, presenting their muskets at the market people and inhabitants. The Captain was yelling to the churning hundreds. 'Get back, stand back, good people of Boston. This is our own private affair.'

'What's happened?' Johnny asked an old hen-wife.

'They've caught one of their own men selling a musket to a farmer.'

'Happens he comes from Medway?'

'So 'tis said.'

'Happens they caught more than the farmer and the soldier?'

'They caught three in all. They are taking them over to the Province House — for General Gage.'

'Gage is in Salem.'

'For some colonel, then.'

No mob gathered to rescue the two Yankees. All, by now, felt a certain confidence in the British way of doing things. A general, or even a colonel, had the right to punish a soldier caught selling his arms, and also anyone who tempted him.

Johnny tagged the marching soldiers, but it was not until they turned into the Province House that he saw the three prisoners. The British soldier was grinning, and Johnny guessed that he had been put up to this game merely to snare 'the yokels.'

The farmer was in his market smock. He had long, straight gray hair and a thin, mean mouth. You could tell by looking at him he had gone into this little business for the love of money, not for the love of freedom. Rab had been shaken out of his usual nice balance between quick action and caution by his passionate desire for a good gun. Otherwise he would not have mixed himself up with such a man. Rab himself was looking a little sullen. He was not used to defeat. What would they do to him? They might imprison him. They might flog him. Worst of all, they might turn him over to some tough top sergeant to be taught 'a lesson.' This informal punishment would doubtless be the worst.

The Province House was a beautiful building and as Johnny hung about the front of it he had a chance to admire it for over an hour. It stood well back from the rattle and bustle of Marlborough Street, with its glassy-eyed copper Indian on top of the cupola and its carved and colored lion and unicorn of Britain over the door. Behind the house he heard orders called and soldiers were hallooing — but worst of all they were laughing. And that was Colonel Nesbit's boy bringing around the Colonel's charger. There was a large group of people still standing in the street. The hilarity of the British soldiers did not ease their fears as to the fate of the prisoners. Johnny could hear the rattle of the men's muskets as they came to attention, and then, all together, four drummers let their sticks fall as one.

Out onto Marlborough Street, with the drummers in black

bearskin caps first, and then Colonel Nesbit on horseback, came almost the entire Forty-Seventh Regiment, surrounding a cart. In the cart sat a hideous blackbird, big as a man, shaped like a man, with head hung forward like a moulting crow. It was a naked man, painted with tar and rolled in feathers. Three times already the Whigs had tarred and feathered enemies and carted them through the streets of Boston. Now it was the British turn. The redcoats marched. The Colonel's horse pranced. The cart with its shameful burden bumped over the cobbles. One glance had convinced Johnny this was not Rab. The hideous blackbird had a paunch. Rab had none.

Before the Town House, Colonel Nesbit ordered a halt, and an orderly came forward and read a proclamation. It merely explained what was being done and why, and threatened like treatment to the next buyer of stolen weapons.

Then (Colonel Nesbit was evidently a newspaper reader) the regiment went to Marshall Lane and stopped before the office of the *Spy*. The threat was made that the editor of that paper would soon be treated like the bird in the cart. Then they were heading for Edes and Gill's office. Johnny guessed the *Observer* would come next after the *Boston Gazette*, and ran to Salt Lane to warn Uncle Lorne. He jumped into the shop, slamming the door after him, looking wildly about for the printer. Rab, in his printer's apron, was standing at his bench, quietly setting type.

'Rab! How'd you do it? How'd you get away?'

Rab's eyes glittered. In spite of his great air of calm, he was angry.

'Colonel Nesbit said I was just a child. "Go buy a popgun, boy," he said. They flung me out the back door. Told me to go home.'

Then Johnny laughed. He couldn't help it. Rab had always, as far as Johnny knew, been treated as a grown man and always looked upon himself as such.

'So all he did was hurt your feelings.'

Rab grinned suddenly, but a little thinly. Johnny told of the tar-and-feathering of the farmer and also that he expected in a short time the Forty-Seventh Regiment would come marching down Salt Lane and stop before the door to read that proclamation about tar-and-feathering seditious newspaper publishers.

'And here they come — those dressed-up red monkeys. But they don't dare do anything but stop, read a proclamation, and move on.'

When this was over and the troops moved on down the lane to Union, Johnny and Rab stood in the street and watched them.

'Luckily,' said Rab, 'I didn't give my money in advance. I'll return it to Aunt Jenifer.'

But he still stood in the street watching the stiff rhythm of the marching troops, the glitter of their guns and bayonets, the dazzle of the white and scarlet disappearing at the bottom of the Lane.

'They'll make good targets, all right,' he said absent-mindedly. 'Out in Lexington they are telling us, "Pick off the officers first, then the sergeants." Those white crosses on their chests are easy to sight on . . .'

His words frightened Johnny a little. Lieutenant Stranger, Sergeant Gale, Major Pitcairn . . . Johnny could not yet think of them as targets. Rab could.

-4-

Back of the Lyte house were apple trees, now heavy with fruit. Johnny and Cilla sat together on a bench. He had missed her that month she had been out in Milton. It was still summer, but everywhere you could smell and feel the coming of fall. It had been an interesting conversation. Madge had run off and married Sergeant Gale, and Ma had been so put to it to keep Mr. Tweedie in the family she had married him herself.

'She said he was too old for me and she knows he's too young for her, but he's a clever smith and she's going to hang on to him — come Hell and high water.' Cilla bent her face over the work in her lap. She was rolling a tiny hem on a tiny handkerchief. One of Miss Lavinia's.

'So she's Mrs. Tweedie now?'

'Yes. Maria Tweedie. That's not so bad. You know you have to marry someone whose last name goes with your first. For instance, if my name was Rue, I couldn't marry a man named Barb, or if my name happened to be Tobacco, I couldn't marry a man called Pouch or Pipe or . . .'

'Nobody was ever named Tobacco.'

'You don't know. If a Southern merchant made a lot of money on tobacco, I think he might name his daughter . . . Tobacco.'

'We make money on codfish around here and I never heard anyone calling his girl Codfish. You're just being silly.'

'But I like to be silly. I like to plan things out; for instance, I . . . couldn't marry a man called . . .'

'Anybody called Priscilla can marry anybody.'

'No, they can't. For instance, I couldn't marry Rab.'

Johnny froze. From being mildly irritated, but interested, he was a little angry.

'Nobody asked you to,' he said shortly.

'I know. But a girl has to think about things like that. Almost anything can happen to a girl. Suddenly. And she has to think ahead so she'll know which way to jump.'

'Rab wouldn't marry *you*. He's too . . . too . . .'

'Wonderful?' Cilla gave him one of her sweet, veiled glances out of the corner of her eye. 'That's what you mean?'

It was exactly what Johnny had meant.

'Of course not. But he's not like any other boy I ever knew.'

Cilla did not look at the work in her idle fingers. She stared off down Beacon Hill. From where they sat, they could see the ocean.

'I know that. But when you get to really know him, he doesn't seem so wonderful. I mean he's just as *wonderful*, but a whole lot nicer.'

Johnny did not want to ask the next question, but he could not help it.

'Have you . . . how'd you get to know him . . . so well?'

She looked surprised. 'Why, he comes here and takes me walking and buys me sweets, and once he took me to Old South to hear Doctor Warren.'

Rab had never said anything about this to Johnny. It was well enough to say Rab was secretive by nature and couldn't help the way God had made him, but Johnny felt piqued. Cilla noticed the shadow on his face.

'Priscilla Silsbee is poor. But Cilla Silsbee is worse.'

Johnny's lower lip stuck out. Seemingly without any action of the wind, his fair hair was rumpled all over his head.

'But Priscilla Tremain is a fine name,' she went on. 'I've thought about that ever since you came to the shop and Mother told me I had to marry you. I was eleven then . . .'

Then they had both been eleven. She a skinny little thing, with a gentle face and disturbing tongue. Her clothes had always been too big for her because they were handed down from Dorcas. She had had to pin her skirts tight about her waist to keep them on. Pretty and shabby, and sweet and sour. Johnny had liked her right off. He had not thought much about what she looked like now. But he looked at her as she bent her face to her work. The little pointed chin settled into the fresh white ruffles about her throat. Somehow her hair was curly around the edges and straight everywhere else. She had a shallow little nose and on either side of the bridge lay those long lashes which could mock him as well as her tongue. And so pretty he could not believe it. He was accustomed to staring at Lavinia Lyte's famous beauty and to feel a pleasant tingle up and down his spine. And now it was Cilla Lapham, just good old Cilla, that was giving him spinal creeps.

When he was eleven, he had said he would marry her — if he had to. And when he was fourteen, he had said he wouldn't take her on a gold platter. He was fifteen now. And soon he would be a grown-up man going courting like Rab.

Cilla was packing up her sewing.

'Miss Lavinia will be wanting her tea and I must get Isannah dressed, brushed, powdered, and perfumed to sit with her.'

One of the soldiers of the Fourth Regiment who were en-camped upon the Common was earning a little money helping at the Lyte stable. As Cilla moved away from Johnny, the groom leaped forward to open the kitchen door for her. Why, that mannered monkey — bowing and flunkying about because of just Cilla Lapham. That red-headed parrot couldn't even talk English right. But he had known what Johnny had not. Cilla was a grown-up young lady — and she was pretty.

'Cilla,' Johnny yelled at her, 'come back a moment — please.' She left the groom bowing and smirking.

'Yes?' she said, standing before Johnny under the apple trees.

'Look here. What's that fellow's name?'

'Pumpkin.'

'That's not a name.'

'Yes, it is. It's his.'

'Nobody ever — no girl could be a Mrs. Pumpkin?'

'Nobody ever.'

There was so long a pause, Johnny's next words sounded awkward.

'You were right about one thing. Priscilla Tremain — that's a fine name.' He had meant to make a joke, but as the words left his mouth, it was not.

They both stood, embarrassed, looking at their feet.

Cilla did not answer, but she reached up through the foliage of the tree and picked a little green apple. She gave it to him.

'I didn't know even winter apples were still so green,' she said, and walked off toward the house without a glance for the admiring Pumpkin.

Johnny put the apple in his pocket. He'd keep it forever. It meant that Cilla really thought Tremain was a fine name. No ... you can't keep even little green apples forever. It would wizen up, or grow ripe, or it might rot. Human relations never seem to stand completely still. This apple, for instance. It

might ripen into something better than it now was, or, unro-
mantically, it might rot away in his pocket.

He put it on the window-sill and a little superstitiously waited
to see what it would do. But Rab ate the apple.

Johnny, already jealous, for the first time in his life, over
Rab's taking Cilla out, buying her sweets — and never saying
anything — tried his best to quarrel with a puzzled Rab over
this apple.

It ended as Johnny might have guessed it would. Rab refused
to be impressed with his crime. All he had done was to eat a
wormy, no-good apple. He'd give Johnny a peck of better
ones, 'just so you'll stop glaring at me.'

'Was it really wormy, Rab?'

'It was.'

He had been a fool to think of the apple as a symbol of himself
and Cilla.

- 5 -

It was fall, and for the last time Sam Adams bade Johnny
summon the Observers for eight o'clock that night.

'After this we will not meet again, for I believe Gage knows
all about us. He might be moved to arrest Mr. Lorne. He might
send soldiers to arrest us all.'

'I hardly think they would hang the whole club, sir. Only
you and Mr. Hancock.'

Johnny had meant this for a compliment, but Sam Adams
looked more startled than pleased.

'It has been noticed that every so often many of us are seen
going up and down Salt Lane, entering the printing shop. We
must, in the future, meet in small groups. But once more, and
for the last time . . . And make as good a punch for us as you
can.'

As Johnny went from house to house talking about unpaid

bills of eight shillings, he was thinking of the punch. Not one ship had come into Boston for five months except British ships. Only the British officers had limes, lemons, and oranges these days — they and their friends among the Boston Tories. Miss Lyte had God's plenty of friends among the British officers. He'd get his tropical fruit there.

Mrs. Bessie listened to him.

'And who's going to eat these fruits or drink them, if I do give you some?'

'Well . . . Sam Adams for one.'

'Don't say any more. Give me your dispatch bag, Johnny.' She returned with it bulging.

'No limes, though. Izzy eats them all.'

'Does she do tricks for them? Like she used to for the sailors along Hancock's Wharf?'

'*Tricks?* Does she do tricks? Lieutenant Stranger has taught her a rigmarole about poor Nell Gwyn selling fruit at a theater. I don't need to tell you how she carries on.'

'What happened to that Cousin Sewall?'

'Gone to Worcester. Joined up with the Minute Men.'

'But he's too fat and . . .'

'Soft? No. From now on nobody's too fat nor soft nor old nor young. The time's coming.'

It would be a small meeting, for of the twenty-two original members many had already left town to get away from the threat of arrest by the British. Josiah Quincy was in England. Of the three revolutionary doctors, only Church and Warren remained. Doctor Young had gone to a safer spot. James Otis was at the moment in Boston. Johnny had not notified him, although he had founded this club in the first place. Ever since he had grown so queer, the other members did not wish him about, even in his lucid periods. He talked and talked. Nobody could get a word in edgewise when James Otis talked.

This, the last meeting, started with the punch bowl on the table instead of ending with it. There was no chairman nor was there any time when the two boys were supposed to withdraw.

They were talking about how Gage had at last dared send out a sortie beyond the gate of Boston and, before the Minute Men got word of their plans, they had seized cannon and gunpowder over in Charlestown, got into their boats and back to Boston. Not one shot had been fired and it was all too late when the alarm had been spread and thousands of armed farmers had arrived. By then the British were safe home again. Yet, Sam Adams protested, this rising up of an army of a thousand from the very soil of New England had badly frightened General Gage. Once the alarm spread that the British had left Boston, the system of calling up the Minute Men had worked well indeed. The trouble had been in Boston itself.

'In other words, gentlemen, it was our fault. If we could have known but an hour, two hours, in advance what the British were intending, our men would have been there before the British troops arrived instead of a half-hour after they left.'

Johnny had been told off to carry letters for the British officers, to keep on good terms with their grooms and stable boys over at the Afric Queen. Somehow he had failed. He hadn't known. Nobody had known that two hundred and sixty redcoats were getting into boats, slipping off up the Mystic, seizing Yankee gunpowder, and rowing it back to Castle Island for themselves.

Paul Revere was saying, 'We must organize a better system of watching their movements — but in such a way that they will not realize they are being watched.'

Sam and John Adams were standing and the other members were crowding about them, shaking hands with them, wishing them success at the Continental Congress in Philadelphia. They were starting the next day. Everyone was ready to give them advice whom to see, what to say, or to prophesy the outcome of this Congress. Paul Revere and Joseph Warren were apart a little, making plans for that spy system which was needed badly. They called Johnny to them, but he could hear one of the men standing about the two Adamses saying, 'But there must be some hope we can still patch up our differences with England. Sir, you will work for peace?'

Sam Adams said nothing for a moment. He trusted these men about him as he trusted no one else in the world.

'No. That time is past. I will work for war: the complete freedom of these colonies from any European power. We can have that freedom only by fighting for it. God grant we fight soon. For ten years we've tried this and we've tried that. We've tried to placate them and they to placate us. Gentlemen, you know it has not worked. I will not work for peace. "Peace, peace — and there is no peace." But I will, in Philadelphia, play a cautious part — not throw all my cards on the table — oh, no. But nevertheless I will work for but one thing. War — bloody and terrible death and destruction. But out of it shall come such a country as was never seen on this earth before. We will fight...'

There was a heavy footstep across the floor of the shop below. Rab leaped to the ladder's head.

'James Otis,' he reported to the men standing about Adams.

'Well,' said Sam Adams, a little crossly, 'no one needs stay and listen to *him*. He shot his bolt years ago. Still talking about the natural rights of man — and the glories of the British Empire! You and I, John, had as well go home and get a good night's sleep before leaving at dawn tomorrow.'

Otis pulled his bulk up the ladder. If no one was glad to see him, at least no one was so discourteous as to leave. Mr. Otis was immediately shown every honor, given a comfortable arm-chair and a tankard of punch. Seemingly he was not in a talkative mood tonight. The broad, ruddy, good-natured face turned left and right, nodding casually to his friends, taking it for granted that he was still a great man among them, instead of a milestone they all believed they had passed years before.

He sniffed at his punch and sipped a little.

'Sammy,' he said to Sam Adams, 'my coming interrupted something you were saying... "We will fight," you had got that far.'

'Why, yes. That's no secret.'

'For what will we fight?'

'To free Boston from these infernal redcoats and . . .'

'No,' said Otis. 'Boy, give me more punch. That's not enough reason for going into a war. Did any occupied city ever have better treatment than we've had from the British? Has one rebellious newspaper been stopped — one treasonable speech? Where are the firing squads, the jails jammed with political prisoners? What about the gallows for you, Sam Adams, and you, John Hancock? It has never been set up. I hate those infernal British troops spread all over my town as much as you do. Can't move these days without stepping on a soldier. But we are not going off into a civil war merely to get them out of Boston. Why are we going to fight? Why, why?'

There was an embarrassed silence. Sam Adams was the acknowledged ringleader. It was for him to speak now.

'We will fight for the rights of Americans. England cannot take our money away by taxes.'

'No, no. For something more important than the pocketbooks of our American citizens.'

Rab said, 'For the rights of Englishmen — everywhere.'

'Why stop with Englishmen?' Otis was warming up. He had a wide mouth, crooked and generous. He settled back in his chair and then he began to talk. It was such talk as Johnny had never heard before. The words surged up through the big body, flowed out of the broad mouth. He never raised his voice, and he went on and on. Sometimes Johnny felt so intoxicated by the mere sound of the words that he hardly followed the sense. That soft, low voice flowed over him: submerged him.

' . . . For men and women and children all over the world,' he said. 'You were right, you tall, dark boy, for even as we shoot down the British soldiers we are fighting for rights such as they will be enjoying a hundred years from now.

' . . . There shall be no more tyranny. A handful of men cannot seize power over thousands. A man shall choose who it is shall rule over him.

' . . . The peasants of France, the serfs of Russia. Hardly more than animals now. But because we fight, they shall see freedom like a new sun rising in the west. Those natural rights God has given to every man, no matter how humble...' He smiled suddenly and said ... 'or crazy,' and took a good pull at his tankard.

' ... The battle we win over the worst in England shall benefit the best in England. How well are they over there represented when it comes to taxes? Not very well. It will be better for them when we have won this war.

'Will French peasants go on forever pulling off their caps and saying "Oui, Monsieur," when the gold coaches run down their children? They will not. Italy. And all those German states. Are they nothing but soldiers? Will no one show them the rights of good citizens? So we hold up our torch — and do not forget it was lighted upon the fires of England — and we will set it as a new sun to lighten a world...'

Sam Adams, anxious to get that good night's sleep before starting next day for Philadelphia, was smiling slightly, nodding his gray head, seeming to agree. He was bored. It does not matter, he was thinking, what James Otis says these days — sane or crazy.

Joseph Warren's fair, responsive face was aflame. The torch Otis had been talking about seemed reflected in his eyes.

'We are lucky men,' he murmured, 'for we have a cause worth dying for. This honor is not given to every generation.'

'Boy,' said Otis to Johnny, 'fill my tankard.'

It was not until he had drained it and wiped his mouth on the back of his hand that he spoke again. All sat silently waiting for him. He had, and not for the first time, cast a spell upon them.

'They say,' he began again, 'my wits left me after I got hit on the head by that customs official. That's what you think, eh, Mr. Sam Adams?'

'Oh, no, no, indeed, Mr. Otis.'

'Some of us will give our wits,' he said, 'some of us all our property. Heh, John Hancock, did you hear that? *Property* — that hurts, eh? To give one's silver wine-coolers, one's coach and four, and the gold buttons off one's sprigged satin waist-coats?'

Hancock looked him straight in the face and Johnny had never before liked him so well.

'I am ready,' he said. 'I can get along without all that.'

'You, Paul Revere, you'll give up that silvercraft you love. God made you to make silver, not war.'

Revere smiled. 'There's a time for the casting of silver and a time for the casting of cannon. If that's not in the Bible, it should be.'

'Doctor Warren, you've a young family. You know quite well, if you get killed they may literally starve.'

Warren said, 'I've thought of all that long ago.'

'And you, John Adams. You've built up a very nice little law practice, stealing away my clients, I notice. Ah, well, so it goes. Each shall give according to his own abilities, and some —' he turned directly to Rab — 'some will give their lives. All the years of their maturity. All the children they never live to have. The serenity of old age. To die so young is more than merely dying; it is to lose so large a part of life.'

Rab was looking straight at Otis. His arms were folded across his chest. His head flung back a little. His lips parted as though he would speak, but he did not.

'Even you, my old friend — my old enemy? How shall I call you, Sam Adams? Even you will give the best you have — a genius for politics. Oh, go to Philadelphia! Pull all the wool, pull all the strings and all the wires. Yes, go, go! And God go with you. We need you, Sam. We must fight this war. You'll play your part — but what it is really about . . . you'll never know.'

James Otis was on his feet, his head close against the rafters that cut down into the attic, making it the shape of a tent. Otis put out his arms.

'It is all so much simpler .than you think,' he said. He lifted his hands and pushed against the rafters.

'We give all we have, lives, property, safety, skills . . . we fight, we die, for a simple thing. Only that a man can stand up.'

With a curt nod, he was gone.

Johnny was standing close to Rab. It had frightened him
when Mr. Otis had said, 'Some will give their lives,' and looked
straight at Rab. Die so that 'a man can stand up.'

Once more Sam Adams had the center of attention. He was
again buttoning up his coat, preparing to leave, but first he
turned to Revere.

'Now *he* is gone, we can talk a moment about that spy system
you think you can organize in Boston.'

Paul Revere, like his friend, Joseph Warren, was still slightly
under the spell of James Otis.

'I had not thought about it that way before,' he said, not
answering Sam Adams's words. 'You know my father had to
fly France because of the tyranny over there. He was only a
child. But now, in a way, I'm fighting for that child ... that
no frightened lost child ever is sent out a refugee from his own
country because of race or religion.' Then he pulled himself
together and answered Sam Adams's remarks about the spy
system.

That night, when the boys were both in bed, Johnny heard
Rab, usually a heavy sleeper, turning and turning.

'Johnny,' he said at last, 'are you awake?'

'Yes.'

'What was it he said?'

'That a man can stand up.'

Rab sighed and stopped turning. In a few moments he was
asleep. As often had happened before, it was the younger boy
who lay wide-eyed in the darkness.

'That a man can stand up.'

He'd never forget Otis with his hands pushed up against the
cramping rafters over his head.

'That a man can stand up' — as simple as that.

And the strange new sun rising in the west. A sun that was to
illumine a world to come.

IX. *The Scarlet Deluge*

THAT FALL Paul Revere did organize a spy system. Thirty artisans, mostly masters, from all over Boston were the center. Each of these men had workmen and apprentices under him. And these had friends and the friends had friends. So this web of eyes and ears multiplied and multiplied again until a British soldier could hardly say he'd like to swim in Yankee blood or a couple of befuddled young officers draw out a campaign on a tablecloth at the Afric Queen but it was reported. It was noted exactly which regiments were on duty in different parts of Boston and how strong were the earthworks Gage was putting up to protect his men if 'the country should rush in.'

All such news, important and trivial, was carried to the thirty, meeting secretly at the Green Dragon.

It had caused comment that so many leading Whigs had been seen ever and anon converging upon the *Observer's* office. It aroused no comment that thirty men of humbler rank — master workmen like Paul Revere the silversmith, Thomas Crafts the painter, or Chase the distiller — met at the Green Dragon. This old stone inn was owned by the Masons. Most of these men were Masons. So why should they not meet in the proverbial secrecy of their society?

Every time they met, each man swore upon the Bible that these meetings be kept secret. That anything they discovered of British plans should be told only to the four men who were looked upon as the leaders of the Boston Whigs. These were Sam Adams, John Hancock, Doctor Warren, and Doctor Church. Already many others had thought it safer to leave Boston. Anything Johnny picked up he usually reported to Paul Revere, but sometimes to Doctor Warren. He had been assigned his own particular duty. This was to keep sharp track of Colonel Smith and the other officers of the Tenth Regiment who were living at the Afric Queen. As long as Goblin was stabled there, no one was suspicious if Johnny hung about the stables, the yard, and the kitchen. He was on good terms with the British grooms and by great good luck, from the point of view of a spy system, intimate with the Colonel's horse boy, Dove.

'Don't you lose track of that Dove, Johnny,' Paul Revere commanded him, 'for if ever the British march out to attack us a colonel's horse boy might well know something is happening, in advance.'

Every day Johnny knew what orders were given to the Tenth and he knew other boys and men and women and girls were as carefully watching the actions of the other ten regiments in Boston. Lydia, the handsome black laundress at the Queen, extended his own eyes and ears into the very bedrooms of the officers, and often, as he helped her hang up sheets, she would tell him this and that, but nothing of any value until one day she called him out of the stable, where he was grooming Goblin.

'Johnny boy,' she called, 'you help me hang up these here sheets and I'll give you a sweet.'

'What's up?' he whispered as soon as he had helped carry out the heavy basket of wash.

'Last night, just before bedtime, Colonel Smith, he sent for me 'cause he says I sent up a shirt as wasn't his. And dat dere Lieutenant Stranger, he was standin' by de fireplace thankin' his colonel for permission to go on de "little business." He was lookin' real happy like young folks do as have been allowed to attend a party.'

'But a little business might be anything.'

'Yes. But Stranger. He likes fightin' real good. He ain't no

cardboard soldier like some of these British boys. And he whistled happy as a robin as he went to his own room, and he sat up
for an hour more writin' letters and tearin' 'em up and writin'
again. And this mornin' he sent one off to Miss Lavinia Lyte by
Dove. But dese scraps of paper I got in my pocket are his trials
and errors. I can't read. And he did tear 'em up. But here dey
are.'

'Lydia, give me your pocket.'

She unpinned the little calico bag from her waistband. Johnny
stuffed it inside his jacket and ran back to the printing office.

It took no time to put together two letters which Stranger had
written and discarded. First he had written Miss Lavinia —
Johnny knew he was dancing attendance on her — a rude note
bluntly declining her invitation to a frolic which on the fifteenth
of December would follow a military concert. Today was the
twelfth.

'Evidently,' said Rab, 'he explained too little in his first letter
and too much in his next. So he tore them both up and tried
a third time.'

Rab, Mr. Lorne, and Johnny all had their heads over the drawing board where the second letter was pieced together and
spread out. The first part was missing and he had never finished
it.

> . . . as Lovelace said so long ago, 'I could not love thee,
> dear, so much loved I not honour more.' 'Tis honour only,
> my dear, my very dear Miss Lyte, which forces me to decline
> your most gracious invitation for the fifteenth of December.
> The honour of a soldier and eyes, even brighter than your
> brilliant orbs, the bright eyes of danger, call me forth. To
> you alone I will confide that on that night I shall be sixty
> miles north of here, for we must have all our forts suffi-
> ciently strengthened so as . . .

Then he had stopped.

'Sixty miles,' said Mr. Lorne. 'That's Portsmouth. Fort
William and Mary. They have only a handful of men on duty
there and a vast store of powder and ball.'

'No wonder,' Rab was saying, 'Stranger tore that letter up. It certainly let the cat out of the bag. Where you off to, Johnny?'

'I'm off to Paul Revere,' Johnny yelled over his shoulder.

He had not stopped for overcoat or mittens. From the lowering December sky handfuls of snowflakes were falling, but as soon as they came to earth they turned to ice. It was a bleak, bad, dangerous day for the long ride north.

Ten minutes after Johnny told him the news, Revere was in the saddle buttoning his fur-lined surtout to his ears. His wife had so recently borne him another child she was still abed. She rapped on a window-pane and Johnny ran to her. 'He forgot this,' she said and handed him the hasty scrawl she had had the wit to write. In it Paul Revere was begged by a make-believe relative in Ipswich to come in all haste. His grandmother was on her deathbed. Johnny had to laugh. The British soldiers at the Neck were asking more and more questions of any known Whig, and sometimes, for a whim, would refuse to let him pass and often again delay the trip. Mrs. Revere's letter would allay their suspicions.

That night, over icy roads and through howling winds, Paul Revere rode the sixty miles. Even before the British got into their transports, word had come back to Boston that the King's fort at Portsmouth had been seized and His Majesty's military stores stolen by the rebellious Americans.

Cilla reported to Johnny that Lieutenant Stranger did, indeed, attend Miss Lavinia's handsome frolic and a more gloomy young man she had never seen.

- 2 -

Even in the old days of the Lapham shop Dove would have been Johnny's friend if Johnny would have had it. The enmity between them was the younger, and smarter, boy's fault. As soon as Johnny began to cultivate Dove, he was surprised at the response. Dove had always been lonely and he still was. The Yankee boys threw bad words and oyster shells at him because he worked for the British. The British horse boys badgered him. Lieutenant Stranger thought he was the stupidest, laziest pig he had ever met, and told him so at least once a day. Colonel Smith was not above knocking him down if his horses were ill-cared for. But Johnny's feelings toward Dove had changed. Dove was garrulous, indolent, complaining, and boastful, but it hurt Johnny when the other boys bullied him and his masters beat him. He was like a man who owns a dull, mean dog. He may punish it himself, but resents it if anyone else punishes it. For better or worse Dove was now his own private property.

Once a day, twice a day, and sometimes three times in one day, Dove would sneak over to the *Observer's* office. Here for a few minutes he could get away from the swearing and cuffing of his superiors and the malice of the grooms. By Rab and Johnny's standards they were often rude to him; by his own they 'treated him fine.' At least he was allowed to slump into a chair, complain, boast, and eat. It was hard to watch Dove swilling their meager food, but the way to his heart seemed to be through his stomach. What they had they shared with him.

Although badly treated by the British and kindly by the two Yankee boys, Dove had become violently pro-British — at least, when talking to Rab and Johnny. He considered himself part of the British army and was always bragging about what 'we' were going to do to rebels.

'Yep. We're going to march right out of here,' he was saying one day. 'And we'll kill every rebel we meet. Skin 'em. Cut off their heads.

'And here in Boston, just as soon as old Gage gives the signal, we're goin' ter string up every rebel. Hundreds of 'em. Yep.'

Johnny yawned. He could not help it.

The yawn may have irritated his guest.

'Oh, they know all about you. You haven't been given any riding to do for them of late, have you?'

True enough, although Johnny had not found out one thing of

genuine value by the letter-carrying he had done for British officers, it had been a good contact and he needed money. He had been sorry to find that he was no longer employed.

'It was I that warned 'em. I told 'em and told 'em that that Johnny Tremain was a rebel of the deepest double-dye.' So Dove had gone out of his way, had he, to be mean?

'Oh, you! . . . Blat, blat, blat. Talk, talk, talk.'

'I know what's my duty to report and what's my duty to keep mum about. Take military secrets. I don't tell them.'

As soon as he had arrived, he had walked over to the cupboard where the boys kept their food, and helped himself. As he talked, the crumbs came dribbling out of the corner of his loose mouth.

'For instance,' he went on, 'you didn't know, did you, that last December Lieutenant Stranger almost went on an expedition to Portsmouth? I knew he was planning to go, but I knew enough not to say anything to you about it. I can keep a secret all right.'

Thanks to Lydia they had known about this. But they had had no idea that Dove, too, had known at the time.

'That's no secret now. But it is a secret where old Gage will strike next. You'd like to know, wouldn't you? I could tell you if I had the mind to. Why don't you give me something to drink?'

Rab and Johnny exchanged a glance. Johnny poured him a tankard of ale. Maybe he knew more than they thought. But would the mild ale loosen his tongue?

'You wait a moment, Dove, I'll be right back.' Johnny ran through the back yard to the Afric Queen. He knew Colonel Smith had told Lydia that one of his young gentlemen was prone to solitary tippling. If ever she found a bottle of brandy in his chamber, she was to take it. He did not say where she was to take it to. Lydia took away the young gentleman's bottle in the morning when she made his bed, but was not above reselling it to him in the evening. Johnny came back, a brandy bottle in his hand.

'Now this,' he promised, 'will pick up that flat ale something fine.' He poured in so generous an amount that Dove's white lashes quivered with anticipation.

'You certainly are a good guy. My, that's great. That's the stuff. Well, as I was saying. Here it is March. That's spring. Armies don't stay cooped up in springtime. They march out and fight' — he hiccoughed for the first time — 'fight battles. And the battle we are going to fight — fight this springtime — me and the rest of the boys! Well, I warn you. If I was you I'd not wait. I'd start running and not stop until I came to the Berkshires.'

'I don't believe they'll move the army all the way out to the Berkshires.'

'Who said anything about the army going to the Berkshires? There are no military stores there. And King's commanded old Grandma Gage to confee — confass — confiscu-late all rebel stores. His Majesty is real mad. Got his royal dander up. He thinks Gage is scared 'cause he don't take action against the rebellion.'

'Gage already has tried three times to seize our supplies. Charlestown, Salem, and Portsmouth. Once he did, and twice we were too quick for him. He doesn't know where our things are hidden.'

'Don't he? Don't he?'

Johnny filled his tankard again with the horrifying concoction. Dove belched with satisfaction.

'They've got maps. Maps in map cases. They've got Worcester and Concord marked in red. They know where to go all right. Don't you wish you knew just how many active troops there are in Boston now?'

'How many?'

Dove's figure was wildly inaccurate. It looked as though they had wasted their ale and Lydia's brandy.

Dove was getting maudlin. There were tears in his eyes as he told them how much he loved them. 'Best friends 'ever had,' he mumbled. 'Best boy-zz in world,' and he suddenly struck out at the British. 'They're mean guys,' he cried angrily. 'I'm goin' to the Berkshires with you two. I'm not a-goin' to stay here in Boston nursemaiding them there horses. Dig a hole. Get in hole. Pull hole in after me. Keep safe till war's over. Boy-zz, boy-zz,' he cried in alcoholic despair, 'you come with me. I can't stand for you ter hang... I can't!' And he burst into tears.

'Pull yourself together,' Rab ordered sternly. He was less easy-going about some things than Johnny.

'Sure I'll pull — I'll pull right outer here.' He got unsteadily to his feet. 'I'm goin' tell that Stranger I quit. Goin' to throw a currycomb in Colonel Swishe's fash... I'm goin' to...'

'Oh, hold on there. No you're not, Dove,' said Rab, blocking the door. 'You're going to sit down, see? And cool off.'

It would never do to let Dove return to the inn in such a state. He'd get fired. The boys had overcooked their own goose.

It took them half an hour to quiet Dove. Over and over they explained to him what a fine job he had and what a glory it was to be part of the British army. Finally Dove began to subside. He was getting sleepy.

'Well, it don't make any difference. I'll get fired anyhow. Stranger told me get the Colonel's horses all shined up good. Told me get Nan around saddled by four somshing, maybe by four-thirty.' He leaned back and slept.

'Looks like I'll have to do his work for him,' muttered Johnny. 'We can't let him get fired. It's four now. Oh, that swill-pig, that louse...'

He ran for the stable. Before this he had often helped Dove with his work.

The Colonel had two horses: the heavy yellow charger called Sandy he had brought with him from England and the light pacing mare Lieutenant Stranger had picked out for him after he had decided Goblin wouldn't suit. Nan, this second horse, had easier gaits than the old war-horse. The Colonel much preferred her for hacking about Boston, but she was not yet well trained for drums and volleys. The Colonel, a poor horseman, never risked his dignity on her when he went out with his troops. Then he rode Sandy.

Nan was beautiful and affectionate: Sandy, sweet-tempered,

old, and wise. Johnny liked them both. As Dove slept, Johnny worked and whistled.

At four-thirty he had Nan saddled and led her to the mounting block in front of the inn. The fat colonel could not mount or dismount from the ground.

'Take her back, boy,' Lieutenant Stranger told him. 'Colonel Smith is bilious.' Then he noticed it was Johnny, not Dove, and his handsome face brightened. He asked no questions.

'Look you,' he said, 'run fetch your horse and I'll take Nan. I want to show you how to jump.'

Stranger had already told him of the hurdles at the foot of the Common. Johnny had wistfully watched red-coated officers schooling their horses over them. He had not dared try them himself. He was afraid they would order him away. But no one would order away any friend Stranger cared to bring with him.

Although the very young officer was proud and class-conscious enough when they met indoors at the Lytes' or Afric Queen, once both were in their saddles they were equals. He was an ardent teacher who had at last met a pupil worth bothering with. Or rather two pupils, for at the end of the first lesson he said Goblin was the finest natural jumper he had ever seen. Johnny knew he longed to own him himself. He could, any moment, by merely saying 'commandeer.' And Johnny knew he never would say it.

From that day he and Johnny spent hours together jumping or exercising horses. Johnny almost worshiped him for his skill and almost loved him, because, ever and anon, he looked so much like Rab; but still it was only where horses were concerned they were equals. Indoors he was rigidly a British officer and a 'gentleman' and Johnny an inferior. This shifting about puzzled Johnny. It did not seem to puzzle the British officer at all.

-*3*-

Now Johnny did not ride all over the countryside on Fridays
and Saturdays, to get back late and tired, taking the last ferry
from Charlestown home to Boston Saturday night. First, there
was no ferry, and, second, the guards at the town gate were too
curious. They would demand to see what was in his dispatch bag
and after looking at the papers dump them in the mud. They
would pretend it was an accident, but it was not. Uncle Lorne
arranged with one of the Silsbees of Lexington to smuggle out
the papers in his farm wagon when he came in every week to
market.

One day late in March, Johnny started out to deliver his
papers, for it was Thursday. But Goblin was so unmanageable,
he decided to take him over to the Common first and let him get
the kinks out of him. As usual he walked the horse through the
British encampment, through the idle men, stacked muskets,
military stores, camp kitchens. The sentry let him by, but the
next moment an officer, half-shaved and in shirt sleeves. was
shouting at him. Something about 'Getting that fool out of here,'
and, 'What's that boy doing here?' 'Heh! Stop him. Grab his
bridle.'

So Johnny knew that the troops were getting edgy. Never
before had they bothered him as he merely walked his horse
through the encampment down to the open fields close to the
Charles.

There was nothing for him to do but sit tight and take what
was coming. The men rushed at Goblin and grabbed him so
roughly the horse was frightened. One man was knocked down
and another kicked before Johnny could quiet him. The dispatch
bag of newspapers fell to the ground at the feet of the burly half-
shaved shirt-sleeved officer.

'Let's see what sort of sedition this rogue is bringing in among
His Majesty's loyal troops.' His face, behind lather, darkened
as he glanced at the paper in his hands. 'Sedition. Incitement to
rebellion. Why, if it isn't that damned *Boston Observer*. If I were

Gage I'd hang the printer of it and this young imp as well. Boy, you're going to get a horsewhipping. Perhaps you still are allowed to peddle such lies about the streets of Boston, but not among the ranks of His Majesty's First Brigade. Sergeant Clemens — thirty lashes on his bare back.'

'Yes, sir.'

Then Johnny noticed that the private holding Goblin's head had orange hair; a freckled-faced little fellow no bigger than himself. It was Pumpkin who earned extra money working at the Lytes' stable. Their eyes met. Pumpkin didn't say the word, only formed it with his lips — 'Spurs.'

Johnny struck his spurs into Goblin. The already excited horse leaped into the air, whirled about, lashing out with his heels, then bolted. Johnny saw redcoats going down in heaps, but one, more persistent than the others, a sergeant, still hung to his bridle. By sheer weight he was wearing the horse down. Johnny, like every boy in Boston, had a claspknife in his pocket. He got it out, reached forward and cut the headstall. So he lost both the sergeant and the bridle as well. Goblin flung up his beautiful head and went off on a dead run.

Johnny never understood how the horse could run so fast without tripping over tent pegs, campfires, stacks of muskets, sheep bought for slaughtering. He heard a pistol shot — that would be an officer. They alone carried pistols. Probably he had fired into the air; they were always doing that. Soon he was off the Common shooting up the Hancock Drive. Without a bridle he had no control whatever over the runaway. Goblin chose to double and weave through fields and orchards, with Johnny flat on his neck to keep from being scraped off by low branches, behind the Hancock and Lyte houses, over a stone wall, down a back alley, over a fence like a tom-cat, frightening an old lady who was hanging up clothes, so she almost swallowed a clothespin, down into West Boston and again up Beacon Hill.

The horse was winded and quieter now. Mrs. Bessie and Cilla were always giving him carrots. It was no wonder that he now turned in at the Lytes' and was ready to listen to Johnny's voice,

'Easy, easy; so, look, Goblin. I'm here. Nothing's going to hurt you. So, quietly, quietly. Softly now, easy, easy.' The bridleless horse came to a stop at the back door of the Lytes'. Soaked with sweat and heaving, he looked about him hoping for a carrot.

One of Lyte's black coach horses was tied in the stable yard. A man was grooming him. It was Pumpkin, his military tunic off hanging on the fence. Pumpkin looked up, grinning, 'I'd rather take those thirty lashes than ride a horse like that without no bridle.'

'Oh, I like riding,' Johnny said airily. He had really been a bit scared, but he wasn't going to admit it.

'You tell your master,' said Pumpkin, 'those papers went where they'll do a deal of good.'

'The British regulars?'

'Yep. Lots of 'em are Whigs, you know. Lots of 'em, just like in England, are on your side.' He knocked his currycomb against the trunk of the tree. 'That's why there has been so much deserting. It's just about getting our officers crazy.'

'But deserters get shot . . . down by the hurdles at the foot of the Common.'

'If they get caught.'

'If it comes to fighting — when it comes to fighting, how'll they fight?'

Pumpkin had little triangular green eyes in his freckled face. He stared at Johnny. 'Oh, we'll fight like hell. We always fight like hell.'

'How about you, Mr. Pumpkin?'

'Me?' The man spat. 'I'm not saying much, see? Actions speak louder'n words.'

'You'd leave if you could?'

Pumpkin screwed up his homely little face. 'Miss Cilla — and ain't she the sweetheart? — and Mrs. Bessie says you can be trusted. When I can get me a smock such as farmers wear. When I can get me an old hat with black hair sewed in it, hanging down like this, see? When I can get a farmer who'll swear I'm his hired man and can take me out past our guard on the Neck . . .'

Johnny stepped closer to him. 'I can get you all that.'

'You sure?'

'Sure. You saved me from a flogging.'

'I sure did. Boy, I like it here. I want to live here forever. A farm of my own. Cows. Poor folk can't get things like that over in England.'

'You can here.' Their heads were close together. Pumpkin, glancing nervously about, picked up a heavy hoof and began cleaning it with his jackknife.

'Sometime I've got to trust somebody . . . Make a break for it. It might as well be you — and now.'

'But if you're caught, you'll get shot.'

'I'll get shot? Hell, what do you expect in the army?'

'Look here. I can get those clothes. Bring them up here, hide them in the hay in the barn. Cilla will tell you when and where I put them. I can get in touch with a Lexington farmer who comes in every Thursday for market. He'll take you out. I'll tell Cilla and she'll tell you. And then . . . then you'll be free.'

'Never hear another sergeant yelling at me as long as I live. A farm. Cows.'

'That's it. And good land can still be had here for the clearing of it.'

'I'm no soldier. I'm a farmer. I hate the smell of gunpowder. What I like is manure.'

'But just one thing, Mr. Pumpkin. I'll do all that for one thing. I want your musket — for a friend of mine. Can you hide it in whatever place I decide to hide the farmer clothes for you?'

'I could do that.'

Before Johnny's mother died, she had made him four smocks. She made them so large she believed they would last him through his indenture. But he had never worn them. Farmers wore smocks, as did teamsters, porters, butchers, brickmakers. But not silversmiths nor printers, and never a horse boy. He had not ever put one of them on. He looked down upon smocks. They were not the fashion in his trade.

He took one of them from his sea chest in the attic. It was a

fine light blue. He had never noticed before how beautiful was
the stitching, and it hurt him to think he had been too proud to
wear them, for now he was old enough to appreciate the love that
had gone into their making. How little his mother had known of
the working world to make smocks for a boy who she knew was to
become a silversmith! She hadn't known anything, really, of day
labor, the life of apprentices. She had been frail, cast off, sick,
and yet she had fought up to the very end for something. That
something was himself, and he felt humble and ashamed.

A hat and an old black wig were not hard to find. He sewed
them together as best he was able. There was a pair of Uncle
Lorne's old breeches Aunt Jenifer said he might have, but he confided only in Rab. Rab must see to it that the uncle who every
week smuggled out copies of the *Observer* also took out the British
deserter.

Ten days later, Cilla told him the farm clothes he had hidden
in the hay were gone. And Pumpkin had left behind him his
musket and uniform.

The musket was smuggled out to Lexington by Rab's uncle.
It was lashed to the tongue of the wagon so cleverly it never
showed. But the British deserter did not show up in his blue
smock and false hair to ride out of town with Rab's uncle. He
seemed to have completely disappeared. At first the British
were much excited and searched Boston from end to end.

When Pumpkin had been gone a week, Johnny stopped worry-
ing about him. Doubtless he had found some other way of getting
out of town.

Rab did not say much when Johnny showed him the musket he
had got for him, but his eyes glowed.

Johnny, trained in a silver shop to do such work, made a bullet
mold. Together at night behind locked doors they cast bullets.
From where they squatted by the hearth in their attic they could
hear the carefree laughing, singing, and sometimes drunken quarreling of the officers billeted at the Afric Queen.

All over New England people were casting bullets. There was
little lead. Women were taking their beautiful pewter from

dresser shelves, stoically watching it melt in crucibles. Porringers, tankards, spoons, teapots, were being re-formed into bullets.

Aunt Jenifer herself gave Rab her pewter. Much of it had been in her family for a hundred years. She loved her pewter, but she stood dry-eyed and looking, for her, a little stern as she saw it disappear in Johnny's crucible.

Gunpowder was even harder to get, but all over New England saltpeter, sulphur, and charcoal were being ground to a paste, made into gunpowder. It was going to be needed.

Each Minute Man made his own bullets, and then his cartridges, to fit his own gun.

The powder and ball were rolled up in a paper cylinder. Uncle Lorne contributed bound copies of sermons to be torn up for paper, but this paper was too tough. The soldier had to bite the end off his cartridge before he loaded his gun. Half the powder was poured into the pan. The rest of it and the bullet and the paper were rammed down the barrel. The sermons were so tough that not even Rab's strong teeth could get through them. Luckily notepaper was more delicate. Cilla collected a basketful of notes that the British officers had written Miss Lavinia. Rab's bullets were wrapped in an assortment of invitations to balls, protests of undying adoration: crude sonnets comparing her to Diana and Aphrodite. Once Johnny recognized Stranger's schoolboy hand.

From now on, when the men drilled at Lexington, Rab would have his box full of cartridges, and, as he said, 'Thank God, a decent weapon in my hands.'

- 4 -

Then March was over and it was April. The tension in Boston grew. Everyone knew that with the coming of spring General Gage would leave the safety of Boston, strike out into the country as commanded by his King, and this time in considerable force.

He would never dare send out a mere handful. He knew how well
the provincials were arming, preparing to welcome him. King
George was in a fury over the dilatory, cautious behavior of his
general. Rebellion had not been put down as he had ordered
and every day it was growing stronger. Few military supplies
had been seized. Everywhere throughout New England men
were drilling. His Majesty had expressly ordered all such militia
companies to disband. Word came to Boston that three generals,
more ferocious than mild General Gage, were already on the way
over to take command — Generals Howe, Clinton, and Bur-
goyne. Doubtless, perhaps against his better judgment, Gage
would make his big sortie before the *Cerebus* arrived with the
three new generals.

Johnny continued to watch every move of Colonel Smith at the
Afric Queen. He listened to every word Dove absent-mindedly
let fall about what he had heard or seen. In spite of a slight fear
that he might, once more, meet that half-shaved shirt-sleeved
officer who had ordered him whipped, he went almost every day
to the Common. Sometimes he exercised Colonel Smith's two
horses, riding Sandy and leading Nan. Until he got on Sandy,
he had no idea that riding could be so tame a sport. He had
rather taken it for granted that whenever you rode a horse you
risked a broken neck. The mildness of all horses after Goblin
amazed him. He had learned the hard way, but he had learned.

- ſ -

Johnny, riding Sandy and leading Nan, came down Frog Lane,
skirting the Common. He was more cautious nowadays about
crossing through the British encampment. Exercising Colonel
Smith's horses was Dove's work, but Johnny always did it for
him and let Dove sleep.

On the Common he could see that Earl Percy was parading
his entire brigade — all three regiments. But Percy was always

doing that. He kept after his men, training and drilling them more than any other commander in Boston. He was a first-class officer.

Although the heights of the Common were filled with men marching, forming columns, and what-not, Johnny believed he could sneak in by the hurdles and let Sandy and Nan graze along the Charles. He knew this fresh grass was as dear to them as sweets would be to him — if he could get them. The day was so warm he rode in his shirt-sleeves. April was more like May that spring. He was filled with lassitude and a sense of peace. As he turned in the path along the lower end of the Common, he was thinking of nothing except only how much the horses would enjoy the fresh grass and how much he would like some sweets himself.

He did notice a small group of redcoats doing something down among the salt marshes. They might be catching eels for all he knew or cared. The horses dropped their heads, spread their legs a little, and tore ravenously at the green shoots of grass.

Then he heard a somber rolling of the drums. Not the usual brisk tattoos. Seemingly all Percy's brigade were marching down upon him. The only place they did not inundate was the patch of hard earth where the hurdles were and where he now sat with Sandy and Nan. They were bringing up platoon after platoon. Sandy, the old war-horse, hearing the drums, the tramp of feet, immediately lifted his head, arched his neck, cocked his tail, and struck a martial attitude. Nan did not hold much by anything connected with the army. She went on eating.

Johnny looked about him. For the first time he took in what that small band of redcoats, so close to the salt marsh, was about. He saw the chaplain reading from his open prayer-book; the wooden coffin, the hastily dug grave. Those eight men and their officer were not out catching eels (as they should have been on so fair and lazy a day), they were a firing squad. That man tied and blindfolded was a deserter. Percy had ordered out his entire brigade to watch, hoping it would cure them of any itch to desert.

A blue smock, a mop of orange hair. So they had caught

Pumpkin. He was not to die in the handsome uniform of the King's Own Regiment which he had disgraced, but in the farm clothes Johnny had procured for him.

The boy gritted his teeth, but he was trapped among the hurdles. He could not get away. Standing at attention, eyes straight ahead, were one or two thousand men in front of him and behind him the firing squad. And the river. The drummers in their high bearskin caps stood with lifted sticks, waiting. The sound of the volley and the roll of the drums came together. What had happened behind his back he saw reflected in the stony eyes, the white and sweating faces before him. One young officer looked positively green. Only Sandy seemed to enjoy the occasion. As he heard the drums and the firing, he lifted his head even higher. Nan squirmed — if Colonel Smith had been on her he would doubtless have rolled off.

Johnny put his hands to his face. It was wet and his hands were shaking. He thought of that blue smock his mother had made him, now torn by bullets. Pumpkin had wanted so little out of life. A farm. Cows. True, Rab had got the musket he craved, but Pumpkin wasn't going to get his farm. Nothing more than a few feet by a few feet at the foot of Boston Common. That much Yankee land he'd hold to Judgment Day.

'Hurrup! Hep! Hep!'

The firing squad was coming up behind him. He did not turn his head. Now they were passing close to him, their backs coming into his range of vision. Grenadiers they were, in bearskin caps, coat tails buttoned back to show their white breeches. Squared scarlet shoulders — and on each shoulder a musket.

Each musket ended with a wicked round eye — watching him so it seemed. Eight cruel eyes. It was like looking into the face of death.

Johnny had always been bold enough, taking about what came, never fearing a fight, and there was much fighting among the boys along the wharves. He had never once doubted his physical courage. But now he did.

He could not see how anyone, certainly not himself, could ever have the courage to stand up and face those murderous little eyes.

That night for one horrible moment he was glad his hand was crippled. He would never have to face the round eye of death at the end of a musket. For days he felt his own inadequacy. Was the 'bold Johnny Tremain' really a coward at heart?

Had Rab ever felt as he did now? You could not guess by looking at him. If he had had any qualms, he would never mention them. Johnny decided to do the same, but Pumpkin's death badly unnerved him.

X. *'Disperse, Ye Rebels!'*

THE fourteenth of April, 1775.

General Gage had sent out spies, dressed as Yankee men looking for work. The spies came back on this day. All the colonels
were at the Province House with General Gage listening to their
reports. Joseph Warren knew this, and so did Paul Revere, even
Johnny Tremain. It was easy enough to find out that spies had
returned, were reporting to the commanding officer — but what
had they reported? This was not known.

The fifteenth of April.

This fell upon Saturday. At every regimental headquarters the
same general orders were posted, signed by Gage himself. All
the grenadier and light infantry companies were to be taken off
duty until further orders. They were to be taught some new
evolutions.

Johnny himself read these orders posted in the lower hall at the
Afric Queen. One man was grumbling, 'New evolutions. What
was Grandma Gage thinking about?' But Lieutenant Stranger
as he read whistled and laughed. 'That,' he said, 'looks like
something — at last.'

Each regiment had two companies picked and trained for
special duty. The light infantry were the most active and
cleverest men in each regiment. Lieutenant Stranger was a light
infantry officer. These men were lightly armed and did scout
and flanking work. In the grenadier companies you found tall,

brisk, powerful fellows, hard-fighting men, always ready to attack.

If you have eleven regiments and pick off from each its two best companies, it adds up to about seven hundred men.

All day one could feel something was afoot. Johnny read it on Colonel Smith's florid face. He was stepping across the Queen's stable yard very briskly and remembering to pull in his paunch. There was ardor in his eye. Was it martial ardor?

Lieutenant Stranger was so happy over something he gave Dove threepence.

Spring had come unreasonably early this year. In the yard of the Afric Queen, peach trees were already in blossom. Stranger was so happy something was bound to happen. Over on the Common Johnny found Earl Percy's regiment unlimbering, polishing two cannons. The soldiers were forming a queue about a grindstone sharpening their bayonets. What of it? They were always doing things like that. Did all this mean something or nothing?

He went to Mr. Revere's, whose wife told him to look for him at Doctor Warren's. The two friends sat in the surgery making their plans and listening to reports that were coming from all directions. Seemingly the excitement among the officers, the preparations among the soldiers, had been noticed by at least a dozen others. But where were they going? Who would command them? No one knew. Possibly only Gage himself although before the start was actually made he would have to tell his officers.

All that day the British transports had been readying their landing boats. This might mean men would be taken aboard, move off down the coast (as Salem had been invaded two months before), or that they were standing by merely to ferry the men across the Charles River, land them in Charlestown or Cambridge. The work on the boats suggested that the men would not march out through the town gates. And yet... Gage might have ordered this work done merely to confuse the people of Boston. Blind them to his real direction. The talk at Doctor Warren's went on into the night.

Johnny relaxed on a sofa in the surgery as the men talked. He was ready to run wherever sent, find out any fact for them. It was past midnight. He would not have known he had been asleep except that he had been dreaming. He had been hard at work down on Hancock's Wharf boiling lobsters — he and John Hancock and Sam Adams. The lobsters had men's eyes with long lashes and squirmed and looked up piteously. Hancock would avert his sensitive face to their distress, 'Go away, please' (but he kept pushing them under with his gold-headed cane). Sam Adams would rub his palms and chuckle.

Johnny woke up and realized that only Revere and Warren were still in the room and they were talking about Hancock and Adams. These two gentlemen had left Boston in March. They were representatives at the Provincial Congress at Concord. The British had forbidden the General Court to meet, but the Massachusetts men had merely changed the name of their legislative body and gone on sitting. But did the British know that both these firebrands were staying at the Clarks' out in Lexington?

'It will do no harm to warn them,' Revere was saying, getting to his feet. 'I'll row over to Charlestown tonight, go to Lexington, and tell them a sizable force may soon move. They had best hide themselves for the next few days.'

'And get word to Concord. The cannons and stores had best be hidden.'

'Of course.'

'Tell them we here in Boston have the situation well in hand. The second the troops move — either on foot or into those boats — we will send them warning in time to get the Minute Men into the field. I'd give a good deal to know which way they are going.'

'But suppose none of us can get out? Gage knows we'd send word — if we could. He may guard the town so well it will be impossible.'

Johnny was still half awake. He yawned and settled back to think of those lobsters. With eyes like men ... long lashes ... tears on their lashes ...

Revere was pulling on his gloves.

' . . . Colonel Conant in Charlestown. I'll tell him to watch the
spire of Christ's Church. You can see it well from Charlestown.
If the British go out over the Neck, we will show one lantern.
If in the boats — two. And come Hell or high water I'll do my
best to get out and tell exactly what's acting. But I may get
caught on my way over. Another man should also be ready to
try to get out through the gates.'

They talked of various men and finally pitched upon Billy
Dawes. He could impersonate anybody — from a British general
to a drunken farmer. This might help him get through the gates.

As Paul Revere with Johnny at his heels left Warren's a man
emerged from the darkness, laid a hand on Revere's arm. In the
little light Johnny recognized the rolling black eye, poetic
negligence of dress. It was Doctor Church.

'Paul,' he whispered, 'what's afoot?'

'Nothing,' said Revere shortly and went on walking.

'The British preparing to march?'

'Why don't you ask them?'

The queer man drifted away. Johnny was surprised that
Revere would tell Church nothing, for he was in the very inner
circle. Seemingly Revere himself was surprised by his sudden
caution. 'But I can't trust that fellow . . . never have, never will.'

- 2 -

The sixteenth of April.

All over Boston bells were calling everyone to church. As
though they had not a care in the world the British officers
crowded into the Episcopal churches and army chaplains held
services for the soldiers in the barracks. Paul Revere was over
on the mainland carrying out his mission. Boston looked so usual
and so unconcerned, Johnny began to wonder if they all had not
made mountains of molehills, imagined an expedition when
none was intended. But Rab was so certain the time was close at

hand that he told Johnny that he himself was leaving Boston for good. There would be fighting before the week was out and he intended to be in it. Now he must report at Lexington.

Johnny took this news badly. He could not endure that Rab should leave him: desert him.

'But as soon as the first shot is fired, no man of military age can possibly get out of Boston. They'll see to it. It's now or never.'

He did not seem to feel any grief at abandoning Johnny, who sat disconsolately on his bed watching Rab. The older boy was cutting himself a final piece of bread and cheese. How many hundreds of times Johnny had seen those strong white teeth tearing at coarse bread. Rab had been eating bread and cheese all through their first meeting — and that was long ago. It seemed he'd be eating bread and cheese to the end. There was a sick qualm at the pit of Johnny's stomach. He couldn't eat bread and cheese, and it irritated him that Rab could.

The older boy was glowing with good health, good spirits. He was eighteen, six feet tall and a grown man. He looked it as he moved about the low attic, stuffing his pockets with extra stockings. Rolling up a shirt in a checkered handkerchief. He is leaving me — and he doesn't care — thought Johnny.

'Perhaps I'll go too,' he offered, hoping Rab would say, 'I'd give everything I've got — even my musket — if you could come,' or merely, 'Fine, come along.'

'No, you can't,' said Rab. 'You've got your work to do right here in town. You stick around with your fat friend Dove. Gosh, I'm glad I'll never have to listen to Dove again. But you'll have a fine time with Dove, while I ...'

'You know I cannot stomach Dove.'

'No? I thought he and you were getting on fine together.',

'And there's not one reason why I can't leave for Lexington too, except you don't want me.'

He knew this was not true, but he could not help badgering Rab, trying to make him say, 'I'll miss you as much as you'll miss me.'

Rab laughed at him. He was going to leave and he wasn't going to be 'slopped over.' Johnny was gazing at him sullenly. Rab took the extra stockings from his pocket, untied his handkerchief, and added them to his shirt and other necessities.

'You *want* to go,' Johnny accused him.

'Yes.'

'Well, then — *go!*'

'I'm going fast's I'm able.'

Oh, Rab, Rab! Have you ever seen those little eyes at the end of a musket? Rab, don't you go. Don't you go!

Rab was singing under his breath. It was the song of the Lincolnshire Poacher that Mr. Revere had taught Johnny and Johnny had taught Rab. There was something about Rab's singing, low, a little husky and not too accurate, that always moved Johnny. It was a part of that secret fire which came out in fighting, taking chances — and dancing with girls! The excitement glowed in Rab's eyes now. He was going into danger. He was going to fight — and the thought made some dark part of him happy.

Johnny wanted to tell him about those eyes, but instead he said, 'I guess you really want to get out to Lexington — and do some more dancing.'

'Here's hoping.'

From then on Johnny said nothing, sitting glumly on his bed, his head bowed. Then Rab came over to him and put a hand on his shoulder.

'Good-bye, Johnny. I'm off.'

Johnny did not look up.

'You're a bold fellow, Johnny Tremain.' He was laughing.

Johnny heard Rab's feet going down the ladder. The door of the shop closed after him. He ran to look out the window. Rab was standing outside the Lorne house shaking hands with his uncle, saying good-bye like a grown man. Now he was bending down to kiss Aunt Jenifer — not at all like a small boy kissing an aunt. He picked up Rabbit, who could toddle about, and kissed him, too. Then half-running, he passed lightly up Salt Lane and out of sight.

One moment too late, Johnny ran out into the alley. He couldn't let Rab go like that. He had not even said good luck, God be with you. Why ... he might not ever see Rab again. He went back to his garret and flung himself on his bed. He half-wished he might cry and was half-glad he was too old for tears.

Today there was no sound from the shops and wharves. No cry of chimney sweep, oysterman, knife-grinder. The town was whist and still, for it was Sunday. As Johnny lay upon his bed, the church bells began to call for afternoon service. They babbled softly as one old friend to another. Christ's Church and Cockerel, Old South, Old Meeting, Hollis, King's Chapel. He knew every one. He had heard them clanging furiously for fire, crying fiercely to call out the Sons of Liberty. He had heard them toll for the dead, rejoice when some unpopular act had been repealed, and shudder with bronze rage at tyranny. They had wakened him in the morning and sent him to bed at night, but he never loved them more than on Lord's Days when their golden clamor seemed to open the blue vaults of Heaven itself. You could almost see the angels bending down to earth — even to rowdy old Boston. 'Peace, peace,' the soft bells said. 'We are at peace ...'

Suddenly close by, over at the Afric Queen, the British drumsticks fell. The fifes struck up 'too-too — tootlety-too.' Even on Sunday they were out drilling. So were other men — even on Sunday. For instance, over in Lexington.

The sixteenth of April drew to a close.

Monday was a quiet day. Lieutenant Stranger looked very solemn. Maybe there was not to be an expedition after all.

- *3* -

The eighteenth of April.

By afternoon the sergeants were going about the town, rounding up the grenadier and light infantry companies, telling them (in whispers) to report at moonrise at the bottom of the Common 'equipped for an expedition.'

The sergeants would tap their red noses with their fingers and bid the men be 'whist,' but it was common knowledge in the barracks and on the streets that seven hundred men would march that night.

This very night — come darkness — the men would move, but in what direction? And who would be in charge of the expedition? Surely not more than one of the colonels would be sent.

Johnny, who had his own colonel to watch, Colonel Smith, hardly left the Afric Queen all day and helped the pot-boy serve drinks to the officers in the dining room. A young officer sitting with Stranger did say, as he stirred his brandy-and-water with his thumb, that he hoped before long thus to stir Yankee blood — and what of that? Colonel Smith did have an army chaplain to dine with him that day. Did that mean he was suddenly getting religious, as people are said to before they go into danger?

Of one thing Johnny was sure. Dove knew much less than he did. Dove was so thick-witted he had no idea anything unusual was afoot. He honestly believed that the grenadiers and light infantry were merely going to be taught 'new evolutions.' As usual, Dove was too wrapped in his own woes to think much of what was happening about him.

By five Johnny thought he would leave the Queen and report to Paul Revere that he had discovered nothing new. First one more glance at Dove.

For once he found him hard at work, his lower lip stuck out, his whitish pig-lashes wet. He was polishing a saddle.

'That guy,' he complained, 'hit me for nothing. He said I was to get to work on his campaign saddle.'

'Who's he?'

'Colonel Smith, of course.'

'Did you do as he told you?'

'I tried. I didn't know he had two saddles. So I went to work on the usual one. I shined it until you can see your face in it. And he takes it out of my hands and hit me on the head with it.

Says I'm a stupid lout not to know the difference between a parade saddle and a campaign saddle. How'd I know? Why, he's
been over here about a year and that campaign saddle hasn't ever
been unpacked. I had to get it from Lieutenant Stranger. How'd
I know?'

Johnny said nothing. He realized he had heard something
which conceivably might be important. Careful . . . careful . . .
don't you say anything to scare him.

'Where's your polish? I'll help with the stirrups.'

The instant Johnny went to work, Dove as usual lay back on
the hay.

'One of the stirrups wrapped round my head. Cut my ear. It
bled something fierce.'

Johnny was studying the saddle on his knees. It was of heavy
black leather, brass (not silver) mountings. Three girths instead
of two. All sorts of hooks and straps for attaching map cases, spy-
glasses, flasks, kits of all sorts.

Colonel Smith is going on a campaign. But perhaps not. He
might merely be riding down to New York.

He leaned back on his heels. 'Say, what if you and I took time
out to eat supper? The Queen's cook has promised me a good
dinner, because I helped them at table this afternoon. Roast
goose. I'll fix it so you can get in on it, too.'

'Oh, for goodness' sake — no.'

'It's past five o'clock. Colonel can't be going anywhere tonight.'

'Oh, for land's sake, Johnny, he says I'm to show him that
saddle by six sharp, and if he don't like its looks he's going to cut
me to mincemeat. He's always saying things like that. He's
the . . .'

Johnny did not listen to what Colonel Smith was. He was
thinking.

'Well, after that — when Colonel Smith has settled down to
play whist. Can you get off?'

'Tonight isn't like any other night. He told me to bring Sandy
around for him, fed and clean and saddled with this old campaign saddle by eight o'clock tonight . . .'

Colonel Smith is going on a long journey. Starting tonight at eight. It might be a campaign. He had an idea.

'I should think if the Colonel was making a long trip he'd take Nan, she's so light and easy to ride . . . if he has far to go.'

'He does like her better — she don't jounce his fat so. He always rides her 'round Boston. But only yesterday he had Lieutenant Stranger take her over to the Common when the men were drilling. Stranger says she still is squirmy when she hears drums and shooting. I heard him say so.'

'Oh.' Drums and shooting. This was not to be a peaceful ride to, say, New York. His cloth whipped over the black saddle leather. He spat on it and rubbed even harder. The one thing he must not say was the wrong thing. Nothing was better than the wrong thing. So for a while he said nothing.

'Sandy's good as gold, but he's an old horse and a little stiff. His front left leg won't last forever.'

'Colonel Smith didn't say he was going off on him forever.'

This did not help much. But Dove went on:

'He and the horse doctor and Lieutenant Stranger were all looking at him just this morning. The horse doctor said old Sandy could do thirty miles easy. And Stranger said, no, he wouldn't swear you could get Nan on and off a boat without her fussing.'

So . . . the campaign would start around eight that night. The Colonel's horse would be put on and off a boat. There would be a risk at least of drums and shooting. They were not going farther than thirty miles. Those men who thought the target of the expedition was going to be Lexington and Concord were right. And it would be Colonel Smith who would go in command.

All Johnny's hidden excitement went into his polishing. The brass mountings turned to gold. The black leather to satin.

'There! You take that in and show your Colonel!'

But he would wait one moment more, Dove might have something more to say when he came back after he had seen the Colonel.

Johnny went into Goblin's stall, but the horse pretended not to know him, and put back his ears and nipped at him.

Sandy next. The big yellow horse carefully moved over to give him room in the stall, nickered a little. He fondled the broad white-striped face, pulled gently at the ears — little furry ears, lost in mane like a pony's.

'I guess,' Johnny said, 'it looks like you'll be seeing that Rab before I do. May be Lexington. You tell that Rab he'd best look sharp. Take good care of himself. Tell that Rab . . . oh, anything.'

Dove came back in a jubilee.

'Colonel says I've done a fine job and so quick he's going to give me tomorrow as a holiday. He don't expect to get back before night.' Certainly this campaign was going to be a short one — if everything went as the British expected.

- 4 -

'It is tonight all right,' Johnny said to Doctor Warren, 'and Colonel Smith will command.' He went on to tell what he had found out from Dove. That the expedition would start tonight and that Lexington and Concord were the likely objects, the men sitting about in Warren's surgery had already guessed. But they were interested to learn that the Colonel and presumably his troops, expected to return to Boston the day after they set out and that he was to command them. Seemingly Gage, a punctilious man, had chosen Francis Smith because he had been in service longer than any of the other (and smarter) colonels.

'Hark.'

Outside the closed window on Tremont Street a small group of soldiers were marching stealthily toward the Common. These were the first they heard. But soon another group marched past, then another. A man whose duty it was to watch the British boats at the foot of the Common came in to say he had actually seen the men getting into the boats, heading for Cambridge.

Doctor Warren turned to Johnny, 'Run to Ann Street. Bid Billy Dawes come to me here, ready to ride. Then go to North Square. I've got to talk to Paul Revere before he starts. Both he and Dawes will be expecting a messenger.'

Billy Dawes was in his kitchen. He was a homely, lanky, young fellow with close-set eyes, and a wide, expressive mouth. He and his wife had dressed him for the part he would play — a drunken farmer. His wife, who looked more like a schoolgirl than a serious matron, could not look at him without going from one giggling fit to another. She laughed even more, and Billy joined her, when Johnny came in and said the time had come. The young man stuck a dilapidated hat with a broken feather on his head and his wife picked up a bottle of rum and poured it over the front of his torn jacket. Then she kissed him and they both laughed. As he stood before them, his expression changed.

His eyes went out of focus. His grin became foolish. He hic-coughed and swayed. He both looked and smelled like a drunken farmer. But he did have money in his pocket which no country blade would have had after a big toot in town. He knew one of the soldiers guarding the Neck that night. He believed he'd get out all right.

The scene in the Dawes kitchen was so light-hearted and so comical — and Johnny as well as little Mrs. Dawes laughed so hard — he wondered if she had any idea of the risk her husband was running. For by any law of any land a man caught exciting to armed rebellion might be shot. The second the door closed after the young man, Johnny knew. Mrs. Dawes stood where her husband had left her, all laughter wiped from her face. Billy Dawes was not the only gifted actor in his family.

From Ann Street Johnny ran toward North Square. This he found crowded with light infantry and grenadier companies, all in full battle dress. They got in his way and he in theirs. One of the men swore and struck at him with his gun butt. The regulars were getting ugly. He could not get to the Reveres' front door, but by climbing a few fences he reached their kitchen door, and knocked softly. Paul Revere was instantly outside in the dark with him.

'Johnny,' he whispered, 'the *Somerset* has been moved into the mouth of the Charles. Will you run to Copp's Hill and tell me if they have moved in any of the other warships? I think I can row around one, but three or four might make me trouble.'

'I'll go look.'

'Wait. Then go to Robert Newman — you know, the Christ's Church sexton. He lives with his mother opposite the church.'

'I know.'

'They have British officers billeted on them. *Don't rap at that door*. Take this stick. Walk by the house slowly, limping, tapping with the stick until the light in an upper window goes out. Then go 'round to the alley behind the house. Tell Newman the lanterns are to be hung now. Two of them. He knows what to do.'

As Johnny stood among the graves of lonely Copp's Hill looking across the broad mouth of the Charles, he could see lights in the houses of Charlestown. And over there he knew men were watching Boston, watching Christ's lofty spire — waiting for the signal. And as soon as they saw it, the best and fastest horse in Charlestown would be saddled and made ready for Paul Revere, who had himself promised to get over — if possible. Ride and spread the alarm. Summon the Minute Men. He watched the riding lights on the powerful sixty-four-gun *Somerset*. The British had evidently thought her sufficient to prevent boats crossing the river that night. She was alone.

The moon had risen. The tide was rising. The *Somerset* was winding at her anchor. The night was unearthly sweet. It smelled of land and of the sea, but most of all it smelled of spring.

Salem Street, where the Newmans lived, like North Square, was filled with soldiers. The redcoats were assembling here, getting ready to march down to the Common — and they would be a little late. Their orders were to be ready by moonrise. A sergeant yelled at Johnny as he started to limp past them, but when he explained in a piteous whine that his foot had been squashed by a blow from a soldier's musket and all he wanted was to get home to his mama, an officer said the men were to let 'the child' pass. Johnny was sixteen, but he could pull himself together and play at being a little boy still.

Downstairs in the Newman house he could look in and see a group of officers as usual, almost as always, playing at cards. Their jackets were unbuttoned, their faces flushed. They were laughing and drinking. There was on the second floor one light. Johnny couldn't believe anyone up there could hear him tapping in the street below. Instantly the light went out. He had been heard.

Newman, a sad-faced young man, got out at a second-story window in back, ran across a shed roof, and was in the alley waiting for Johnny.

'One or two?' he whispered.

'Two.'

That was all. Robert Newman seemed to melt away in the dark. Johnny guessed what the little tinkle was he heard. Newman had the keys to Christ's Church in his hand.

The two friends, Paul Revere and Joseph Warren, were standing in the Doctor's surgery. They were alone. Revere was urging Warren to cross with him that very night to Charlestown. If there was fighting tomorrow, Gage would not hesitate to hang him — at last — for high treason. But Warren said no. He would stay and keep track of the British plans until the very last moment.

'The second a shot has been fired, I'll send a messenger to you,' Revere promised.

'I'll wait until then. Why, Revere, I never saw you worry about anything before. I'll be a lot safer tonight than you'll be — catching crabs out on that river. Being shot at by the *Somerset*. And falling off horses — I'll not forget you and Parson Tomley's ambling jade.'

He was always ragging Revere about falling off horses. It was some old joke between them which Johnny did not know, and both the men suddenly began to laugh. The mood between them had been heavy when Johnny came in, but now it lightened. They parted as casually as any friends who believe they will meet in a few days. But each knew the other was in deadly peril of his life. It was ten o'clock.

Doctor Warren told his colored man to make up a bed for Johnny in the surgery. The boy could not think of bed. He stole down to the Common to see the 'secret' embarkation. It was almost over, and was no secret. Hundreds of townsfolk stood about silently watching the boats returning from Cambridge shore and taking on yet another scarlet-coated cargo. But where these men were heading and who commanded them, scarce a man in the crowd knew except Johnny. Farther down the river he knew the *Somerset* was on guard. By now Paul Revere was in his boat, trying to steal around her. In Charlestown the horse waited for him.

He saw Sandy step into a boat with never a quiver. He recognized Lieutenant Stranger's own horse and for a moment saw the young man's dark face in the moonlight. Being a horse-minded boy, he noticed that there was a little trouble with a showy white horse built like Sandy, but much younger. This was Major Pitcairn's. Were the marines being sent as well as the grenadiers and light infantry companies? Or was the rough, genial, stout-hearted old major merely going along for the fun of it?

At least, he thought this observation important enough to report to Warren. Other spies had been bringing news of the embarkation. It had been noticed that Pitcairn was not in his usual tavern. He had been seen with a civilian cape wrapped about him heading for the Common. Doubtless he was going. Gage had sent him either because he knew he was a better officer than Colonel Smith or because he had a way with Yankees. Everyone liked the pious, hard-swearing, good-tempered Major Pitcairn.

A barmaid from Hull Street came in to say she had been watching the *Somerset* at just the time Bentley and Richardson were rowing Paul Revere to Charlestown. Not a shot had been fired. It was also known that Billy Dawes had woven and bribed his inebriated way past the guards on the Neck. And the horse he was leading and pretending to try to sell had not looked like much — a thin bony beast in a bridle patched with rope. It was one of the fastest horses in Boston.

Then Doctor Warren told Johnny to lie down and get some sleep. It was almost midnight.

Johnny took off his jacket and boots, rolled up in a blanket on the bed the black man had made for him. The night before and the night before that he had been much upset over Rab's leaving. His thoughts had turned to the empty bed beside him. He had slept badly. Although people were still about the surgery, exchanging ideas, trying to guess what the future might be, he immediately fell asleep.

It was dawn. He was alone in the surgery and still sleeping. But out in Lexington on the Village Green the first shot was fired. One shot and then a volley. And Major Pitcairn was saying, 'Disperse, ye rebels, ye villains, disperse! Why don't ye lay down your arms?'

The war had begun.

It was the dawn of the Nineteenth of April. But Johnny Tremain still slept.

XI. *Yankee Doodle*

So Johnny slept. It was daylight when he woke with Warren's hand upon his shoulder. Outside on Tremont Street he could hear the clumping of army boots. A sergeant was swearing at his men. The soldiers were paraded so close to the house, which stood flush with the sidewalkless street, that Johnny at first thought they must be in the room.

Doctor Warren dared speak no louder than a whisper.

'I'm going now.'

'Something's happened?'

'Yes.' He motioned Johnny to follow him into the kitchen. This room was on the back of the house. They could talk without danger of being overheard by the troops in the street.

Doctor Warren had on the same clothes as the day before. He had not been to bed. But now his hat was on his head. His black bag of instruments and medicines was packed and on the table. Silently he put milk, bread, herrings beside it, and gestured to Johnny to join him.

'Where did it begin?' asked Johnny.

'Lexington.'

'Who won?'

'They did. Seven hundred against seventy. It wasn't a battle. It was ... just target practice ... for them. Some of our men were killed and the British huzzaed and took the road to Concord.'

'And did they get our supplies there?'

'I don't know. Paul Revere sent for me just after the firing on Lexington Green.'

The young man's usually fresh-colored face was haggard. He knew the seriousness of this day for himself and for his country.

'But everywhere the alarm is spreading. Men are grabbing their guns — marching for Concord. Paul Revere did get through in time last night. Billy Dawes a little later. Hundreds — maybe thousands — of Minute Men are on the march. Before the day's over, there'll be real fighting — not target practice. But Gage doesn't know that it's begun. You see, long before Colonel Smith got to Lexington — just as soon as he heard that Revere had warned the country — he sent back for reinforcements. For Earl Percy. You and I, Johnny, are just about the only people in Boston who know that blood has already been shed.'

'Were many killed — at Lexington?'

'No, not many. They stood up — just a handful. The British fired on them. It was dawn.'

Johnny licked his lips. 'Did they tell you the names of those killed?'

'No. Did Rab get out in time?'

'Yes. Last Sunday.'

The Doctor's clear, blue eyes darkened. He knew what was in Johnny's mind. He picked up his bag. 'I've got to get to them. They'll need surgeons. Then, too, I'd rather die fighting than on a gallows. Gage won't be so lenient now — soon as he learns war has begun.'

'Wait until I get my shoes on.'

'No, Johnny, you are to stay here today. Pick up for me any information. For instance, out of my bedroom window I can see soldiers standing the length of the street 'way over to the Common. You find out what regiments are being sent — and all that. And today go about and listen to what folk are saying. And the names of any the British arrest. We know Gage expects to move his men back here tonight. If so, there'll be a lot of con-

fusion getting them into town. You watch your chance and
slip out to me.'

'Where'll I find you?'

'God knows. Ask about.'

'I will do so.'

'They've begun it. We'll end it, but this war ... it may last
quite a long time.'

They shook hands silently. Johnny knew that Warren was
always conscious of the fact that he had a crippled hand. Everybody else had accepted and forgotten it. The back door closed
softly. Warren was gone.

Johnny went to the surgery, put on his boots and jacket. The
wall clock said eight o'clock. It was time to be about. There was
no leaving by the front door. The soldiers were leaning against
it. Through the curtains of the windows he could see the muskets.
He noticed the facings on their uniforms. The Twenty-Third
Regiment. The narrow course of Tremont Street was filled to the
brim and overflowing with the waiting scarlet-coated men. Like
a river of blood. He left by the kitchen.

- 2 -

On Cornhill Johnny could feel the subdued excitement. Everyone knew something was happening. No one knew what. Doors
and windows were open. People hanging out, calling back and
forth or gathered in knots in the street. Johnny kept his eyes and
ears open. Everyone knew about that 'secret' expedition last
night. Colonel Smith had embarked with seven hundred men
and landed in Cambridge. That Gage was sending over at least
a thousand fresh troops to support him anyone might guess. But
the people of Boston knew no more than Gage that the fighting
had begun.

Johnny went to the Province House. All was as usual. The
sentries were on guard. Young officers lounged about. One was

already in his cups. Johnny could see that a group of them were playing at cards in the south parlor. Perhaps they were finishing off the game they had begun last night.

He knew which was General Gage's bedroom. The curtains were still drawn. Colonel Smith's early call for reserves evidently had not upset the commanding officer. He had given the order which set Percy's First Brigade in motion, had rolled over and gone to sleep.

Johnny went to the Common. He had already seen the tail of Percy's brigade lashing around Doctor Warren's house. The head of this scarlet dragon lay upon the Common. The men were restless, grumbling, spitting, shifting their heavy equipment. Some had already been standing about for three hours. Johnny learned from one of their camp women what was causing the delay. They were waiting to be joined by a detachment of marines. He looked about and saw for himself these twelve hundred men were taking with them cannon and baggage wagons.

The tension among the inhabitants was growing. What had happened? What was going to happen? Shops and schools were closed, and Johnny met a wreath of tiny children advancing and chanting, 'School's done. War's begun.' It looked to him they were shrewder guessers than their elders who were trying to believe that not a shot had been, or would be, fired.

Then from over North Boston way came the brisk rattle of drums. The five hundred marines, billeted all about North Square, arrived at double-quick. They took their places in the ranks. Some were still buckling their equipment or eating the bread that had been tossed to them. They had been hours late, but when they had been notified they came fast.

Tagging after them, looking half-awake and half-dressed, Johnny recognized an old acquaintance. It was Madge, even fatter since her marriage and seemingly more in love than ever. Tears streamed down her thick, red cheeks and, all old animosity forgotten, she flung herself upon Johnny.

'I c-c-can't bear it. But he says he's g-g-got to go.'

Near-by tough little Sergeant Gale was strutting about like a bantam cock, roaring at one of his men whose buttons did not shine. He was pretending not to know that his wife was so near-by. He was really showing off in front of her and approved her presence. Men went to war and women wept. All was as it should be.

'Sure he's got to go,' Johnny comforted Madge; 'but people say Gage is just sending out the brigade for exercise. They've been sitting about barracks catching fleas all winter. Why were the marines late?'

'Gage sent a letter to Major Pitcairn telling him to parade his men. But Pitcairn wasn't to home.'

'Pitcairn went off last night. Second in command to Colonel Smith.'

'Did you know that? The marines didn't know until about ten minutes ago.'

Johnny had to laugh. It certainly would hearten Doctor Warren when he heard how stupid the British had been. Gage had forgotten the marine major had already gone, had sent him a letter, and then turned over for another snooze.

Suddenly there was silence along the whole great length of the brigade. Slim Earl Percy on a white horse, escorted by a group of officers, was cantering slowly across the Common.

Five mounted men. The sun was bright that day with only breeze enough to ruffle the horses' manes, flaunt scarlet riding capes, float the flag of England. Johnny was an Englishman. The sullen, rebellious people standing about watching Percy and his staff approaching, waiting for the brigade to march, all were Englishmen. That flag — it stood for Magna Charta, the Bill of Rights, Charles the First's head upon a block, centuries of struggle for 'English liberty.' But over here there had grown up a broader interpretation of the word 'liberty': no man to be ruled or taxed except by men of his own choice. But we are still fighting for 'English liberty' and don't you forget it. French slaves to the north of us, Spanish slaves to the south of us. Only English colonies are allowed to taste the forbidden fruit of liberty — we who grew up under England. Johnny thought of James Otis's words. Upholding the torch of liberty — which had been lighted on the fires of England.

Not since the soldiers had come to Boston had Johnny removed his hat when the British flag went by except once when it had been knocked off his head by a soldier. He started to remove it now — for the first time and doubtless the last. Thought better of it —— It was too late. He knew the shooting had begun.

The sword in Earl Percy's hand flashed. There was a command which was instantly picked up and repeated and echoed and repeated again. The regimental drummers struck up. The artillery horses threw their weight against their collars. Wagoners cracked their whips and the scarlet dragon swung forward, sluggishly at first, heading for the town gates. Thousands of separate feet merged into only one gigantic pair. Left, right, left, right. The earth shook to their rhythm. Johnny watched them pass. Every button was sewed on. Every buckle in place. Every cartridge box held exactly thirty-six cartridges. Every musket had a bayonet, and there was not one old fowling piece among them. Every horse had four new shoes. It was a magnificent sight, but Johnny felt a little sick.

What chance — what shadow of a chance — had those poor, untrained, half-armed farmers at Concord? O God, be with us now. But even as he prayed, he kept an eye out for the regimental markings on the men's uniforms. It was the Fourth, the Twenty-Third, and the Forty-Seventh who were being sent out, plus five hundred marines, plus a small artillery train, and a few baggage wagons. Twelve hundred for a guess.

The drums throbbed. The heavy dragon marched on its thousands of feet, and now above the drums came the shrilling of the fifes. They played a tune they always played when they wished to insult Yankees. For once more Yankee Doodle was going to town on a spanking stallion, with that forlorn feather in his cap, asking those unmilitary questions.

Poor Yankee Doodle. Whatever could he do against this great scarlet dragon?

- 3 -

The hundreds gathered to see the departure of the brigade stood about gazing at the empty space they had occupied. Far away, growing faint and fainter, came wafting back the last sound of the tune they played. A man, standing by Johnny with clenched hands and head thrust down and out like a bull's, said thickly, 'They go out by "Yankee Doodle," but they'll dance to it before night.'

Johnny saw a group of women, and they were nodding their heads, whispering a prophecy, 'Before night they'll be dancing.' This catch-phrase was everywhere. It did not seem to have gone from mouth to mouth, but from mind to mind.

Old Meeting struck nine. Earl Percy and his laggard brigade were gone.

This day, this unreal day, in which Boston waited hour upon hour for news — any news, good or bad — was well begun. Suddenly, people were saying, 'Have you heard? At sunrise this morning over at Lexington the British fired on us.' No one seemed to know where this rumor had started, but it was everywhere.

Although half of Gage's forces had left town for the battlefield, there were more officers than usual hanging about the streets and taverns. And their faces were so bland and they reassured the people so glibly that not a shot had been fired, not a person killed and begged all and sundry so smoothly to keep calm and go to their shops or their homes, Johnny was confident that the British as well as the inhabitants had heard now that the war had begun.

And by noon little bands of soldiers appeared on the streets going quickly from house to house. Too late General Gage had given orders that the leaders of the opposition should be arrested. But the leaders were all gone. The angry, frustrated soldiers might scare Sam Adams's black handmaiden out of her wits. They could break John Hancock's fence. But these gentlemen had quietly left Boston a month before. They stormed into

Joseph Warren's house. He was gone. And so was Paul Revere. Not one of the principal leaders was left. And seemingly no rebel printers. Isaiah Thomas's shop was empty. He and his press had left the night before. At Edes and Gill's, where the *Boston Gazette* was published, they did grab young Peter Edes. His father and press had been smuggled out to Watertown.

Robert Newman, suspected of having hung the lanterns in Christ's Church the night before, was thrown into jail, and John Pulling, merely suspected of having helped, was forced to hide in his grandmother's wine butt. Paul Revere's cousin was in jail. And every minute the temper of the soldiers was growing shorter and a queer feeling of jubilation was apparent among the people. You couldn't see, you couldn't guess, why they began feeling so confident. Confidence was in the air.

As soon as Johnny heard that arresting parties were on the streets, he sent a message to Uncle Lorne. Uncle had best make himself scarce. Soon after, having stood about the jail and noted exactly who was put in it, he himself headed for Salt Lane. There was not a person on the street, but at every window he saw a face. The lane itself had changed. He glanced about him and saw what was wrong. There was no little man in a blue coat observing Boston through a spyglass. The familiar sign had been torn down, stamped to kindling. The door of the shop was shattered. He went in. The presses were broken. The type pied. Upstairs his and Rab's bed had been ripped open by bayonets. Frightened, he ran across the street.

Aunt Jenifer sat in her kitchen. Half in her lap and half on the floor was an enormous feather bed. She was peacefully sticking on it a new ticking. The only unusual thing was the great number of feathers this deft housewife had carelessly spilled over her kitchen floor.

Rabbit, enchanted with these new toys, was constantly picking up a feather, putting it in his hair, and saying, 'Yankee-do.'

'They've been here?' asked Johnny.

'Yes. Are they gone?'

'Not one in sight.'

'We got your message just as they were turning down Salt Lane.'

The feather bed began to heave on the floor.

'You can come out now,' Aunt Jenifer whispered to it.

Out of the bottom rolled Uncle Lorne, choked with feathers and looking more bird than human. Rabbit shrieked, 'Da, Da.' He evidently thought his father much improved. Still trembling, for Uncle Lorne was a timid man, he kissed his wife and hugged his child.

'It was all I could think of,' Aunt Jenifer said to Johnny. 'Mr. Lorne just stood here and said he wasn't afraid to die. We could hear the men marching down the street . . . it was terrible. So I just popped him in and went on sewing.'

'Were the soldiers rough?'

'Rough? They were furious.'

'Good,' said Johnny grimly. 'That means they are really scared. Something pretty awful has happened to all those men Gage has sent out. Some of the officers may know already, but the men have guessed it, and they are running about with uniforms unbuttoned and yelling, "If they want a war, we'll give it to 'em. And they won't pay taxes? We'll collect in blood." '

'You don't say! Are you sure the fight's going for us?'

'Pretty sure. I was down by the ferry slip and saw a British major coming over from Charlestown. Well, he had a civilian coat over his uniform — sort of disguised — and he tore off the boat and he ran for the Province House. He'd come to tell Gage Colonel Smith's and Percy's men are getting licked.'

'Boy, you're jumping at conclusions.'

'Not I. I saw his face. It was just done in and tied up with disgust. His uniform was a mess. His feelings had been hurt. People who have been winning battles don't go around with faces like that, but British officers who have been beaten by "peasants" and "yokels" do.'

'Oh, Johnny, I do like to hear you talk like that. But I'm not counting much on one man's face. Where you off to?'

'Beacon Hill. I've an idea that major got back to Gage to
tell him one thing. The British are going to try to get to Charlestown, just the way he did, and under protection of the *Somerset's*
guns. They won't back-track the way they came. Too dangerous. If I've guessed it right, before long from Beacon Hill we'll
be able to see them — running, and our men after them.'

'Johnny, here's half a mince pie for you. You're a real smart
boy.'

Uncle Lorne came back from the bedroom where he, with
Rabbit's help, had been picking off feathers. 'Even if they hang
me,' he said in a proud tremolo, 'I will feel I have not lived in
vain.' He was still pretty scared.

Out on the street, Johnny met officers yelling at their men,
trying to get them back into their barracks, striking at them even
with the flat of their swords. You couldn't say the British regulars lacked fight. All they could talk about was how many
skulking cowards and damned rebels they were going to kill.
In one day all was changed in Boston.

On both sides the gloves were off and the hands underneath
were bloody. War had begun.

The pastures and orchards back of Beacon Hill were crowded,
and all eyes turned northward. Johnny was not the only person
who had guessed that Percy would not attempt to get the remains
of Smith's troops and his own brigade back through Cambridge,
but only to Charlestown, where they could be protected by the
Somerset's guns.

Then Johnny saw running down Cambridge road through
the bushes on Charlestown Common a scurry of red ants. Had
he really seen them or imagined them? But all about him people
were exclaiming, 'Look, there they are!'

Those red ants were British soldiers.

To his left the last moment of sunset light was dying. The
day had been amazingly warm, but with night a fresh breeze
came up off the ocean. Lights began to glimmer in Charlestown
and on warships. Seemingly there was nothing more to be seen
from Beacon Hill. Silently people turned to go to their houses.

'Look!' Johnny cried.

You could see the flash of musket fire, too far away to be heard. Fireflies swarming, hardly more than that.

- 4 -

Getting two thousand men (or what was left of them, for gossip was saying they had been 'well chewed') into boats and back to Boston would create just the confusion Doctor Warren had promised. But it would not be easy for Johnny to slip over. The soldiers were cross and frightened. He would wait a little until they were more relaxed. Say about midnight. Before him, lighted from top to bottom, he saw the Lytes' house and he remembered Pumpkin's uniform. Dressed in that, he might slip aboard in the confusion.

He went to the Lytes'. In front of the house he saw wagons and carts and men loading them with furniture, chests, trunks, boxes — even old portraits. The Lytes were moving and by night and in a hurry. He went to the kitchen door.

Mrs. Bessie, who certainly ought to have been superintending this moving, was sitting idly in the kitchen — doing nothing. Cilla sat beside her. She was doing nothing.

Mrs. Bessie jerked her thumb toward the front of the house.

'Scared,' she said. 'They are all going to London until this insurrection, as they call it, is over. The *Unicorn* leaves at dawn tomorrow. Gage has given permission.'

'Cilla,' said Johnny, 'don't you go with them.'

'Never. We all had a terrible fight this afternoon when word first came that us Yankees had beaten them hollow. All the other servants are Tories and are going with them. But Mrs. Bessie and I are Whigs, and we are not going with them. In the end Mr. Lyte said he was glad we are Whigs because he will leave us here to look after his property. Gage has promised nothing up here will be touched.'

'But they don't want us around. Can't bear the sight of us,'
Mrs. Bessie said smugly. 'The very sight of a good Whig makes
them furious. Mr. Lyte did have another fit — just a little one.
Miss Lavinia is afraid, if she doesn't get her papa right out of
town and off to London, he'll die. She always did like London
better than Boston anyway. They are leaving tonight, and fast.'

'What's Isannah going to do?'

'Izzy?' Mrs. Bessie's lips curled. 'She'll go with them.'

'She will not,' said Cilla. 'Miss Lavinia has gone down to
Hancock's Wharf to ask Ma to let her take her. But Ma couldn't
give her away — just as though she was a kitten.'

Miss Lavinia was standing in the doorway from the dining
room to the kitchen. She had on a black cloak with the hood to
it over her head. She stood a moment looking about and said
nothing.

Johnny was on his feet. He knew he would never forget her —
never. Even when he was an old man he would remember
Lavinia Lyte standing, framed in that doorway, saying nothing.
Her eyes were angry and tired. The chisel mark was deep between the low-sweeping black brows. He had never seen her
look so worn and old and never been more aware of her beauty.

'Isannah is going with me,' she said at last. 'Your mother,
Cilla, has too many kittens.'

'Miss Lavinia,' said Cilla, 'you can't do that.'

'Can't? Your mother signed the paper — and you're a wicked
girl to stand in the way of your sister's good fortune.'

A little diffidently Isannah herself emerged from behind the
lady's great dark skirts.

'Isannah,' said Cilla gently, 'you can't go off and leave me
like this. It's no matter what Mother says. Look, dear, if you
go to London, maybe you will never come back. Isannah . . .
don't go away . . . from me.'

Lavinia was smiling under her dark hood.

'I will leave the decision entirely to her. She shall be perfectly free to choose between us. Precious, would you rather go
with me to London and be a great lady and wear silks and

jewels and ride in coaches, or stay here and be just another poor working girl?' And then, to make the choice doubly hard for the child, she added a little maliciously, 'Which do you love most, Cilla or me?'

Still Isannah said nothing. But even in her silence Johnny could detect something of her desire for drama. At the moment silence was more dramatic than anything she could say. Izzy is no good, thought Johnny. She'll go.

Cilla was standing quietly, well away from the child. She was too proud to make any further appeal to her. Perhaps like Johnny she knew what the answer would be.

'Well,' said Lavinia, 'I haven't got all day. Which do you love the most?'

Isannah began to cry. It was perfectly natural crying. Not even Johnny could believe it was done for effect.

'I don't know,' she sobbed.

'Which would you rather be, a common person like your sister or a fine lady?'

'Fine lady,' she sniffled, and went on dreamily, 'and I'll have a gray pony and a pony cart. I've got the gold locket already.' Her hand went to her throat. Next she'd be saying she wanted a little sailboat. Even now she was only reflecting old desires of Cilla's. Isannah never could think up anything for herself.

'Yes, dear, you will — when I am Lady Pryor-Morton and you my little protégée.' She explained to the others: 'I've been betrothed to marry my lord ever since I last came back from London. Papa is a very sick man. He could never live through a civil war over here. Never. He doesn't want to leave all his property to the mob — but what does it matter? My lord is so rich — this miserable house, our ships, shops, are nothing to him. And my lord never liked it that my papa was in trade. Until now Papa would not give up his trade — nor could I bear to leave him.'

She turned to Cilla, 'And I promise you, I will be in a position to give your sister the best care and training.'

'Training,' said Johnny. 'What's she going to be trained for?'

'Isannah shall be an actress. I would have been myself —
but my station in life prevented me. And then, I am too tall.
And, besides, I can't act. Isannah shall be the toast of London.
You'll be proud someday. Even over here in this dreary wilder-
ness you shall hear her name and boast that once you knew her.'

Mrs. Bessie said smartly, 'I'd welcome the day I was proud
to know that Izzy.'

Cilla was not taking the parting as hard as Johnny would
have expected. Now he knew that she had been through the
worst of it months before when first the two sisters had come
to the Lytes'. She had lost Isannah long ago.

'Now, Cilla,' said Miss Lavinia, 'I want you to have some
time alone with Isannah. You've been a good girl, Cilla — better
than Isannah — but happens she is what I fancy. Now go with
her and help her pack her duds.'

Cilla said nothing, but curtsied and went upstairs with
Isannah who was once more sobbing.

'You, too,' said Lavinia irritably to Mrs. Bessie. 'You leave
me. For I must talk to Johnny alone.'

Mrs. Bessie heaved herself up out of her comfortable chair
and shut the door after her.

The young woman sat at last and murmured, more to herself
than to Johnny: 'I must talk to you, Jonathan Lyte Tremain.'

Johnny raised his eyes in amazement.

'I wanted to tell you before we left. First of all, Papa never
meant to trick you out of your cup. He honestly thought it was
an attempt at swindle. I mean that someone here in Boston
stole the cup and then found a boy to pretend to be a long-lost
relative — and used the cup as proof. Your mother did leave
Boston with one of those cups. Papa did not mention that fact
in court. There really were five! He implied no more than four
ever came to this country.'

'He didn't imply it,' said Johnny. 'He swore it in court.'

'Oh, well — what of it? Let me talk.

'You see, he never knew that his niece, Vinny Lyte, had a
child. He had it from your father's family that both she and her

husband died of cholera almost as soon as they reached Marseilles. You see, your father was a naval surgeon, a prisoner of war while here in Boston. Oh, nothing very much,' she added scornfully, 'no great fortune or title. And Vinny Lyte fell in love with him. He was everywhere in society that year, although a prisoner of war, and, of course, the Lytes wouldn't hear of a marriage. He a Frenchman and a Catholic. And they told her if she ran off with him she would be cut off and she was never, never to return.'

'But she did?'

'Vinny was so wild she went right ahead. A ship's captain married them. Then his family, of course, would have none of her, she being a heretic. And then he died. They sent word to Papa — your grandfather was dead — that both had died. But his family sent Vinny to a convent — hoping the sisters would convert her, and there — three months after your father died — you were born. You were born in a convent in the south of France. Odd, isn't it?'

'Why do you call my mother Vinny?'

'We all did. Vinny Lyte, the wildest, handsomest girl in Boston. I was only a schoolgirl, but she was so beautiful and so gay. Oh, if you could but have seen her . . .'

'But I did . . .' He remembered the sweet, sad face of his sick mother. Was the wild and beautiful Vinny Lyte really the same woman? His mother patiently sewing and sewing to keep life in her son's body. She wanted no more life for herself. Teaching him to read. Making him those smocks. Knowing she had changed so much in such few years, she dared as Mrs. Tremain return to Boston, so her boy could grow up there, learn a decent trade. He thought of her agreeing with Mr. Lapham for his indenture. Smiling as she told him that when she died he was to go there.

'When I first saw you,' Miss Lavinia went on, 'I noticed one thing — but it set me thinking. I did nothing for a while, but this spring I asked one of my father's captains, bound for Marseilles, to feel about and find out the truth. I did so behind

Papa's back. Papa was already too ill to be bothered, but I knew he would want to do right.'

'Like swearing in court there never were but four Lyte cups.'

She colored angrily.

'Please let me do the telling. Don't you dare criticize the best man ever lived.'

Johnny had his own opinion on that.

'What was the one thing?' he asked.

'The way your hair turns down upon your forehead. That little peak. She was a dark girl. That widow's peak on her was very striking. And then that day in Mr. Dana's court. I did notice you walked like her, light and wild — like a panther, or' — she shrugged — 'maybe only like a tom-cat. I admired my cousin so, I may tend to exaggerate her qualities.'

'And what did your captain find out?'

'What I have just told you. And one thing more. Your father, the naval surgeon, was ashamed to be a prisoner of war. He told folks here his name was Latour. That's why your name Tremain meant nothing to us.'

'That is my true name?'

'Yes. But I haven't much time to talk. Only yesterday I told Papa. He's too ill to speak to you himself. He does want you to know that he did not deliberately cheat you — steal your cup.'

'Mother did take it with her?'

'Yes. It belonged to her. And her maid, Mrs. Dennie, went with her. It was Margaret Dennie who got her and you out of the convent and onto a ship her brother commanded and so to Townsend, Maine.'

'That's where I grew up. I remember Aunt Margaret. She died just before Mother took me to Boston.'

'Yes. And Papa says I am to promise you that he will write the whole thing out in black and white. When the war's over' — she shrugged — 'you can put in quite a claim for property — if there's any property left, which I doubt. Anything more you wish to ask me?'

'Yes. What relationship are you to me? What ought I to call you?'

She laughed out loud. 'Mercy, I don't know. What am I? Why, I suppose I'm sort of a cousin — but you'd better call me Aunt. Aunt Lavinia.'

He said it tentatively.

'Aunt Lavinia?'

You couldn't even secretly have a romantic passion for an aunt. The queer hold she had had on him for a year snapped.

She went to Johnny, stretched out a hand, and touched the widow's peak — all that he had ever got from the beautiful Vinny Lyte. Then she was gone.

- ʃ -

Johnny almost forgot the principal reason for his visit to the Lytes. He would have liked to sit quietly for a moment, brood over what Miss Lavinia had told him. Now was not the time to brood. Cilla and Mrs. Bessie came back together. He told them he must have Pumpkin's uniform. Mrs. Bessie said he was not to think of such a thing.

'If they catch you, Johnny, they will shoot you for impersonating a British soldier in wartime.'

'Lots of better men got shot today — Lexington — Concord . . . The British are sending boats back and forth tonight, taking off their men from Charlestown. I can sneak along over with them.'

'No, I forbid you, Johnny. You're going to stay right here and help Cilla and me look after this house.'

'I've got to go.'

'Who's going to look out for the Lyte horses if you walk out on us? General Gage has given his word no person or horse or any household gear will be touched, but we need a man to mind the stable.'

Johnny had an idea.

'Cilla, there is a thing you can do for me.'

'What?'

'Go to the Afric Queen and get my Goblin. Take him up here and turn him out to pasture with the Lyte horses. I guess he won't mind being a Tory for a while.'

'Can I ride him?'

'Yes, if you don't mind falling off.'

'I don't mind.' She looked excited and pleased.

Mrs. Bessie shook her head. 'And who's to care for the animals? You adding your Goblin makes things worse — not better — for us two womenfolk.'

'The coachman's going with the Lytes?'

'Of course. He's English-born.'

'Look here, Mr. Lorne, the printer — he's not what you'd call a coachman, but he was reared on a farm and he's in trouble.'

'British haven't arrested him yet?'

'He hid in a feather bed. But he can't stay there until we've driven the British out of Boston. Couldn't he and his wife and child move up here into the coachman's quarters and you sort of act as though he had always worked here?'

'Of course, they could. I'd be proud to have them. Cilla, just as soon as the *Unicorn* sails, you go to the Lornes and tell 'em to come right up and settle in.'

The girl nodded.

Johnny said, 'If he can get his little press to working again, I think he might like to bring that with him — go on with his "sedition," as they call it. He just about has to print.'

'We can hide his press, too. Nobody would dare hunt here for sedition — not after what Gage promised.'

'He'll be a very happy man, and now I've got to go. Cil, where's that uniform of Pumpkin's?'

'I hid it under my bed. I'll fetch it down.'

Mrs. Bessie shook her head, but she wasn't going to argue any more.

'How old are you, Johnny?' she asked.

'Sixteen.'

'And what's that — a boy or a man?'

He laughed. 'A boy in time of peace and a man in time of war.'

'Well, men have got the right to risk their lives for things they think worth it. God go with you, my young man. But if they shoot you, remember, I warned you.'

'I'll remember all right.'

Pumpkin had been a little stouter than Johnny. The uniform went on easily over the boy's breeches and jacket. Mrs. Bessie braided his hair for him and tied it tightly as the British regulars wore theirs.

'You couldn't say, could you,' Cilla asked him, 'why it is you have to get out tonight?'

'Yes. Doctor Warren told me to. 'Told me things to watch for and report on to him. I've got to find him — and Rab.'

'*Rab?*' The girl's voice sounded frightened.

'He was with the Lexington men. They stood up at dawn and the regulars killed quite a few of them.'

'Oh, but Rab?'

Johnny did not answer immediately. He was sitting at the kitchen table and Mrs. Bessie was still fussing with his hair. Not once since Doctor Warren had left had he spoken his name. He hadn't dared to let himself begin thinking about him. If he did, he knew he could not think of anything else. Now he had spoken his name, and emotions, fears, that he had held in check all day surged up through him. But he said quietly, 'I've got to find him. So be a good girl, Cil, and mind Mrs. Bessie.'

He stood up and put on a shiny black hat with a silver cockade on it and saluted smartly. He knew that the last man to wear this uniform had been shot for putting it off and there was a chance he'd get shot for putting it on.

The scarlet tunic, with its pale blue facings, the white cross-bands on his chest, the white breeches, made him feel like a different person. Now he was a private of the King's Own. He felt confident and happy. And Rab? Of course, he was all right.

You couldn't kill a fellow like Rab with just a handful of bullets.

He shook hands with Mrs. Bessie and, because his uniform made him feel grown up, he kissed Cilla good-bye just as he had the Sunday before seen Rab kiss his aunt. Not at all like a child being kissed by female relatives. But Cilla said mischievously, 'Why, I feel as if I were kissing Pumpkin.'

So Johnny stalked off down Beacon Hill with the proper martial strut. The littler they are, he thought, the more they strut. The physical act of strutting lifted his spirits. Made him feel bigger than he was. Of course that was why the little fellows do it.

And he wondered what had happened to Sergeant Gale.

XII. *A Man Can Stand Up*

BY INSIGNIFICANT back alleys and little-trod lanes, Johnny made his way to the ferry slip in North Boston. From there to Charlestown boats were going back and forth. The wounded were taken off first.

No civilian except only the Boston doctors, who had offered their services, were allowed close to the wharf. It was well Johnny had thought to put on Pumpkin's uniform. Mrs. Bessie had been right about one thing. A Yankee caught impersonating a British soldier would be shot. He kept well out of the moonlight and away from the flare of torches, and huddled between a warehouse and a tanning shed.

His uniform said he was a private in the Fourth Regiment — the King's Own. Pumpkin had not been big and bold enough for a grenadier nor clever enough for a light infantryman. Just a simple footsoldier. Obviously, a footsoldier of the Fourth would have left Boston that morning with Percy, would have mucked about for twelve hours shooting and being shot at. And he would not already be back in Boston unless he had been wounded. The smartness of the uniform which at first had delighted him he now saw was a danger. He lay down and rolled in the muck of the tanning shed. Tore his jacket on a nail and pulled off a button. The black and silver hat he stamped on, banged out of shape, and pulled on well over his eyes. He put mud on his face; pricked his wrist, and smeared his cheek with blood. Then he stepped out on the wharf.

An officer who had been in town all day moved up to him. Johnny saluted.

'Wounded?'

'Not much, sir.'

'Well, better report to the medical officers. They are using that house as a temporary hospital.'

'Others are worse off than I. I'll wait till the bad ones have been tended to.'

'That's the spirit. How was the fighting?'

'Very heavy, sir.'

'Can those damned Yankees shoot straight?'

Johnny had been around the regulars enough to know that was a question that should be answered by oaths (in spite of Mr. Lapham's training).

The officer laughed and moved down the wharf.

Although no townsmen, except only the doctors, were permitted on the wharf, Johnny knew that hundreds of them stood well back and in darkness, gloating. They were not saying much, only watching. Then one man began to whistle and the next took it up and the next and the next. The whistling was shrill as a fife. They had not forgotten the prophecy of that morning, 'They go out by "Yankee Doodle," but they'll dance to it before nightfall!'

'Yankee Doodle' filled the darkness as the eerie shrilling of the hylas fill black swamps in spring.

Four more boats were coming in. Johnny dared move out onto the wharf, but he still kept well in shadow. More wounded. Could these be the very men who had started out so confidently? Bedraggled, dirty, torn uniforms, torn flesh, lost equipment. Faces ghastly with fatigue and pain. Some were twisting and crying out. The first two boats were filled with privates. They had been packed in, and now were being tossed ashore, like so much cordwood. Most of them were pathetically good and patient, but he saw an officer strike a man who was screaming.

Johnny's hands clenched. 'It is just as James Otis said,'

he thought. 'We are fighting, partly, for just that. Because a man is a private is no reason he should be treated like cordwood.'

The third boat was moving in with a creak of oarlocks and he heard an exclamation, 'Colonel Smith.' There were only two wounded in this boat, for both were officers. Getting the fat colonel up and off the bottom of the dory was heavy work. He was rolled upon a stretcher and carried to the hospital. He had been shot through the leg. Johnny had never seen Colonel Smith except when he was rosy with good brandy, pompous with pride in himself and the men he commanded. Now he was tallow-colored and as deflated as a pricked bladder.

The other officer crawled off unaided. The torch suddenly lighted his face. A dark young face, his lips locked to keep down any cry of pain. One arm in a bloody sling. Rab — oh, Rab ... Of course not. It was Lieutenant Stranger.

Instinctively Johnny started forward to help him, for everyone else was so busy with the wounded colonel, Stranger was left to shift for himself. The boy thought in time of his own danger. How curious a thing is war! Last week — no, yesterday — this man was, in a way, his friend. Lieutenant Stranger walked stiffly and in agony toward the hospital.

And then another boat, more wounded. The sight of them sickened Johnny. Gray and twisted lips. Hollow eyes. 'But I can't leave ... I've got to stay about, watch my chance for a ride over.'

Next what was left of Colonel Smith's command began to arrive. They had been marching, and much of the time under fire, for twenty-four hours. They had gone without food or water. As the men stumbled off the boats, there were plenty of questions and answers. Johnny would not be able to tell Doctor Warren the exact number of casualties the British had suffered, but he could tell him that they thought they were heavy.

The very last man of Colonel Smith's command to return was Major Pitcairn. His face still looked cheerful and confident. They had been licked, had they? All right. The tough old marine had been licked before. As he stepped ashore, suddenly the soldiers about the ferry slip began to cheer. 'Let's get back at 'em, Major,' they yelled.

He grinned and stuck out his jaw. 'We'll take another try,' he said, 'and if next time we don't clean up on those . . .' he went off into the profanity for which he was famous to describe what he thought of their enemies, and a roar went up from the men.

Now Johnny learned that the bulk of Percy's Brigade would be left over in Charlestown camped on Bunker Hill until the next morning. Johnny believed the time had come for him to act.

The sailors from one of the boats were standing about arguing whether or not they were supposed to go to the *Somerset* for the night, or over to Charlestown. Johnny ran up to them. 'I've a message for Earl Percy.' He was breathing hard from excitement, but it might have come from running. 'Get me over quick, boys.'

'Oh, you go whistle for your general,' said one of them. 'You go whistle for your mama. We're sailors, not soldiers, see?'

'Just let me take your boat . . .'

'That's irregular.'

'Well, I've got to get over and I can't swim, can I?'

'You ask Lieutenant Swift. He's in charge of us.'

The last thing Johnny wanted was to be questioned by an officer.

'Will you or won't you take me across?'

'Not without orders — you little wabbler.'

'What's up, men?' a quiet voice asked. The sailors saluted.

'This here baby-boy says he's got a message for Earl Percy. He wants us to row him over.'

'Then you will do so.'

'Aye, aye, sir.'

Nobody had asked to see Johnny's letter.

Johnny was rowed across and landed at a wharf in Charlestown. Quickly he slipped up a cobbled street, turned into a garden, stripped off his uniform and hung it on a clothesline. He found a pump and washed his face.

Although past midnight lights showed in all but the abandoned houses. The people of Charlestown were in a panic. They dared not go to bed with over a thousand British soldiers suddenly camped upon them — defeated soldiers whose mood might turn ugly. These soldiers only wanted to be let alone, allowed to sleep, but the inhabitants thought they might butcher them all.

Johnny glanced in at two or three taverns. British officers were sleeping in chairs, on benches, on the floors, but he remembered that one of the tavern-keepers was a prominent Son of Liberty. There he tiptoed in among the sleeping guests, found a nine-year-old girl servant hidden behind a flour barrel in the pantry and got her to lead him to the summer house where the tavern-keeper and his wife had moved for the night.

From the tavern-keeper he learned for the first time what had happened after the skirmish at Lexington. Colonel Smith had indeed marched on to Concord, possessed the town, destroyed such military stores as had not yet been hidden. And there had been another skirmish. You might even call it a battle, at North Bridge. But from everywhere, all about, had come the Minute Men. Obviously Smith had been a little afraid of leaving the safety of the village. He would wait where he was for the reinforcements he had sent for, even before Lexington.

But Percy did not come and did not come. Every moment more and more Minute Men were arriving, surrounding the village. At noon Smith had decided to try to take his men back. He dared wait no longer. Then the shooting began. The Minute Men, from behind stone walls and barns, trees, bushes, had opened fire. Beaten and bloody, almost in a panic, Colonel Smith's troops struggled through to Lexington. Not until then did Percy's reserves arrive. If they had not come, every one of Smith's command would have been killed.

And from Lexington the British had drawn back to Menotomy. And from there the wounded scarlet dragon had crawled over Charlestown Common, crossed into safety at Charlestown Neck, and were covered by the *Somerset's* guns. And here they were. They had been badly beaten.

'What of Doctor Warren?'

He had been everywhere, one moment fighting and dressing the wounds the next. He had fought like a wildcat. But the inn-keeper had no idea where he was now.

'He didn't get hurt?'

'I'm told he had a lock of hair shot away. He came that close to death.'

'Have you, by any chance, heard how it fared with the men of Lexington?'

'I believe seven or eight of them were killed in that first volley.'

'Do you know their names?'

'No. But by the time the British got back to Lexington from Concord, the Lexington men were ready for them. And they fit 'em and harried 'em all the way to Charlestown.'

- 2 -

Johnny knew he had no chance of leaving Charlestown until the few hundred fresh men who had been rowed over to hold the Neck had been withdrawn. Next morning he watched them go and waited his chance. It was ten o'clock when he left the town. People were running about. Each had a story to tell. Many women, children, and timid folk had spent the night hidden in the clay pits. They, too, were coming out of hiding.

Johnny, from sheer high spirits, jumped the now deserted breastwork the British had thrown up so hastily the night before. He had seen so much of the British army he had come half to believe that they were, even as they said, invincible. No Yankee farmers could stand up to them. He had been impressed with their perfection of equipment, discipline, grand gaudy uniforms, the pride of their officers. 'We beat them. We Yankees did. God *was* with us.'

He took the road for Cambridge, crossing desolate Charles-

town Common with its salt marshes, clay pits, gallows and
gibbet. Everywhere he saw signs of the retreat: The heavy
tracks of cannon. The road itself beaten to muck under anxious
feet. He saw lost hats, uniforms, muskets even, and he saw a
group of men getting a horse out of a pit. The horse was taking
the matter sensibly, not struggling, seeming to understand that
the oxen being tackled would pull him out. It was Colonel
Smith's Sandy. Johnny looked upon this as a good omen and
walked forward whistling, but his whistling stopped abruptly.
He had met his first burial party. He noted the faces of the men
and women following the dead countryman. Next he saw a cellar.
hole with smoke and stench still rising from it.

There was a tavern, and in the taproom men sat about drinking rum and boasting of their great deeds. Johnny did not doubt
but they all had done as well as they said, but he was in no
mood to listen. So, having bought bread, a handful of salt
alewives, and asked if anyone knew where Doctor Warren was,
he quickly left. They told him to try Cambridge.

Here a strange thing had happened apparently overnight.
Milling about were hundreds upon hundreds, perhaps thousands
of Minute Men. They had come as they were from the plow,
the shop, even from the pulpit. Most of them had guns in their
hands, but there were hardly a dozen overcoats among them.
No blankets. They had no food except the little their women
had tied up for them — enough to take a man through one
day's fighting. No tents, no extra munitions. What now was to
be done with them? What were they to do with themselves?
Should they go home now — having accomplished the mission
for which they had been summoned — or were they to stay and
undertake the siege of Boston? They had no cannon. Seemingly
they had nothing but the guns in their hands and the fire in
their hearts.

A man, who told Johnny he was a colonel — he did have a
pair of home-made epaulets sewed to his old hunting shirt —
said that the Committee of Safety was sitting at the Hastings'
house, trying to work out some way these civilians might be

turned into soldiers. Doctor Warren was chairman of this committee. Johnny went to the Hastings' house, where he met Paul
Revere, who told him Doctor Warren had left for Lexington.

Lexington! It was to Lexington of all places in the world
Johnny wanted to go. Now he had an excuse for it. This day
like the one before was warm and beautiful. It was one of those
silent, dreamy spring days when sunshine pours down upon the
yet-cold earth and the earth turns in its sleep. No cloud in the
sky. Not one cat's-paw of breeze.

He stepped along rapidly. Not until he reached Menotomy
was he once again following the tracks of the defeated British
army. A parcel of folk were standing about a stout old grandame.
Six grenadiers had surrendered to her and asked for her protection. She had no idea the battle was moving in so close. Old
Mother Batherick had been out digging dandelions.

In every house left standing, Johnny saw bullet holes and,
once again, a burial party. Twelve men, hastily thrown upon
an ox sled, were being drawn to their single grave. And there
were British dead to bury. Where should they be buried? The
minister said they were to be laid in the lot set aside for slaves,
but all who had hats doffed them as friend and foe passed by.
Johnny had no hat, but he stood with bowed head.

He walked on. The sight of a young woman drawing water
was too much for him. He stopped and asked her for a drink.
As he sat on a wall and drank from a wooden bucket, she answered his questions. Was he now in Lexington?

Yes, he had just crossed the town line.

'Those Lexington men. How many were killed on the Green
yesterday?'

'Eight,' she said.

As he asked his next question, his voice sounded unreal, to
himself.

'Happens you know their names?'

She turned a stony face and stared at him. 'These are their
names,' she said. 'Let them never be forgot.' She stretched out
her hands and counted on her fingers. 'Jonathan Harrington,'

she said, 'and Caleb, too. Robert Munroe, Jonas Parker, Samuel Hedley, Isaac Muzzy, Nathaniel Wyman, John Brown.'

Rab's was not one. Johnny smiled.

'Do you know how the Silsbees fared?'

She said the women and children had, like so many others, gone away to hide. She believed they had gone to Woburn, but by now they might be back again at Silsbee's Cove.

'And the men went out fighting?'

'Of course. All except Grandsire. He wouldn't hide with the women and farm animals and he couldn't go fight. He was sot on sitting it out under his own roof.'

Then Johnny went on his way passing Munroe Tavern where Percy had joined Colonel Smith — he could see the marks of the cannon and the destruction they caused. So he was in the village. The first thing he noticed as he stood looking down at the Green was that the old meeting house had been knocked into a cocked hat by a cannon ball.

-3-

So late in the afternoon of the gentle April day, Johnny came down upon Lexington Green. The smashed meeting house with its tiny wooden belfry was before him. Buckman Tavern was to his right. The Green itself was laced over with the shadows of new leaves. It was here the men had stood; here upon this Green they had formed a thin pathetic line, a handful of farmers to resist the march of seven hundred British regulars. Here they had died. Oh, it was so hopeless and so brave, you might laugh. And you might cry. The inside of Johnny's nose began to prick and he brushed his arm across his face.

But it was his duty to find Doctor Warren — not to stand gawking at the little battlefield. Thus far he had had no luck at all in locating the Doctor, but at last his luck turned. He recognized his chaise and that rabbit-ear little pacing mare of the

Doctor's, hitched before the Harrington house. The Doctor was standing on the steps, and about him were a group of women all crying. Johnny knew why. Jonathan Harrington, wounded in the skirmish, had been able to drag himself thus far to his own house and die upon that threshold. Doctor Warren was leaving them now.

He had on no hat, but a bandage about his thick fair hair. The bullet had grazed his scalp. Johnny went up to him and handed him the lists he had had time to write down during the night at Charlestown. The Doctor read it, nodded, and put it in his pocket. He was too tired to say much, but there was one question Johnny had to ask.

'Doctor Warren . . . when the Lexington men stood here . . . and the British over there and fired at them . . . I know the names of those who were killed. But when the British came back from Concord and the fight went on all the way to Charlestown and the Lexington men went after them . . . I don't know who was killed then.'

'You are hunting for Rab?'

'Yes, I've got to find him. Nobody seems able to tell me.'

'I'll tell you, Johnny.' Tired as he was and surfeited with the sight of blood and suffering, he broke the news as best he could.

'Rab stood here . . . just about where we are standing now. He did not go when Major Pitcairn told them to disperse, he kept on standing — with the other men — his musket in his hands.'

Johnny could see him, clear as in the flesh. Rab standing unafraid in the cool gray of earliest dawn, the musket in his hands, the 'look' in his eyes — that fierce sudden look.

'But after that. Did Rab follow the British to Charlestown?'

'No. He was wounded in that first volley. He got it pretty bad.'

'You mean very bad, don't you?'

'Yes, very.'

'I see,' but Johnny saw nothing. The fresh spring world

turned black before him, but even in this darkness he could
still see Rab, chin up, shoulders squared — not afraid.

'Where? . . .' he asked.

'He was carried to Buckman's Tavern. I saw him yesterday.
I was about to go there now. But . . . don't expect too much.'

'No.'

'Rab played a man's part. Look that you do the same.'

'I will.' He knew the Doctor meant he wasn't to cry or take
on. He'd got to take it quietly.

-4-

Doctor Warren whistled to his mare who followed him like a
dog. Johnny entered the tavern on Warren's heels and to their
right was the taproom, full and overfull. Johnny half-heard the
same conversation going on here that he had listened to when
he had stopped to buy food at that other tavern. Had they all
been heroes? Or did they just talk — and do nothing? Rab
never had said much, but he had done all a man might.

The boy had been carried to a back chamber on the second
floor. He was not in bed, but sitting up in an armchair propped
with pillows. A woman of the inn had been sitting with him,
quietly knitting. She got up when the Doctor and Johnny
entered the room and left without speaking.

Johnny had been fearful that Rab would be suffering, crying
out, struggling like other wounded men he had seen: afraid that
with death so close something of that aloof dignity he had always
had would be shattered. He had lived with Rab a year and a
half, and yet he had never really known him — not known him
inside out as, say, he had known the hated Dove.

But half-sitting as he was, Rab did not seem at first very different from always. His face was white but not drawn. The eyes
very dark and wide. Rab smiled.

'You got out all right?'

'Yes.'

'How's Boston?'

'The British are furious that we licked them so.'

There was a sudden trickle of blood at one corner of his mouth. Rab wiped it away. In these few hours his hands had grown white, weak, thin. And as he turned his face, the afternoon light fell across it. Johnny saw the flesh seemed translucent. There were lavender circles about the eyes.

'I've had a lot of time to think,' said Rab at last. 'Just lying here. Do you remember that marketwoman who lost her pig? Its name was Myra and it could do tricks . . . then I looked up and you were standing there looking like a robber-boy with your hand in your pocket?'

'I remember.'

Rab lay with his eyes shut for a little while, remembering other things — things perhaps Johnny did not share. Back into his childhood in Lexington — the important and unimportant things jumbled together. A favorite dog. The death of his father. The first day he went to school and the first day he drilled with the Minute Men. He moved a little restlessly and said, 'Colonel Nesbit . . . remember. And he told me, "Go buy a popgun, boy." Well . . . a popgun would have done me just as well in the end.' This idea fretted him a little. Doctor Warren wet a cloth in a basin of water and wiped his bloody mouth.

'There's my musket — over there. It's better now than any *they* have. I was always kind of bothered to think I might have to stand up to them without a good gun in my hands. But I had it all right.'

He was thanking Johnny for getting it for him.

'But I never did get to fire it. They shot first.'

The trickle of blood became a stream. Doctor Warren was bending over him, holding his shoulders. Johnny walked disconsolately about the chamber. He looked out the window. He picked up a pewter candlestick and examined the maker's mark. He heard Warren saying, 'Steady, boy,' and, after a moment, 'Is it better so?'

'It is . . . better so.' Rab whispered. But the next moment he said, quite naturally, 'Johnny.'

Johnny went to him, sat on the floor beside his chair and put his hands over Rab's thin ones.

'Yes, Rab?'

'You can have that musket. I sort of like to think of its going on. I've put a better stock on it, changed the angle of the steel. Look at that flint. The one it had was too smooth. I've knapped it.'

'I'll take good care of it.'

'And there's another thing you can do for me.'

'Anything.'

'Go to Silsbee's Cove. See if the women have come back yet from hiding. Grandsire will be about . . . he said he wouldn't go off hiding. He'd sit it out — in his chair.'

'I'll go.'

Then Rab began to smile. Everything he had never put in words was in that smile.

But as he was leaving the room, Johnny saw that once more Doctor Warren was bending over him. He heard him say.

'How is that? Is it better?'

'Yes . . . it is better so.'

- *5* -

At Silsbee's Cove there were no women, children, or farm animals about, except a couple of weaned calves in the calf pasture. When the warning came, it had probably been decided they were too hard to catch and cart. Johnny looked at the deserted barn. Hens were about. They could live for days on the spilled oats and rye. There were two dogs who came up to him, telling him they had not been fed. 'I'll bet they took you with them,' said Johnny, 'and you sneaked back home, eh, boys?'

The cat stuck close to him. It was a big orange tom and Johnny knew it was Grandsire's favorite. It was mewing and rubbing about him. He picked it up. 'You wouldn't be bothered to go out and catch a mouse in the barn like other cats, would you?' he said. But if Grandsire had not gone away to hide like the other noncombatants, he wondered why he had not fed the animals. He entered the old house, which was unlocked. The tom, confident that now he would be fed in the elegant way he was accustomed to, began to knead his paws and his purring grew hoarse with triumph.

'Grandsire?' Johnny called.

There was no answer, and the red armchair, where the old gentleman usually sat since his game leg had grown so bad, was empty. Major Silsbee was not there. Johnny went to the larder and found bread and sour milk for the animals. He welcomed this small duty. It kept him from thinking. The tom he fed in the kitchen. The basin of food for the dogs he put in the yard. Where, where, was the old gentleman? Suddenly he had an idea, and he ran back into the kitchen and looked over the hearth. Grandsire's old gun was gone, and so was the powder-horn he had carried to Louisburg back in 1745. And so was Grandsire Silsbee.

Johnny walked back to the village, his head bent and his hands in his pockets. A numbness, half-emotional, half-physical, was stealing up through him. His feet felt like lead. His mind seized upon little trivial things, like that orange tom-cat of Grandsire Silsbee's. He noticed a jubilant little girl with a grenadier bearskin hat on her head, half over her face. He could not help but notice the regimental number on the cap. The grenadier likely dead by now, had been a soldier of the Tenth.

He saw Doctor Warren's chaise before Buckman's Tavern. In the lower entry Doctor Warren was waiting for him.

'Rab?'

The Doctor dropped his eyes. 'Sometime,' he said, 'we will know how to stop bleeding like that. We don't now.'

'He sent me away because he knew he had to die?'

'Yes. He knew.'

Doctor Warren moved into the empty parlor of the inn away from the noisy group in the taproom — telling over and over of their great deeds.

'There's no need for you to go upstairs.'

Johnny nodded. He had moved off into a strange lonely world where nothing could seem real — not even Rab's death.

The woman of the inn came in on tiptoe. She had a tray of food for the Doctor. Tired out, the young man sank into a chair, his fair, bandaged, aching head in his hands.

'You remember that night,' he said, 'that last meeting of the Observers. James Otis came, although we didn't want him. I can't remember much of what he said, but I remember how his words made the gooseskin on my arms.'

'I'll never forget it. He said . . . so a man can stand up.'

'Yes. And some of us would die — so other men can stand up on their feet like men. A great many are going to die for that. They have in the past. They will a hundred years from now — two hundred. God grant there will always be men good enough. Men like Rab.'

The quiet woman came in again. She had tossed up an omelet for the Doctor and silently put it before him.

'Will you go up and fetch down the musket from the back chamber?' he asked her. She nodded and did as he asked.

Doctor Warren began to eat as doctors will even under greatest strain.

'Can't you eat, boy?'

'Not yet.'

'Try and get some sleep.'

'No.'

Johnny was on his feet pacing about the room. He was too stunned to feel much now. Later, he thought. Tomorrow, next day. Then I'll know that Rab is dead. But it can't hurt me now. But next year, all my life . . .

His eye caught on the musket. He took it up, holding it close to the light of the window, fingering and examining it to see those improvements Rab said he had made on it. Rab had not taken one shot with it on Lexington Green. Never had a chance. Doctor Warren was standing beside him.

'Johnny, put down that gun. Here by this window. Lay your right hand down like that, so.'

Johnny felt no more shame over his burned hand. He did as the Doctor bade him. He felt the cool, clean hands bending his fingers, twisting his thumb until he gritted his teeth.

'Johnny, that hand is not as bad as you think. Burned, wasn't it?'

'Yes.'

'As you stood there holding that gun, it was the first time I've had a good look at it. Was it kept flat while healing?'

'No.'

'I suppose your master called in some old herb woman to care for it?'

'A midwife. Yes.'

'Bah . . . these midwives! Any doctor in Boston would have known . . . You see, the thumb is pulled about like that, not because of any basic injury, but by scar tissues.'

'What do you mean?'

'I mean that if you have the courage I can cut through the scar — free the thumb.'

'My hand good and free once more?'

'I can't promise too much. I don't know whether you can ever go back to your silver work. But not even Paul Revere is going to make much silver for a while.'

'Will it be good enough to hold this gun?'

'I think I can promise you that.'

'The silver can wait. When can you, Doctor Warren? I've got the courage.'

'I'll get some of those men in the taproom to hold your arm still while I operate.'

'No need. I can hold it still myself.'

The Doctor looked at him with compassionate eyes.

'Yes, I believe you can. You go walk about in the fresh air, while I get my instruments ready.'

Johnny stood upon the Green and looked about him. He heard a woman calling, 'Chick, chick, chick.' From a near-by cow shed he heard milk spurting into a pail. A tap of metal on metal: his trained ear told him a gunsmith was at work.

He could smell turned earth and gummy buds. And sweet wood somewhere burning. His nostrils trembled. Almost could they recapture the gunpowder of yesterday. So fair a day now drawing to its close. Green with spring, dreaming of the future yet wet with blood.

This was his land and these his people.

The cow that lowed, the man who milked, the chickens that came running and the woman who called them, the fragrance streaming from the plowed land and the plowman. These he possessed. The skillful hands of the unseen gunsmith were his hands. The old woman throwing stones at crows who cawed and derided her was his old woman — and they his crows. The wood smoke rising from the home-hearths rose from his heart.

He felt nothing could hurt him on this day. Not Rab's death nor the surgeon's knife. He felt free, light, unreal, and utterly alone.... Tomorrow — next day — it would be different, but today is today.

Then far away, but coming nearer and nearer down along Menotomy road, he heard the throb of a drum. Men coming back from Charlestown. He stood, turned his head to listen. The shuffle of feet. A fife began to toot. It was ill-played. Maybe a foolish tune, but Johnny warmed to hear it. For once — once more — Yankee Doodle was going to town.

Everywhere else in the village was silence. The music, small as the chirping of a cricket, filled that silence. Down the road came twenty or thirty tired and ragged men. Some were blood-stained. No uniforms. A curious arsenal of weapons. The long horizontal light of the sinking sun struck into their faces and made them seem much alike. Thin-faced in the manner of Yankee men. High cheek-boned. Unalterably determined. The tired men marched unevenly, but Johnny noticed the swing of the lithe, independent bodies. The set of chin and shoulders. Rab had been like that.

Please God, out of this New England soil such men would forever rise up ready to fight when need came. The one generation after the other.

Close on the heels of the marching men was an old chaise containing their commanding officer. For if you couldn't get to the fight on foot, you went on horseback — and if not on horseback, you went in a chaise.

It was Grandsire Silsbee, with his old gun across his knees.

Johnny started to run to him, to shout, 'Grandsire, Grandsire, you haven't heard yet . . . Rab is dead.'

But he knew the old Major wouldn't stop. He had to get his men on to Cambridge and the siege of Boston.

True, Rab had died. Hundreds would die, but not the thing they died for.

'A man can stand up . . .'

THE END

Turn the page for a special preview
of the
1996 NEWBERY HONOR BOOK

(ISBN 0-385-32175-9)

Enter the hilarious world of ten-year-old Kenny and his
family, the Weird Watsons of Flint, Michigan. There's
Momma, Dad, little sister Joetta, Kenny, and Byron, who's
thirteen and an "official juvenile delinquent." When Momma
and Dad decide it's time for a visit to Grandma, Dad comes
home with the amazing Ultra-Glide, and the Watsons set out
on a trip like no other. They're heading south. They're going
to Birmingham, Alabama, toward one of the darkest
moments in American history.

**Don't miss *The Watsons Go to Birmingham–1963*
by Christopher Paul Curtis.
On sale now from Delacorte Press!**

1. And You Wonder Why We Get Called the Weird Watsons

I t was one of those super-duper-cold Saturdays. One of those days that when you breathed out your breath kind of hung frozen in the air like a hunk of smoke and you could walk along and look exactly like a train blowing out big, fat, white puffs of smoke.

It was so cold that if you were stupid enough to go outside your eyes would automatically blink a thousand times all by themselves, probably so the juice inside of them wouldn't freeze up. It was so cold that if you spit, the slob would be an ice cube before it hit the ground. It was about a zillion degrees below zero.

It was even cold inside our house. We put sweaters and hats and scarves and three pairs of socks on and still were cold. The thermostat was turned all the way up and the furnace was banging and sounding like it was about to blow up but it still felt like Jack Frost had moved in with us.

All of my family sat real close together on the couch under a blanket. Dad said this would generate a little heat but he didn't have to tell us this, it seemed like the cold automatically made us want to get together and huddle up. My little sister, Joetta, sat in the middle and all you could see were her eyes because she had a scarf wrapped around her head. I was next to her, and on the outside was my mother.

Momma was the only one who wasn't born in Flint so the cold was coldest to her. All you could see were her eyes too, and they were shooting bad looks at Dad. She always blamed him for bringing her all the way from Alabama to Michigan, a state she called a giant icebox. Dad was bundled up on the other side of Joey, trying to look at anything but Momma. Next to Dad, sitting with a little space between them, was my older brother, Byron.

Byron had just turned thirteen so he was officially a teenage juvenile delinquent and didn't think it was "cool" to touch anybody or let anyone touch him, even if it meant he froze to death. Byron had tucked the blanket between him and Dad down into the cushion of the couch to make sure he couldn't be touched.

Dad turned on the TV to try to make us forget how cold we were but all that did was get him in trouble. There was a special news report on Channel 12 telling about how bad the weather was and Dad groaned when the guy said, "If you think it's cold now, wait until tonight, the temperature is expected to drop into record-low territory, possibly reaching the negative twenties! In fact, we won't be seeing anything above zero for the next four to five days!" He was smiling when he said this but none of the Watson family thought it was funny. We all looked over at Dad. He just shook his head and pulled the blanket over his eyes.

Then the guy on TV said, "Here's a little something we can use to brighten our spirits and give us some hope for the future: The temperature in Atlanta, Georgia, is forecast to reach . . ." Dad coughed real loud and jumped off the couch to turn the TV off but we all heard the weatherman say, ". . . the mid-seventies!" The guy might as well have tied Dad to a tree and said, "Ready, aim, fire!"

"Atlanta!" Momma said. "That's a hundred and fifty miles from home!"

"Wilona . . . ," Dad said.

"I knew it," Momma said. "I knew I should have listened to Moses Henderson!"

"Who?" I asked.

Dad said, "Oh Lord, not that sorry story. You've got to let me tell about what happened with him."

Momma said, "There's not a whole lot to tell, just a story about a young girl who made a bad choice. But if you do tell it, make sure you get all the facts right."

We all huddled as close as we could get because we knew Dad was going to try to make us forget about being cold by cutting up. Me and Joey started smiling right away, and Byron tried to look cool and bored.

"Kids," Dad said, "I almost wasn't your father. You guys came real close to having a clown for a daddy named Hambone Henderson. . . ."

"Daniel Watson, you stop right there. You're the one

who started that 'Hambone' nonsense. Before you started that everyone called him his Christian name. Moses. And he was a respectable boy too, he wasn't a clown at all."

"But the name stuck, didn't it? Hambone Henderson. Me and your granddaddy called him that because the boy had a head shaped just like a hambone, had more knots and bumps on his head than a dinosaur. So as you guys sit here giving me these dirty looks because it's a little chilly outside ask yourselves if you'd rather be a little cool or go through life being known as the Hambonettes."

Me and Joey cracked up, Byron kind of chuckled and Momma put her hand over her mouth. She did this whenever she was going to give a smile because she had a great big gap between her front teeth. If Momma thought something was funny, first you'd see her trying to keep her lips together to hide the gap, then, if the smile got to be too strong, you'd see the gap for a hot second before Momma's hand would come up to cover it, then she'd crack up too.

Laughing only encouraged Dad to cut up more, so when he saw the whole family thinking he was funny he really started putting on a show.

He stood in front of the TV. "Yup, Hambone Henderson proposed to your mother around the same time I did. Fought dirty too, told your momma a pack of lies about me and when she didn't believe them he told her a pack of lies about Flint."

Dad started talking Southern-style, imitating this

Hambone guy. "Wilona, I heard tell about the weather up that far north in Flint, Mitch-again, heard it's colder than inside a icebox. Seen a movie about it, think it was made in Flint. Movie called *Nanook of the North*. Yup, do believe for sure it was made in Flint. Uh-huh, Flint, Mitch-again.

"Folks there live in these things called igloos. According to what I seen in this here movie most the folks in Flint is Chinese. Don't believe I seen nan one colored person in the whole dang city. You a 'Bama gal, don't believe you'd be too happy living in no igloo. Ain't got nothing against 'em, but don't believe you'd be too happy living 'mongst a whole slew of Chinese folks. Don't believe you'd like the food. Only thing them Chinese folks in that movie et was whales and seals. Don't believe you'd like no whale meat. Don't taste a lick like chicken. Don't taste like pork at all."

Momma pulled her hand away from her mouth. "Daniel Watson, you are one lying man! Only thing you said that was true was that being in Flint is like living in a igloo. I knew I should have listened to Moses. Maybe these babies mighta been born with lumpy heads but at least they'da had *warm* lumpy heads!

"You know Birmingham is a good place, and I don't mean just the weather either. The life is slower, the people are friendlier—"

"Oh yeah," Dad interrupted, "they're a laugh a minute down there. Let's see, where was that 'Colored Only' bathroom downtown?"

"Daniel, you know what I mean, things aren't perfect

but people are more honest about the way they feel"—
she took her mean eyes off Dad and put them on Byron—"and folks there do know how to respect their
parents."

Byron rolled his eyes like he didn't care. All he did
was tuck the blanket farther into the couch's cushion.

Dad didn't like the direction the conversation was
going so he called the landlord for the hundredth time.
The phone was still busy.

"That snake in the grass has got his phone off the
hook. Well, it's going to be too cold to stay here tonight, let me call Cydney. She just had that new furnace
put in, maybe we can spend the night there." Aunt
Cydney was kind of mean but her house was always
warm so we kept our fingers crossed that she was home.

Everyone, even Byron, cheered when Dad got Aunt
Cydney and she told us to hurry over before we froze to
death.

Dad went out to try and get the Brown Bomber
started. That was what we called our car. It was a 1948
Plymouth that was dull brown and real big, Byron said it
was turd brown. Uncle Bud gave it to Dad when it was
thirteen years old and we'd had it for two years. Me and
Dad took real good care of it but some of the time it
didn't like to start up in the winter.

After five minutes Dad came back in huffing and
puffing and slapping his arms across his chest.

"Well, it was touch and go for a while, but the Great
Brown One pulled through again!" Everyone cheered,

but me and Byron quit cheering and started frowning right away. By the way Dad smiled at us we knew what was coming next. Dad pulled two ice scrapers out of his pocket and said, "O.K., boys, let's get out there and knock those windows out."

We moaned and groaned and put some more coats on and went outside to scrape the car's windows. I could tell by the way he was pouting that Byron was going to try and get out of doing his share of the work.

"I'm not going to do your part, Byron, you'd better do it and I'm not playing either."

"Shut up, punk."

I went over to the Brown Bomber's passenger side and started hacking away at the scab of ice that was all over the windows. I finished Momma's window and took a break. Scraping ice off of windows when it's that cold can kill you!

I didn't hear any sound coming from the other side of the car so I yelled out, "I'm serious, Byron, I'm not doing that side too, and I'm only going to do half the windshield, I don't care what you do to me." The windshield on the Bomber wasn't like the new 1963 cars, it had a big bar running down the middle of it, dividing it in half.

"Shut your stupid mouth, I got something more important to do right now."

I peeked around the back of the car to see what By was up to. The only thing he'd scraped off was the outside mirror and he was bending down to look at himself in it. He saw me and said, "You know what, square? I must be adopted, there just ain't no way two folks as ugly as your momma and daddy coulda give birth to someone as sharp as me!"

He was running his hands over his head like he was brushing his hair.

I said, "Forget you," and went back over to the other side of the car to finish the back window. I had half of the ice off when I had to stop again and catch my breath. I heard Byron mumble my name.

I said, "You think I'm stupid? It's not going to work this time." He mumbled my name again. It sounded like his mouth was full of something. I knew this was a trick, I knew this was going to be How to Survive a Blizzard, Part Two.

How to Survive a Blizzard, Part One had been last night when I was outside playing in the snow and Byron and his running buddy, Buphead, came walking by. Buphead has officially been a juvenile delinquent even longer than Byron.

"Say, kid," By had said, "you wanna learn somethin' that might save your stupid life one day?"

I should have known better, but I was bored and I think maybe the cold weather was making my brain slow, so I said, "What's that?"

"We gonna teach you how to survive a blizzard."

"How?"

Byron put his hands in front of his face and said, "This is the most important thing to remember, O.K.?"

"Why?"

"Well, first we gotta show you what it feels like to be trapped in a blizzard. You ready?" He whispered something to Buphead and they both laughed.

"I'm ready."

I should have known that the only reason Buphead and By would want to play with me was to do something mean.

"O.K.," By said, "first thing you gotta worry about is high winds."

Byron and Buphead each grabbed one of my arms and one of my legs and swung me between them going, "*Wooo,* blizzard warnings! Blizzard warnings! *Wooo!* Take cover!"

Buphead counted to three and on the third swing they let me go in the air. I landed headfirst in a snowbank.

But that was O.K. because I had on three coats, two sweaters, a T-shirt, three pairs of pants and four socks along with a scarf, a hat and a hood. These guys couldn't have hurt me if they'd thrown me off the Empire State Building!

After I climbed out of the snowbank they started laughing and so did I.

"Cool, Baby Bruh," By said, "you passed that part of the test with a B-plus, what you think, Buphead?"

Buphead said, "Yeah, I'd give the little punk a A."

They whispered some more and started laughing again.

"O.K.," By said, "second thing you gotta learn is how to keep your balance in a high wind. You gotta be good at this so you don't get blowed into no polar bear dens."

They put me in between them and started making me spin round and round, it seemed like they spun me for about half an hour. When slob started flying out of my mouth they let me stop and I wobbled around for a while before they pushed me back in the same snow-bank.

When everything stopped going in circles I got up and we all laughed again.

They whispered some more and then By said, "What you think, Buphead? He kept his balance a good long time, I'm gonna give him a A-minus."

"I ain't as hard a grader as you, I'ma give the little punk a double A-minus."

"O.K., Kenny, now the last part of Surviving a Blizzard, you ready?"

"Yup!"

"You passed the wind test and did real good on the balance test but now we gotta see if you ready to graduate. You remember what we told you was the most important part about survivin'?"

"Yup!"

"O.K., here we go. Buphead, tell him 'bout the final exam."

Buphead turned me around to look at him, putting my back to Byron. "O.K., square," he started, "I wanna make sure you ready for this one, you done so good so far I wanna make sure you don't blow it at graduation time. You think you ready?"

I nodded, getting ready to be thrown in the snowbank real hard this time. I made up my mind I wasn't going to cry or anything, I made up my mind that no matter how hard they threw me in that snow I was going to get up laughing.

"O.K.," Buphead said, "everything's cool, you 'member what your brother said about puttin' your hands up?"

"Like this?" I covered my face with my gloves.

"Yeah, that's it!" Buphead looked over my shoulder at Byron and then said, "*Wooo!* High winds, blowing snow! *Wooo!* Look out! Blizzard a-comin'! Death around the corner! Look out!"

Byron mumbled my name and I turned around to see why his voice sounded so funny. As soon as I looked at him Byron blasted me in the face with a mouthful of snow.

Man! It was hard to believe how much stuff By could put in his mouth! Him and Buphead just about died laughing as I stood there with snow and spit and ice dripping off of my face.

Byron caught his breath and said, "Aww, man, you flunked! You done so good, then you go and flunk the Blowin' Snow section of How to Survive a Blizzard, you forgot to put your hands up! What you say, Buphead, F?"

"Yeah, double F-minus!"

It was a good thing my face was numb from the cold

already or I might have froze to death. I was too embarrassed about getting tricked to tell on them so I went in the house and watched TV.

So as me and By scraped the ice off the Brown Bomber I wasn't going to get fooled again. I kept on chopping ice off the back window and ignored By's mumbling voice.

The next time I took a little rest Byron was still calling my name but sounding like he had something in his mouth. He was saying, "Keh-ee! Keh-ee! Hel' . . . hel' . . . !" When he started banging on the door of the car I went to take a peek at what was going on.

By was leaned over the outside mirror, looking at something in it real close. Big puffs of steam were coming out of the side of the mirror.

I picked up a big, hard chunk of ice to get ready for Byron's trick.

"Keh-ee! Keh-ee! Hel' me! Hel' me! Go geh Momma! Go geh Mom-ma! Huwwy uh!"

"I'm not playing, Byron! I'm not that stupid! You'd better start doing your side of the car or I'll tear you up with this iceball."

He banged his hand against the car harder and started stomping his feet. "Oh, please, Keh-ee! Hel' me, go geh Mom-ma!"

I raised the ice chunk over my head. "I'm not playing, By, you better get busy or I'm telling Dad."

I moved closer and when I got right next to him I could see boogers running out of his nose and tears running down his cheeks. These weren't tears from the cold either, these were big juicy crybaby tears! I dropped my ice chunk.

"By! What's wrong?"

"Hel' me! Keh-ee! Go geh hel'!"

I moved closer. I couldn't believe my eyes! Byron's mouth was frozen on the mirror! He was as stuck as a fly on flypaper!

I could have done a lot of stuff to him. If it had been me with my lips stuck on something like this he'd have tortured me for a couple of days before he got help. Not me, though, I nearly broke my neck trying to get into the house to rescue Byron.

As soon as I ran through the front door Momma, Dad and Joey all yelled, "Close that door!"

"Momma, quick! It's By! He's froze up outside!"

No one seemed too impressed.

I screamed, "Really! He's froze to the car! Help! He's crying!"

That shook them up. You could cut Byron's head off and he probably wouldn't cry.

"Kenneth Bernard Watson, what on earth are you talking about?"

"Momma, please hurry up!"

Momma, Dad and Joey threw on some extra coats and followed me to the Brown Bomber.

The fly was still stuck and buzzing. "Oh, Mom-ma! Hel' me! Geh me offa 'ere!"

"Oh my Lord!" Momma screamed, and I thought

she was going to do one of those movie-style faints, she even put her hand over her forehead and staggered back a little bit.

Joey, of course, started crying right along with Byron.

Dad was doing his best not to explode laughing. Big puffs of smoke were coming out of his nose and mouth as he tried to squeeze his laughs down. Finally he put his head on his arms and leaned against the car's hood and howled.

"Byron," Momma said, gently wiping tears off his cheeks with the end of her scarf, "it's O.K., sweetheart, how'd this happen?" She sounded like she was going to be crying in a minute herself.

Dad raised his head and said, "Why are you asking how it happened? Can't you tell, Wilona? This little knucklehead was kissing his reflection in the mirror and got his lips stuck!" Dad took a real deep breath. "Is your tongue stuck too?"

"No! Quit teasin', Da-ee! Hel'! Hel'!"

"Well, at least the boy hadn't gotten too passionate with himself!" Dad thought that was hilarious and put his head back on his arms.

Momma didn't see anything funny. "Daniel Watson! What are we gonna do?